Hampton,

Thanks for the blurb and for opening a door to your agent, and for answering some silly questions along the way.

Hall

Points on a Line

Points on a Line

D. L. GENTSCH

iUniverse, Inc.
Bloomington

Points on a Line

iUniverse books may be ordered through booksellers or by contacting:

iUniverse
1663 Liberty Drive
Bloomington, IN 47403
www.iuniverse.com
1-800-Authors (1-800-288-4677)

ISBN: 978-1-4759-2177-9 (sc)
ISBN: 978-1-4759-2179-3 (hc)
ISBN: 978-1-4759-2178-6 (ebk)

Printed in the United States of America

iUniverse rev. date: 05/09/2012

For my high school teachers—Renate Gerken and Jack Pepin—who inspired me to connect the dots.

ACKNOWLEDGEMENTS

To George, Brian, Karen, Bob, and Paul for their enthusiastic encouragement and constructive input after reading an early draft. To Linda, who applied her degree in economics and experience at the Federal Reserve to ensure the authenticity of the novel. To Mado and Ramiro, who provided their first hand experiences and knowledge of Argentina's Dirty War. To Mike, who pointed out unrealistic scenarios. And to Candelora, for giving me lessons in fiction writing as she edited the manuscript. Finally, to my daughter, without whose goading I may never have written *Points On A Line*, and who tired of my talking about this novel long ago. She was right—it was time to move on.

PART ONE
Seeds of the Beast

1

Present Time

"COLONEL RINCON, WHERE are we headed?"

We were in a C-130 transport twenty minutes out from the city of Buenos Aires. Colonel Rincon had commandeered me at my apartment an hour earlier to take part in what he called "a little exercise." You didn't say "no" to the higher ups in the Argentine military—especially if you were an American advisor to the country's economic team.

"Señor Anders, tonight we are doing God's will . . . and the will of your *presidente*. You will soon see." He smiled. "You will see how we in my country deal with our mutual problem."

I sat quietly in the cockpit pondering the possibilities of our "mutual problem" as we flew low to the ground headed eastward toward the dusk. In the far distance, I saw the last vestiges of sunlight glimmering on the Rio de la Plata. When we crossed the land boundary of Argentina and were surrounded by water, the plane banked sharply right and began a circling pattern, gradually descending until the force of the mighty engines whipped up waves across the giant river.

"Come with me, Jude Anders."

Obligingly, I unbuckled myself and moved toward Rincon, already at the cockpit door, and followed him and his heavy scent of Old Spice cologne into the enormous cargo hold of the C-130. There were more than a dozen people sleeping on the floor fully clothed amidst green and blue plastic tarps strewn about the hold. Rincon nodded to a corporal standing about half-way down the length of the vast space. He and several soldiers began prodding the sleeping bodies awake, kicking them in their sides and, if that didn't work, in the head. The corporal slid open the mid-plane cargo door, and a loud rush of cool air quickly circled inside, flapping the plastic tarps.

"*¡Tírenlos vivos al río!*" Rincon commanded.

The corporal grabbed the nearest body by the arm, a half-asleep young man with dark stubble, and pulled him to a kneeling position, his sleepy face looking out the door of the plane. Rincon nodded his approval, and with the force of his large army boot on the man's butt the corporal shoved him overboard.

A dark haired man, older than the first and dressed in jeans and a black sweater, struggled to his feet in the middle of the cargo hold.

Rincon glared at him, hatred in his eyes. "*¡El proximo!*" Rincon pointed directly at him.

A soldier kept shoving the dark figure until they reached the open door. The man gazed outside, but suddenly turned to Rincon and me, his eyes glued on mine. I couldn't pull away from his cold, dark gaze.

"*El cuervo,*" he said. It wasn't more than a whisper. But before another word could pass his lips, the corporal grabbed him by the back of his jacket and with one swift motion tossed him out of the plane.

The corporal nodded toward another body on the floor as the plane banked hard in a tight circle. This time, he'd selected a woman, probably late twenties, like the man before her. A soldier nudged her with his boot, and she slowly got to her feet. Her long, wavy brown hair slightly obscured her face as she was pushed toward the open door. Was it the hair or the sharply chiseled features of her profile that vaguely reminded me of someone? I strained my memory, but the corporal tossed her over the side of the plane before I could figure it out.

The corporal gazed around the hold at the remaining souls. A teenage boy near the door had gotten to his feet and looked wide-eyed around the plane as though desperately searching for someone. Rincon's man grabbed the boy by his arm and flung him out the door with a single hand. One after another I watched as each one—seven men and almost as many women, somewhat awake now but stunningly silent—was dragged to the door, only to disappear across that thin line that separated the inside from out. They were all so young. None complained. They were free.

Rincon smiled. "Young men and woman, in a nice little sleep, and now going for a swim on a warm spring day. See, Señor Anders, we solve our mutual problem!"

I looked around, but the cargo hold of the C-130 was empty. The sleepers had gone for their swim.

"Ladies and gentlemen, we are making our initial approach . . ."

I turned to see who was speaking, but only Rincon and three of his men were talking to each other.

"At this time we ask that you buckle your seatbelts, put away your tray tables, and return your seatbacks to their upright position."

Rincon's mouth was moving, but it was a woman's voice that I was hearing. I felt a hand on my shoulder.

"Mr. Anders . . . Mr. Anders."

I awoke with a start; the flight attendant continued to jostle me before withdrawing. "We have begun our initial descent into Athens. Please bring your seatback to its upright position." She smiled, pausing a moment, then continued navigating the aisle with a trash bag in her hand.

I stared at the TV screen on the seatback in front of me, my mind moving sluggishly back to reality. It was explaining custom procedures to expect in Greece. I moved the lever to raise my seatback. The dream was over, but its horror lingered.

The wheels of the plane met the concrete runway with a shudder, and I quickly tucked the book I had tried to read before falling asleep into my backpack. After a long taxi to the gate and equally long disembarking of the crowded plane, I finally made my way up the jet way and through the terminal—a labyrinth of twists and turns that eventually led me to baggage claim. At customs, the line was shorter than I expected; almost immediately a customs agent beckoned me forward. Hurriedly I pulled my passport and declaration form from my backpack and waited while he looked them over for what seemed like forever. Was his thoroughness just an act?

"How long will you be staying in Greece, Mr. Anders?" he finally asked.

"I have a three month lease on a small house on Amorgos outside of Lagada."

"So, three months then. What is the purpose of your trip?"

"To get away from the U.S. for awhile. Relax. Maybe do some writing."

The agent gazed at me for a long moment. He looked back at my passport. "Well, Mr. Anders, you will be far away from your country on Amorgos." He looked back to me square on. "How are things in the U.S. now?"

My first instinct was to ask which one, but decided against a flippant response. "Marginally better, I guess."

"It is not much better here. But I suspect you know that. Do you have the address of the house where you will be staying?"

I quickly pulled out the rental agreement from my backpack and handed it to him. He typed the address of my rental house into the computer, closed my passport, and handed it and the rental paper back to me.

"Have a nice visit," he said as he waved at the next person in line without another glance at me.

I picked up my luggage but tried not to rush as I exited customs. Once inside the main terminal, I adjusted my watch to the local time and changed my cash into *drachmas*. The bills were worn and faded, and smelled as though they were just pulled out of storage. While I checked the information kiosk for ferry departure times, a cabby waved at me from the curb. A ferry to Amorgos was leaving in an hour and thirty minutes; the cab was my only option if I was to catch it.

The taxi driver approached me and took hold of my roller bag.

"Do you speak English?" I asked.

"Small," he responded.

"How long to get to the Port of Athens where the ferries leave?" I hoped he understood more English than he could speak.

"Take back road. Sea, then port."

"How long?" I asked again.

The cabby put up a single finger in the air, which I took to mean one hour. That would be cutting it close.

"Okay, let's go."

I hurriedly opened the door to the back seat of the green Fiat, presuming this route would bypass the historical sites and traffic of Athens. If I missed this ferry, there wasn't another leaving for Amorgos until morning. I could stay a couple of days in Athens to see the tourist attractions on my return home; right now, all I wanted was to get to my final destination.

The cabby squealed out of the parking lane and maneuvered southward toward the Aegean Sea on a two-lane road paralleling the hills in the near distance to the west. Athens and its famous ruins lay on the other side. On this side of the hills, the countryside was arid—covered with scrub pines and olive trees. It reminded me of the landscape of New Mexico; I had seen it once during a summer trip to Santa Fe with my mother when I was twelve.

I leaned back and lit a cigarette—my first smoke since departing from Dulles yesterday—hoping my cabby was right about the time to the Port of Athens. Besides the long plane trip from D.C. to Athens, this journey had been no less hectic and time-constrained than the rest of my life, an irony that was not lost on me. Even before leaving yesterday, I furiously finished loading several new albums on my iPod and put a change of clothes in my backpack just in case. After my cabby had honked his horn three times encouraging me to get a move on, I finally locked the door to my condo. Surely when I got to Amorgos the pace could do nothing else but slow down. How long would it take my mind to ease into a corresponding rhythm?

The car swerved in and out around slower traffic, sometimes scaring the hell out me when it barely missed an oncoming car. Was the whole world in a rush to go somewhere? I smiled. Of course it was, just like me on this journey. Still, I could tell we were making good time; it took less than half an hour for us to reach the sea and turn north on the road that hugged the coastline.

The driver downshifted and began navigating the curves that followed the rocky coastline, sometimes faster than I would have dared to take them even in my old Z. Shifting to the other side of the back seat to get a better view of the Aegean Sea, brilliantly blue, exactly as I had imagined it would be, I could see a few small islands in the distance. Before selecting Amorgos for my retreat, I had researched all of the Greek Islands, wanting one that was not overrun with tourists, but was large enough to provide reasonable accommodations. That was Amorgos—the Greek island farthest from its mainland. While I treasured its remoteness, I now questioned whether I should have picked an island nearer to Athens. Six and a half hours stood between the Port of Athens and my island of choice, and I was anxious to get there.

I gazed at the tiny islands off the coast. What would my life be like on Amorgos? For that matter, what would it be like to have an extended vacation—for more than a week or two? Even my honeymoon had been cut short by a crisis. Now, here I was, off for three months. I could have made it longer, but it was long enough to give me the time I needed to get away from the chaos, to clear my head, and most important, to find that sense of myself that used to hover with me like a shadow in the sunlight—a feeling that had gradually dimmed with age. Was that, whatever you name it, even a part of me anymore? If it was, how would

I find it again? Maybe by reading, writing, or just listening to the waves of the sea collide endlessly with its rocky coastline as I drank my coffee in the morning and a glass of wine with the setting sun that gave way to the canopy of stars overhead. But most of all, by being far away from the United States and its politics.

After passing through several fishing villages, the car finally entered the southernmost part of Athens, filled with houses and commercial buildings. Traffic thickened, but we were ahead of schedule, and when the cab finally pulled up to the ferry terminal in the Port of Athens, I had forty minutes to spare. I smiled at my cabby and thanked him with a generous tip. He pointed to his watch with a wide grin. He had beaten his own estimate.

Inside the terminal it took me a minute to figure out where to buy tickets before inching my way forward in the long line and checking my watch often. I had to stand in line yet again before boarding the *Albion,* but finally settled into a window seat half way down the portside aisle of the boat five minutes before its scheduled departure. The ferry was only about half full, but there were two island stops along the way to pick up additional passengers.

When we finally maneuvered away from the dock and moved to open sea, I pulled the book I had been reading on the plane from my backpack, intending to finish it during the journey across the Aegean, and opened it to *Part Three: From Food to Guns, Germs and Steel.* I only managed a few pages before I was distracted by the dream of Colonel Rincon and his C-130. I understood where it came from. But why now after so many years?

The shoreline of the Greek mainland retreated from view; I could feel my mind begin to release its intense focus that had controlled it most of my adult life. Would this trip mark a new path? Was another path even possible at my age, or was this the end of a line that tapers off gradually without a clear demarcation? I reclined my seat and gazed out at the open sea. A kaleidoscope of memories flickered past like random thoughts—some brought a smile, others were sad, and too many were just painful, like the C-130. How many of those relics from my past had been so embellished over the years that I couldn't be certain whether they really happened the way I remembered? Even those memories surrounding Gillian, Anton, Fallon, and Lex. But I guess it didn't matter—they were real, as was my work, for good or bad, and its consequences.

I turned back to my book, determined to push the thoughts from my mind. After all these years, this was my time—my time to reclaim some peace of mind that I hadn't known since I was a teenager. But as I started to read the opening paragraph, another memory flashed into my head, an old one of a cool June day in Missouri. I was lying in the thick green rye grass of my backyard, staring into the powder blue sky and making faces out of the puffy cumulus clouds hovering overhead. I couldn't remember exactly how old I was then; still, on that day I felt that something had changed—profoundly. Up to then, life had been a big party that I enjoyed without any thought of duties to attend to the next day. But on that day, the party ended, and all the accoutrements of my youth lay around me like empty cups, cigarette butts, and disarranged chairs. I stared at the clean, sharp line of the roof of my house against the sky. As my mind walked that line I could feel myself stepping through a great gate that was closing behind me. What lay ahead took no visible form.

2

April 1970
Columbia, Missouri

I ROLLED OVER to pull a cigarette from the pack of Marlboros on the end table next to the bed and lit it. Why did a smoke taste so good after sex?

"Got one for me?" Kathy asked.

"Sure thing."

I reached for another butt and lit it for her with the old Zippo lighter my grandfather had given me. I rolled back over and handed it to her.

Kathy took a deep drag and ran her fingers through her long blond hair. She let the cigarette dangle from her bottom lip. She took another puff as she laid back and exhaled toward the bedroom ceiling.

"That was good. Let's go again."

"You've got to be kidding. Give me some time, will you."

"You know me, Jude. When I get something I like, I want more."

"Is that just you or a female thing in general?" I took a drag on my cigarette and exhaled a gray cloud. "Tell me, Kath, what else do you like?"

"Besides fucking? Eating, I guess, and some good dope."

I had worked up an appetite. Sex often had that effect, especially after smoking a joint, and I forgot we had escaped to the bedroom without any dinner, tensed out from a long afternoon of hitting the books.

"Then maybe we should try eating. I assume you can cook."

"Sorry, mama never taught me. Why do you think I still live in a dorm?"

"Figures." My stomach started to rumble. "Let's get a burger at The Shack."

"I just want to stay right here for the rest of the night. If we get hungry, we can find something to munch on. Know what I mean?"

Someone pounded on the apartment door, causing it to rattle in its jamb. I choked on the smoke from my cigarette, and saw my stash lying out in the open on the dresser.

"Jude, are you there, man? It's Paul."

Another pounding.

"Shit! Goddamn it."

Relieved it wasn't a bust, I rummaged around for my jeans and pulled them on, hobbling my way to the living room as the pounding persisted.

"Yeah, I'm here. Just a minute."

"We need to talk, man. Did you hear what happened?" he asked loudly from outside.

I had known Paul since I was a sophomore and he was a new freshman in the dorm. We got to know each other watching TV in the lounge in the evenings instead of studying, and then one night he asked me if I wanted to get stoned. I never had up to that point, but quickly appreciated the insights pot seemed to provide. Before I knew it, both he and I had a little business going—just enough for spending money. The next year we both moved out of the dorm and into a small apartment off-campus. That's when the business got a little more serious—pot, hash, and an assortment of hallucinogens and amphetamines.

When the Vietnam War started to get really intense so did we, attending protests and rallies, and eventually planning the protests with the leaders of various campus groups. We were both committed to doing something to end the war, but for Paul the protests held the promise of a larger cause—revolution against capitalism. Maybe it was his constant rants against markets and corporations, or maybe it was the remnants of his long black hair that he always left in the bathtub, sink, or on the bathroom floor that led us to part ways at the end of my junior year. Not that we weren't still friends; we were, and we remained staunchly aligned against the war as well.

I opened the door and Paul rushed into the apartment. He wore his tattered jean jacket, the American flag sewn upside down on the back; his long dark hair, greasy as usual, was tucked behind his ears.

"It's happened, man, it's really happened!"

"Yeah, now what?" Paul typically overreacted to events. I assumed this was another one of his rants.

"That goddamn Nixon has done it this time." Paul paced the room like a pinball. He was always getting pissed about Nixon; he had an endless laundry list of grievances—as we all did—but I had just gotten out of bed and my stomach was growling. The last thing I wanted to do was have a political discussion.

"Done what?"

"Just started another goddamn war, that's all."

"Another war?" I had no clue what the hell Paul was talking about but I admit he got my attention and I quickly forgot about Kathy and food.

"Yeah, man, he invaded Cambodia. It's on the news. Haven't you heard?"

"How would I know, man? I don't have a TV."

He looked down at the floor chuckling. "Oh yeah, I forgot. They're calling it an interdiction."

"Inter what?"

"Interdiction."

"What the hell is that?"

"It's when we send troops and B-52s into a country. It's a goddamn invasion, man. Nixon invaded Cambodia!"

"Why would he do that, especially now?"

Paul was still pacing from one corner of the living room to another. "I don't know, but we gotta do something. We can't let this stand without a fight!" He clenched his fist and lifted it to his side.

I stared at Paul's bellbottom jeans—he had sewn green and red fringe along the hems because they had shrunk—and I tried to get my mind around the news he had just delivered. None of it made sense. We were making progress on ending the war and public opinion was changing in our favor. Nixon was promising peace and wouldn't expand the war if he wanted to get re-elected.

"Who have you talked to?"

"No one. I ran over here as soon as I heard the news. Man, Bill's gonna go ballistic when he hears. What are we gonna do?"

"Hell, I don't know. Let's get the facts, then we'll figure it out." I had no idea, and I was still a little buzzed from the joint I shared with Kathy before we screwed. I never thought clearly after sex anyway. "Get in touch with Bill and Sasha, and Doug, too, if he's straight. Let's meet at Mark's place in an hour."

"Sure thing, man." Paul left more agitated than when he arrived, cussing as he walked down the sidewalk away from the apartment. "Goddamn Nixon; mother fucking army, sons o' bitches."

When I returned to the bedroom Kathy was smoking another cigarette, only partially covered by the sheet and her long wavy blond hair. She really looked inviting, but I didn't have time. I stared into her deep blue eyes.

"Sorry, Kath, I have to go. There's some left over mac and cheese in the fridge, if you get hungry." I sat on the edge of the bed, pulled on a t-shirt, and slipped into my sneakers. "Nixon's invaded Cambodia."

"Cambodia. Next to Nam. Where are you going?"

"Mark's place. We need to talk things through; make a plan." I said, tying the last bow of my shoelace. "I don't know when I'll be back. You can stay here or go to the dorm, whichever you want, but I have to go and probably won't be back till late. See ya later." I doubted she would stay here alone; that wasn't her style. I headed out the door.

"JUDE, COME ON in, man. What's up?" Mark asked, surprised to see me.

I repeated Paul's story. Mark had been working on a paper for Elizabethan Literature and didn't see the news either. He got up quickly and turned on his TV, dialing through the channels. A couple of inane comedies, a cop show, and some nature film, but no news.

"We'll have to wait for the 10 o'clock news to see what's up," he said, as he flicked off the set and resettled into his favorite reading chair.

"None of this makes any sense," I insisted.

"People who exhibit psychotic tendencies often do bizarre things. Why do you think they call him 'Tricky Dicky'?"

Mark and I first met at a protest meeting last year. Like Paul he was a year younger than me. He had a low lottery number, but had another year to wait it out and hope the stupid war would end.

There was a quick single knock and Doug, Sasha, Bill, and Paul came hustling through the screen door. Paul was still cursing the government. Doug and Paul were the only ones who had seen Nixon's press conference on TV, and for once Doug wasn't stoned.

"Yeah, it's true," Doug said. "The fucking U.S. Army invaded the southeastern part of Cambodia. Nixon claims the North Vietnamese Army and the Viet Cong are using that part of Cambodia as safe haven and as a supply route from the north to South Vietnam. He insists that part of Cambodia is a 'communist headquarters', whatever the fuck that means."

"Have there been any protests?" I asked.

"None reported. I got Tricky Dicky's announcement from the Oval Office, a brief recap by Brinkley, then back to a rerun of *Ironside*." Doug plopped down on Mark's couch. "We'll have to wait for the local news."

I looked at my watch. "It's almost 10. Mark, can you turn the TV back on—channel 4. It's bound to be the lead story."

I lit a cigarette, running the options through my head. We needed to find out how other campuses were going to respond to this; it might give us some idea of how we should react.

"Hey, Sash, how about giving your friend at Berkeley a call?" I asked. "Kind of interested in what they're thinking."

Sasha had an on-again, off-again boyfriend in Berkeley who allegedly was a key SDS member there. She really didn't need a boyfriend in Berkeley; she had more than one lover on campus, and plenty more who would be happy to accompany her into the sack. Sasha was attractive, especially when she wore those tight, slightly dirty jeans and that leather halter-top, but like most of the smart girls on campus, she often hid her intelligence, especially when she was with the guys. I thought she and Mark had something going, but when I pressed the idea over a couple of beers, Mark insisted they were just friends. Yeah, some friendship I thought.

Sasha moaned from her cross-legged position on the floor, leaning against Mark's old coach. "Sure, why not." She got up from her comfortable seat and looked at Mark. "Can I use the phone?"

"I know you can, but yes, you may." He said it with such a straight face that Sasha couldn't be sure if he was teasing.

"What else would I get from a fucking English major?" Her deep set green eyes flashed beneath her long stringy auburn hair; she shot Mark a knowing smile as she headed for the bedroom phone.

Bill, normally outspoken and often angry over the war like Paul, remained strangely quiet. I wondered if he was stoned. Finally he turned to me and, in an unusually calm voice, said, "You thinking another protest—or something a bit more intense?"

"Intense?"

"Yeah, you know, like Plan B."

Plan B was our euphemism for blowing up the university ROTC building, which a number of us had quietly discussed at the beginning of fall semester. Aside from the sheer audacity of it, that kind of action would require a lot more planning, not to mention time to procure the necessary materials to do the job. I was pissed-off enough to blow up a building, but we needed to do something *now*. And then there was my future to think of. If we were caught, it meant prison time. While a felony conviction would keep me out of Nam, it would also destroy any future in my chosen field . . . or any profession, for that matter. Four years of studying and one month from graduation, I wasn't going to throw it all away now.

"Maybe something more within the law this time," I answered. "What are our options?"

Bill seemed to take my response in stride. "Well then, the usual protest in the Quad. If we get a big turnout, we could step it up a bit and take over Jesse Hall. Unless you think a panty raid would be more appropriate?"

We all chuckled as though it was only a joke, but I got his message—Bill thought I was copping out.

"Hey, shut up. We got the news," Mark interrupted the laughter just as Sasha was coming back into the living room.

We sat around the TV, some on the couch, some on pillows on the floor watching excerpts from Nixon's announcement. Paul, for all his ranting, was essentially right. We did initiate a series of aerial and ground incursions into Cambodia, and for the reasons Doug said. What was unclear was how long they would last. Was this temporary or a deliberate attempt to widen the war?

Bill stood up and shook his clenched fist at the TV, finally showing the Bill we all knew and loved. "Wow! Can you believe the balls on that motherfucker?"

I cut Bill off before he could launch into a tirade and asked Sasha what she learned from our friends out West.

"They're not sure yet, but they think maybe starting tomorrow with a rally—crowds will be small because there's little time for publicity, but they'll use that rally to get the word out for bigger protests over the weekend. They're talking about boycotting classes next week. They think they can get a huge turnout on Monday, especially if the boycotts take hold." Sasha looked down at her jeans, picking at a sewn-on patch. "But they have something else in mind."

SDS. Berkeley. She definitely had our attention. The room went silent.

"They intend to occupy their administration building with enough people and for long enough to get a good dose of national news coverage, even if the boycotts don't work. But if the boycotts take hold and the protests get big enough, they might be able to shut Berkeley down."

"When?" I was beginning to formulate my own plan, and piggybacking on the SDS was part of it.

"Tuesday, Wednesday, if enough people get pissed off."

"Any well-known speakers?" Doug asked.

"Not at this point," Sasha answered. "Too soon to know who will show up though. Berkeley's as good a forum as New York for the press. Somebody's bound to show up, especially if they live in the area. But they're not sure they'll need them. They think this is just the issue we've been waiting for."

Heads nodded. We all liked their plan, but this was the Midwest. Could we ever get people pissed off enough to occupy Jesse Hall, much less boycott their classes? None of us believed that shutting down the University of Missouri would ever happen.

"Let's see how many people will show up for a protest tomorrow," I said. "Who knows what might happen? Doug, how soon can we get the word out?"

"It's too late tonight except to notify the usual players. We need to make up some flyers and get them out in the morning. We might be able to get it together by mid-afternoon."

I nodded. "The timing on that would be good. Most of us will be out of classes by 2:00. But we can't go any later than that. Once everyone's gone home for the day, they won't come back. It's Friday—people will be ready to party. Doug, can you mock up and print a flyer at *The Maneater*?"

"I think I can sneak that in." He leaned back in the overstuffed couch. "If I draft it tonight and get it there early in the morning."

Doug was the editor of the student newspaper, and we often hung out in his office late at night running off flyers, smoking joints, and listening to The Rolling Stones. It was the best way to get the word out quickly on campus, whether for a protest or a concert.

"Bill, can you round up a crew to post them?"

Bill leaned back against the couch from his pillowed seat on the floor with the ease of a cat and a devilish smile on his face. "I'll get some help. There will plenty of pissed off people. Anyway, I was looking for an excuse to cut my Anthro lecture."

"Okay. I'll lead off the speaking. Sash, I need you to speak, too. See if Tim Glazny can say some words—you know, from a vet's perspective."

"Yeah, sure, no problem."

"Another rally at 1:00 on Saturday, and the same time on Sunday to keep the fire burning until Monday. We'll announce times and locations at tomorrow's protest, and meet again after the protest to fine tune next steps?"

Everyone agreed.

"Okay, see you on the Quad tomorrow," I said as we all got up to leave. My heart was pounding; I was jazzed; I knew I wouldn't sleep much tonight. "I have to make a few calls to fill in some of the other protest groups."

"Hey, Doug," Mark called as we were walking out the door. "Wanna smoke a number?"

"Not tonight, man. I need a clear head."

We all did.

3

ALTHOUGH IT WAS still April, the bright sunshine made it feel warmer than it really was. The redbuds and dogwoods were in early bloom, while the grass around the Quad was beginning to green up and fill in the paths that students created all winter, shortcutting their way to and from the classroom buildings around it. Some students were still walking to class or heading home for the day, but a couple hundred, maybe more, were milling about the steps up to Jesse Hall, waiting for the protest to begin. As more classes were dismissed at 1:30 the ranks of students filling the Quadrangle began to grow. By 2:00 their numbers had more than doubled, and students were still flocking in from other parts of the campus.

Sasha, Paul, Mark, and I, and leaders from other war resistance groups on campus had gathered to the side of the steps to Jesse Hall to discuss the order of our speeches and when we should start.

"We should give it another fifteen minutes," Mark insisted. "People are still coming."

"If we wait too long, we're gonna lose some of them—it's Friday," Paul countered.

The crowd was not only getting bigger, but louder. Chants and yells were heard throughout the Quad. But now a single chant was unifying the crowd: "No more war! No more war! No more war!"

"Jude, I think it's time to go," Sasha interjected.

She was right.

"Okay, let's do it." I picked up the bullhorn and climbed the steps.

The crowd chants grew exponentially. When the shouts of "No more war!" in unison became deafening, I raised my arms in the air. The shouts continued for more than a minute until they gradually subsided and I could only hear a handful of jeers and chants from the crowd. I raised the bullhorn.

"My name is Jude Anders. Many of you have heard me before. I am a person of few words, and I am tired of talking. So what I have to say will be brief." The crowd grew quiet. "Over a year and a half ago, our president promised an honorable end to the war in Vietnam. Since that time more than 10,000 Americans have died there—most not by their choice. Last year we found out that our Army troops had massacred an entire village of women and children at My Lai while we were seeking an honorable end to the war. And while we wait for the war's 'honorable end', B52s continue to bomb North Vietnam and our jets continue to drop napalm over villages in the South. Thousands of our fellow human beings have been killed and maimed at the hands of the United States of America. And why? Because of the economic interests of American and foreign corporations, the military industrial complex, and the paranoia of a false belief—the domino theory. Communism has been around for at least fifty years. As an economic theory we all know it hasn't worked. So what are we afraid of?"

Chants of "No more war!" rose again, gained strength, and as I put my left hand in the air, subsided. Before I began again someone from the center of the crowd yelled, "Kill Nixon!"

"We won't be like them," I shouted in response and waited for the crowd to settle. "But some equate communism with dictators and totalitarian rulers, and they claim that is why we are fighting in Vietnam—to stop them. They say we are fighting for democracy. But who is the president of South Vietnam? A military general! And how many dictators does the U.S. prop up all over the world today? Lies, all lies!"

"Lies! Lies! Lies!" the crowd echoed.

"What the hell are we fighting for? We've been asking that over and over and over again. This war has been going on for more than seven years. And now instead of winding down this war as Nixon promised to do, he's expanding it. It's not just Vietnam anymore, people. Now it's Cambodia!"

The sea of protesters booed; the sound was deafening, and then began their chant of "No more war!" again. I let it go on, listening for the crescendo.

"And once again we know why our dear president is called Tricky Dicky. He promises an end to the war but expands it. Now, please tell me how invading Cambodia is going to end this war? I for one have had enough. If Nixon and the Congress won't end it, then we will! The time has come. The time is now!"

"Now! Now! Now! Now!" The crowd erupted.

"If not now, then when?" I paused, letting my words hang in the charged air. "We have to act together. We must focus on only one thing—end this war now. And we can't stop until the war is over! How can we continue to write papers or get ready for finals as long as this war continues? It's time to get serious! Yeah, it's fun to protest the war on a sunny spring afternoon and then go home and continue business as usual. But I ask you, how you can go to class when this war destroys lives and our country? Sure, you can burn your draft card—that's a nice symbolic action, but it won't end the draft. That's not being serious. You want to end the draft? Then refuse to go. Let the government fill its prisons with all of us. How long do you think that would last?"

The crowd quieted. It was more than a thousand strong, but hardly enough to achieve our objectives. What could I say to mobilize them? I pushed those doubts out of my mind. Right now it was my job to motivate them to show up tomorrow.

"I know most of us can't vote, but we have to think, eat, and breathe only one thing until we put an end to this madness! And so today we begin. And tomorrow we continue, and Sunday, and Monday. We continue right here, right now until we shut this place down!"

The crowd erupted with "Shut it down!" over and over.

"Yes, we *will* shut it down; we'll shut it down because we have no business here as long as this war continues!"

I had more to say, but my job was done. They were fired up, ready to go. I put down the bullhorn, held my right arm with fist clenched in the air. Many of the crowd followed suit. As I started down the stairs, Sasha headed up surrounded by the drone of "Shut it down!" It was her turn to keep them going.

THE CROWD WAS even bigger for Saturday's protest, and by the time Sunday's rolled around there were over two thousand people and not all were students. We recognized some professors, and there were many adults from the town of Columbia, home to the university. Some protesters had come earlier in the day with picnic lunches, played Frisbee, and smoked dope. Some of the students, as expected, were even tripping. As we watched the news at Mark's place on Sunday night, we finally saw the same thing being reported from campuses all over the country. Throngs of protestors had rallied, vowing to shut down their colleges and universities. We all knew that mere protests would not galvanize the nation enough to force Congress to intervene and end the war, although it was an important start. But on Monday the gods gave us a gift—unimagined and horrific.

The protests over the weekend had some impact on class attendance on Monday. There were obviously fewer students on campus. In the morning there were incidents of students harassing others who were trying to enter classrooms. Several professors—mostly from liberal arts classes—had not shown up for their classes. I boycotted my classes in advance of the afternoon's protest, as much in solidarity for the effort as to set an example for others. Instead I had a sandwich and a cup of coffee in a booth near the front windows of the Student Commons where I could watch the people outside and see how many would go into the General Classroom Building across the mall. Bill and Doug were coming up the sidewalk toward the heavy glass front doors of the Commons. Just outside the door they stopped and continued what looked to be a very intense debate.

"Join you?"

Tim Glazny, one of the few vets on campus and a fierce voice against the war, had come up from behind, surprising me.

"Sure thing." I gestured him to join me and quickly looked back toward the doors for Bill and Doug. They had just entered the Commons and made a beeline for my booth.

"We got a new headline for the protest today," Bill said as he slipped into the booth beside Tim while Doug sat next to me. "We are now in a police state. The fucking U.S. Army killed protesters in Ohio."

"It was the National Guard," Doug interjected.

"Like I told you, Doug, same fucking difference. They mowed 'em down. Killed four and injured god knows how many."

"This was at a campus protest?" Chills ran through me and I could feel the hair stand up on my arms.

"Yeah, just like ours. The protestors were ordered to disperse by some general, and when they didn't, the Army gassed them." Bill squirmed in the booth and leaned across the table. "But it didn't work. They moved out of the area to another and continued the protest. But the Army followed and shot 'em down."

"When did this happen?"

"About an hour ago," Doug said.

This didn't happen in this country, certainly not in our lifetimes and through all our demonstrations. I dropped my sandwich on the plate and gulped down my remaining coffee.

"Let's go upstairs."

There was a large lounge on the second floor of the Commons with soft sofas and chairs and a TV. A number of students were focused intently on the TV, with several standing in doorway. Two girls hovered nearby, their arms around each other's shoulders. One was crying. We found some space near the set in time to see some live footage from Ohio as the reporter delivered the news.

"At 12:24 pm today, members of the Ohio National Guard opened fire on approximately two hundred students at the campus of Kent State University who were protesting the U.S. interdiction into Cambodia. The students had been ordered to disperse, and when they refused, the National Guard opened fire, killing four and injuring many more. We do not yet have the numbers of those injured or the names of those killed. As you can see, ambulances are on the scene attending to the injured. We are awaiting comment from the governor of Ohio. We understand that a press conference will be scheduled for some time this afternoon."

Doug nudged me with his elbow. "Jude, we don't have a lot of time before today's demonstration."

Like all the others in the room, I wanted to stay and hear as many details as I could. But what more was there to know? College students shot down on their own campus. "Let's find a place to talk." I hurried down the stairs, the others behind me.

The four of us found a small circle of benches in the rear of the Commons. I pulled a cigarette from my near empty pack.

"I guess this changes a few things," I said after a long silence while I organized my thoughts. "People are going to be angry. We're nearing a very fine line here."

"There's bound to be a lot of police at the rally after Kent State. This could get really ugly!" Doug interjected.

"I get it. We need to provide a constructive outlet. Remain peaceful."

"Good luck with that," Bill chimed in.

"Listen, Bill, the pigs are looking for violence. Let's keep it calm for now. Renew the call for a campus-wide boycott of classes and memorial protests each day to honor our dead and injured brothers and sisters."

"Bullshit!" Bill responded. "Enough of this fucking protest shit! It's time to break things. That'll be my memorial to the fallen."

"Like what?"

"Windows, cars, heads. Anything that will break."

"You don't think I feel like bashing heads? We have time to get violent, but not yet. Let's try this plan first. If it doesn't work, we can talk about Plan B or something else."

"You guys do what you want. I'm going back to my apartment to get a goddamn baseball bat."

Bill stormed off and the rest of us walked to the Quad where thousands of students, professors, and others had shown up for a third day of protests. Obviously, the word of Kent State had gotten out. The Quad was surrounded by cops—campus, city, and state pigs with their cars everywhere. They kept their distance. The protest, though angry, remained peaceful. Nobody, except Bill, was into breaking things—at least not yet.

ON TUESDAY THERE was virtually no one in class except for the ag students and the engineers. By the time the demonstration began that afternoon, the number of protestors had almost doubled again. Until I saw all these people gathered in one place, I had no idea how big the university really was.

Once again, we stood at the base of the steps to Jesse Hall, lining up the order of our speakers. The police were back in force again, forming a line in front of the doors to Jesse and ringing the perimeter of the Quad—more cops in one place than I had ever seen. There were rumors the National Guard had been mobilized, but there wasn't any sign of them around the Quad. We were about to begin the protest when a member of the administration came down the front steps of Jesse Hall and walked over to us. He was thin, balding and wore a dark suit that was a size too big for him. He patted his forehead with a white handkerchief to wipe away the drops of sweat beading on his forehead.

"The chancellor would like to have a brief word with your leader." His voice was timid.

Sasha got into his face. "We have no leaders here."

He stepped backward a couple of steps.

"Okay, okay . . . then how about a couple of you. He would like to talk briefly before you start the . . . your protest."

We all looked at each other dumbfounded. What could the Chancellor want to talk with us about?

"Jude, maybe you, Doug and Sash should go," Mark suggested quickly.

"I'm going too!" Bill interjected as he lifted his bat in the air.

The suit cautiously withdrew several paces, and several state cops moved to the edge of the steps, hands on their Billy clubs.

Mark stepped in front of Bill. "Bill, three's enough. And I don't think that bat will get you past the pigs standing up there."

Bill looked up at the state police at the top of the steps ready to make their next move. "Yeah, maybe you're right. I might kill the motherfucker."

Sasha, Doug, and I walked up the steps and through the front doors of Jesse with the crowd yelling and screaming behind us in the Quad. The chancellor was standing near the entrance of the hall, well primped and suited.

"People," he said, trying to sound stern, his voice echoing in the near empty atrium. "I would like a couple of minutes to address the crowd before you begin today."

I traded surprised glances with my comrades.

"What do you want to say?" I asked.

He cleared his throat and fiddled with his tie. "We are closing the university . . . for the remainder of the school year. I think you can understand why." I could see the beads of sweat popping out on his forehead. "We cannot afford violence, and believe this is the best solution. Other universities and colleges around the state are also closing for the remainder of the term."

The three of us just stared at each other. It couldn't happen this easily.

"What about grades? People will want to know what's going to happen to them," Doug asserted after the chancellor's words had finally registered.

"Everyone will get the grade they currently have. If they wish to improve their grades, they can mail in any papers to their professors between now and the end of the semester. Anyone wishing to take final exams can do so at the beginning of summer semester . . . in June." The chancellor paused but not long enough for me to lodge a complaint. "I am sorry, but this is not negotiable. The university is closing today, and all students living in university housing will be expected to vacate by the end of the weekend."

The chancellor buttoned his suit coat and turned to walk outside, but turned back to me.

"Oh, I almost forgot. Mr. Anders, there will be no commencement ceremony this year."

He knew my name. Did he have a file on me? The concerns for my future that I had kept at bay during the frenzy of the weekend's protests rushed into view. Would all of this go on some kind of permanent record?

"Graduating students will receive their diplomas by mail. Now, I need to inform the crowd of our decisions. Then I would ask that you disperse the crowd as soon as practical. All classroom buildings will be locked within one hour and police will be posted to prevent any, uh, vandalism that some might wish to do."

We hurried out the doors, following the chancellor, stunned by the sheer size of the crowd and the realization, sinking slowly in, that we had won this round. The chancellor's fear was evident on his face and in his voice as he made his announcement. At first the protestors were silent, but then, as if everyone got it at once, they erupted . . . "Shut it down! Shut it down! Shut it down! Shut it down!"

I could hear the chants reverberating throughout the Quad from our perch just outside the doorway, standing in the midst of the state police. After the chancellor had returned to the safety of Jesse Hall with the small army of police surrounding the doors, Doug, Sash, and I moved to edge of the top step. When the elation of the crowd began to subside, I addressed the crowd one final time.

"This was your doing, your effort. This is what happens when we act as one voice. Now it's time to go back home for a long summer and continue our efforts there. Remember, the pigs will still be out in force until we leave the campus. Our work here is done, so let's keep it peaceful. And never forget Kent State and the four who died there!"

A BUNCH OF us headed over to Mark's house to celebrate, and we started getting stoned as soon as we got there. There were bottles of

Ripple—pink, red, and white—and Thunderbird. Paul was pacing around in circles in Mark's living room, ranting that this was the beginning of the revolution. Some hoped he was right; others believed that wasn't going to happen—not now, not over Vietnam, but maybe some day. I listened to Paul, wondering if I really wanted it to happen at all. Kathy showed up about 4:00 and eagerly joined in the party. She was already mostly packed to go home—she hated the dorm.

"You going to take your grades as is?" Mark asked me.

Kath, Mark, and I were slumped in Mark's old red mohair couch, listening to Led Zeppelin II on the stereo.

"Guess so." I hadn't really thought about it until he asked. "As and Bs. Not sure raising a couple of Bs to As is worth it, or possible for that matter."

"So what are you going do?"

"Hang around town for a couple of weeks, I guess. I've got no reason to rush back home."

"No, I mean this summer or the rest of your life for that matter, Mr. Graduate."

He was right—it just hit me that I had officially graduated. I reached into the pocket of my army surplus fatigue jacket and handed Mark a neatly folded piece of paper.

He unfolded the paper and read it. "Bummer, man. Anyone know about this yet?" He nodded toward Kathy.

"Nope."

"Come on, let's go outside."

I looked over at Kath; she was finally exhaling her last hit on a number Paul had handed her.

"Mark and I are going outside for some air. I'll be right back. Okay?"

"Sure." She coughed slightly as she handed the joint back to Paul, who parked himself on the couch as soon as Mark and I got up.

Outside I pulled out a couple of cigarettes and handed one to Mark.

Mark took the offered light from my Zippo. "Jesus, Jude, 'your fucking friends and neighbors have selected you'. What are you going to do?"

"Not sure. I just got this on Saturday. You would think my mother could have kept it until I got back home rather than forwarding it to me. Some news to get before finals, and with all this going on."

"Shit, man. I'm sorry." Mark looked down at the ground. "I'll be facing the same thing next year. Prison's not my thing. And you know how much I hate cold weather." Mark took a deep drag on his smoke. "Canada's an option for you though—*America, Love It or Leave It*, you know, the bumper sticker. Besides, you like snow. Hey, what about a grad school deferment?"

I flicked the ash from the end of my cigarette, took another drag, and watched the exhaled smoke drift in the breeze. "They're hard to get since the lottery went into effect. I guess I could apply for one to delay it, but in the end, I'd probably be facing the same options I have now."

I never felt I would have to go to Vietnam; I knew I'd get out of it somehow. But now . . . maybe my intuition wasn't as good as I thought. I didn't love America, but I didn't want to leave either. I took another drag off the Marlboro and looked at Mark.

"I'm really scared, man."

When the draft notice first arrived, I could barely finish reading it before getting sick to my stomach. Since then, the news had sat like an iron ball in my gut.

Mark was silent. We smoked.

"I don't know what to do." I stared at my shoes as I ground out the butt of my smoke.

He nodded.

4

Fall 1970
Toronto, Canada

I WAS LEFT alone to man the server line of the Student Union cafeteria at the University of Toronto just before closing for the night. My hair was in a ponytail; I wore jeans with frayed ends and an old button-down shirt my mother bought me before my senior year in college. It was covered with a starched white servers jacket.

It wasn't busy. Mostly I just stood there, gazing out at the empty tables and booths, my mind a blank until I was interrupted by a student clacking his plastic tray noisily along the metal slide that wound around the buyer's side of the entrées, side dishes, and desserts. It was 7:45 pm, almost closing time for the cafeteria line.

"Well, what have we tonight?" the customer asked. He looked to be about my age but had short dark brown hair and was clean-shaven, wearing dress slacks, and a tattersall shirt with, of all things, a black v-neck sweater.

I pointed to the entrées with my tongs. "Well, as I assume you can see, fried chicken and roast beef."

"Which would you recommend?"

"This time of night they're both a bit dried out from sitting under the heat lamps. But I can pour *au jus* over the beef to make it taste like wet shoe leather." I gave him a slight smile.

He chuckled. "Okay, my man, give me the beef with potatoes and whatever that green stuff is."

"Well, *my man*, the green stuff is allegedly broccoli." Did he think that just because I worked in the serving line I was nothing more than a servant? Did he wait on himself at home or have a cadre of hired help to support his every whim? I didn't like people who acted like they were superior either in intellect or wealth, and I wasn't his *man*. If he was rich, he shouldn't be eating here in the first place. I pulled a plate from the stack, and slapped on a pile of roast beef, covered it with *au jus*, added a spoon full of mashed potatoes ladled with brown gravy, and spooned the over-cooked broccoli on to the remaining empty spot on the plate.

"Here you go. Enjoy." A dash of sarcasm wouldn't make the food any worse than it already was, but it did make me feel better.

He took the plate and put it on the tray. "Thanks, man," he said with a sheepish smile.

He proceeded down the line, selecting a chocolate pudding for dessert and a cup of coffee before getting to the cashier. My eyes followed him as he found a booth in the quiet of the empty Union cafeteria. There were no more potential customers that I could see, so I started to move the food to the containers used to save them for some concoction that would be served if not tomorrow, then probably the next day. When I finished closing up the serving line, I put on my army surplus jacket, grabbed my backpack, and headed out through the near-empty cafeteria.

"Join me for a cup of coffee?" my last customer asked as I walked past his booth.

I turned to look at him. Who was this guy? Rich, condescending, and now asking me to join him. I intended to go back to my apartment and finish my reading assignments. I was tired, not just from today's full load of classes and several hours working in the Union, but from days and weeks of keeping my nose in my books and trying to stay off the radar of anyone who might wonder what I was really doing in Canada. This guy didn't look like he'd even remotely have anything in common with me—he wasn't my kind of people. I was about to say "no thanks," but another night alone in my sparse apartment? There was no one I knew in Toronto other than my teachers, advisor, and the cafeteria help. I guess I could do worse than this well-dressed snob. Besides, a cup of coffee would keep me awake for the little bit of studying I ahead of me.

"Okay. Why not?"

I dropped my backpack on the floor by his table and helped myself at the coffee station. I added my usual portion of sugar and a bit more cream than normal to turn the stale coffee to a light brown and headed towards Michelle at the cash register. She waved me away, just happy her long workday was finally over. I returned to the booth and scooted in on the opposite side.

"I am Anton Tomasin." He reached his hand across the table.

"Jude Anders." I shook his hand.

"You were right about the beef, Jude. One needs a chainsaw to cut through it, but I did not expect much better." We both chuckled.

He set his fork on his plate and took a sip of coffee. "I have seen you in the Union a few times. What are you studying?"

"I'm working on a masters in theology." Hearing my own words made me cringe—an atheist studying to be a minister.

"Here at U of T?"

"Yeah, the Toronto School of Theology."

"Yes, I heard about that. It is a consortium of seminaries or schools of religion isn't it?"

"They just started it this year." TST turned out to provide exactly the kind of haven I was looking for. I stirred my coffee; the bottom of the urn was never a good choice.

"Do you have your undergraduate degree in theology or philosophy?"

"No, economics."

He gave me a curious look. "Well now, that is an odd mixture. Where did you get your undergraduate?"

I told him, and he quickly replied, "Oh, I get it. A Yank, conscientious objector."

"Working on my masters before becoming a preacher or a teacher." I was matter-of-fact, not knowing who this guy was or what he wanted. For all I knew, he worked for the U.S. government rounding up draft dodgers. I had probably said too much already.

"And you? What are you studying?"

"I am getting a masters in political science. I may go on to law after that."

"Is the program a part of the Philosophy Department or the Business School?"

"Actually, it is its own department, and I may say, the political science program here is well-respected. Besides my parents live in Toronto, so I can keep the comforts of home."

Comforts of home. That certainly confirmed my initial suspicions of his economic status. I warily sipped my coffee. Anton looked oddly familiar, but I couldn't place where I had seen him. Maybe he had eaten here before; perhaps we had crossed paths on campus and I didn't remember.

"Living at home was the last thing I wanted when I chose a university." I hoped we were treading onto safer ground. "In fact, I gave up a scholarship to a very good private college in the city where I lived."

"And where is, I mean was, that?"

"St. Louis."

"Well, Jude, how do like the new School of Theology?"

He sat there drinking his coffee and staring at me as though he could see right through me. I felt my walls going up and tried to make my expressions as flat as I could. "The program seems promising." I took another sip of the stale coffee. "I have a few interesting courses this semester. The professors seem first rate, coming from Knox, Trinity, and Wycliffe."

He pushed his plate aside. Anton apparently had had about as much of his entrée as he could stomach. Half of it remained on his plate, cold by now. "Do you live on campus?"

"I have a studio apartment about six blocks away, but spend most of my time here in the Union, working or studying."

He sank his spoon into the pudding, a gelatinous glob I had mixed up hours earlier from an enormous carton of chocolate powder and a gallon of skim milk.

"I was thinking about getting a beer before I head home." He stirred the pudding but didn't bother to taste it. "Would you be interested?"

I checked the time; like my treasured Zippo, my watch was a gift from my grandfather, one of his old ones. Anton made me wary—still, I had not made any friends since coming to Toronto. And I admit I was always a sucker for good conversation with Poli Sci majors.

"I guess a quick one would be okay. I only have some light reading to do tonight."

"Great. I know just the place."

It was just a few blocks to a small bar on Yonge Street that was mostly patronized by students. Along the way we talked about the courses we were taking this semester, and we began an interesting discussion of Hume's political philosophy. Anton admired Hume because he didn't believe in natural rights—there weren't any except for those one could claim and hold on to with force, if necessary.

"That's why I admire what you're doing in the States. Fighting your government's claim that they have the right to draft you to serve in a war. Although there might be more effective methods."

"We're fighting against the war," I interjected.

"Yes, but it is the draft really when you think about it. If people were not forced into conscription, there would be no protests."

I rubbed my cold hands together and thrust them back into my pockets. "I'm not sure I agree. But, at any rate, the alternatives to being drafted are pretty onerous."

"Like getting a 4D deferment and attending a lovely little institution like TST far away from the insanity of the States these days."

I didn't respond; he held the door to the bar open, and I went in ahead of him. The place was fairly crowded—unexpected for a weekday night. We got a couple of beers at the bar and found a table against the back wall.

"What does your father do?" I asked. Although he seemed adept at turning the conversation back on me at every chance, I was done providing information until he gave a little more about himself. But my question made him look a little uncomfortable. Was that too personal a question to ask in Canada?

"Which one, my adoptive father or the real one?"

His answer surprised me. "Both . . . I guess."

"My adoptive father whose name I bear is in the export/import business, mostly industrial metals. My real father, who I rarely talk to, is into a number of enterprises, but I guess you could say he is chiefly into media."

"Media?"

"You know, newspapers, radio stations, television stations."

"Yeah, I know what media is. And your adoptive father. What kind of metals?"

"The standard stuff: aluminum, zinc, copper."

"They must both do very well," I said as I took my first sip of the Molson. Industrial metals, export/import, media baron . . . not your standard middle-class jobs, that's for sure.

"And I do benefit," Anton concurred. He tapped his beer bottle against mine in a toast. He not only was wealthy, he was apparently proud of it too.

I took another drink of my beer. "What about your mothers?" If his fathers were that interesting, I wondered what kind of women they would be attached to—middle-age matrons who stayed in the background or expensive pretty young things?

Anton was staring at the waitress with her short skirt and tight top. He turned back to me. "My adoptive mother is . . . well, she is best described as a socialite, probably with little redeeming value from your point of view. I guess she is good at planning parties."

What did he mean, my point of view? Was he now sniping at my middle-class background?

"But she raised you, didn't she?"

Anton took a sip of his beer. "I was adopted at birth. But my nanny raised me. You get the picture."

He showed no reluctance to answer any of my admittedly personal questions. If anything, I was more curious about him than before.

"Any brothers or sisters?"

"No, just me. I think my parents just wanted to have the appearance of a normal family. But not one that included screaming kids fighting each other. How about you?"

"Only child. And your real mother—what about her?"

"My real father either does not know much about her or will not tell me."

He swirled his beer bottle along the edges of the wet rings it left on the table. Someone had just put a coin in the jukebox and *The Letter* was now blaring throughout the bar, reminding me of the Shack and the many times Kathy and I had gone there for a burger and a beer.

"He says she was just some college girl he met at a business conference in your country. When she delivered me, she gave me up for adoption. My father tracked me down about a year ago. He said he was curious about me and also felt some obligation to support my future. He has plenty of money and his wife died a year earlier. It sounded to me like now he had room in his life for me, you know what I mean? Still, I rarely talk with him. I guess it will take some time for us to get to know each other."

This was an interesting story. Too much like my own in some ways. "Did you ever try to find your real mother?"

"I did not see the point. What would be accomplished? And what about your parents, Jude? I mean, what do they do?"

I took a long pull on my beer and equally long look at Anton. "I was raised by my mother—you know, one of those single-parent kids. I honestly don't know who my father is. When I was little she told me that he died in the Korean War. Since I didn't have his last name, I became suspicious when I got older. When I finally pressed her for an answer, she told me he was really a guy she met in a bar in Boston. She didn't relate the details, but you get the picture. And she wasn't going to seek out some back-alley butcher . . . know what I mean? Anyway, she didn't know his last name so she gave me hers."

Anton leaned back in his chair, lifting the front feet from the floor. "What does she do?"

"Works in the assembly line of the Chrysler plant." I couldn't wait for his reaction to that one. A rich kid out for a drink with the blue-collar crowd.

Anton finished the last of his beer. He seemed to have run out of steam. "That must be a tiresome job."

"You do what you have to in order to survive." I tipped my bottle of Molson in salute.

I'm sure survival was never an issue for him. I downed the last of my Molson and pulled my stuff together to head out. It had begun spitting rain and I had a bit of a walk home. I pulled up the collar of my jacket to the back of my neck as we walked outside.

Anton handed me his business card. I smiled as I took it; I had never actually seen a business card, let alone been handed one by a fellow student.

"If we don't see each other on campus, give me a ring and let's get together." He started walking back toward his car on campus, but stopped and turned. "Oh, I assume you have a phone."

OVER THE NEXT several weeks I went to classes, worked on my assignments and served food at the Student Union. Each evening on my way home from work I checked the mail, nervously waiting to hear from the draft board. I had indeed, as Anton had joked, applied for a 4D—a deferment reserved for those who were pursuing a career in the ministry. Just in case the 4D was rejected, I enrolled at a seminary in Canada instead of one in the States as a backup. It didn't hurt that the TST was in its first year, looking for applicants, and had some financial aid to dish out. Honestly, I expected the deferment would be denied. I filled out the forms in July and received only one letter from the draft board, requesting proof of my enrollment in seminary. That was in October. Now it was coming on December and still no word.

Christmas came and went. I spent the holiday break alone in my small apartment without a tree. My mother sent a package with some new jeans, a sweater and some homemade cookies. We talked briefly on Christmas day, mostly about how I was getting along in Toronto.

I ran into Anton again on my way into the Student Union shortly after classes got underway in January. We had coffee and talked for an hour or so, mostly about politics and some economics—the inflation in the States, a result of paying for the war and social programs at the same time. He obviously knew a lot more about economics than I did about political science, although I kept my own when discussing political philosophy—that was the one philosophy course I had taken as an undergraduate.

Back at home, the protests continued, but I was content to read about them from the sidelines. Congress debated the repeal of the Gulf of Tonkin Resolution and in January it followed through, but Nixon continued the war anyway, claiming the powers of the executive branch of our government. Then there was talk about defunding the war and limiting the powers of the president. Debate after debate. I was happy to be away from the continued rancor over the war, but was anxious for it to end so I could get on with some semblance of a normal life. Everything seemed to move so slowly, and still there was no word from my draft board.

Through the winter, my meetings with Anton became a regular occurrence. We saw each other at least a couple of times a week, sometimes over coffee in the Union, sometimes for a beer in the bar on Yonge Street. Come March, I was sick of the cold and gray of Toronto, and had even less enthusiasm for my job in the cafeteria.

"I have talked about you so much my father would like to meet you," he said one night in the Union near closing time, surprising me with an invitation to dinner at his home on Saturday. "It is not a big deal, really. Besides I thought you might like a nice meal." He nodded to the cafeteria food I was eating, "And some decent wine, of course."

"I guess so." I hesitated, not being sure I wanted to mingle with the upper crust. "Do I have to get a haircut?"

"Please do not be ridiculous, Jude."

"Do I need a dinner jacket? Because I don't have one."

Anton smiled. "In spite of what you may think, my friend, we are not snobby rich. Just wear a sweater."

"Oh, so I don't need pants?"

We both laughed and agreed he would pick me up at 6:00 pm.

I SPENT SATURDAY morning pressing my one pair of dress slacks and an oxford-cloth shirt I hadn't worn in all the months I'd been in Toronto. My new Christmas sweater would come in handy, although my old navy pea coat would have to stand in for an overcoat. The outside still looked fine, but the acetate lining was torn in several places. I knew not to put my keys in the coat pockets—they'd fall inside between the lining and the outer wool and be hard to root out later. My coat added to my image as a hippie, but it was all I had. Anton was right on time in his little orange BMW.

"Well, Mr. Judas Anders, don't you look dapper. It almost looks like you are going on a date."

I flinched. Even my mother never used my full first name. Running away from the draft and my country, I guess some could consider me a traitor.

"Just Jude, okay? And to answer your question, Mr. Tomasin, I *am* going on a date . . . with you and your parents." I opened up my coat as we stood outside his car to show Anton the torn lining. "I'm sorry, but this is the only winter coat I own."

He chuckled. "It looks fine. Speaking of dates, have you found a nice Canadian woman to your liking yet?"

"There's a lot to look at, but I've been busy and, frankly, not in the best state of mind to start a relationship."

"This draft thing is really wearing on your head?"

"Yep."

"Well, maybe we should check out some of the prostitutes on Yonge Street." He laughed as he opened the driver's side door.

"Are you buying?" I joked as I slid into the passenger seat.

I certainly could use the warmth of a woman. I hadn't had that since my last night with Kathy before she left the university. Maybe a one-night stand would relieve some of the tension I lived with every day.

Anton put his car in first gear and sped off. News about the Vietnam War was on the radio, and he quickly turned it off.

"Now tell me again what your father does?"

"Export and import of industrial and commercial metals." He maneuvered easily through the light Saturday night traffic.

"Is it his company or a corporation?"

"Oh, it is his. My father would never turn decisions over to shareholders."

I tried to recall the definitions of small, medium and large privately-held companies. "How big is it?"

"Well that depends on how you define 'big', I guess. He does not employ a large number of people, but the revenues are substantial."

"How substantial?" I paused, realizing as soon as I said it how nosey it sounded. "Never mind, that's just the economist in me coming out."

"No, no, it is quite okay to ask. I would say his business is worth in the hundreds of millions of dollars. Canadian, of course."

"That is substantial." I looked over at Anton.

"Please, Jude, he and my mother will not put on airs with you. Just relax. We will have some good food, wine, and conversation. Okay?"

"Yeah, sure." Even so, I imagined sitting at a formal dining room table big enough for twenty, being served by a butler.

Anton and his family were better off than I could have possibly imagined. And now I was going to their house for dinner. We were leaving the city limits and entering a wooded area north of Toronto. Anton turned off the highway and onto a twisty two-lane road. He downshifted the BMW, taking each curve with the skill of a Grand Prix driver.

When we got to Anton's house, I felt a little more at ease. It wasn't what I would call a mansion, but it was quite large—a two-story brick and stucco Tudor on several acres with lots of pine, aspen, and birch trees—very private and with the winter snow, very quiet. Anton parked in the drive near the garage, and he and I entered a breezeway connecting the house and garage. It took us into a hallway running between the kitchen and what appeared to be a small office. Anton took my coat and ushered me down the hall to the spacious foyer surrounded by a second floor balcony on three sides. Anton's mother was halfway down the last flight of stairs, wearing a modest blue dress. Even without heels, Mrs. Tomasin was on the tall side, and every strand of her brown hair was neatly in place as though she had just been to the beauty parlor. For a woman in her forties, she looked well-taken care of.

"You must be Jude," she said offering me her hand.

"Yes, Mrs. Tomasin."

"Oh, please call me Laurel. This is not a time for formality."

I smiled. "Thank you, Laurel."

"Jack," she called toward the living room. "Anton and his friend, Jude, are here. Why don't you boys go on in and have a drink. I have to finish in the kitchen." She turned to go as Anton's father appeared at the living room entrance.

"Jack Tomasin," he said with his hand out stretched. He looked at me strangely, his hand frozen in mid-air, but he quickly put on a smile. His handshake was firm and businesslike. "You must be Jude."

"Yes, sir. Jude Anders." Maybe Anton never told Jack that I had hair down to my shoulders, so unlike his son's short haircut.

"Have a drink, Jude?"

"Love one, thank you."

"Hard or soft? And you, Anton, your usual or something else tonight?"

"The usual, but please, Father, with only two cubes."

Jack Tomasin, a man of slight stature with salt and pepper hair, made his way to a wet bar in the living room. He wore a gray wool sweater over a starched button-down collared white shirt, khaki chinos, and cordovan tassel loafers. The look was casual, yet elegant in a way. When he reached the bar, he looked back at me.

"Just a beer, Jack, thanks." I didn't have a whole lot of experience with hard liquor so I decided to play it safe.

"American, Canadian, or European?"

"A Molson if you have it."

"No problem, good choice."

He reached into a small refrigerator hidden within the cabinetry surrounding the bar sink, pulled out a bottle, and slowly poured the beer into a chilled glass—a first for me—then he tonged some ice from a small bucket on the bar into a rocks glass and filled it halfway with scotch.

"Here you go," he said, handing the drinks to Anton and me. "Jude, Anton tells me you're studying at the Toronto School of Theology. Are you intending to preach?"

I was taken a little off guard by his directness and looked at Anton. He obviously hadn't told his father the real reason for me being in Canada.

"Not unless I have to. I guess it depends on how long the war and the draft last."

"Aah." Jack smiled at Anton, who nodded back. "Anton tells me you have a degree in economics. Why aren't you working in your field while you're here in Canada, you know, part-time?"

I took a quick sip of the ice-cold beer. "School keeps me pretty busy, and I'm not a Canadian citizen. I doubt I could get a visa to work for a private company."

Jack nodded. "I don't mean to be insensitive, but maybe you should stay here and finish your theology studies even when the war ends. There might be a future in the church for you. With your background in economics and the size of the pockets of most of these churches, you might be able to make a good living. Even the pope could learn a few things from Milton Friedman."

I looked at him quizzically as I downed half the Molson.

"You know, Friedman's theory of unfettered capitalism? Quite the rage in today's economic circles. But, of course, you know all about that. Seriously, when the war ends, what will you do?"

Maybe I had drunk too much of the beer too fast; I could feel the alcohol relaxing away some of my tension. "To be honest, sir, I haven't thought about it. I've been focused on staying out of fatigues, if you know what I mean."

Jack chuckled heartily.

"But it's a good question. I look forward to the time when I can think about what I am going to do with the rest of my life."

"Well, Vietnam is a sad state of affairs. As you might guess, there are a number of companies making some real money off of it. But I am afraid that your government, and mine for that matter, have taken their eye off the real threats."

"Real threats?"

"Oh, here we go, Dad, again?" Anton interrupted.

Jack ignored Anton's plea. "Seriously. I don't worry much about Vietnam. Hell, give Ho Chi Min the damn country; it's nothing but jungle and swamp anyway. I doubt that little communist could threaten Suharto's rule in Indonesia. We worry about the fall of Southeast Asia to the communists when they are in our backyard. No one is paying any attention to South America. That's where the real problems lie. Just look at Chile. The stupid people there just elected a . . ."

"Jack, you and the boys need to come into dinner," Anton's mother announced at the living room entrance. "Jude will not be impressed by a cold roast."

At Jack's lead we put our drinks on the bar and made our way into the dining room on the other side of the great foyer. The conversation that began over cocktails was not continued over dinner or after, but I was curious about what Jack had said. Was something going on in South America that was more dangerous to us than Vietnam?

Although I was itching to prod Jack to continue, Mrs. Tomasin controlled the dinner conversation with numerous questions about my mother and her own views on the poor Americans who were stuck in Canada because of "this terrible war." The Tomasins made me feel comfortable, and I enjoyed their company, not to mention the food. I hadn't had a good home-cooked meal in many months. I also realized this was probably the first time I had experienced this end of the economic spectrum. Considering how pleasant the evening was, a notion I had not thought of before began to sink in. Beyond the money, the cars and the mansions, maybe the rich were just like the rest of us.

5

Spring 1971
Darien, Connecticut

"THAT BASTARD WANTS 60% of the profits for mining and refining his ore. It's nationalization, Joseph. When that happens the company stock is going to fall through the goddamn floor. I thought we had some control over those boys in D.C. How can they let Allende nationalize U.S. businesses? We're the ones who built up their economy—the fucking peons."

"Yes, yes, the battle against the Communists, or Developmentalists as they call themselves in Chile. First Russia and Eastern Europe, then China and Southeast Asia, and now in our own backyard." He turned away from the window behind the large, burled walnut desk overlooking his Connecticut estate and met the angry eyes of his compatriot sitting in an over-stuffed chair in his paneled study. "It's going to be a long struggle. But, in the end, you know we will win."

"Yeah, how do I know that? The evidence seems to be going the other way. So many poor people in so many back-assed countries, dominated by dictators, warlords, most of them corrupt. The people don't know the fucking difference. So whoever gives them the most they support."

"In the short term, yes." Joseph moved to a small side table and poured two glasses of whiskey, offering one to his guest.

"Thanks. I can use a drink. But for god sake, do you expect those ignorant bastards to look at the long run?"

"No, I expect them to take what they can get now, just like you and most other people. But some of us are a little more patient. We wait. We see a bigger picture. We know they will eventually fail, and when they do we step in and double, even triple our share."

"That may be, but right now I have a bigger problem. My stock in the company is going to . . ."

"Listen." Joseph handed his guest the drink. "We have people inside and out. We work both ends at the same time, quietly. We stop what we can, and plant the seeds that position us for the longer term. And we take advantage of the short term. We can always make money. Even under the worst of circumstances."

"So how do we do that? Or better how do I do that?"

Joseph took a seat in the chair next to his guest's and sipped his drink. "I would suggest that you buy some military stock like Sicorsky. After Allende nationalizes the copper business, you should consider dumping copper to drive the price down. Yes, this will hurt your bottom line in the short run, but it will put going-concern pressures on their new business. Who knows, maybe it will get bad enough that he will give it back." He chuckled.

"I get the dumping, but why buy military stock?"

He gazed into his study's empty fireplace. "Because in due time there will be a coup in Chile and the military will run the country. They will need equipment and weapons to root out the opposition and restore and maintain order in the country."

"And just how can you be sure of that? You think you're the goddamn CIA? You think you're going to just get on the phone to George or that Nazi and tell them what to do?"

A wry smirk covered his middle-aged face, distorting the lines beginning to form into the sides of his mouth. "No, I do not think I am the CIA . . . and I do not like talking on telephones."

6

Fall 1971
Toronto, Canada

IN JULY THE Congress chose not to renew the Selective Service Act as an outright act of rebellion against Nixon's handling of the Vietnam War. Draft boards across the country put their "call ups" on hold through the summer, and the anxiety that I had gradually pushed to background over the past six months began to rise again. Finally, in October, after intense negotiations with the White House, the Act was renewed, but only after commitments were made to substantially reduce the number of draftees. I remembered when I received the news. I was in my third semester at TST and still had not heard any news from my draft board. The days were warm but the leaves were changing from green to yellow, burnt orange to brown, some beginning to gather on the ground. One late afternoon while I was, as usual, working in the cafeteria, Anton walked into the serving line, but instead of a tray, he had a newspaper tucked under his arm.

"Hey, Jude. Can you take a break? I have some news you might be interested in."

I asked one of the other servers to fill in my position, got a cup of coffee, and met Anton at our usual booth by the windows.

"What's up?" I asked.

He handed me his copy of *The Globe and Mail.*

"Page 2, second column."

I opened the paper.

"Shit!" The headline read "US To Renew Draft."

"No, no," Anton insisted, "read on."

A few paragraphs down I understood.

"The Pentagon announced today that it will substantially reduce the number of draftees this year. Previous estimates were that individuals with lottery numbers up to 200 would be issued notices of military service induction. As part of negotiations with the U.S. Congress that number will be reduced to 125. Individuals with a draft lottery number greater than 125, and eligible for the draft this year, will not be drafted."

I sat there in a haze.

"You told me once that your lottery number was 141, didn't you?"

I shook my head, making sure this wasn't a dream. "Yeah, that's the number."

"Well, then, my friend. It is over for you. You are free."

"I don't believe it. There must be a catch."

I read through the rest of the news article. Nope, no catch. I flashed on that day we shut down the university; all those people assembled for the protest and the chancellor telling us he had closed the school, just like that. I remembered waiting for the other shoe to drop then, too. But Anton was right; it really was over for me.

"Wow!" I tried to drink some coffee, but my hands were shaking too much.

"So what are you going to do?" Anton had the joyous smile of a small child on his face. Mark had asked me that same question after we shut down the university. I didn't have any clearer idea how to answer now than I did then.

"Anton, Christ, man, I don't know. Give me some time to think about it."

"Well, you can think about it in the serving line until 8:00. I will be back then to take you out for a celebration. Oh, and you can forget about going to class tomorrow. You will not be up to it."

I HUNG AROUND TST for another couple of months, wanting to be certain that the government would not draft beyond number 125 during the remainder of the year. I attended classes and continued my job in the cafeteria. Anton and I spent more and more time in our favorite bar on Yonge Street, talking politics, economics, and the options for "my next life."

The Tomasins, whom I had visited frequently during the summer, held a belated celebration of my newfound freedom. Every time I went to Anton's house, Jack and I had lively debates over global economic issues, and this time was no exception. Jack avidly supported the widely-held position that government had grown too big and was interfering in the market place. There was too much government spending, crowding out capital in the private sector; there was too much government intervention with rules and regulations on what business could and could not do; the "goddamn unions" were driving labor costs through the roof.

"That's what's causing your inflation, Jude. The regulations and the unions are driving up the cost of doing business."

"What about the cost of the war?"

"The war is a very small percentage of your GDP. And the military spending creates more jobs, just like World War II. It brought us out of the Depression. But the unions . . . the damn unions are demanding not just higher salaries, but more benefits, from healthcare to pensions. Most of the top economists are saying the same thing. Friedman has it right. You're an economist; you should know that. And just look at Chile. They're nationalizing all of the key sectors of their economy. Communism, on our continent!"

This was one more variation on the economic discussions Jack and I had. Why was everyone so preoccupied with communism? Did people have to have something to fear? Or even hate?

"Jack, you know communism as an economic theory hasn't worked anywhere in the world. So why should we be worried? Give it time if you really believe Chile's turning communist, which I think is unclear. It won't work and will turn into something that will." I lit a cigarette. "But to tell you the truth, I have a certain sympathy for what Chile is doing. Foreign corporations have pillaged the natural resources of their country, leaving them with a miniscule percentage of the profits."

"Pillage!" He threw his shoulders back. "These countries would still be in the Dark Ages without the help of our corporations. You think these people are smart enough or have the capital to extract and process those natural resources? Both parties in the deal have benefited. And you have to keep in mind which party has taken all the risk." He was just getting warmed up, and I knew what was coming. I tried to reason with him.

"Jack, if the country has more income, it can invest in capital projects and industrialization that will position it for a stronger, self-sustaining economy in the future. If the people have higher wages, they can buy more goods and services that in turn create more demand and more employment. Everyone will benefit. As I understand it, these countries want strong economic growth from the private sector, but they want to be able to develop from within. They are not rejecting capitalism, they simply want to direct it to benefit the majority of the people rather than a few."

Jack was having none of it. "The only way to have strong growth is to let the marketplace work without interference from government. And the businesses that have long-term investments in those countries deserve to recoup their costs through profit. But it is even worse in Chile; they are appropriating the businesses that were created and are owned by the businessmen that made those investments. It's not the government's to take!"

I didn't remember seeing him so exercised before. I was not in the mood for a heated argument, and was a guest in his home. I decided to end the debate.

"I understand, Jack. I'm not sure what the right answer is."

"Well, you're still young and haven't been out in the real world yet. Get a job, earn some money, and find a girl. Then you will begin to understand." His voice quickly calmed to its normal tone. "By the way, have you thought any more about what you are going to do when you get back to the States?"

He sounded like a father giving counsel to his son. And sure, I more than anyone wanted a life made of something other than fear. But what made Jack think the world I had lived in the last two years was any less real than his?

"Yeah, some. I was thinking about applying for an analyst position with the Federal Reserve."

"The Federal Reserve?" Jack's voice heated again. "Jesus, talk about the ultimate controller. Every time business gets going, here comes the goddamn Fed to put a damper on things. You would be better off finishing graduate school."

"Anything but that." I laughed. "As you said, I have to get out into the real world. I want experience—not more theories."

"Well, why don't you try the IMF or the World Bank? At least they are doing the real work for developing economies around the world."

"Except for one thing, I only have an undergraduate degree, and it's not from the University of Chicago."

"No, no. You might be surprised. At least submit an application."

I knew all about Chicago-style economics, with its emphasis on monetary theory and free-market capitalism. The World Bank and the IMF were completely dominated by theories promoted by its adherents. It was almost as though there was an inside track for economists who came out of Chicago to head straight to Washington.

IN THE MIDDLE of November I sent a letter to my draft board, dropping my application for a 4D deferment, and notified my advisor at TST that I would be quitting at the end of the semester. He seemed to know why without any explanation from me. I had two months to think about what to do next. Mom would help me out once I got back home until I found a job. Anton took me to the bus terminal on an overcast morning in late January. I was ready to get on with my life, but would miss him. He had become a dear friend, the kind I never had before.

7

Present Time
Andros, Greece

ANTON, ANTON. DID you care more about me than yourself? I turned away from the woman seated beside me and wiped away a tear drizzling down my right cheek. Outside the window of the *Albion* a large island was coming into view. The ferry was slowing, coming into port. This must be Andros. One more stop after this one, then finally on to Amorgos.

It was early afternoon when we docked, and we had about thirty minutes before departing again. Passengers, continuing on to further ports, could disembark or stroll around the upper deck. I took the latter option, placing a laminated "occupied" sign on my seat before scooting past the woman next to me.

It was good to be outside. Perhaps the fresh air would help my exhaustion. The sun was bright and there were only high wispy clouds parading through the blue-sky canopy. The air was crisp but warm under the sun, and the smell of diesel fuel from the boats in the harbor filled the air. I stood at the rail and pulled out the old Zippo. I twirled the wheel and the flame jumped to life, licking the edge of my cigarette. From the top of the ferry I had a good view of the town—whitewashed stucco buildings no more than two stories high giving shape to narrow, winding cobblestone streets.

My conversation with Jack at my celebration party so many years ago bounced around in my head. He was not alone in his economic views; they were the same views and opinions being repeated over and over again like a mantra from many quarters. Even I was beginning to question my own convictions. After all, these were the positions held by so many respected and experienced economists, politicians, and businessmen. I shook my head. I also remembered thinking back then that maybe Jack was right about where I should go to work.

A huge burden had been lifted from my shoulders when I beat the draft, and I had two months hanging out with Anton to relish in my newfound freedom. But a new anxiety was beginning to grow inside me—I had to face the working world like most of my friends. Like Jack said: the "real world." I had part-time jobs while in high school, worked for the railway in the summers, and even sorted bones for the Anthropology Department during college to make ends meet. That is, before Paul and I started our lucrative little business. But these never seemed like real jobs, just like my cafeteria gig at the student union in Toronto. It was hard to imagine what working a full-time job year after year would be like, and frankly, it didn't sound appealing. But I had no choice. That's what we did when we grew up.

It was funny how I just fell into my career. Sure, I received a degree in economics, but I only studied it because it was more interesting than anything else, and maybe because I was good at math. Still, I had no real idea what economists did beyond teaching at the university.

I thought back on the major decisions I had made throughout my life. Most of the time I just threw myself into a new situation, sensing it would turn out okay—just like I did with high school, college, even moving to Toronto to dodge the draft. After facing the prospect of Vietnam, I thought for sure my good karma had abandoned me. That had shaken my confidence in my intuition and my future. But every time, things worked out—and generally to my advantage. Even my years in Toronto had given me connections that shaped the rest of my life.

I took the final drag on my cigarette and studied the waterfront, the blue sky against the whitewashed houses, the gulls careening towards the shore. Did things happen to me for a reason or were they just a series of coincidences?

The ship's public address system announced that it was time to be reseated. A small number of new passengers were boarding with their luggage and packages. I took my seat and pulled *Guns, Germs and Steel* from my backpack—an epic attempt at explaining why some civilizations succeeded at the expense of others. I had wanted to read this book since it first hit the *New York Times* Best Sellers list over a dozen years ago. At the rate of my reading, I would not finish it by the time I got to Amorgos.

8

April 1972
Washington D.C.

"FIRST DAY?"

I looked up from the New Employee paperwork that I had been working on for the past half hour. A redhead in a tight black skirt and matching heels stood in the doorway of my cubicle, giving me a mocking look. She looked taller than I was, but I couldn't be sure with the heels and her hair piled up atop her head.

"Pretty obvious, huh?"

She gave a slight laugh. "Actually, I was kidding. I thought you were the son of one our employees. Must be the baby face."

"I am twenty-three." I don't know why I was so defensive; she couldn't be much older.

"Really? Wow, you are young, at least for this department. My name is Fallon, Fallon Connelly."

"Jude Anders," I replied, getting up to shake her hand.

Fallon leaned against the corner of my cubicle doorway. "Well, Jude Anders, how did you come to the IMF?"

"I applied. You know, filled out an application."

She took an erect stance and put her left hand on her hip. "Just filled out an application? So who do you know?"

"What do you mean?"

"For someone your age to be assigned to this department, you have to know someone."

That was an idea I hadn't considered when reading the offer of employment from the International Monetary Fund in Washington D.C.

"No one that I am aware of."

"I guess you'll find out eventually." Her tone sounded sarcastic and the words "tough cookie" rolled through my head. "What's your first assignment?"

"Right now, filling out these forms from Personnel." I pointed to the stack of paper on the desk. "They handed me the paperwork, then showed me to my cubicle. After that I don't know. How about you? I mean what are you working on?"

"Finishing some work on the Indonesia account."

"Indonesia?" I remembered that a communist dictator was overthrown there sometime in the late '60s, and the new president was supported by the United States.

"Rule number one, Jude, no details. We keep our work confidential except when we work with other economists at the IMF or our clients. You will get your dos and don'ts when . . . Have you met with Simpson yet?"

"No, who's he?"

"Personnel didn't tell you?" She turned abruptly and waved, saying "Later" as she disappeared in the maze of cubicles. I returned to my paperwork, more confused than ever.

In about an hour the phone in my cubicle rang. It was Brent Simpson's secretary, setting a time for me to meet with him. Of course I had to ask where Simpson's office was located in this confusing cityscape of temporary walls, and the directions were so complicated that I asked her to repeat them while I took notes. It seemed like everything was confidential here, including where my boss's office was located.

At the appointed time I picked up a notebook and pen and made my way down a series of hallways, around corners and through sets of doors. I tried not to be distracted by the several glass-walled conference rooms I passed, some of them occupied with my new colleagues pointing at flip-charts, others with lights on but curtains pulled over the glass. Finally, at the end of a long carpeted hallway, a dark-haired woman in her fifties greeted me and picked up her phone announcing my arrival. In less than a minute she ushered me into Simpson's prestigious corner office. The two walls of windows looked out onto a small triangular-shaped park that bordered Pennsylvania Avenue; the other two walls were filled with bookshelves. The only pictures were those of him and, I assumed, his family, framed and neatly arranged on the credenza behind his desk.

"Please have a seat," Simpson said, pointing to the chair opposite his desk. "Have you gotten settled in, Anders?"

"I think so, sir." Was it common that people at the IMF called each other by their last names?

"Good. Just a few more things in addition to all the nondisclosure forms you signed this morning, before I give you your first assignment." Simpson ran his hand over the top of his mostly baldhead and leaned back in his black office chair. "First, all documents that you use in your work or create as a part of an assignment are never to leave these premises except when you have to travel on business. Security, you understand. Second, the work we do here is for member countries and their leaders. As such, your work must be kept in strict confidence. Unless you are working with another IMF employee on a particular assignment, please do not discuss your work with your fellow employees. Third, *never* discuss your work with a non-IMF employee, except an authorized official from the country whose requests you are processing. Understood?"

"Yes, sir."

"Good. Now your first assignment."

That was it? Those were the only dos and don'ts? Fallon Connelly had made it seem like the rules came in a 3-ring binder. Simpson reached to the left corner of his desk and pulled a folder in front of him.

"The government of Chile has requested short-term financing to cover a small financial imbalance. Normally this would be handled by one of our South American analysts, but one is out on maternity leave and we're a bit short-handed. I want you to run a fairly routine analysis to determine that the amount of their request is within acceptable parameters, and the estimated time frame for repayment is reasonable and based on valid assumptions."

"Sir, is there guidance on the parameters?"

Simpson looked surprise. Maybe he had forgotten that I was not just a transfer like most of the other new employees in his department, as Fallon Connelly had suggested.

"Good question, Anders. Typically people assigned to this department . . . well, I guess that is not important."

He opened a drawer in the credenza behind his desk and pulled out a thin black notebook.

"You need to study these. They are the IMF's operating guidelines for loan requests. I think you will find what you need in here. Check in with me if you have questions. I would like some preliminary results by the end of the week—sooner if you finish early."

My first impressions of Brent Simpson were pretty much what I expected from a boss—matter of fact and to the point—all business without being very personable. But after Fallon Connelly's question about how I got this job and Simpson's allusion that someone right out of college does not get assigned to his department, I began to wonder just how I had been accepted to the IMF and assigned here after all.

I spent the next two days pouring over the loan request submitted by Alejandro Baca, Chief Economist, and Roberto Menendez, Senior Economist, of the Central Bank of Chile. The country had not anticipated the current steep decline in copper prices, which was created by large stockpiles and reduced demand, and a sell-off of those copper stockpiles by U.S., Canadian, and British companies. There were requests for loans from the usual cadre of U.S. and European commercial banks, but the loans were denied without clear explanation. On the surface, the loan amounts and time frames for repayment were appropriate, considering they were based on future projections of copper prices and projected economic growth in Chile for the remainder of the year. I was reasonably sure that tax revenues and other actions the Chilean government were taking to shrink its growing budget deficits would provide enough income to make interest and principal payments. I gave the results of my analysis of Chile's loan request in writing to Simpson a day early. Mid-morning on Friday he called me into his office.

"Good job, for your first assignment. Your analysis was thorough and to the point. I will have something new for you on Monday."

"Thank you, Mr. Simpson."

"You have just moved to D.C., haven't you?"

"Last week."

"Well, I am sure there are things you need to do to get settled into your apartment. I don't often do this, but why don't you take off this afternoon. You finished sooner than I had anticipated, and, frankly, I am still working on your next assignment."

After thanking Simpson, I went back to my desk to gather up my things and put away my analysis work. I wanted to know if Chile would get the loan, but I dared not ask.

MOST OF MY first year at the Monetary Fund was spent analyzing loan requests from Third World countries—usually Africa. The more exciting stuff dealing with countries on the European continent, in Southeast Asia or the southern-most countries of South America, known as the Southern Cone, was usually given to the experienced analysts and frequently involved consultations with IMF senior and junior economists. They gathered daily in the conference rooms with one wall of interior glass, which we affectionately called "fish bowls." If I passed by one of these conference rooms hurrying down the hallway, sometimes I snuck a glance at the flip charts filled with writing and drawing, but quickly looked away, remembering Simpson's cautions on my first day at the Fund. Most of the time I kept my head down and focused on my work. There was a lot I had to learn. And frankly, after the anguish of the last few years, I was happy to have discovered what having a job and a steady working life was like, which included lunch with work associates and an occasional cocktail or dinner after work. Sure, there were some dates too, and a few with a sleepover, but nothing with an emotional tie.

I especially appreciated how much I was learning about the world around me. During the '60s there had been military coups in Brazil and Indonesia, and I knew the IMF was involved in various financial arrangements with those new governments. Fallon Connelly owned the "Indonesia account," as it was referred to. She and other economists were busy each day, often working late into the night. I just wished I could be involved in one of those accounts—with something more exciting than the bits and pieces I was working on for African countries.

The Vietnam War protests continued, but America had turned a corner. Most Americans were now against the war, according to opinion polls, and Nixon talked about "peace with honor" during his campaign for re-election. The Democrats had nominated McGovern, vowing to end the war immediately. My mom often called to tell me about working with my grandmother at the phone banks at the McGovern campaign headquarters in St. Louis. They even worked the polls on Election Day before Mom started the night shift at the Chrysler plant. There were rumors of "dirty tricks" by Nixon's campaign before the election at the Democratic Headquarters in the Watergate Building in D.C., but it didn't matter. Nixon was re-elected anyway. I supposed there would always be people who voted against their own best interests. In January of 1973, a peace accord ending the Vietnam War was signed. Our troops were coming home. The "long war" was finally over. For me it was over that morning in Toronto when Anton showed me the newspaper article—now the rest of America could share the same sigh of relief.

With the Vietnam War behind us, we were all anxious to turn the page on that dark side of our recent history—maybe that's why there weren't any ticker-tape parades in New York as the last troops came home. It seemed as though the war was an event that never happened. The pictures of the bloodied bodies in the fields with choppers hovering above the smoke of battle to swoop in and ferry them away, or of the men without limbs lying in beds or shuffling down the hallways of Walter Reed in wheelchairs, suddenly disappeared from the press. We acted like a people happy to forget the whole affair.

The feel and smell of spring was in the air. The famous D.C. cherry trees had bloomed early and were now dropping their blossoms. They reminded me of the redbuds and dogwoods three years ago during the protests in Columbia when we shut down the university over Kent State and the invasion of Cambodia. But at the end of the April, events in Washington took another sinister turn, reminding us that while the war was over, the darkness of the last decade was not—the Watergate hearings, covering the clandestine activities tied directly to the White House began on Capitol Hill. Both Bob Haldeman and John Ehrlichman resigned their positions of Chief of Staff and Counsel to the President as their role in the Watergate scandal began to come to light. Elliot Richardson, a WWII vet with a degree from Harvard Law, was appointed the new Attorney General of the United States. A month later, Richardson appointed a special prosecutor to investigate the Watergate incident.

At the end of each workday I went back to my small apartment, with its lumpy Murphy bed and postage-stamp kitchen, and turned on the small 12-inch black-and-white TV. A gift from an associate from work who had upgraded to color, it was my first set, and I watched the rebroadcast of the Watergate hearings every night at my kitchen table.

One night after work, several analysts and a couple of junior economists invited me to drinks at our usual watering hole. I wanted to catch the replay of the Watergate hearings that evening, so after finishing a Heineken and a little chitchat, I put on my jacket and prepared to leave.

"Only one, Anders? Are you a wimp or just boring?" Fallon asked in her typically abrupt manner.

"Probably both. I want to get home to watch the hearings. Dean was testifying today."

"I've been catching some of them too. Pretty interesting, all in all. Want some company?"

"Are you kidding?" Fallon's company certainly would add another dimension to the proceedings.

"I'm ready to blow this pop stand anyhow. What do you have to eat?"

"I was going to pick up a pizza on the way home."

"Make it pepperoni and sausage and I'm in."

I offered Fallon a beer as we made our way into the tiny kitchen of my apartment, parking dinner from the neighborhood pizzeria on the counter.

"A beer seems appropriate." She accepted a bottle of Molson and popped the cap off with the bottle opener before I could do it for her. "These hearings are finally getting down to the meat and potatoes."

It was clear from John Dean's testimony that there had been a cover-up of the Watergate break-in. Dean was the White House Counsel. Just how high the scandal went was unclear. But it looked like Haldeman and Ehrlichman knew more than they had said. Whatever did happen was beginning to unravel, and fast.

"Motherfuckers," I muttered as Dean unraveled a key piece of information.

Fallon was already half way through her beer. "Yep, the real motherfuckers."

I looked at Fallon, surprised by our sudden frankness with each other.

"Jude, you have no idea of the shit that goes on here."

"Here?"

"In D.C. At the Monetary Fund."

"D.C. I get, but the IMF?"

"I've seen you sneaking a peep into the glass conference rooms when you pass by. Who do you think all those people are in the room?"

Fallon fidgeted in her purse for a cigarette. She lit it, took a long drag and leaned back in the chair to the point I thought it would tip over. A wry smile crossed her face as she sipped her beer.

I wondered what she was getting at. "Economists, right?"

She blew the smoke from her cigarette into the air. "Yeah, some of them. But there are others that are not from the IMF."

"You mean there are economists from other agencies? I assumed some of the economists would be from member countries."

"Not all of the people, even from member countries, are economists. Some of the guys in suits wear uniforms in their country." She winked. "And there are some who are American but not economists either."

"Do they normally wear uniforms too?"

She smiled. "Only if it fits an assigned undercover role."

It took me a few seconds to square the circle. "CIA?"

"Or Military Intelligence, or NSA, or, or who knows what agency. Or what position in which member country's military apparatus." Fallon leaned forward until all four legs of the kitchen chair regained their footing on the floor. "And then there are the secret economists."

"I hadn't really thought about it, but I guess the foreign military thing fits. A number of countries requesting loans come from military-run governments. But why U.S. intelligence?"

U.S. intelligence service, secret economists, military uniforms. I thought the IMF was a body of professionals trying to stabilize a country's economy when it started to fall over the edge. Fallon was making it sound like an arm of a spy ring. All my attention was focused on my colleague; this conversation was counter to everything I had been told over the past year and yet here we were.

"First thing, Jude, not all these countries come to the IMF to request loans or interim financing. In fact, in some cases they argue *against* financial assistance, at least in the usual way. So, for example, we have a general from Chile who, with the CIA, argues against giving loans to Allende, Chile's president. I bet you didn't know that the Chilean loan you processed was put on hold. Not because it wasn't needed or couldn't be paid back, but because it wasn't politically acceptable."

"What do you mean, politically acceptable? What did politics have to do with Chile getting help from the IMF?"

"It means that the interests-in-charge did not think it was a good idea to assist the Chilean government."

"Huh? Who are these interests-in-charge?" I could feel my understanding of the IMF and my own job shifting into something else entirely.

"I have no idea who they all are, but you can put some officials of member countries, the intelligence agencies of the U.S., and maybe most of the executive branch of our government on the list. Then there are the capitalists, whether commercial banks, corporations, or various kinds of influential economists. What they have in common is that they want to use the IMF to promote their agendas, whatever those are."

"You said secret economists. Who are they?"

"Influential thinkers who have the ears of political leaders and economists from around the globe. Usually from the University of Chicago or associated with the economic theories it teaches, or maybe I should say 'preaches'. You know, reduce the size of government, slash debt levels, sell off state-owned businesses and utilities to private business, open economies to free trade and private investment, eliminate regulation, kill unions—the usual stuff coming from those circles."

The Watergate hearings were still going on, but neither of us was listening anymore. My conversations with Jack Tomasin ran through my mind.

"I need another beer." I leaned forward to open the refrigerator door.

"Me, too."

Spooks, manipulation of governments by other governments and people with a hidden agenda—and the IMF was a player in the clandestine operations. This was not like our feel-good, college-kid protests, and was much more sinister and consequential than even our old Plan B. This was hardball.

"Why are you telling me this?" I finally asked her. "What about IMF disclosure policy?"

"I don't know, maybe the alcohol is making me loose-lipped. Maybe because you've been with the IMF for half a year, and you're about to get more deeply involved in the shit that goes on there. I want to spare you the shock that I had during my first exposure to . . . to the world of global economics."

9

May 1973

JUST BEFORE LUNCH, I was beckoned to Simpson's office by his assistant. After acknowledging the time for our meeting, I hung up the phone. I still got a little nervous when I had to meet with the boss. Now I had a couple of hours to think about why he wanted to talk with me. At 2:00 on the button I entered his office. Fallon Connelly was seated in one of the chairs opposite Simpson's desk.

Fallon and I had passed in the hall many times since our conversation at my apartment, but I could tell she didn't want to discuss it further at work. She always politely said hello, but she wouldn't look me in the eyes. It was as though our conversation that night never happened.

"Please have a seat, Anders. I have asked you to join Connelly and me because you will be assisting her on the next assignment."

"Afternoon, Fallon," I said as I sat down next to her.

"The IMF has been asked to study the economic progress in several South American countries. These countries include Brazil, Chile, Uruguay, and Argentina, although Brazil will not be included in this study because of recent changes in their economic and political . . . uh, institutions. Each of these countries has implemented a form of developmentalism. While not recognized as a unique economic theory, there are common components that set it apart from established economic theories."

That was a new one on me; I didn't recall the term from any of my college courses, but as Jack Tomasin had frequently reminded me, real world economics had little to do with textbooks.

"Excuse me, Mr. Simpson, what is developmental . . ."

"Developmentalism, Anders. There have been several economists that . . . Well, I guess that's not important. I will try to give you a simplified explanation."

Simpson's explanation was not simple, but I got the gist of it: an economic theory that, if implemented consistently, would help Third World countries develop their economies by maintaining ownership of their natural resources—oil, gas, minerals, and the like; nationalizing foreign-owned industries; developing their own industries without relying on global companies to develop or operate them; and limiting imported goods from other countries so the government-controlled industries producing the same goods and services could flourish. All of this meant more jobs for the people who lived in these countries, jobs with better wages since much of the profits that typically went to the big companies could be reinvested to expand the business or make it more commpetive, or paid out in higher wages instead.

With more people employed, they could buy more goods and services from their own companies. The more they bought, the more their companies would grow. That increase in demand would cause wages to increase, so people would have more money to buy even more. As personal income and business volume grew, so would tax revenues to support the needed services of a civilized society. It sounded plausible, assuming a government had enough power to limit the endless desire for larger profits and higher salaries.

Simpson continued, this time reading from a document he held in his hand.

"The IMF will trace the historical roots of developmentalism, understanding the socio-economic and cultural conditions that have given its rise in Chile, Uruguay, and Argentina. It will describe the significant components of developmentalism in each country, with an eye on similar and disparate forms and methods of implementation. It will assess its progress in developing the economies of each country in terms of: gross national product (GDP); impact on federal revenues, deficits and inflation; employment (public vs. private), personal income, and wealth distribution among the populations; unionization; types, methods, and financing of social programs; literacy trends and impact on higher education; types and growth of businesses; impact on the balance of trade; and impact on foreign investment and capital formation. The IMF is requested to assess the likelihood of success or failure of developmentalism in each country and the expected time frame for either."

Fallon interrupted Simpson: "Do we need to write this down, or will we get a copy of the request?"

"I will provide you and Anders a copy of the specifics of the request."

"And who is our client, Mr. Simpson?"

"I'm sorry, Connelly, I am told the client requests confidentiality, at least for now."

"What?" Fallon asked in surprise. "Then what is the purpose of this analysis? What is the background of the request?"

"To be frank, I do not know. Just as I cannot reveal all I know, I am not privy to what my superiors at the IMF may know."

Fallon rolled her eyes. This was not a usual request of the IMF. She was about to speak when Simpson spoke again.

"I'm sorry, but this is all I can provide you for now. It's your assignment." He glared at Fallon and me, cutting off any more pushback from our end. "We have two months to complete our work. Come to me with any specific questions. I want weekly progress reports from you, Connelly. And, Anders, remember, confidentiality. No one can know what the two of you are working on, not even other IMF personnel. Okay, that's all."

We left Simpson's office in silence, and Fallon guided me to a "fish bowl" conference room complete with flip charts. She closed the glass door, plopped down in the chair at the end of the long table and put her feet up on the chair next to her, whisking a strand of her long red hair out of her face.

"Welcome to the glass bubble, Jude. I warned you," she said, at last acknowledging the conversation in my apartment.

"At least it's an intriguing assignment compared to African loan requests, although it may be above my pay grade. I'm going to need some guidance." I was excited not only by the assignment, but also by the prospect of working with Fallon. "But why me?"

"Good question. Maybe because you worked on the Chilean loan request; maybe because of your age, you're closer to the world of academia than the rest of us. This almost sounds like a PhD dissertation topic, doesn't it?"

"I wouldn't know. I only have an undergraduate degree."

"Who knows, maybe Simpson wants to see what you can do. But aren't you the least bit curious who is behind this assignment?"

"In spite of the fact that we may never know, I assume it is U.S. intelligence. But why?"

"Hmm, well, we're on the same page there. I have to tell you this is not like any assignment I've ever had. I didn't know the IMF did this kind of stuff. Right now I'm more interested in the who and why than the specifics of the analysis."

"I can't figure out why someone would be interested in analyzing the forces that gave rise to developmentalism." I looked over my notes from the brief meeting with Simpson. "How did they put it: the cultural and socio-economic conditions that led to its adoption? And why look only at these three countries? Some of the same economic constructs have been tried in other developing countries even though they never called it developmentalism." The talks with Jack Tomasin once again raced through my mind.

"Puzzling." Fallon agreed.

"I had a friend in Canada whose father insisted the real threat to the U.S. and Canada was South America. Fear of communism. Anyway, how do you want to structure our little project? Two months is not a long time."

"Normally, we'd figure a way to divide the work in half and touch base once or twice a week. But this time I think we should work together on each topic. There's a lot to kick around, and a ton of data that we have to pull together. Maybe we should focus on one of the countries first to figure out how best to attack this."

Fallon paused as if lost in a thought. "You know, if I didn't know better, I'd say this assignment is somebody's set-up. If it is, we have to figure out how to spin our results."

"Set-up? Spin?" While Fallon seemed energized by the special complexities of this project, I was beginning to feel uneasy. I was glad to let her hold the reins.

"Let's just say that I've been around long enough to know this kind of assignment usually doesn't end up with black and white conclusions. Lots of gray, especially in projecting outcomes over time. Someone has an agenda here. We need to figure out who and why. Then we have to decide how to play their game."

Fallon and I spent the rest of the afternoon and the entire next day compiling a list of all the data we would need as a starting point. Simpson had arranged for a conference room with four real walls and a door that locked for us to work in—our home for the next two months. We were assigned two junior analysts to assist with data gathering and limited analysis. When there was data that we couldn't find, Fallon went to Simpson. Usually, we got what was needed even if it took several days.

By the time we were halfway through the time allotted for our analysis, we had most of the data we needed, but going through the research and documents took a lot of time. We needed to quit analyzing and start concluding or we wouldn't finish our work on Simpson's schedule.

I picked up the next document from the stack of papers I had been reading. It was from the Argentina Ministry of Justice, disclosing information on certain groups that were opposing agrarian reform.

"Fallon, look at this. Half the information has been redacted."

Fallon grabbed the document from my hand and read it. "This isn't new. I've seen this kind of thing many times, from Indonesia. It's from the Ministry of Justice. Figures."

Once again, the scope of our project was shifting, and I began to wonder just how deep Fallon and I were getting into something we obviously didn't understand.

PART TWO
Rise of the Mantra

10

May 1973
Santiago, Chile

CALIDA IPOSA, HER brother, Felipe, and her boyfriend, Roberto Menendez, were having an early dinner at a small restaurant in the Ñuñoa district of Santiago. They sat at a table on the sidewalk outside, smoking cigarettes while finishing a bottle of the local cabernet they had ordered with dinner. The leaves from the sycamore trees lining the street were beginning to turn, and the musty smell of autumn was in the air.

The waiter brought the bill, laid it on the table, and returned inside the restaurant.

"Split it?" Felipe asked.

"I'll get Calida's." Roberto snagged the bill from the table.

"Such a gentleman."

"Well, of course. I have to sleep with her tonight." Roberto displayed a boyish smile as he looked at Calida.

The men laughed, but not Calida. She just glared at Roberto, her dark eyes fiery.

Roberto quickly scanned the hand-scribbled ticket with the skill of an accountant. "*Madre Dios.* Before too long I'll have to bring a briefcase with me just to hold the money." He reached in his jacket pocket for his billfold.

Felipe grabbed the bill from Roberto's hands, his eyes going to the bottom line. "No problem for you, Roberto. You guys at the Central Bank can just print some more *escudos.*"

"But then we would need a suitcase."

Felipe just chuckled. Each of them was aware of the current economic conditions in their country. The steel wire manufacturing company owned by Felipe and his father was selling its wares in the black-market to avoid what his father claimed were ridiculous fixed prices. Because Felipe managed plant operations at the company he was very much aware that production was down over last year—way down.

Calida worked at the Production Development Corporation—called Corfo by its employees, which was responsible for spurring internal industrial production through tax credits, government investments, and stiff tariffs on imported products. She believed in the direction her country had taken when it began the program to strengthen Chilean industry and improve the employment opportunities for its citizens. The middle class of Chile was growing and the quality of life for most Chileans was improving. President Allende's nationalization program at first seemed to be successful, but the tax revenues from industrial production and higher wages were not keeping pace with the growing government expenditures. The deficit was rising at an unsustainable level. The government printed more money to pay off the debt, but that only reduced the value of their currency and increased inflation in spite of price controls.

As an economist with the Central Bank of Chile, Roberto had a bigger view of how things were going in his country. Foreign capital investment had crawled to a near stop, and it was difficult to get loans from foreign banks. Even the *Yanquis* had pulled the plug on most aid to the country, not looking favorably on the kind of economy the Chileans were developing. The standard-of-living gains made over the past five years were gradually eroding under inflation and a slow-growing economy. Roberto was hopeful the newly implemented economic program might reverse the current direction. But the country needed time for it to work. A bridge loan from the IMF that he and his colleagues had submitted would have helped, but it had been over a year since their application. There were periodic requests for new data and continuous pressure for various austerity measures before a loan would be approved. Allende and his Economic Council would not go for it.

Roberto paid the bill and the threesome started walking down the block to Felipe's car. Roberto and Calida lived only about a mile away. Felipe lived in a small town just outside the southern edge of Santiago.

"Roberto, did you see the graffiti on the walls surrounding the stadium?" Calida asked.

"No, what did it say?"

"Kill Allende."

"The kids are getting a little violent with their language these days."

"I do not think it is funny. Maybe it is not teenagers, Roberto."

"Sure it is, sis," Felipe chimed in. "Who else does graffiti?"

Calida stopped suddenly and grabbed hold of her brother's arm. "Someone who wants us to be scared, Felipe. There are forces in this country that want Allende out, not to mention foreign interests. Like the military. And the rich who see their land, their business, their wealth going to the rest of our society. The bastards who controlled everything before Allende."

"Yeah, maybe it was the CIA. Like they are behind every evil in the world and this country? The *Yanquis*, the CIA. Christ why would they care about our little country?" Felipe turned and started walking again toward his car.

"I do not know. Calida may be right," Roberto interjected. "I see and hear things at the bank. The rumor is that Nixon wants to break our economy and bring down Allende because he thinks he is a communist. I even heard the U.S. had plotted a coup against him. And there are economists teaching over at the Catholic University who were educated in the U.S.—*laissez-faire* capitalists from the University of Chicago. You know, free-market types who want to tear apart all we have done in Chile. Even at the bank we have some economists who studied in the States. And I can tell you, they argue very forcefully for opening up our markets to foreign investment and businesses."

"Wake up!" snapped Calida. "We all sense something is going to happen. There is anxiety in the air. People are not smiling."

Felipe put his arm around his little sister's shoulder as they continued walking. "Calida, please, not so angry and morose. It is a tough time. We will get through it, and our people will smile again."

11

June 1973
Washington D.C.

FALLON AND I worked double overtime on our assignment. Every night was a late night with an occasional exception on Friday. On those nights Fallon often had an "engagement" with a girlfriend or some mysterious guy that she refused to talk about. I used Friday nights mostly to chill out and catch up on the latest news, especially the Watergate hearings. During the week, it was not unusual that we would go out for a quick dinner and then return to the IMF offices to continue our research and analysis. And there was plenty of weekend work as well. We were both tired and close to burnout, but when one of us discovered a tidbit of new information that provided another piece to our puzzle, it renewed our excitement and our energy.

With the help of our assistants we had pulled together the past and current statistics on economic growth rates, inflation rates, employment, poverty levels, wealth distribution, balance of trade, and foreign investment in Chile, Uruguay, and Argentina. In my analysis of historical conditions and the factors that gave rise to developmentalism in each of the countries, I could not detect any common root causes besides the historical conflict between the landed gentry that began in colonial times and the aspirations of a growing middle class in this century. Somehow the indigenous poor always remained poor with little political or economic clout. At Simpson's most recent request following Fallon's last status meeting, we were now focusing our analysis solely on Chile.

Like many South and Latin American countries, Chile had a history of military *coups d'état*. They returned to democracy, but then there were more coups. Since 1932 it had a democratically elected government, and there was a distinct trend to have the government more involved in economic matters. Chile, more than most countries in recent history, had a great amount of foreign investment, especially in mining of raw materials like copper, iron, and nitrates. It wasn't a very balanced deal between the investors and their host country. The investors took most of the profits, leaving the government with a very small piece of the pie—just as I had suggested to Jack Tomasin on more than one occasion during our debates on the Chilean economic direction.

Perhaps it was because of this history that Allende rose to power. Once he became president, he accelerated the economic and agrarian reforms begun in '64. He nationalized most of the banking system, began a program of expropriating foreign-held interests in the country's valuable minerals, developed Chilean industries like steel manufacturing by placing high tariffs on foreign-produced goods, and funded numerous business start-ups. Perhaps most controversial at the time, he continued a program to redistribute land owned for decades by a small group of wealthy land barons.

During the early years under President Allende, GDP rose substantially, unemployment dropped below 4%, and inflation was falling. But now things were going the other direction. In addition, private investment was diminishing and bank depositors were moving their cash offshore to protect themselves from taxes and inflation. The cash-strapped government continued to run huge deficits to promote its program of reforms. But without private investment or financial assistance from other governments or financial institutions, Allende's government could not afford its aggressive economic and social programs without printing money. Even with price controls, inflation was out of control.

I sat in our little conference room, thinking of how Chile's loan request could have helped them over their inflation crisis at the time.

"Fallon, you told me the IMF never approved the loan to Chile I worked on last year."

"Yes. Why?"

"A year ago it might have helped to stave off their financial crisis. It seems to me that either the IMF believed the loan would only postpone the inevitable, or they weren't interested in helping Chile through their crisis."

"Why wouldn't they be interested in helping one of their member countries? That's part of the IMF charter."

I stared out the only window in the room. The sun had begun to set and I could see shadows fall over the city's streets. Fallon had just contradicted something she told me herself that night over pizza and beer. Her nose was buried in a stack of papers, and it made me wonder if she had heard me correctly.

"You said it before—not politically acceptable. Maybe they wanted to expedite the crisis."

"The IMF? But that's not . . ." She looked up from the reports and stared blankly at me.

"Remember when you wondered who our client was on this assignment?"

"I'm still wondering."

"Well, how about the Agency. And Treasury, State, and god knows who. It's no secret that Nixon's paranoid of communism. What if they're working the IMF to bring down Allende, and the governments of Uruguay and Argentina, too?"

I could see the wheels turning. Fallon got up from her chair and paced quietly back and forth in the small conference room until whatever she was considering finally took form.

"That's way out there, Jude. That would be a conspiracy and against the IMF charter. And how would they sneak that by the board of governors, much less the managing director? He's French, you know."

Of course I knew that, but had already connected the dots. "And the deputy managing director is American. It's always been that way. And France is a U.S. ally."

"But there's the board."

Fallon had a point, still . . . "What if the Board didn't know or was lied to?"

"As a member country, Chile could bring it up to the Board directly. It would be hard to cover it up."

"But even if they protested, the IMF could obfuscate the facts or bury the analysis. Even better, they could set such austere terms for the loan that the Allende government would never accept it," I said, pressing my theory. "They could at least drag it out long enough to do the damage."

"That's plausible, but not convincing."

Fallon flopped back into the conference chair. She sat there, a blank look returning to her face. I could see she had her mind wrapped around something.

"This puts the Indonesia account in a different perspective," she said finally.

"Different perspective? What do you mean?"

Fallon had never spoken to me about her Indonesia project, but she had made veiled references from time to time about its challenges. Now she revisited it, divulging more details than I knew what to do with.

"I thought the feds were trying to stabilize the country after Sukarno was overthrown. Especially with Nam going on. That's why I thought they had the IMF involved—to stabilize the economy to prevent the country from turning communist. I knew a couple of the guys in the room were from State and Treasury, but I believed what I was told at the time."

Deep in concentration, I could see she was furiously trying to fit the pieces of some puzzle together. Finally she got up, and started pacing the room again.

"Jude, if your suspicions are correct, then we weren't picking up the broken glass in Indonesia. We helped to break the bottle."

"Why would the IMF do that?"

"You mean the U.S. government, don't you?"

"Both, I guess. But why?"

"Because Sukarno was against the West, and was cozying up to the communist factions in the country in order to hold on to power."

"They were afraid Indonesia would become another domino in Southeast Asia if Sukarno stayed in power?"

"Or something like that."

"And you think they're going to try to do the same thing with the Southern Cone?"

"It was you that started us down this line of thinking, but it makes sense."

"Christ, and we're in the middle of their plot."

"We're just the pawns, Jude. The pieces in a chess game that are easily sacrificed for the win. The first movers are used to assess the game plan of the opponent. God, I hate being played."

She had been played with the Indonesia account, and the way she said it, it wasn't the first time.

Fallon flopped back into her chair and sighed. "And Chile is first on the board."

"We need to tell Simpson," I finally said after a moment.

"Yeah, right."

"Maybe he doesn't know."

Fallon shook her head. "Whether he knows or doesn't, he's going to tell us he doesn't know and to continue with our work. Simpson's not a guy to go up the chain anyway. Besides, the guys at the top would just tell him a lie or it's none of his business. And if your little conspiracy theory is right, the guys at the top are in on it anyway."

Fallon made sense. Somebody at the top knew exactly what was going on. But what were the options if our bosses were in on it?

"We could refuse to continue the assignment."

She collected the reports on the table and stacked them neatly. "Do you want to continue working at the IMF? Or at least in this department? Do you want to process African loan requests the rest of your stay with the IMF? Well, not me, my friend."

I thought back to the Cambodia and Kent State protests again and the caution I had felt with graduation so close. I had proposed a safe approach, and it worked out. What safe approach was available to us now? Vietnam, Watergate, and overthrowing democratically elected governments—would we ever have a government I could be proud of? I was free of the draft. I could just leave; go live anywhere I liked. I mentally ticked down the list of countries I'd always wanted to visit—Germany, England, France, Italy, Spain, Ireland, Greece.

"No, we have to finish the assignment," Fallon insisted, interrupting my escape reverie. "But we don't have to do the best job of it."

"I'm not following you."

"Let's say there's some data or conclusions we reach between the two of us that would be helpful to a coup. Nothing says that has to go in our report." She looked at me pointedly.

"But anything we put in our report could help them. Besides, the U.S. government already knows the basics—it has its spies in those countries. And most of the current economic data is well known." None of this made sense to me. I felt a burning creep up from my stomach to my throat. "So why do this analysis to begin with? What are they looking for?"

"Indonesia, Jude; don't you get it? Something that makes the coup easier. Something that makes it more acceptable to the people."

". . . or specific groups that need to be targeted—dealt with early on."

"Like?"

"Like the groups that supported and benefited from Allende's policies in Chile: students, intellectuals, unions, the professional class—doctors, lawyers. It's mostly the same for Argentina as well."

Fallon was already moving ahead of me. "And those that hate Allende. Those that could help the coup—the land barons and business owners before Allende's reforms."

WE SPENT THE remainder of the week going back over our analysis and draft report, trying to identify anything that would be useful to a coup attempt in Chile. There wasn't a lot, but there were some things that could be stated or presented differently to hide any benefit to those who planned a violent intervention in the affairs of the country. When we finished with Chile and were satisfied that our report was as oblique as possible, we started in on Argentina and Uruguay with the same suspicions in mind: whoever requested this analysis had the same agenda for all three countries.

At the end of July we turned in our final report. A week later Simpson called Fallon and I into his office and offered his congratulations. He said the reports were well received by our client—a client who he still refused to name—and gave us a couple of days off wrapped around a weekend before our next assignments.

I knew one thing: I couldn't go back to doing simple economic analysis of loan requests. In spite of the fact that we had done work that ran contrary to my beliefs, the challenges and intrigue of the assignment made me feel alive. If this was what my career as an economist was going to be like, I craved more.

12

August 1973
Santiago, Chile

ROBERTO STOOD IN the bedroom doorway wrapped in a towel after his shower. Calida was sleeping deeply, so small cuddled beneath the cover of their bed. Her long, wavy brown hair covered most of her face and shoulders. Roberto could not believe such a beautiful and intelligent woman could fall in love with him. He cherished his good fortune and he cherished her.

"Cali, time to get up," he whispered in her ear, as he shook her gently with his hand on her shoulder.

Calida moaned softly and turned onto her back. "Beto, what time is it?"

"7:30."

"Ugh. Why not just stay home from work today? Lie in bed."

"I cannot do it, my love. I have an important meeting today. But you can."

Calida was slowly waking up. "Would you make me an espresso?"

"Of course I will. Just stay there."

Roberto went to the kitchen still wrapped in the towel to make a double espresso for Calida. He gently pressed the ground coffee into the filter holder, twisted it in place, and pushed the red "on" button. The machine came alive with steam.

As he waited for the demitasse cup to fill, Roberto suspected his meeting today would be grim; the new inflation numbers he got on Monday meant action needed to be taken immediately before things spiraled out of control. The problem was how to curb the inflation. Nothing they had done seemed to work. Roberto added a cube of sugar to the cup, stirred it, and placed it on a small saucer. Returning to their bedroom, he set the drink on the nightstand and sat on the bed next to Cali.

"Here you go," he said. "Enjoy. I have to finish getting ready for work."

Calida reached out for his arm as he was getting up to leave. "Stay with me a minute, Beto. What is this meeting you have that is so important that you cannot stay home with me today?" She patted his side of the bed and took her first sip of espresso.

"Trust me, Cali, I want to stay, make love to you, and just cover my head from the world outside. Stay here with you in our own room with shutters closed and the noise of the streets made silent. But I cannot. Our economy is in serious trouble and I have to go to this meeting. If we cannot turn it around and soon, we may have another coup attempt like in June."

"Beto, we can fix anything that we want to. What has happened to your optimism? You will see. You guys will come up with a plan just like before."

"Yes, just like before." He looked at his lover, his mind running through the data he had reviewed last night. Yes, just like the stabilization programs implemented last year to continue the growth plan while cutting inflation. They had not worked, and now the deficits, growth, tax revenues, and inflation were all moving very fast in the wrong direction. Calida did not understand how bad things truly were.

"But anyway, Cali, you stay home. You need the rest after all of your late nights at the office. Besides there is a big protest planned today near the Development Corporation supporting the physician and lawyer strikes."

"That is right. I read something about it a couple days ago. Now I have my perfect excuse to lie in bed all day—maybe read this book that has been sitting on the nightstand for a month." She nodded toward the book.

"That sounds good, my sweet. But I have to finish getting ready."

"Yes, yes, I know. But, Beto . . . I love you. I will cook you a special dinner tonight. Call me to let me know when you will be home."

"DO YOUR PEOPLE have the necessary votes in the Chamber of Deputies?" A stiff suit with a thin black tie and white shirt stood at the small kitchen table of a Santiago apartment.

"You people worry too much," the man insisted, getting up from his seat. "With the Supreme Court proclamation in May and current crackdowns on economic activity, we got both the Christian Democrats and the National Party on our side."

"The right vote gives us cover and rallies our supporters. The time to go is soon. If this goes the wrong way, it will set us back."

"Presidente Allende has played into our hands, Señor Thomas. Chileans want justice, and we have made sure that every action he takes to control the economy turns into an act of political and legal repression. He is ignoring our constitution!" He slammed his fist on the table. "The people will see him for what he is—a tyrant."

"We have dumped millions into this. We cannot afford failure."

"And what about us? We lost our lands. And the government tells us how to run our businesses, setting wage levels, controlling the prices of our products, setting production quotas, and, of course, taxes. We lost more than millions, *señor*. We are losing our country and our way of life. Now we will take it back. And you, have you arranged for the gathering after the Chamber votes?"

"We have taken care of that."

ROBERTO'S MEETING STARTED at 13:00 with the most recent economic data displayed on flip charts around the bare room except for a single picture of President Allende. Each Central Bank economist offered his interpretation of the data and a prescription for action. Some believed this was the bottom of the trough, and pointed to key data that supported GDP growth next month, with a reduction in inflation coming on its heels by the end of the year. Others were not so sure, including Roberto. There were no good answers, he thought as he listened to the presentations. Nothing that could turn things around quickly—nothing that would be politically acceptable to the president. Gradually throughout the meeting, a general consensus built in the belief that the worst was behind them and things would gradually move on a more positive line. Roberto wasn't entirely certain that this wasn't more than a bit of wishful thinking dressed up with a few statistics to make it official.

As the meeting began to wind down, Señor Baca's secretary knocked on the door of the conference room and handed him a folder. "You need to see this," she said.

Baca stepped into the hall and partially closed the door. Roberto kept an eye on his superior in the hallway as he shuffled some papers on the conference table. He watched Baca skim through several pages in the file the secretary had handed him and wondered if this was going to up-end everything they had just talked about. Baca spoke quietly and the woman rushed away, her heels clacking noisily in the tiled hallway as Baca returned to the room.

"*Señoras y señores*, the Chamber of Deputies has just denounced our government and called for a return to the Constitution. I have seen only a synopsis of the resolution, but I am told the full text will be published in tonight's newspapers. Based on your political persuasion, you can decide which one. I think we are done for the day."

For a moment, no one moved, and then in a flurry of papers and briefcases, the men hurried out of the conference room.

There was no point in hanging around the office. Roberto called Calida to let her know he was on his way home, packed up his briefcase, and left the bank. He headed to the metro station, a short walk that twice a day took him past La Moneda Palace. An imposing edifice built in the 18th century, it occupied several city blocks and housed the office of the president and his cabinet. This afternoon, Roberto was surprised to find hundreds of protestors in front of La Moneda, carrying signs denouncing Allende and yelling angrily. "*¡Tirano! ¡Abajo con el tirano!*" Down with the tyrant. Between them and the palace were armed security guards—Allende's last line of defense. Roberto stopped to watch, as the crowd got more agitated. Soon more guards came from both sides of the palace and proceeded to surround the mob on three sides.

This was not where he wanted to be, Roberto realized, and he walked quickly down Morande past the palace grounds, then over to his metro stop where thankfully nothing appeared out of the ordinary. When he got off in the Ñuñoa district near his apartment, he stopped by a small grocery store to buy a copy of the evening's *La Prensa*.

When he arrived at the apartment, he found Calida preparing paella, her specialty. A dish of ceviche and an open bottle of slightly chilled white wine were on the kitchen table. Calida put down her wooden spoon and rushed to hug Roberto even before he could set down the paper and his briefcase.

After a long kiss she asked: "Did you solve our economic problems, Beto?"

"As a matter of fact we did."

"And how did you do that?" She seemed light-hearted, almost giddy.

"By deciding there were no problems to fix."

She pulled away from him and looked into his face. "Seriously?"

"I am being serious. Since none of us could figure a solution, we decided to be like ostriches. All you have to do is interpret the data optimistically." He shrugged out of his suit coat and began loosening his tie.

"Do you really believe the economy is on the right track?" Her tone had turned serious.

"No." Roberto took in her dark eyes, her soft hair, her sweet-smelling skin, flushed and damp from standing over her paella on the stove. "We cannot fix it."

Calida looked at him in disbelief, while Roberto picked up the newspaper and showed her the headlines.

"Have you heard about this yet?"

Calida grabbed the paper and began reading while Roberto poured two glasses of wine. Deputies Denounce Allende!

"No! No, no, no." She threw the newspaper on the floor, and started pacing around the kitchen table. "*¡Mi dios!* This is just what the right wants. They will use it to topple Allende."

Roberto picked up the newspaper from the floor. There were follow-up articles on subsequent pages, but the front page had captured the gist of the issue: pressure Allende to reform or resign. He tossed it on the counter, wondering how things could have escalated this quickly, or whether he simply had not been paying enough attention to see this coming.

"There was a big protest in front of La Moneda Palace this afternoon, after the resolution was announced. A couple hundred demonstrators calling Allende a tyrant. When the security guards surrounded them, I left."

"You were there?"

"Yes, on my way to the metro station."

Her eyes flashed. "Thugs! CIA-paid thugs!"

"Cali, you do not know that. There are many on the right who want Allende out."

She fumed in silence, flipping angrily through the paper and skimming several articles. Roberto sipped his wine and gazed out the window behind her. Was it still peaceful out there? Had the protests spread?

"The paella!" she yelled as she put down her wine and rushed to the stove to stir the dish. "I hope it is not ruined. I know it is one of your favorites."

"It is my favorite, and thank you so much. Not just for dinner, but for your friendship and your love." He wrapped her in a warm embrace. At least they have this moment, he thought.

Her eyes welled with tears. "Beto, I love you so much. What is going to happen to our country? What is going to happen to us?"

"I am not a fortune teller, but I think our country will go through some big upheavals. I just want you to be safe."

"What do you mean, safe? Who would want to hurt me?"

"You have worked for the Development Corporation for five years. The right and the rich both hate Corfo. Even as much as I do not want to believe it, I am sure the Americans hate it, too. You could get caught up in retaliation if anything really bad happens."

"Oh, come on, Roberto. You cannot believe . . ."

"Listen, Cali. It could happen." She hastily spooned paella into two bowls and set them on the table. "I can see the anger and frustration. You sense the tension. I know what is going on over at the Catholic University with their economics department. The military is not Allende's friend. There is just too much pent-up hostility and determination to bring the government down."

"Then what do you want me to do?"

Roberto had secretly thought a lot about that lately. Cali was not going to like what he had to say, but she had to hear it.

"Quit your job and go live with your parents in Buin. Get out of harm's way."

"Move away from you? No way, Roberto."

"Buin is not that far away. We can still see each other on weekends."

Calida looked at him for a long moment. He could see her fiery resistance drain away as reality set in. "Do you really think so?"

"Yes. My days at the Central Bank are numbered, too."

"But what would you do? You have worked for them since graduating the university."

"I do not know. Maybe I could start a consulting business. At a minimum, I could get a financial position at a company. But, please, go to Buin. When you get settled, I will make plans to join you."

Calida and Roberto ate in silence and left the dishes in the sink to soak. The news of the day weighed heavily on their lovemaking, and Roberto could feel Calida's tears on his neck as they fell asleep.

Two days later, Allende defiantly responded to the Chamber's resolution. With his queen taken by his opponent's bishop, he moved his last knight to protect the king.

13

September 11, 1973

TUESDAY MORNING WAS sunny and clear but clouds and rain were predicted for the afternoon. Roberto got dressed for work, listening to the news on his favorite radio station. Just as he had urged her, Calida had quit her job at Corfo and went to work for her father's company as the senior accountant. She had packed up her things and moved in with her folks, an arrangement they both hoped was temporary.

Roberto was growing increasingly uncomfortable with his position at the Central Bank; if there was to be a coup, Allende's economists would, at the very least, be fired. He hated to think about what else could happen to him, but he just couldn't quite make himself resign. "Not yet," he kept telling himself.

He was having an espresso at the kitchen table when the radio broadcast suddenly turned to static. He got up to change the station, but it was the same on the others. That was strange. Occasionally, a radio station would suffer from a brief outage, but not all of them at the same time. It was time to leave for work anyway. Roberto put on his coat, grabbed his briefcase and headed out. From the metro station, he walked the four blocks to the Central Bank, passing La Moneda Palace on his way. Cars moved up and down the avenue, and on Morande, people made their way by foot to work or school.

Arriving fifteen minutes before starting time, as was his usual habit, he bought an espresso from a cart vendor on the street and headed up to the third floor.

He briefly scanned a paper on last week's economic data, while sipping his espresso, and when he finished reading, picked up the phone to call Calida. Unlike every other morning, this time there was no dial tone.

This was odd, first the radio, and now this. Something is up, thought Roberto as he slowly replaced the phone.

He was about to go down the hall to the office of Señor Baca when a sudden rumble rattled the windows of his office. Situated near the southwest corner of the Central Bank building, Roberto's office had a decent view of the grounds on the northern edge of La Moneda, and he glanced out the window but saw nothing that could have made such a noise. Just as he was about to head out down the hall again, he heard a second, continuous rumbling sound coming from the direction of the Palace. Again he looked out the window and this time, movement caught his eye off to the left of the government seat. Roberto could see a line of tanks coming up Morande, making their way toward the presidential palace.

Before he could decipher what was going on, he heard the thunder of jets overhead. Two Hawker Hunter jets banked from the north toward the southern end of the palace then moved away beyond his view. The tanks were proceeding one by one to surround the palace. Then two more planes, or maybe the same planes making a second pass overhead. Roberto saw army soldiers getting into position behind the tanks around La Moneda, as they turned their turrets on the palace. Then another pass of jets. The Army was moving forward. Roberto's stomach knotted up and he gasped for air. In his mind there was no doubt what was happening—a *coup d'état* was underway.

There was a brief crackling of gunshots from the roof of the palace, then silence. Then more gunfire, this time from the infantry on the ground. Exchanges of gunfire between the roof and the ground came sporadically. To Roberto, who was glued to the window in disbelief, time seemed to have stopped. Everything was in slow motion—the march of the troops, the army tanks rumbling toward the palace. The engines of the two jets got louder, announcing their approach again toward the palace. He first saw them from the right side of his window and followed them as they moved west, banked, then headed for the south side of the palace. They flew directly over the palace, shaking the entire Central Bank building as they passed overhead. The paper cup that held the last of his espresso rolled over the edge of his desk just as a concussion of noise and air blew out some of the glass panes of his window. Roberto turned away just in time to keep the shattered projectiles from hitting him in the face but he couldn't resist another look. Ducking below the windowsill, he peered over the edge and saw smoke coming from La Moneda.

Roberto could not believe they would bomb the presidential palace. "*Jesús Cristo*," he said aloud. "I need to get out of here—now!"

He grabbed his coat, leaving behind his briefcase full of economic data and notes he had made last night. People in the hallway of the Central Bank were panicked and running into each other as he made his way to the back stairway at the end of the hall. Running as quickly as he could, he skipped half the steps on his way down the three flights and emerged into the lobby as his colleagues were rushing towards the front doors that opened on Morande.

He stopped short suddenly, thinking: not this way. Instead he turned right and headed for the side doors exiting to Agustinas Street. Once outside he quickly tried to determine which would be the best route to take him away from the encroaching army vehicles and the soldiers.

People were pouring out of the nearby government buildings and scurrying away from the palace as fast as they could. Roberto fought his way through the terrified crowds as they ran in between the cars and trucks. Traffic had ground to a halt. When he reached Bandera, the crowds began to thin. He took a left on to Paseo Huerfanos where there were even fewer people, and quickly hurried the two blocks to Ahumada. As he approached the Plaza de Armas, he slowed his pace and looked back. For the first time since seeing the tanks and the army around La Moneda, Roberto was conscious of taking a breath. Here there was no army, no police, and only a hand full of people. But he could still see the jets circling overhead, and then he heard the concussion of more bombs.

He leapt down the steps of the metro station to the platform and waited. And waited. Where was the train? What if they have cut the train service? Roberto's only thought was to escape the army. The economists would surely be seen as accomplices of Allende, or worse. If he stayed in Santiago, they would eventually find him anyway. But what would they do to him? Why should they want to arrest him? What had he done?

Just as he was thinking of returning above ground and finding an alternative route home, he heard the eastbound train approaching. It stopped at the platform and he could see through the windows that the cars were virtually empty. At least there were no soldiers, but where was everyone else?

He jumped an empty car of the eastbound train, knowing it would be easier to get to Ñuñoa in this direction. The train lurched forward.

With each stop, he shuddered at the thought that the military would be on the platform, waiting to board the train and arrest him. But the platforms were mostly empty, and only a few of his fellow citizens joined the train headed east. He rode the train four stops to the Manuel Montt station. From Manuel Montt, he walked crisply south some forty blocks toward Ñuñoa and his apartment. Hardly anyone was out. It was like walking in a city after some weapon had wiped out all of the people but left the buildings intact. Although eerie, it made his travel quicker. Block after block, the images of the jets, the tanks, and army ran through his mind. By the time he reached his apartment, soaking wet from the promised shower that started before he was halfway there, he had convinced himself that Allende's economists would be arrested. And maybe tortured or killed. Roberto knew he had to get away. But where could he go?

CALIDA AND HER brother sat with their father in his office at the steel wire manufacturing company, watching the news reports on a small black and white TV setting on top of a small bookshelf filled with supplier catalogues. A stern looking spokesman dressed in full Chilean Navy uniform was seated at a desk.

"My fellow citizens, today we have demanded that President Allende resign his post as President of Chile. After condemnation by the Chilean Supreme Court and Chamber of Deputies, President Allende has defiantly refused to yield to the authority of our Constitution. He has deliberately defied all legal measures to restrain his actions that turn our country into a communist state and usurp the power of democracy guaranteed to the Chilean people by our constitution.

The military forces of Chile have gone to La Moneda to arrest President Allende for crimes against the constitution and the Chilean people. The military has taken temporary control of all major government functions and the television and radio media in this country. A new government will be formed as soon as possible. To reduce the possibility that some may take advantage of the situation by looting or robbing, we are imposing a temporary curfew that begins now and will continue until tomorrow morning. The civil police will continue their duties to enforce our laws during this period of transition. All non-emergency travel is prohibited tonight. We understand that many of you are already at your place of work, but following work today, we ask that you go immediately to your homes and stay there.

We will have further information about the length of the curfew later in the evening. Thank you for your cooperation in these very trying times for all of Chile. *Puede dios bendecir el país de Chile.*"

"*Oh dios*, Roberto! I need to call him right away." Calida jumped from the sofa and reached for the phone on her father's desk. "It . . . it is dead!" She looked at her family, fear rising in her throat.

Felipe took the receiver from her hand, put it to his ear, and replaced it on the cradle. "Of course, the phone service is down. They will not let us communicate until they are in control."

"But, what will happen to him? He needs to get out of the city. They have his address on file. They will find him!"

Calida's father interrupted. "That means they will also have your name—you lived there, too. It will not take them long to find you as well. I saw this in the last coup when I was a teenager. They rounded up all of those who opposed them. They will come for all of us."

"Father, we have a legitimate business," Felipe interrupted. "They have no reason to bother us. Just make sure you burn that stack of old leftist newspapers you keep on the back porch," he added with a dry chuckle.

Felipe's father looked at him sternly. "It is not really us I am worried about. It is Calida. They will know she worked for the Corporation under Allende. They will check her out."

Felipe remained calm and was quick to make up a story the authorities would believe. "And what will they find? A bureaucrat doing her job. Who quit because she got fed up with the policies of the administration, taking our economy and country in the wrong direction? Let us not get too paranoid, Father."

"But what about Roberto? He is part of Allende's economic team," Calida said.

"Roberto is another case," Felipe responded. "They will go after him early. If they cannot find him, they may not bother with him. It is not like he would be a leader of a counter-offensive against the military."

"But how do we find him?"

"Certainly you cannot go back to his apartment. That would be too dangerous, and anyway, there are travel restrictions tonight and probably tomorrow." Felipe tried to reason with her. "And you do not want to lead the security forces to us. Calida, I think we just have to wait. Wait for Roberto to contact us."

ROBERTO LOCKED THE door and heard the radio in the kitchen, which he had left on this morning. The station was back on the air and there was some kind of announcement relating to the coup. A curfew. No travel tonight. God bless Chile. He turned the radio dial and found a station that was repeating the announcement. He listened to the entire message.

He paced the kitchen. The facts were correct, just not the reasons. He picked up the phone. Still no dial tone. He started to make an espresso, but quickly decided he needed a glass of wine to calm him instead. He sipped the wine and continued pacing the floor—round and round the small table where he and Calida shared their breakfast on so many mornings. He began to mutter out loud the same conversation he had with himself as he walked to his apartment from the metro station. I must leave the city. They will soon find where I live. They will come for me. Or maybe not. Why am I important to them now? No, no. They will want to stamp out resistance and contrary views. They will come for me. So, I have to leave the city. I need to talk with Calida. She could be in danger also. No. Did she leave the Corporation soon enough for anyone to notice her? Probably. When the phone service is restored, I will call her. But they could trace the call. Not safe. I will go to her parents' . . . but how? There is the curfew.

Still in his wet clothes, Roberto paced around the apartment. It was getting late in the afternoon and he needed a plan. He headed into the bedroom and reached for the light switch but stopped himself.

"No light!" he said aloud. He knew they could already be looking for him, perhaps watching the apartment from the street below.

He went to the closet for a suitcase. No, no. Too obvious. Instead he got his small backpack that he used for day hikes in the Andes. It would not hold much, but it would have to do.

He stuffed a pair of pants, three pullover shirts, two pairs of socks and underwear, and a toothbrush and toothpaste into the bag, then took off his wet clothes and took a hot shower in the dark. He put on a clean pair of slacks and long-sleeved shirt and waited in the dark of his apartment until the next news announcement. He would try to escape Santiago when the curfew was lifted.

The news came at 10:00 that night. Roberto had barely changed positions all evening and was still sitting in the darkened apartment when the announcement began. At first he thought it was just a recording because the reasons for the coup remained the same. But there was a new piece of information this time: President Allende had apparently committed suicide rather than being taken into custody for his "traitorous actions." Roberto rubbed his eyes and ran his hands across his tired face. The curfew would continue through tomorrow; all businesses, government offices, and train and bus services would remain suspended.

Roberto checked the phone periodically for a dial tone until he could no longer keep his eyes open. He lay down on the bed in the dark solitude of his apartment, thinking of Calida, and fell asleep.

14

Washington D.C.

I LEFT THE IMF about thirty minutes early and headed home, stopping by the grocery store and the dry cleaners around the corner from my apartment on O Street. As was still my ritual these days, I turned on the little black-and-white in the kitchen to watch the replay of the Watergate hearings on PBS. A breaking news alert caught my attention.

"Today the military forces of Chile took control of the government of that country. A spokesman for the Navy said the military *coup d'état* was necessary because the president continued to defy the constitution and the rule of Chilean law. The president was asked to step down, but he and his private security forces fought tenaciously from the presidential palace. Finally, the Chilean Air Force bombed the palace to end the standoff. According to a Chilean military spokesman, President Allende committed suicide."

I pulled a beer from the fridge without taking my eyes off the TV.

"President Salvador Allende was democratically elected in 1970 as a known socialist, and was moving the country's economy in a socialist direction. This had angered many politicians in the U.S., as well as many companies that had interests nationalized by the Chilean government. In recent months, the Chilean economic experiment had faltered with rising unemployment, slow economic growth, and a rate of inflation over 100%.

Earlier this year Chile's Supreme Court accused Allende of violating the country's judicial process. Last month the Chilean congress accused the president of usurping the powers constitutionally assigned to them and abusing the powers of the presidency. Allende refused to yield, blaming the right-wing factions of his country for trying to sabotage the country's economic reforms.

In other news today . . ."

"It's started," I said aloud. "Suicide my ass."

15

September 12, 1973
Santiago, Chile

ROBERTO AWOKE WITH the sunlight seeping through the closed slats of the bedroom shutters. There were no dreams from last night that he could remember. But he did remember yesterday. He went to the kitchen and turned on the radio, then the espresso machine. The radio was playing music—a song by Victor Jara. He turned the dial until he found a station with news. Same propaganda to support the coup; curfew to remain in effect through tonight. Allende's suicide. That one he wasn't so sure about. He picked up the phone and was surprised to hear a dial tone. His heart jumped, but he quickly hung up the receiver. No, he could not call her from here, but he could call from the pay telephone at the end of the block. But what about the curfew?

Roberto went to the bedroom window overlooking the street below. There was no one out. No people. No police. No army. No one. He looked at the clock on the dresser—8:13. Calida would not be at work because of the curfew; she would be at her parent's house.

Should he risk it? He checked the dish on the kitchen counter where he and Calida dropped their spare change. There was enough. He could only chance going out once. He made an espresso and waited until 9:00, pulled on a jacket, checked the street below again from the bedroom window, and quietly left his apartment, leaving the door slightly ajar so it wouldn't make any noise. He walked down four flights of stairs, tiptoeing in his sneakers. No noise. Carefully opening the heavy glass and metal front door to the building, he peeked up and down the street. It was empty except for the typical jam of parked cars on the street. They would provide some cover.

Roberto pulled out a slip of paper from his jacket pocket, folded it twice and slipped it between the latch and its keeper on the doorjamb to prevent the heavy glass door from slamming shut and locking. He crept slowly down the block toward the phone booth, staying close to the cars parked along the street and looking through the glass windows of the storefronts to make sure no one was looking out. Finally reaching the end of the block, he was five feet from the telephone booth, hiding behind a pillar at a corner entrance to the liquor store. Roberto looked around from behind the pillar—up and down each street, up to the windows of the apartments above the stores, and into the storefront windows that lined the streets. All empty and all closed.

Making a quick move to the telephone booth, he deposited the coins and dialed the number of the Iposa's house, then crouched as low in the booth as the receiver cord would permit. The phone rang, rang, rang.

"Come on, answer." He could hear his heart pounding in his ears almost as loud as when the jets first bombed La Moneda.

"Hello." Calida's father's voice seemed so cautious that Roberto barely recognized it—as though he was a man Roberto had never met.

"Señor Iposa, this is Roberto."

"Roberto! Are you all right? Where are you?"

Roberto could hear him yell. "Calida, Calida, Roberto is on the phone!" He imagined Cali's father holding the receiver to his side as he bellowed his call to his daughter.

"I am okay." He kept his voice barely above a whisper. "May I speak with Calida?"

"Sure, sure she is coming. But what is happening in the city?"

"It is very quiet. Listen, I am outside in a phone booth and do not have much time before I am discovered.

"Outside! Oh, here she is." His voice trailed off as he handed the phone to his daughter.

"Beto, are you okay?" Cali's voice was a strange mix of excitement and fear, but its sound brought a moment of calm.

"Yes, but I do not have much time."

"Where are you?"

"In the phone booth at the end of the block."

"In the phone booth! Are you crazy? There is a curfew."

"Calm down, Cali. I could not risk calling from the apartment. Now listen to me, please. As soon as I can I will make my way to you. I need your parents to hide me for a while until I figure out if it is safe for me."

"Yes, yes, we will do it, but the curfew. You cannot leave now."

"I will leave when it is lifted tomorrow, or *dios prohíbe*, if I think they are coming for me before then. I will not try to call you again before I leave. I cannot risk it. I will just show up. Please do not worry."

Just then Roberto could hear a car coming but could not tell its direction.

"Got to go now. I love you." He slammed the receiver into its cradle, and laid on his side in the tiny booth, trying to conceal himself behind the metal plates at its base. He rolled his body in a ball, trying not to look like a human figure—more like a large package left behind by the previous user in a rush to escape. The car got louder as it approached, but he dared not look out.

The car slowed as it neared the intersection. Roberto could not leave now, could not run. He forced himself lower into the booth. The car stopped, the engine idling. This is it. They will take me in for violating the curfew, then find out who I am.

But no sooner had the thoughts raced through his mind, he heard the engine rev and the car drive off. Roberto stayed frozen in place until the silence of the streets returned, then quickly got up and sprinted back to the apartment, not caring who saw him.

Roberto waited in his apartment all day, listening to the news on the radio and pacing the tiny rooms. The curfew would have to be lifted soon—people had to eat and the economy needed commerce. They would lift it tomorrow, he was certain.

Later that night the news broadcasts told stories of extremists being detained, but the interim government insisted the country remained peaceful and stable. The military Junta was now in charge of the media, so what could Roberto really believe? The broadcast announced, as he expected, that the curfew would be lifted for work and business during the next day but reinstated for the nighttime hours. Universities would remained closed. Trains and bus service would resume but operate on a normal schedule only until 18:00. That meant Roberto had to find a way to Calida's while it was still light. But the army would be in full force at Santiago's bus and train stations, closely observing those coming into and leaving the city. He pulled out a map of Santiago that Calida had kept under the phone book and began searching routes. He could take the metro east and south as far as it went near the southern boundary of the city, blending in with the other citizens going to work. That left him another fifteen or so miles to the Iposa's. He could get a cab from there.

He checked his wallet. He did not have enough cash and could not risk going to the bank. He would have to hitchhike.

THE NEXT MORNING Roberto rose before sunrise and repacked the clothes in the backpack, making sure to add his passport, which he had forgotten the day before. After showering, he made an espresso and turned on the radio, waiting for other people to appear on the streets before he left. The news anchor was announcing appointments to various posts in the government. Of utmost importance was the news that General Pinochet would serve as interim president until elections could be held. In the meantime, all political activity was in recess, whatever in the hell that meant. There were reports of numerous skirmishes with the military in various parts of Chile by extremists, most of them aligned with the Popular Unity coalition, which had attacked the army with guns. The most spectacular attack was on a police station in Neltume the night before, but apparently, the military had been able to put it down before things got too far out of hand.

After a long walk through the near-empty streets to the station at Plaza Egana, Roberto took the metro south to Vencuna. Traffic on the subway was light and his fellow passengers sat silently with their eyes glued to their feet. He got off at Vencuna and walked five blocks to the Ballevista De La Florida station, passing only a couple of older women braving the outside with their shopping bags. When he reached the metro station there was only a single man waiting, like him, for the next train. At the end of the line Roberto got off and began walking down Avenue Trinidad, pointing his left thumb toward the street and occasionally turning around to face the few cars that came past. It did not take long. An old rusty pickup truck slowed then stopped next to him.

"Where are you headed?" The driver was a man in his late fifties or early sixties. He showed no sign of curiosity at a young man hitchhiking his way out of Santiago the day the curfew was lifted.

"Just this side of Buin."

"Come along, then, I will take you there. I am going to my sister's in Paine."

"Wow, that is my good fortune. Thank you very much." Roberto opened the squeaky door of the old pickup and climbed in. He had made it this far without any trouble. Hopefully, there would not be any on the way to Buin.

"My name is Alonso. Yours?"

"I am Felipe," Roberto said, cautious about giving his real name. "I am trying to get back to my home."

"I guess you got stuck in Santiago."

"Yes. I was there on business during the coup."

"What kind of business do you do, Felipe?" Roberto was happy for the ride; he was less sure of the questions.

"My family manufactures steel wire. I am the salesman."

"Did you take the train into the city?"

Roberto hadn't exactly expected to be grilled on every detail of his story. He fine-tuned his awareness as he huddled against the door of the old truck.

"Yes, yes. I did three days ago."

"And now you are hitchhiking with a backpack?" You could have taken the train back to Buin."

"I was going to be in Santiago only one night, and I heard train service would not be available until the afternoon. I wanted to get home as quickly as possible. I really appreciate the ride; I know my family is worried about me."

Alonso smiled and offered Roberto a cigarette, which he gladly accepted. They talked about the coup, Allende, the mess of the economy as Alonso referred to it, and the fears of what might happen next. To Roberto, it was refreshing to hear an ordinary Chilean's understanding of the affairs of the past several years. He had been ensconced in government offices for so long, he had forgotten what the world looked like to regular people going about their day. Alonso offered no solutions, but made it clear that he had seen the good of Allende along with the complaints.

A few kilometers outside Buin the cars in front began to slow; brake lights flashed for as far as the eye could see. The line was so long that the cause of the slow-down could not be determined.

"Felipe, it looks like an accident ahead, or maybe a road block."

Anxiety gripped Roberto. Whether an accident or a roadblock there would be police and maybe the Army. "Yes, it does." To Roberto his voice sounded shaky. He had gotten this far. So close. And now this.

"I do not very much want to be slowed down, especially for a car wreck or something stupid like asking us where we are going and what we are doing. Who knows how long this could take." Alonso looked over at Roberto. "If you do not mind, I think I know a road we can take to get around this mess. It is out of our way, but with the look of the line ahead, we will probably make better time."

"That sounds good to me."

Roberto was relieved by the plan and breathed a little easier. At the next intersection Alonso turned left and proceeded east on a dirt road. They drove that road for a kilometer or so, turned right onto another dirt road, bouncing along with the mountains in the distance on their left. After about twenty minutes, the truck turned right again, this time onto a paved road.

"I hope there are no roadblocks coming into Buin from the east," Alonso offered.

And there weren't. Once in Buin, Roberto gave Alonso directions to the Iposa's manufacturing plant. He did not want anyone to know the location of the Iposa's home, and his story looked better by dropping him off at the plant. Hopping out of the truck near some large rolls of steel wire, he thanked Alonso repeatedly and wished him safe travels as his old pickup truck pulled away.

Señor Iposa was standing in his office door, talking to one of his employees when he saw Roberto approach. He quickly finished the conversation and waved Roberto into his office, made him sit, and then shut the door.

"Roberto, my boy, you made it! You are safe."

"For now, maybe. How is Cali . . . and Felipe?"

"We are all fine. Have you eaten?"

"Just coffee this morning."

Señor Iposa got on the intercom with his secretary and directed her to go out and buy some empanadas. "And please call my wife to tell her Felipe and a guest will be joining us for dinner."

He then picked up the phone and called Felipe, who was somewhere in the plant.

"Now, come with me, my boy."

They headed down the narrow hallway to Calida's office. Roberto walked in, a smile on his face. Calida jumped out of her seat and ran over to him. She hugged him so tight he thought his lungs would collapse.

"How did you get away from the bank? How did you get here? Did you have trouble on the way? When did you leave Santiago? Are you okay? Have you eaten?"

"Whoa, whoa, one question at a time. Which question do you want me to answer first?"

"Have you eaten? You look so thin."

"Your father has ordered empanadas and I am fine. I left about 9:00 this morning, and had no real trouble, although there was a small incident which we avoided."

Señor Iposa looked concerned. "Incident?"

"I took the metro all the way to the end and got a ride in a rusty old truck driven by a man named Alonso. Then, just when we were a little way outside of Buin, there was a roadblock, or maybe an accident, so we took a detour on some side roads and nobody stopped us. I guess there are too many roads for the army to guard them all."

"What happened the morning of the coup?" Calida asked. "How did you get away?"

"I got out of the bank as soon as they assaulted La Moneda, ran in the opposite direction, grabbed the metro, and then walked to our apartment in Niñoa. Why?"

"Because the rumor was they were arresting anyone on the streets around the palace that morning."

"Well, that would have been hundreds of people. I did not see them arrest anyone."

Calida sighed with relief as she hugged him again, this time with a quick kiss. Felipe showed up at the door of Calida's office and grabbed Roberto in his large arms.

"Brother, you are safe now," he said as he squeezed him tightly.

"Let us go to my office," said Señor Iposa. "We will have some empanadas."

Over a very late lunch, all four discussed the events of the last few days. Roberto was questioned again about the tiniest details of what Santiago was like the morning of the coup, how he got away, where he went, how he got to Buin. They also talked about the latest news, including Pinochet's appointment and the disbanding of the Popular Unity Coalition. Just since Roberto had left the apartment this morning, there was even more news: Congress had been dissolved and all political activity had been suspended. Political parties had been outlawed. So much for the Chilean constitution.

"Have you had any news on resistance?" Roberto asked.

"Only in Valparaiso and Neltune. Both put down," Felipe said.

"Have they started to arrest any of Allende's people?"

"You mean like the economists at the Central Bank?"

Roberto nodded. "Yes, Felipe, people like me."

"We have heard nothing about that . . . yet." He smiled. "Do not be paranoid. Why would they want you?"

Roberto could tell Felipe was trying to put him at ease, but it wasn't working. "They should not, but maybe they want to make us an example of what is wrong with the country and the economy."

"That is nonsense. You were there to support Allende's program."

"Not entirely. We helped to develop the economic program. From the start. Even before his election."

Felipe paused. "I guess that is true, but why would the Junta be interested in arresting you now? They can just fire you and replace you with their hacks. How do you call them—the Chicago Boys?"

Señor Iposa interrupted. "Now, now enough about such grim possibilities. We are here and you are safe, Roberto. You will stay with us, and we will give you work here to do."

"Thank you very much, sir. But if they do come looking for me, I will be a liability to your family. I cannot have that."

"We will not talk of that, at least, not now. Tonight Isabel will cook a feast and we will celebrate your safety and being together."

IN THE WEEKS and months to come, the people of Chile went about their day-to-day business and were quiet about politics and the coup. They were afraid. There were rumors of people being arrested by the army or the police in their homes or at work, dragged off, never showing up again—just disappearing. There were rumors of torture, and students and those with leftist beliefs being held at the National Stadium. The military dictatorship had instilled a harsh and penetrating fear into the hearts and minds of the Chilean people. But that was mild compared to the economic reforms that were to come. The Friedmanites from the University of Chicago were poised to initiate their grand experiment. Life in Chile would become as austere as the peaks of the Andes that divided Chile from the next target—Argentina.

16

December 1973
Darien, Connecticut

A GROUP OF three middle-aged men drank whiskey in the paneled study of a large Connecticut estate after a sumptuous meal. It was their annual Christmas holiday gathering.

"Three down and two to go." Benjamin lifted his glass.

The others raised their glasses in a toast. Thomas drew a line through Indonesia, Brazil, and Chile, names on a list he had earlier scrawled on a cocktail napkin. Argentina and Uruguay remained. "Two in this hemisphere." He tossed the napkin into the fireplace.

"And beyond?" Benjamin asked.

"Yes, there are more, but they will take time." Joseph turned to look out his study's window at the falling snow on the estate grounds.

"You mean the Soviet Union? I doubt it," Thomas said as he watched his list curl and dissolve in the flames.

"We don't care too much about the Russians anymore. Their collapse will come on its own. And outside of oil and gas, what do they have? So many years fighting the communists—for what? Let them retreat into their deep freeze of a country."

Thomas looked over at Joseph. "Then who?"

"Where the largest number of workers and buyers in the world are and will be for the foreseeable future," Joseph answered. "But for now we must focus on immediate situations. Our next objective has a long history of leftist thinking and we are a small minority there. It will be difficult. And we haven't prepared like we did with Chile, especially with our student exchange program."

They all laughed.

"But we have a strong ally there," Benjamin insisted. "And he is a lot more brutal. Are our contacts in place in D.C.?"

Thomas sipped his drink. "Even more determined after the success in Chile."

"Then they should move it along. We have elections in three years. And this Watergate incident could be a distraction."

"The oil embargo isn't helping either. Goddamn Arabs and Jews."

"Doesn't your driver fill up your car, Benjamin?"

"You know what I mean."

Joseph interrupted their banter. "I am afraid that genie is out of the bottle, but they are beyond our influence for now. They present a new problem, but one we cannot yet resolve. Let's not get distracted."

"Our people are starting to plant the seeds now for the next phase of the plan," Thomas began, this time seriously. "It shouldn't take as long as Chile."

"Good." Joseph lifted his glass of whiskey. "Merry Christmas."

"Merry Christmas." The other two lifted their glasses.

Joseph lifted his glass again. "Gentlemen, The Deep."

"The Deep," they echoed in salute. And all three took a long, deep draw on their whiskies.

17

January 1974
Santiago, Chile

"¡MALDITA SEA!" MAJOR Araya exclaimed. "What do you mean you cannot find him? He had an apartment in the city. A bank account. Has he paid the rent? Has he made deposits and withdrawals? He did not just disappear."

Sergeant Soto said he had followed the logical steps to find the missing man. "He has not paid the rent on his apartment since the first of September, and there have been no bank account transactions. His landlord served a formal eviction notice last month. It was still in his mailbox when the police came to evict him. There is little in his personal effects to help locate him. There was a picture of a girl. We're still trying to find out who she is."

"Did he have parents? Brothers, sisters?"

"Parents dead. No siblings."

"Phone calls?"

"We pulled his records from just before the coup. Nothing for two days before and nothing since."

"Then go back further and check his office phone records. Find out whom Roberto Menendez has talked to. Maybe a girlfriend, the one in the picture. And take the picture of the girl to the neighbors. See if they know who she is."

Major Araya ran the Junta's security force in Santiago. He was charged by the Navy admiral with finding the key players in Allende's socialist transformation of the Chilean economy. His forces arrested numerous members of Allende's economic advisors in an attempt to "root out the promoters of the Marxist cancer"—most of them on the very day of the coup. Still, some slipped away. Araya's group compiled a list of names taken from name plates on office doors of the Central Bank and Corfo, signed documents from executive office files, or given to the Junta by the new economists from the Catholic University, then cross-referenced with those already arrested. Their orders were to "find and eradicate the communist plague that had permeated economic thinking in Chile." Roberto Menendez was one of the few names left without a face . . . or a body. The others had been corralled and put in the National Stadium. Some died there. Those that survived the initial roundup were shipped to Colonia Dignidad prison.

ROBERTO WORKED ODD jobs in the plant and filled in for employees who were ill. It was a welcome change to work with his hands, move around the plant floor, and have some physical labor to do. One of Felipe's men taught him how to drive the forklift. That was his favorite job, and he volunteered to move the big rolls of steel wire and cable at every opportunity. Occasionally, he worked with Calida handling accounts receivable or payable or preparing financial statements at the end of the quarter.

Señor Iposa converted a small storage area next to the employee kitchenette into a bedroom for Roberto, and added a metal shower to the plant's bathroom for him. As strict Catholics, Calida's parents gamely tolerated the fact that the young couple had lived together in Santiago, but there was no way they would allow the same thing in their own home. Calida often made excuses to work late so they could find time for each other after the employees had left for the day.

Some four months after the coup, hushed stories of round-ups and arrests persisted, but with less frequency. There were rumors of terrifying screams coming from the National Stadium and various military detention centers around the country. And then there was the oft-repeated tale that Pinochet's henchmen traveled to military prisons throughout the country, slaughtering any prisoner known to have extremist views. But these were rumors. The people did not know what to believe.

Roberto watched the news every night, sometimes with Calida when she stayed after the plant had closed. There was little information on military actions taken unless there was a failed insurrection. The emphasis of the news reports was on "brutal" and "putdown." Most of the news programs broadcast changes in the economic policies of the new regime—promises of job growth and bringing inflation under control, but not without austere measures to put Chile's economy on a solid footing. Social programs were being reduced because the country could not afford the out-of-control spending of the Allende years. The Production Development Corporation, which previously owned a substantial stake in Chilean industries and utilities, was selling off nationalized industries and businesses to private investors as a necessary step to operate them more efficiently and to recapitalize the economy. Barriers to free trade were being torn down to ensure that Chilean business would develop in such a way as to compete in the world economy. The number of public employees was slashed. Unions were outlawed. Market forces would set wages and prices.

Roberto, as an economist, had studied this approach to economic development at the Technical University. He certainly had heard a lot about it from the economists educated in the States and the Catholic University in Santiago. Allende had ushered in a grand economic experiment. As it was constructed, or at least carried out, it did not work. Now Chile was apparently in for a second grand experiment. Roberto could see some of its flaws. Most Chileans seemed to accept it, especially since things had been so bad last year.

"What are you thinking?" Calida asked one night after the news was over.

"I was wondering what has happened to Señor Baca and some of the economists from the bank—Sergio, Raul, and Isabella." Sometimes he retraced the events of that day the windows blew out of his office just as he was getting ready to head down the hall to Señor Baca's.

Calida got up from the chair in Roberto's tiny quarters and turned off the TV. "I also wonder what has become of many of my former work associates at Corfo. I hope and pray they are each okay."

"I want to call Sergio and Raul but know it is too risky. Their phones could be tapped—incoming calls could be traced. That would lead the army right to here."

"You could use a pay phone in town."

"Even that might raise a suspicion that someone they are interested in might be living in Buin. No, no. We must be silent, disappear. Blend into fabric of the country. At least for now."

He was quiet for a minute as his worst thoughts re-emerged. "I wish I knew if the Junta was looking for me. At least then I could put together a plan."

"A plan for you! What about me? Would I be in your plan?"

"Cali, of course. If they do not care about me, we will stay here, work, eventually marry and get our own place." He wished he could still believe in the vision he had held for so long.

"And if they are hunting you?"

"I have thought about that day and night. The country is too small. I cannot see how going underground for the rest of my life would work, even in a remote area. They would find me, and if I am with you, they would find us both. No, if they are hunting me and if we are to be together, then we must leave Chile."

"MAJOR ARAYA, SIR." The sergeant clicked the heels of his boots as he approached the desk.

Araya, annoyed at the interruption, looked up from the paperwork on his desk. "Yes, sergeant?"

"We have a lead on the girl. Sir, the Menendez case."

Araya leaned back in his chair, waiting for more details.

"A neighbor says she used to live at the apartment with Menendez. Moved out in August and has not been seen since. The neighbor thought she worked for the Development Corporation."

"And?"

"We looked at the employment records of the Corporation, looking for terminations and resignations of female employees in August. Only one, sir. A Calida Iposa."

"And where is Iposa now?"

"We are not sure, but we got a telephone number that Menendez called at least every other day from his office right up to the ninth of September. It is the number of a business owned by an Atilo Iposa in Buin. And, according to Calida Iposa's birth record, her parents lived in Buin at the time of her birth."

"Do you have an address of the home of Señor Iposa?"

"Yes, sir."

Araya drummed his fingers on the papers spread across his desk, planning his next move. Buin. If Menendez is there, how did he get out of Santiago undetected?

"I think that you and a few men should make a visit to the Iposa family. But go in the morning. Very early before they go off to work. And sergeant, Señorita Iposa worked for Corfo. That is reason enough to bring her in for questioning."

Araya smiled as the sergeant left the room. Two birds, one stone. He liked it when his job was so easy.

ATILO IPOSA WAS in his kitchen at 6:00 making his first espresso of the day when a sharp rap on the front door startled him. Was this it? Was this what they had been waiting for? He took a moment to gather his composure and went quietly to the door, where he peeked out a small glass window. Three uniformed men stood on his front porch. He took several deep breaths before opening the door.

"Yes? How may I help you?"

"Atilo Iposa?"

"Yes."

"Father of Calida Iposa?" At the mention of his daughter, his heart stopped.

"Yes." He could hear his voice trembling.

"I am Sergeant Soto of the Chilean Security force. We want to speak to your daughter. Is she here?"

Atilo hesitated again. Should he say no? But they might want to search.

"Yes, but she is still in bed."

"Please wake her now, sir." Sergeant Soto seemed determined.

"But . . ."

"Now!"

Señor Iposa partially closed the door. He could hear the sergeant directing the officers to the side and rear of the house as he made his way to Calida's bedroom. Calida would be unable to sneak away, that was certain. His stomach was in a knot. Was this what he had feared since the coup, or was he overreacting? He put an optimistic thought in his head. They have just come to ask about Roberto.

"Calida, Calida, are you awake?" Atilo's voice was barely above a whisper at her open bedroom door.

"Yes, father, who is here?" Calida was sitting up in her bed, and based on the look on her face, Atilo could tell that she sensed there was a problem.

"The Security Force. They want to speak with you."

"Roberto. You didn't tell them anything, Father?"

"No, no. But you must go speak to them." He moved to her side, this time he whispered. "Remember the story as we rehearsed it. I will call Roberto at the plant, if we think they are going there too." He and his daughter believed that some day the army would come looking for Roberto and had developed responses to the questions they were almost certain to ask.

Calida pulled on a pair of jeans and tucked in the t-shirt she had worn to bed. She met Sergeant Soto on the front porch, leaving the front door slightly ajar.

"I am Calida Iposa." Her tone was polite, appropriately so, Atilo thought as he lingered in the kitchen close enough to overhear the conversation, puttering with the espresso machine, his awareness fine-tuned to the presence of soldiers surrounding his house. He wondered if his daughter could deliver their story convincingly.

"Señorita Iposa, we have information that you are acquainted with a Señor Roberto Menendez. Is that true?" His question was direct, the tone of his voice matter-of-fact.

"Yes." She paused a moment. "He used to be my boyfriend. Why do you want to know?"

"And you lived together in Ñuñoa in Santiago?"

"Yes, until last winter when we split up."

"You mean last August."

"Yes, August. August is in winter."

Atilo winced, but Soto seemed to ignore the sarcastic remark. "Have you seen or talked with him since?"

"We talked frequently after our separation." This time her reply was more respectful. "Roberto took it hard."

"And have you seen him since?" Soto asked.

"No." Maybe a little too emphatic, Atilo thought. "Is he alright? I have not talked with him since the . . . you know."

"Do you have any idea where he might be?"

"No. I was hoping you might know. I have been worried about him." Her voice was more calm and persuasive.

"Señorita, we know you quit Corfo about the same time you left Santiago. Could you tell us why you left the Corporation?"

Atilo had told Calida they would ask this. As he listened, he prayed Calida's response would be convincing.

"I left because I did not want to be with Roberto." She replied quickly. Perhaps a little too quickly for Atilo. "And I was disgusted with all of the politics and infighting at Corfo. I had a chance to work with my father at his business. I just had to get away."

"I see."

Surely the sergeant would think Calida's story reasonable enough. Atilo peeked at the sergeant from the kitchen. He could see the indecision on the military man's face. He tried to steady his shaking hands as he finished making his coffee.

Finally Soto said matter-of-factly: "Señorita Iposa, we would like you to come with us back to Santiago. We have some additional questions about your position with Corfo."

"Surely I can answer your questions here." Atilo could hear the panic in his daughter's voice.

"No, señorita. You will come with us. We will wait for you to finish dressing."

Atilo used both hands to put his cup on the counter. He did not want to drop it, although in his head he could hear the sound it would make as it shattered on the tile floor.

18

CALIDA WAS DRIVEN off in the sergeant's car followed by the other soldiers in the jeep. Señor Iposa protested only modestly to the sergeant when they insisted on searching his house—he knew it would do no good—and he had to get word to Roberto and Felipe. Being taken into custody himself would make matters worse.

Once Atilo told his wife what was happening she became hysterical. "My daughter, my daughter, Calida. No, no, no. Calida."

"Calm down! I have to tell Roberto and Felipe."

"I will call Felipe." She wiped her eyes and reached for the phone.

"No, my dear, it is better this way," He took the receiver from her hand and put it back on its cradle. "They may already have a trace on the phone. I will get dressed and go to the plant like I do every morning. Felipe should be there within the hour."

Señor Iposa took his time getting ready, just in case the sergeant had left behind an officer or two to watch the house. Any sudden or unusual movement would be suspicious. The security forces must know where his plant was located. They did not seem interested in going there, as far as he could tell. He finished dressing as he normally did for a workday, and stood in the kitchen drinking his coffee with still-trembling hands. A few minutes after his normal time to leave for the office, he got into his car parked in front of the house and drove off. All the way to the plant he looked around to see if he was being followed. He prayed the security forces would not be there.

When he drove into the parking lot in front of his office, he was relieved. No army. No police. Just Felipe's car. He slowly got out of the car and walked normally through the office door, just in case he was being watched from afar. He walked down the hall and onto the plant floor where he found Felipe and Roberto in Felipe's office. He rushed in and closed the door behind him, relieved to finally release the tension that had been building inside since early this morning.

"It has happened! They came! The Security Force came to the house looking for Roberto. They took Calida to Santiago for questioning. They took Calida!"

"What?" both Roberto and Felipe said in unison.

Felipe kneeled in front of his father, who had covered his face in his hands. "Father, be calm."

After a moment, Atilo Iposa told them what had happened and as much of the conversation between Calida and the sergeant that he heard.

"But why take Calida?" Felipe insisted. "That makes no sense."

Roberto began pacing Felipe's small office. "There can only be two reasons to take her. They do not believe her and want to interrogate her to see if she will give up information on me."

"She will never do that," Felipe interjected. "She would never betray you."

"Unless they torture her. *Dios prohíbe.*"

"And the second?" Felipe got up to close the blinds of his office windows that looked out into the plant.

"Calida worked for Corfo. I have told you before that its leaders might be blamed just like the economists at the Central Bank."

"But Calida only ran the numbers. She was not a decision-maker."

"I know that, but maybe they do not, at least not yet."

Atilo sunk into Felipe's desk chair, looking for any sign of hope. "And when they find that out, they will let her go."

"Yes, yes, Señor Iposa. Probably so," Roberto agreed.

Atilo poured a glass of water from the pitcher on Felipe's desk, beginning to feel slightly relieved. A loud crash suddenly exploded across the plant floor and all three jumped. Felipe rushed outside his office to find that a large steel roll had slipped off one of the forklifts as it was being moved.

"Anyone hurt?" Felipe asked his foreman.

"Just the steel, Señor Felipe."

Felipe closed the office door and continued although all three men were visibly shaken. "Roberto, what will you do?" They had lived with uncertainty for months; at least they now knew this one thing.

"I must go. I must keep your family out of further danger."

While Atilo had come to the same conclusion, Roberto was family; they were sending one of their own out into the woods—to the wolves.

"Let us think this through," Atilo said. He had finally calmed himself and was ready to strategize. "You could find another place to hide."

"I have thought about that a hundred times. Except perhaps for a remote cabin in the mountains, there is no place to hide in this country. Maybe I should turn myself in. Tell them that I did not know they were looking for me."

"And the moment you do that, they will suspect Calida of hiding you," insisted Felipe. "That would be too coincidental. No, you cannot do that. And anyway, who knows what they would do to you."

The three men sat silently in the office, each realizing there were no good alternatives.

Roberto finally spoke. "I think it the best plan that I should leave Chile. I have suggested this to Calida many times; under the circumstances, this is the best option. I will go to Argentina. I know some people there. The political climate is okay."

"But there will be the army at the border, Roberto. Surely, your name is on a list," Atilo said.

"What I really need are fake documents."

"Do you know how to get them?" asked Felipe.

"Of course not. And, even if I did, they would be impossible to get these days. I have to chance a crossing with what I have. Maybe I could avoid border guards by crossing the mountains on foot."

Atilo rolled his eyes. Young men, they think they are invincible.

"Yeah, right. The Andes. Why do you think we feel so safe in Chile?" Felipe said. "No way, Roberto. You would die."

"And I will likely die if I stay in Chile. I have to risk a crossing past the guards. Maybe if I take a remote road across. There the guards may not have a list, or at least one that is old without my name on it."

Reluctantly, Felipe agreed. "But how will you travel?"

"I hadn't thought of that. Bus?"

To Atilo Roberto seemed to be grasping at straws. Walking across the Andes? Taking a bus? Atilo thought about Calida, taken away this morning by the security forces; who knew when she would be home? These boys and their plotting, like it was some big adventure. He stood, preparing to leave, but Felipe put his hand on his father's shoulder, stopping him.

"We could smuggle him out with one of our shipments to Argentina."

"Come on, Felipe. Our trucks have flat beds for the steel wire and we do not cover the wire. Even if we did, that would raise suspicion. Besides, I am certain the army is closely checking all shipments that go out of the country."

"What about a bus through a remote crossing? Father, you could get Ceci to see what buses go to Argentina and which routes."

Who knows, maybe that was crazy enough to work, Atilo thought. "Sure, sure," he said, dialing his secretary from the phone on Felipe's desk. The more he thought about the idea, the more he began to like it.

"Ceci, I am thinking about some of our distribution routes into the south of Argentina. Perhaps I will go myself and look at some roads." He turned to Felipe and winked. "Can you get me some bus routes? They would already know the best roads, especially through the mountain passes. Perhaps we can avoid some of the major highways, take smaller trucks, I don't know, just a thought. Just bring them to me in Felipe's office."

No sense letting everyone know what he and the boys were discussing. At least this way there would be a cover story, if it ever came to that. Atilo had another idea. "Felipe, would you go get us some breakfast? Maybe, drive near the bus station. See if and how many of our 'friends' might be there. And while on your journey, check to see if anyone follows you."

"I understand, Father. Good idea."

"If anyone is following you, go to your apartment and call me. In the meantime, Roberto and I will look at bus routes and schedules." He rolled up his sleeves. No longer panicking, he knew now was the time for serious planning. Roberto's life was at stake, and maybe his daughter's as well.

Felipe hugged his father, shook hands with Roberto and headed out, almost colliding with Ceci in his haste. She delivered an armload of materials to Señor Iposa, already sitting at Felipe's desk. Maps, schedules, pamphlets; he had to acknowledge the efficiency of his shipping department, although he knew they would not ask why he was considering something so preposterous as to truck steel wire across a remote mountain road, when there were probably plenty of perfectly good highways to use instead.

Señor Iposa sat with Roberto pouring over the bus options. There were very few routes to take from Chile to Argentina. The main and most popular route near Santiago was unacceptable—it would be heavily patrolled with up-to-date lists. The other paved routes were in the north of the country, but most crossed into Bolivia or Peru. Roberto pointed out the two southern routes. "What about these? They would seem the least likely to have a lot of guards." The bus on those routes ran only once a week. On the most promising route a bus left from Los Angeles, but that was a large city and the army might be at the bus station. However, there was a small town on the way, Quilleco, where the bus stopped to pick up passengers.

When Felipe got back with the breakfast, he informed Roberto and his father that there were security forces at the bus station, checking papers of people arriving and departing.

"We have found the right route," Atilo told his son. "The bus leaves Los Angeles in two days. Roberto needs to get to Quilleco, a village east of Los Angeles small enough for the security forces not to bother with. He can board there. It is a long passage to the border, dirt road the whole way. But I think it is Roberto's best chance."

"That is a long way. How will he get to Quilleco?"

"You must drive him, my son. I understand the risk, but there is no other reasonable way."

Felipe nodded. "I agree, but tonight Roberto must come stay with me. The plant may no longer be safe for him. We will start our drive tomorrow."

CALIDA WAS TAKEN to the National Ministry of Defense in Santiago and put in a small locked, windowless room. There was a hard chair and a cot. She could hear voices coming from the open room outside that she had passed through when they brought her in, but when she put her ear to the door, she could not make out what they were saying. She paced back and forth across the floor. Certainly they wanted information about Roberto; but why were they interested in Corfo? What would she tell them about Roberto? She ran through what she told the sergeant at her parent's house—she needed to be consistent. Were there any holes in her story? She could not think of any. Just stick to it, she thought, as she sat down on the hard chair. They could not prove she was lying; what could they do?

Calida was there about an hour when a soldier brought her a sandwich and some water.

"How long are you going to keep me in here?" she asked as the soldier set a tray on the cot.

The soldier left the room without responding, and Calida could hear the door lock behind him. She angrily kicked the door and walked around the tiny room, wandering what the security forces would do with her. All the rumors she had heard since the coup paraded through her imagination. No, no, she thought, they create fear and I will not let fear inside. She sat on the edge of bed and picked at the meager lunch.

In the early evening Calida was brought a small dinner. Her watch was her only connection to the passage of the day. It was 18:20.

"Hey, how long are you going to keep me here?" she asked the solder again, this time more forcefully.

The soldier set the tray on the cot and again left without a word. She ate even though her stomach was in knots, paced the small room, sat down, and paced again. Her watch told her it was 22:00. She lay down on the cot, pulled a lightweight blanket around her, and soon fell asleep.

19

ROBERTO AND FELIPE left at 6:00 the next morning, after a quick breakfast of cereal, bread, and espresso. It would take them at least twelve hours to get to Los Angeles and then another hour to Quilleco. After they made the rest of their plans yesterday afternoon, Atilo Iposa and Felipe each went to the bank and made withdrawals, neither withdrawal by itself large enough to arouse suspicions. Together they gave Roberto enough money to get into and through Argentina to the city of Buenos Aires. That night Felipe and Roberto had shared a bottle of wine over dinner, talking about Calida, the coup, what would happen next in Chile. This helped to keep Roberto from thinking about the next day or the potential outcomes of his attempted escape. There was no use talking about it anyway; they had a broad plan—the details would unfold as they went. It was likely they would have to improvise along the way, especially if there were checkpoints on the highway leading to Los Angeles.

After eleven hours of hard driving and long silences, stopping only for gasoline and sandwiches that they ate on the road, they turned off the main highway just before Los Angeles. They had not encountered a single checkpoint along the way. Roberto and Felipe had considered sleeping in the car somewhere outside of Quilleco, but since there were no army or security forces in the town, they decided to stay in Quilleco's lone hotel. It appeared to be barely more than a few rented rooms in a family home.

It was a restless night. This time Roberto could not stop tomorrow's journey from taking control of his thoughts. The bus was scheduled to leave at 10:00 in the morning. He needed his rest so he would be alert for anything that might happen on the trip. When he finally fell asleep, his dreams hinted at disaster, but he could not remember their detail when he woke up. He checked his watch; only an hour had passed since he had last looked at it. Felipe snored softly in the single bed next to his. Roberto reached over to the nightstand to grab the glass of water he had taken to bed with him. As he put the glass to his lips, his trembling hands spilled water down the front of his t-shirt. He pummeled his flimsy pillow, trying a different sleeping position and hoping it would help him to fall back asleep. He imagined security forces coming to town just as he was boarding the bus and pulling him off. He imagined the bus having mechanical problems half way up to the mountain pass that led to his freedom, and the army coming to rescue the bus and finding him. He could see the little wooden shack at the border to Argentina. He imagined it empty with no guards, but he also saw it surrounded by army trucks and soldiers with machine guns. Roberto turned his thoughts to Calida and the day they walked in the park near their apartment in Santiago, holding hands in the yellow sunlight of autumn and kicking the fallen leaves. He fell asleep, finally.

The morning came too quickly for Roberto, who awoke to Felipe's nudging on his shoulder. He was groggy and felt an inner burning that ran from his stomach to his throat. His reckoning was finally upon him.

While Roberto dressed and repacked the suitcase filled with new clothes he had bought while staying with the Iposas, Felipe went across the street to a small general store to buy a loaf of fresh baked bread and a slab of butter. They met at a picnic table in a park across from the gas station where the bus stopped and ate silently while Roberto frequently checked his watch and stared down the road to where the bus would come from. About half past nine, Felipe wrapped up what was left of the breakfast and gave it to Roberto for the trip. Roberto threw his pack on his back and picked up the small suitcase which Felipe had given him.

"I guess it is time to buy your ticket," Felipe said.

"Yes, you are right. We say goodbye here then."

They shook hands and then hugged. Roberto started toward the gas station, stopped, and turned back to Felipe.

"When Cali comes home, please tell her how much I love her."

"I will. Good luck, my brother, and please call when you get settled. If they trace the call, they will have no clue who it is from in Argentina."

Felipe sent him away with a positive outlook, Roberto thought as he walked through the small park, across the street, and into the gas station. But it did no good; as he reached for his billfold to pay for the ticket, he could only think about the worst of what might happen. He even imagined the clerk looking at him suspiciously when he handed him the *escudos*, as if he were a criminal trying to escape.

The bus arrived at 9:53, two minutes early. He was the only passenger getting on in Quilleco. The driver put his suitcase in the storage beneath the bus. Roberto looked at Felipe for a brief second before he got on the bus, but did not wave. Felipe watched as Roberto took his seat. The driver put the bus in first gear and pulled away, the gray smoke from diesel engine trailing the green bus as it moved down the road toward the Andes.

CALIDA WOKE TO a strong knock on the door. A flood of light rushed onto her face. Perhaps it was the anxiety that helped her to sleep deeply without dreams she could remember. But she did have to pee.

"You will come with me," snapped a young army soldier.

"What? No breakfast?" Calida retorted. "I have to go to the bathroom."

The soldier ignored her and escorted her down a hallway, up a flight of stairs, then down another hallway. He stopped in front of a door with half glass and bold black letters—*Inteligencia Militar*. He escorted her in and told her to take a chair along the wall; she faced a window where she could see the bright summer morning outside. The soldier knocked on one of the inner doors and went in, closing the door behind him. In less than a minute, he came back out.

"In here," he commanded.

Calida walked into the office as the soldier closed the door behind her.

"Good morning, Señorita Iposa. I trust you slept well." Major Araya sat behind a large desk, the Chilean flag on a pole behind him. Calida could hear the morning traffic outside the window; had she driven past this same building herself many times before?

"Of course. I love roughing it on a cot. But you know, I missed breakfast, and I have to pee."

"Those will have to wait. First I need to ask you a few questions."

"Ask away." She was calm, forcing down her fear. She could feel her full bladder pressing on her pelvic bone. She tightened her muscles to hold back the urge.

"My name is Major Araya." He drummed his fingers along the edge of the desk almost as if he were playing the piano. Calida's stomach growled loudly. "I am entrusted with finding certain individuals who may be considered enemies of the state."

"Who, me?"

"Now, now Señorita Iposa. I did not say you. For now, we are more interested in your boyfriend, Roberto Menendez."

"He is no longer my boyfriend, Major Araya. I told your people that."

"Still, it is a curiosity to me that he continued to call you on a regular basis after you moved from Santiago to your parents in Buin. How do you explain that?"

"As I told your man yesterday, Roberto took it hard when I broke up with him. We were still friends." She had repeated it to herself so many times yesterday while locked in the small room that she was almost ready to believe it herself. Just a few more minutes, she told herself. They'll let me out of here and I will go home to Mother and Father, and Roberto will be safe.

"And being friends, as you call it, you were inclined to help him were you not?"

"Help him how?"

"Do not play games with me! Help to hide him."

"Why would I need to hide him?"

"*Señorita*, surely you know that as a member of President Allende's subversive economic team, Mr. Menendez would be subject to questioning by authorities and possibly face criminal prosecution."

"Prosecution. Just what crime has Roberto committed, Major?"

"I should advise you to be as cooperative as possible. At this point we are not looking at you for any criminal activity, but that is not to say that further investigation may not change our minds. After all, you were a key employee at Corfo."

Araya pushed his chair away from the desk and stretched his legs. She had not seriously considered that she might also be wanted by the new government. She could hear people moving through the hallway behind the closed door and wondered how many other innocent professionals and government employees had been swept up for questioning, for being "subversive."

"Key employee? Surely you are joking with me. I kept track of the government's investments in various businesses and utilities. The level of investment, and the profits and losses of those businesses. You know, something called return on investment."

"But you had input on which investments to make, did you not?"

He picked up a pencil and rolled it around in his fingers. She tried to concentrate on her story. "No, sir, I did not. I only put the data together. It was up to others in the Corporation to make those decisions. Just ask them."

"We will, Señorita Iposa. But for now, I want to know about Roberto Menendez."

Araya got out of chair and walked over to Calida. "Where is he!"

Calida instinctively took a step backward and almost peed her jeans. "I do not know."

"Very well, *señorita*. Very well. Perhaps some more time will help you remember."

He had stepped closer to her, so close she could smell the morning coffee on his breath. His eyes were cold and empty. For the first time, Calida felt a fear she could not name.

"There is nothing to remember," she protested. "I have told you all I know." She felt herself grow hot suddenly, a prickly heat that rose through her body like a fever, followed almost instantly by an unexplainable chill.

"That I doubt. Guard!" Araya shouted.

The soldier who escorted Calida to Araya's office appeared at the doorway.

"Please escort Señorita Iposa to San Miguel prison where she can rot for awhile."

She felt her stomach lurch. This can't be happening. It was Roberto they wanted; he was the one that was hiding. All she did was move to her parents' home. How could this be happening to her?

He turned to face Calida. "I hope you enjoy your stay. Perhaps, after a few days, or weeks . . . or months, for that matter, you may feel like being more cooperative." He turned his back to her and gazed out the window.

"Prison! But I have done nothing."

"We shall see, *señorita*, we shall see." He didn't bother to turn around.

The guard grabbed her arm at the elbow and forcibly led her out of the major's office. She did not want to be locked in the windowless room again, but this would be worse. Months, the major had said, and there were stories about San Miguel even before the coup. She trembled and her bladder finally gave way as she was escorted down the stairway and into a waiting army truck.

20

ROBERTO'S BUS TRIP from Quilleco to Las Maquinas, Argentina, was long and rough. At its best, the road had a thin layer of gravel to help with the mud during rainy season. At its worst, it was rutted from dried mud. Even when the road was obviously going over nothing more than bare rock, it was better than the dried ruts that shifted the bus dangerously side to side. The bus route ran east for many miles and then turned south where it intersected a slightly better road—the road to the border. Turning east again, the bus shifted frequently as it began a long uphill journey of hairpin turns through a pass and then down the other side, again via sharp turns. The road followed a river for many kilometers on level ground before it started up again toward the mountain peaks. At the top of this climb was the border . . . and its guards. Roberto looked at his watch. It was 13:35.

Roberto counted only fourteen people on the small bus, slightly more than half full. He pulled out his backpack from where he had stored it beneath the seat in front of him and removed the leftover bread. A woman in the seat on the other side of the aisle handed him a bottle of water—a welcomed offer, considering he had forgotten to bring any with him. He smiled, thanked her, and drank. He pulled some bread from his loaf and gave it to her when he handed back the bottle. He could tell she was hungry.

The bus turned left 90 degrees, then right, then left, then right, then left again. The bus was in a steep ascent, downshifting its way to the summit of the pass. Roberto sat calmly, but inside his anxiety was growing. He could not look nervous when they reached the crossing. Taking steady deep breaths, he could feel his nerves quiet. The woman across the aisle was watching him. He smiled at her. She half smiled back. The bus leveled off and Roberto looked anxiously forward. He could see nothing ahead, but soon the bus started climbing again, this time with less sharp curves. The bus was well above the tree line now. It made a sharp turn left, dropped to the lowest gear, and lurched forward. This was a steep grade—the summit would be at the top.

The brakes screeched as the bus ground to a halt in a pull-off area next to a brown wooden shack. The small outpost was flanked by a single army truck. This was it. Familiar with the routine, the bus driver turned off the engine and told the passengers this was the border and papers would be checked. "It should not take too long, but please be patient."

The door to the shack opened and two soldiers walked to the bus. The driver opened the door and exchanged pleasantries with the one soldier who climbed the bus stairs—the other stood guard outside the door. The soldier stood in the front staring at the passengers one by one. He carried a clipboard in his right hand that hung to his side.

"*Señoras y señores,*" the soldier said, "I will come down the aisle and ask each of you a series of questions. I will also see your papers."

The soldier started in the front with an old man seated next to a woman who appeared to be his wife. He took his passport, asked some questions which Roberto could not hear, and looked at his clipboard. The old man motioned to the woman next to him. The soldier looked at her passport, checked the clipboard, handed them back, and then moved on to a woman on the other side of the aisle. Roberto was seated about two-thirds of the way back in the bus. He watched the guard cautiously as he questioned each of the passengers. When the guard was about half way down the aisle, Roberto could hear the questions.

"Where are you coming from? What is your destination? What is the purpose of your trip? Are you wanted by the country of Chile for any criminal activity?"

This last question sent a shudder through Roberto.

The soldier was now in the row in front of him, asking the same questions of a young couple as he looked at their passports. He stepped to Roberto's aisle, looked at Roberto, and then turned to the woman in the seat on the opposite side of the aisle. He finished with her. Now it was Roberto's turn. He looked at Roberto and smiled as though he knew. He asked the same questions. Roberto had rehearsed his responses and delivered them as he handed the soldier his passport. Roberto was visiting an aunt and cousin who lived in Neuquén.

"And where do you currently reside, Señor Menendez?"

Roberto was not prepared for this question. He thought quickly, then said: "Temuco, sir."

That seemed to satisfy him, but he pulled up his clipboard, scanned it with his eyes, handed Roberto his passport and moved to the next aisle.

I have made it! Roberto said to himself. I have made it through!

The soldier had finished with each aisle. He moved toward the front of the bus, said something to the driver, and then exited into the shack while the bus sat there under the guard of the second soldier.

Roberto wanted to scream at the bus driver: Why aren't we moving? But he remained silent, seated stoically in the bus like the other passengers.

In about ten minutes, the soldier came out of the shack again and stepped back onto the bus, saying something to the driver before proceeding toward the rear. He stopped at the aisle in front of Roberto.

"Señor Menendez, you will come with me."

"Why?" Roberto asked, his voice trembling.

"You will come with me now!"

The woman across the aisle turned her head as Roberto picked up his backpack on the open seat next to him, stepped into the aisle in front of the soldier, and walked to the front of the bus. The driver sat in his seat, gazing straight ahead. The soldier nudged Roberto with his hands as he stepped off the bus. He was ushered into the guard shack. Another guard was on the phone in the shack as he entered.

"Yes, it is Menendez. We will detain him, Major."

21

February 1974
Washington D.C.

AT THE BEGINNING of the year I was promoted from senior analyst to the position of junior economist. The work didn't change much, but the addition to my paycheck made me feel a little more comfortable with dining out and buying better bottles of liquor. I sat in my small office at the IMF, reviewing the latest economic forecasts of certain South American countries that were the beneficiaries of IMF and other commercial loans. The IMF was concerned that the debt these countries were piling up would call into question their ability to pay the principal and interest on notes coming due. Some of the commercial banks had requested the IMF to review the data and determine whether programs to restructure their debt would be feasible and appropriate. Or at least, that's what I was told.

Just as I glanced up at the glass wall of my new office—something I was still getting used to—Fallon Connelly stormed down the hall, still bundled up in her green winter coat, her long red hair splayed across her shoulders. She had just gotten to work—an hour late. As she hurried past my office, I hollered to her.

"Hey, Fallon."

She stopped short at my door and glared as though any interruption right now was distasteful. I lifted my left arm in the air and pointed to my wristwatch.

Fallon stepped into my office. "Screw you, Jude. It took me three gas stations before I could find one that had gas, and then I had to wait in line for thirty minutes."

"Gotta love the Arabs."

"You love 'em. As far as I'm concerned, you could round them all up and send them back where they came from—under a rock."

"You mean sand." I always enjoyed jousting with Fallon; she was one of the bright spots in our world of gloomy economic news.

"Rocks, sand, whatever." She reached down to wipe a little dried slush from the toe of her high heeled boot.

"Why don't you move back into the city?" I asked, only half joking.

"Yeah, right. You're a guy. I'd rather wait in a gas line than worry every night about getting mugged or raped."

"Really, that's a bit of an overstatement, don't you think? It's not that bad." Her comment caught me a bit by surprise; it was hard to think of Fallon Connelly as being particularly vulnerable.

"As long as I worry about it, it is that bad."

"Point."

"How much longer is this embargo shit going to last anyway?"

I guess I spent more time reading and listening to the news than Fallon. Anyone who was paying attention already knew the answer to that one. "When the Israelis get out of occupied lands or when we drill the oil in Alaska. I guess that would be either never or ten years. I think that's the estimate for drilling and building a pipeline from the north shore of Alaska."

"You know what really sucks?" Fallon asked, taking off her coat. "Getting to work just as the sun is coming up. Permanent daylight savings time. Boy, Nixon sure has some great ideas."

"Wait until the 55 mph speed limit goes into effect. You'll love that. So much for your new little sports car." I grinned at her.

"Like I said when I got here: screw you."

She pivoted and stormed out, her green coat slung over her arm like Robin Hood on a coffee break.

"How about lunch? I'll buy," I yelled as she huffed her way down the hall to her office.

I shook my head and smiled. I did feel sympathy for those who relied on their cars to get around. But I felt the pinch too, especially with the escalating cost of groceries. The oil countries were making a point about our support of Israel, but it couldn't last; they needed the oil revenues or the kings and dictators would eventually be overthrown.

I went back to analyzing the debt picture of Chile and Argentina, remembering the assignment Fallon and I completed less than a year ago. How much of our work helped to overthrow Allende? And what was being planned for Uruguay and Argentina? All three countries carried significant debt on their books, most of it owed to foreign commercial banks in the U.S. and Europe. The best solution for those countries would be to default; at least on part of their debt, and let the bondholders take the loss. Instead, we were looking for mechanisms to keep the banks whole—extending principal payments on the notes or reducing interest rates on the longer-term bonds. Of course, this would hurt the bank's quarterly bottom-line, but it kept them whole in the long-term.

Fallon called an hour later and agreed to have lunch with me. She had gotten over the effects the oil embargo had on her normally well-planned and controlled life. We ate a late lunch at a place specializing in soup and salads—the kind of place Fallon had taken to lately.

"We have to start eating healthier, Jude," she replied to my less than favorable comment on the menu. "Just think of the impact on health care costs."

"It couldn't be that you like the way you look in your new mini skirt. It's a little short for the office, by the way. Or maybe Geoff prefers women on the thin side." I continued scanning the menu options: nothing but soups and salads. I peeked above the menu to see her reaction.

Her glare quickly changed to a demure smile shaping her lips. "Well, there's that too, I guess."

"You guys have been going out for almost a year, Fallon. When are you going to get married?"

"I don't know. I'm not sure I want to."

"Sure you do. All women want to get married."

"What kind of a sexist comment is that?"

"I didn't know there was more than one kind." I laughed. She didn't.

"You know, you're nearing thirty. You've had a good career. I just assumed you wanted kids." I knew I should probably abandon this train of thought, but I was genuinely curious about Fallon's plans. I knew so little of her private life; I wondered what she really wanted.

"I have thought about it on and off . . . I'm not sure what I want. Let's change the subject, okay?"

We ordered lunch, if you could call it that; I had decided to give the broccoli cheddar soup a try, while Fallon ordered a chicken Caesar salad. I tore into the miniature loaf of sourdough bread the waiter left on the table.

"So what do you want to talk about?"

"How about you for a change?" Fallon asked. "When are you going to get out of that postage-stamp apartment? You've been promoted. You can afford it."

"What, move to the burbs like you? Buy a car? Wait in gas lines? No thanks."

She shot me a dagger. "There are plenty of nice places in the city you could move to."

"Yeah, and pay 50% of my disposable income on rent. And then there would be the taxi fares."

"You are tight, Jude. Do you take your dates to McDonalds?"

"What dates?"

"That's the point. You need to get a girlfriend. Why don't you buy one of those leisure suits and go to a disco bar? We all need love. Well, at least companionship and an occasional . . . you know."

I looked at her with a wry smile. "No, Fallon. What do you mean?"

"Oh, shut up. Get a girl, will you?"

She flagged down the waitress for more iced tea while I struggled to regain the advantage in our sparring match.

"I've had dates."

"Yeah, how many? One in the last three months?"

"Sorry, Fallon, I'm picky."

"So what are you looking for? Blond, brunette, re . . ."

"Yeah, someone like you." That stopped her short. If she wanted to play this game, I was happy to go along. "Redhead, Fallon, like you."

"No, seriously. What do you want?"

"I don't care about the color of their hair, but they have to be attractive. I hate to be crude . . . but not overweight."

Fallon rolled her eyes.

"I'm serious. You get it. That's why we're eating here."

"Okay, okay, I get it." She pushed her bread plate away and poked at her iced tea with a straw. "What else?"

"Well, I need someone my equal. You know, intellectually."

"Like me? Again?" Fallon smiled and leaned forward with her elbow on the table.

"Yes, my dear, like you. But someone with emotion—not an egghead, thinking type."

"You think I'm an egghead?"

"That's not what I meant, and you know it."

"Well, at least thank you for that."

"Just once I'd like to find a woman who was as interested in me as herself," I ventured, hoping I wasn't being too confessional here. "And, I guess, I need someone with some spunk."

"Spunk?"

"You know, sparky, fiery."

"So I get it, you want a thin, red-headed Leo, who is probably a cyborg designed to cater to your unique needs, mental and physical. Sounds like a fantasy to me. Sorry, I don't know anyone who fits that description."

She was right. But what reality was better than our fantasies?

I SPENT WHAT was left of the afternoon wrapping up my reading. When the phone rang, I was surprised to see it was almost five.

"Jude?"

I recognized the voice but couldn't place it. "Yes, this is Jude Anders."

"This is Anton. Anton Tomasin."

I hadn't heard from Anton since I left Toronto and had pretty much written off his friendship. I guess I could have called him, but I didn't—just like I hadn't tried to maintain contact with Mark, Doug, Bill, Paul, or Sasha. I wondered what I did with the business card he had given me that night in Toronto?

"My God, Anton. What have you been up to? Are you still in school?"

He laughed. "No, my friend, I finished my master's last year. I had enough of the book stuff, like you. It just took me a little longer."

"So what are you doing?" I leaned back in my chair and settled in for what I hoped would be a long catch-up session.

"Working for my father."

"Which one?" I asked without thinking.

"I hadn't thought of that. Good question. For Jack actually." I smiled at the thought of Anton working for Jack Tomasin. "Listen I'm in D.C. for the day."

"In D.C.? What are you doing here? Are we allowing Canadians in now?"

"It sounds like you have developed a sense for sarcasm. That coupled with your innate cynicism will make a dangerous cocktail. Anyway, I was wondering, if you don't have any plans, could we get together for dinner tonight? My treat."

"Hey, Anton, I can afford it," I replied laughing. At least some things had changed for the better. I had money now and didn't have to rely on him to pick up the tab.

"Of course you can. Junior economist with the IMF. Quite impressive, my man."

"Anton, you know I'm not your man."

"Sorry, old habits. Anyway, how about dinner?"

"And how did you know about my position at the IMF?"

There was a pause. As much as I enjoyed hearing from him, I also remembered the discomfort I often felt around Anton. There was always something going on beneath his surface that I was never able to reach.

"Come on, my father has connections."

Fallon's words that first day at work came to mind. How did she put it—Who did I know to get this job?

"So, I'm being watched?" I tried to make a joke out of it, but my words were strained.

"Listen, both my father and I like you. In Toronto, you were like the brother I never had. Of course we are interested in your well-being and success."

"So your father knows people in the IMF?"

"Yes, Jude. That is obvious."

I wondered who it might be. There was silence on the phone. What else did Fallon say that first day—influence in the hiring process?

"Jude, are you still there?"

Now my curiosity was piqued. Did I get this job on my merits, or did someone call in a chip to put me here? "Yes, Anton. Dinner would be great; it will be great to see you. What time and where?"

WE ARRANGED TO have dinner at 7:30 at the Old Ebbitt Grill near the White House. I went back to my apartment briefly to pick up the mail and clean up a little, changing into a clean white shirt and putting on a red and black striped tie. I didn't know whether to ask Anton whom Jack knew at the IMF or if he had pulled strings to get me hired. The whole thing kind of disturbed me and overshadowed the excitement I felt at seeing my old friend. At 7:00 I put on my wool overcoat, left the apartment, and hailed a cab out front. I had heard about Ebbitt's—a place for politicians, celebrities, and elites. Anton and the Old Ebbitt, this was going to be a trip.

Arriving a bit early—with the D.C. traffic it was hard to be precise—I pulled out a cigarette and moved away from the entrance. I was nearly finished with the smoke when Anton pulled up in a cab. I half expected to see him arrive in a limo.

Anton saw me right off.

"Jude." He walked over and shook my hand. "Mind if I join you for a quick one?" He pulled a pack of Dunhill cigarettes from his inside coat pocket. Of course, Dunhill's were the most expensive cigarettes one could buy, and you had to go to a pipe and cigar store to purchase them.

"I didn't know you smoked."

"Only occasionally." He stared at me oddly.

"What?" I turned around to see if he was looking at something or someone behind me.

"Of course," he concluded. "It is your hair. You had it cut."

"Give me a break. Do you really think I would turn up at the IMF with a ponytail?"

We both laughed and went inside. The whole place was glass and wood; glittering chandeliers threw muted lighting on the brass rails and velvet banquettes. Exceptionally posh, especially for me. We checked our coats and were escorted to a quiet table with a starched white tablecloth in the rear of the restaurant.

"Don't you look spiffy," Anton remarked. "The IMF has certainly helped to dress you up. Do you like steak *au poivre* or lobster? The Old Ebbitt has the best in the area."

I remembered having a lobster tail at a fancy restaurant with my mother to celebrate my graduation from high school. A lot of trouble for something so small, I thought at the time. I flipped through the elaborate leather-bound menu looking for something familiar.

"What is steak *au* . . ."

"*Au poivre*. I guess the old adage is true: you can dress them up but you cannot take them out." I obviously looked annoyed because he quickly followed: "Jude, I am joking. It is a strip steak encrusted in black peppercorns. Very tasty. And, how about a Bordeaux?"

"Sure." I continued to look through the menu. The wine list was a separate affair, even more elaborate than the menu. I was happy to let Anton choose.

"Gentlemen," the white-coated waiter said when he approached our table. "May I bring you a cocktail tonight?"

"I will have a Macallan, two cubes," Anton replied.

I ordered a Heineken, my usual.

"Very good. Thank you, gentlemen. I will bring your drinks right away."

Before he could leave, Anton ordered a bottle the Chateau Margaux '62. "Could you open it now and decant it?"

"Certainly, sir." The waiter smiled. "That is a very fine wine."

I put the menu on the table, having decided on the steak since Anton had ordered the Bordeaux. "So what are you doing in town?"

"I had a couple of meetings."

"Uh-huh, with whom?"

Anton smiled. "Ah, the first meeting was with some businessmen at your Chamber of Commerce, and then, with some low-level officials of your State Department."

"State Department?"

"Yes, we were discussing some of the privatization in Chile."

"Chile? Pinochet?"

"No, not Pinochet. We are working with other businessmen from the U.S., Canada, and Europe and some officials of the Chilean government to return some of the mining assets that were appropriated under Allende, and to bid on some other public business assets."

Anton paused, staring at me. I wondered if he knew of my involvement with Chile at the IMF. Of course he did, I was sure of it.

"They are only financial transactions," he said.

"Sure they are. Tell that to the Chilean people."

"Jude, their way is over. It did not work. You are an economist. You, better than I, understand what went wrong."

The waiter silently delivered our drinks. I pulled out a cigarette.

"Maybe their way didn't work, maybe they pushed too fast. Or . . . maybe their way needed more time to work. Anton, you remember what I told your father. It was economically sensible for them protect their assets from exploitation."

Anton put his glass down on the table. "Exploitation."

"Yes. Exploitation. That's when I buy something that you own for a $1 and sell it for $8. That's a bad deal for the guy who gets the $1. And it's not just that. They believed if you raise the standard of living for everyone, then everyone would contribute to the commerce of the country."

Anton gave me a puzzled look, but I knew the concept was not beyond him. Even so, I spelled it out for him, giving him a remedial economics lesson he had not asked for.

"It's like this: would you rather have a hundred people buying widgets, especially if those widgets were made in your country, or ten people. It's about demand, Anton."

"Then what went wrong?" He looked me square in the eye, his fingers gripping his glass.

From the way he asked the question, I couldn't tell if he was genuinely interested or just sniping at my point of view. It had been over two years since I had last seen or talked with Anton, so I wasn't sure where he was coming from. Based on his financial status, I suspected he was being critical. This was going to be a contentious reunion.

"To start with, the rest of the developed Western world stacked the deck against them. Dumping copper to drive the price down. Cutting off short-term commercial capital needed for investments and ongoing operations. Restricting imports from their country. I think Chile tried to do too much too quick. That was one of their mistakes. As a result, wages went up too much too soon. There was a very uneven balance between production and demand. That kind of thing requires time to get it right, even in a free-market economy." I stubbed out the butt and resisted the urge to reach for another.

"They tried price controls, but they didn't work," I continued. "The black market deprived the government of tax revenues. Inflation caused a monetary flight from the country. Agrarian reform was chaotic at best, and Allende's indecision on how fast to proceed with it affected food production. Tax rates on wealth and profits were probably too high, while tax revenues were not commensurate with government expenditures. The deficits that grew could not be sustained over the short run, especially with the lack of foreign investment and capital."

I took a long drink of my Heineken. Even to my own ears, I sounded more intense than I expected. But hey, if Anton was going to start right out talking about Chile, he was going to get the full picture from me. I had, after all, been spending the last two years on the whole Chile situation.

"Sounds like a lot was wrong. You have obviously studied the situation." He looked serious as he swirled the ice cubes in his scotch.

"Yes, I have. It's my job, remember, and a lot did go wrong. Someday I would like to talk with some of the economists under Allende to get their take on it. But like I said, it's something that perhaps, just perhaps, could have been worked through over time. But no. The financiers wanted their pound of flesh, the wealthy Chileans wanted their lifestyle back, and the military was brainwashed by . . . let's just say, by the incessant fear of communism propagated by the U.S."

The President of the United States could have walked into Ebbit's by then and I would not have noticed. I was back in the zone like I used to be with Anton, only this time our theoretical discussions were based on my real world experience.

"I am sure it is not that simple, Jude." He sipped at his drink.

"You're right, Anton, it isn't that simple. The workings of an economy are very complex . . . especially when other countries are involved and there are internal interests chomping at the bit to regain power. But you know the thing that pisses me off more than any other?"

"What is that?"

"The people of Chile freely elected their government. They were a democracy. What they were doing with their economy was their decision. The U.S. and a small group of determined, selfish bastards had no right to destroy it!"

Anton was quiet. I suspected that this last comment drew his father, and maybe Anton himself, into the mess now known as the "Chilean Experiment"—the grand economic correction that was underway. How many experiments could one country tolerate over such a short period of time?

"And you do not believe the far left of the country had anything to do with its downfall?" Anton asked after a moment.

How had I left myself open to that one? My work was focused almost entirely on the economic situation; the political framework had always been less important.

"Probably so. Both the far right and left. Extremists on both sides wanting it their way—no compromise, like compromise was an evil word. What is sad is the vast majority who are politically in the middle will continue to pay the price for the extremists' intransigency—the middle class, well-off, and poor alike."

Anton was quiet, taking another sip of his scotch. He set his glass back on the table. "So, will you continue to do work for Chile at the IMF?"

"Shit, I don't know. They are still a member country. I've done work on their behalf in the past. And I still work at the IMF. Why?"

"It is just that you sound so passionate about what is going on there."

"I may not agree with what they are doing there now, but it is my job to serve the member countries of the IMF."

The waiter brought Anton's decanted bottle of wine. This was going to be a delicious dinner—I was expecting a lettuce wedge with bleu cheese with my steak, while Anton had ordered beefsteak tomatoes with mozzarella. I didn't want to spoil it thinking about my role in the toppling of Allende and his economic model.

Anton wisely changed the subject. "Well, Jude how is your love life in D.C.?"

I was eating a breadstick and almost choked.

"What is this with my love life today? First Fallon, and now you."

"Fallon? Sounds juicy. I cannot wait to hear about her."

22

Present Time
Aegean Sea, Greece

SURROUNDED BY THE endless circling of gulls, the *Albion* cut through the peaceful waters of the Aegean Sea. Had this sometimes angry sea laid down just for me, at this time in my life? I pushed the button to lower my seatback, thinking I could take a nap. As if the long flight to Athens wasn't enough to make me tired, all these memories were making it worse. But they were flowing like the lava that formed these islands. I couldn't stop them, even if I wanted to.

That first reunion with Anton was so combative that frankly, I thought I'd never hear from him again after our dinner at the Old Ebbitt Grill. But I was wrong—very wrong. That night I didn't anticipate getting into the Chile discussion and was surprised by my strong emotional reaction to what happened there. Maybe it was the contrast between Anton's life of luxury and the struggles of the people of Chile that stirred my vehement reaction. Most important, that night re-ignited my sense of justice. Where had it been? Somewhere between my last year at college and that night, it had slipped away. Or had it just gone underground, waiting for the right time to raise its head again? Regardless, from that night forward, I viewed my work at the IMF through a different set of lenses. I was less excited, and certainly more wary of whom the IMF was actually trying to help. And now Jack's words were ringing again in my ears: "The IMF was doing the real work for developing economies around the world."

Two names stuck with me during those days: Roberto Menendez and Señor Baca, names on the IMF loan forms from the Central Bank in Chile that ultimately had been turned down. I wanted to discuss the details of Chile's economic experiment with both men to understand the details of their model and what went wrong. I could only speculate from afar with facts and figures. For the most part, their economic model made sense to me; it seemed structurally sound. So what really happened? These men were a part of the conversations then—the weighing of pros and cons over various actions before they took their fateful decisions. That is where their program must have failed.

Again I remembered a comment I had made to Anton that night at the Old Ebbitt: maybe they just didn't have enough time. Enough time? Certainly not with Nixon, the CIA, the IMF, and Chile's commercial creditors breathing down their necks, and taking actions to topple the regime. My hatred for Nixon that began in college had only intensified, and I struggled to find even a few things that made me proud to be an American. Even the fact that my government was holding hearings on Nixon's illegal activities didn't make me feel any better about it. But finally it came; an enormous event that promised a new day for my country.

I remembered it clearly. It was late when I finally got home from the office that sultry August night. I took off my suit coat, loosened my tie, and opened a beer. When I turned on the TV, the announcer was saying President Nixon would address the nation at 9:00 pm. And at 9:00 sharp Nixon appeared on the screen from behind his desk in the Oval Office of the White House. By the time he had concluded his speech, I had nearly finished my beer. It was over. All of it. Vietnam and Nixon's presidency as well.

I couldn't believe it, no more than I could believe we shut down the university in 1970. Nixon had fucking resigned. It was unbelievable, an unheard of moment in the history of our country. The President of the United States resigned. I wanted to scream it from the rooftop, but I settled for calling Fallon. She couldn't understand my emotional reaction to the event, but she went to Harvard before the Vietnam protests got into full swing, and she never had to face the draft. But I knew what this meant, not only to me but also to an entire generation forced to deal personally with that hideous war. It was the end of the misery that had followed me for more than eight years. Nam and now Nixon were finally over.

I could hear the drone of the *Albion*'s engines and feel the ship's steady forward motion. I rested my head against the small window and dozed off.

23

August 1974
Santiago, Chile

CALIDA COULD HEAR the cart rolling down the long corridor of the prison wing. The guard was coming with her breakfast as he had every morning about this time. But this time, just before the cart reached her cell, another guard approached her door and opened it.

"You are being released. Grab your belongings and come with me."

Calida didn't have to be told twice. She quickly grabbed the cloth sack that held the few things she had been allowed to have in prison and followed the guard to a room where she was given the clothes she had been wearing that terrible day, the day she was sure she would never see her mother and father or Roberto again. Her jeans were tight fitting when she came in. They hung loosely around her thin hips now. It was summer when she came in. It was winter now.

She was given ten *escudos* and escorted to the front gates of San Miguel prison. It was cloudy and cold, and Calida did not have a coat. She walked hurriedly down the avenue to the first restaurant she could find ten blocks away—a small coffee house. Shivering as she opened its heavy glass door, she entered into the warmth and bought an espresso and a pastry, and counted out some change for the pay phone she had spotted in the back of the shop near the restroom. She took a table, placed her sack on the chair, and sipped her espresso. Picking up her pastry, she moved to the pay phone, and struggled with her trembling hands to insert the coins into the pay phone to call her father.

"Señor Iposa's office," his secretary answered.

"Ceci, this is Calida. Is father there?"

"Calida, *ay mi dios*. Are you all right, child? Where are you?"

"I am in Santiago. Is father in yet this morning?"

"Yes, I will get him. Hold on, please."

She tore into the pastry while she waited, hungrily stuffing the sweet dough in her mouth.

"Calida! Where are you? Where have you been?"

She felt her eyes well up at the sound of her father's voice. "I have been in San Miguel prison, Father. Where is Roberto?"

"Those bastards. They said they released you weeks after your arrest and had no idea where you were. We have tried our best to find you, old friends and acquaintances in Santiago and here, but no one had heard from you. Calida, my daughter, are you okay?"

"Yes, I guess." She knew she was lucky; she hadn't been beaten, she hadn't been tortured or raped. More than anything, she thought she had been forgotten, except for those two meals a day. "What about Roberto?" There was a pause.

"Calida, we do not know."

Calida could not figure out what her father meant. What does he not know? Where Roberto is? Whether he is safe? Roberto's situation would have to wait until she got home.

"I am cold. I have no coat. I am holed up in a little coffee house by the prison. Will you come get me?"

"Sit tight, my child. I will be there within an hour."

Calida got into the front seat of her father's car for the drive back to Buin. She had barely closed the car door when she started in.

"So, where is Roberto?" It had been the only thing that sustained her those long months in the cell; thinking about Roberto, dreaming about their plans for the future, worrying about him, praying for his safety.

"Calida, like I said, we do not know." His eyes were more on her than on the road. "Felipe drove him to the bus stop in Quilleco. He got on the bus and Felipe drove home. He was taking the back road to La Maquinas. He and I concluded that was the only safe way to try to escape the country."

She could see how the fear and worry of the past several months had taken its toll on him. He looked thinner, grayer, sadder.

"That was the last time any of us saw or heard from Roberto. He was going to call Felipe when he got settled in Buenos Aires. He never called."

So Roberto had decided to flee the country without her. There was no way he could get out; the military had the country locked down tight. She wavered. Who knows? Back then, maybe? Through the pass to La Maquinas, it was an outside chance. It is remote. But then why hadn't he called? A traced call from Buenos Aires would not mean much to the government. No, it was obvious he did not make it.

"That means he must be in jail . . . or worse."

"Please, Calida, do not talk of such things." Atilo reached over to pat her hand while he drove.

"Father, facts are facts; logic is logic. Even if they have him in prison, I cannot help him. If he did get to Buenos Aires, I may be able to find him there."

"You are going to Buenos Aires? You just got out of prison. You must stay home for a while; your mother has been sick with fear and worry. Half the time she does not even eat anymore."

She ignored his concern; she was not a child. This was a war, a war by a government against its own people. She would do whatever she had to do to be with Roberto.

"First I will try to contact some of Roberto's old acquaintances, assuming they are still alive, and assuming I can even find them. If Roberto is alive and hiding in Chile, I will go to him. If he is dead or in prison, or just 'missing', I will go to Argentina. He may have made it across the border. In any event, I cannot do him any good by living here anymore."

"Do you think the government will allow you to leave?"

Atilo turned off the highway onto the road to Buin.

"Why should they care about me anymore? They did not get what they wanted from me in prison. How can I be any further use to them?"

"But if Roberto did make it to Buenos Aires, they may follow you. You would lead them to him."

"Who would follow me, Father? A soldier in a uniform?"

"They may be collaborating with the police or army in Argentina."

Calida had not considered that possibility. "Then I must be careful in Buenos Aires until I am sure I am not being followed." Though her words were strong, Calida felt her energy fade. There was so much to do, and she was so tired.

"Are you sure about this? At least take some time at home to think about it. You need to eat and regain your health. You look so . . . thin."

Her father had always told her she was too headstrong for her own good. *I never argue with you,* he had told her once. *You just get even more determined to get your way.* Was she thinking straight? *Madre Dios,* she thought, I have just this day gotten out of prison, and I want to begin a new journey in another country.

"Okay, Papa," she finally acquiesced. "I will stay for a while and eat Mamá's cooking." Yes, she would stay . . . for a while at least. She knew she needed to plan carefully; there were so many variables and what-ifs to take into account, and as she had said, she must try to contact Roberto's friends anyway.

OVER THE FOLLOWING weeks and months, Calida tried to contact each of Roberto's known friends, acquaintances, and work associates, but had little luck. Most had apparently moved or their telephone numbers were no longer in service. Roberto's fellow economists and a few analysts who worked at the Central Bank had just disappeared. Finally, she found the wives of two remaining economists on her list and met them for coffee the following week. Their stories were heartbreakingly similar. The army came to their homes the day following the coup and arrested their husbands. After several days they tried to find out where they were. Army officials told them that they did not know. They had not been heard from since.

She worked hard trying to find people who could help her and amassed a large file of newspaper clippings, notes and scribbled leads, but it all went nowhere. As the holidays drew near and Calida resigned herself to spending Christmas without Roberto, she knew she had to take action. At Christmas dinner, she announced she would go to Buenos Aires after the first of the year.

"I will find a job there and make a new life, whether I find Roberto there or not."

Her mother and father tried to reason with her to stay in Buin, but Calida was determined to leave. She was angry at her country; she wanted nothing more than a fresh start in a new place. This nightmare had gone on too long.

"If you must go, then please contact Imelda, your cousin," her mother insisted, dabbing at the tears in her eyes. "She is your age and has her own apartment, and maybe she can put you up for a while until you get settled."

Calida nodded.

24

January 1975

ON THE TWELFTH day of the New Year, Calida took the 19:00 bus from Santiago to the city of Buenos Aires. It was midnight when the bus reached the border. The bus driver pulled over, waiting for the border guards to check the passengers' papers. The guard walked down the aisle, checking passports against a thick binder. She assumed it was a list of names.

He handed her passport back after checking it against his binder. "Enjoy Argentina, Señorita Iposa. We hope you stay there."

Before she could check the look on his face, the soldier passed to the next row. She could not fathom that she was being told to leave and never come back. Chile was her country, too, as much as this soldier's. She had spent most of her adult working life trying to make Chile a better place to live. Now she was more trouble than she was worth. *¡Basta!* I have had enough of Chile.

Imelda met Calida at the bus terminal in Buenos Aires at noon the next day. They had not seen each other in eight years, the last time Imelda and her mother visited them in Buin. Imelda gunned her little well-worn Ford through the busy boulevards of the city on the way to her apartment while they caught up on the news of various relatives. Imelda already knew of Roberto's disappearance and her time in prison from their phone conversation in December.

"There was no need for you to take off work to pick me up," Calida said, as Imelda maneuvered into a parking place on a crowded street. "But thank you so much."

"Do not worry, Calida, I work the night shift at the Ford assembly plant. Sometimes a double shift on weekends. So we have all afternoon. We will take your things to my apartment and then go for something to eat."

After Imelda helped Calida carry her bags up to the apartment they walked down the street, Imelda in tight jeans that accentuated the lovely curves of her svelte body. The firmness of her biceps and triceps, which had developed from using an impact wrench to attach doors to the cars on the assembly line at the plant, showed through her short-sleeved blouse. Calida noticed that Imelda received more than one long glance from the men as they walked to the restaurant past boutiques, bars and hip little cafes that lined the street, and she realized just how starved she had been for excitement in sleepy Buin.

"What do you think happened to Roberto?" Imelda asked after they had ordered tapas and sangria.

"Either the military caught him or he is here in Argentina, probably in Buenos Aires."

"And if they caught him?"

"There are so many stories, rumors mostly. Prison. Torture. Murder. I do not know, and it does me little good dwelling on them. He has just disappeared."

Imelda squeezed a wedge of orange in her sangria. "Did Roberto have friends in Buenos Aires?"

"He told my brother that he knew people here, but he never mentioned them to me. So if he made it here, I do not know where to look for him." The restaurant was packed; Calida was surrounded by more people right now than she had seen in weeks in Buin. With the noise from all the chatter around her, she was having a hard time concentrating on the misery of Chile.

"He is an economist, right? Maybe in those circles. Or at the university."

"That is worth pursuing," Calida nodded. "Perhaps you can tell me how to make contacts. I would not know where to start in your country."

"Probably like in your country, but I will give it some thought."

"How are things in Argentina?" Calida wanted to change the subject. And she genuinely wondered whether the two neighboring countries would have anything left in common. After she left Corfo and the Junta took over, she was so focused on what was happening in Chile she had lost interest in keeping up with the larger region.

Imelda laughed. "Actually I do not know whether to laugh or cry. Isabel is no Juan Peron. She tries to make peace with both the right and the left, giving into each. There are clashes and violence. One group explodes bombs—banks, car dealers, drug laboratories. Another group kills trade union leaders, journalists, and lawyers. Even the Peronists are at war with each other. But we Argentines are used to it. We have grown up with these conflicts."

"And your economy?"

"*Mierda*. But then we are used to that too. Recession, inflation, growth, stagnation, contraction, and blah blah blah. All we know is wages go up, then down, the value of our money goes down, and inflation always goes up. As I said, the government politicians try to find a middle ground, but the compromises pull against each other. So nothing works more than a few months."

To Calida this sounded all too familiar; like Chile before the coup.

IT TOOK CALIDA a little less than three weeks to find a position as a financial analyst for Chase Manhattan Bank of Argentina. Going back to work was a relief, not only because she now had money to buy more fashionable clothes and go out for dinner or to a club periodically, but because her job helped take her mind off of Roberto and her life in Chile. She lived with Imelda for another couple of months until she found an affordable apartment near the bank headquarters where she worked. One night a week Calida took a course in monetary theory at the School of Economics at the University of Buenos Aires, hoping to make some contacts with people who might know Roberto. She often fantasized that one night she might run into him while walking to or from class or in the library or student union. No such luck.

Imelda was not much help either with finding anyone who might have some clue whether Roberto was in Buenos Aires or not. As it turned out, Imelda did not have a single acquaintance who had even taken an economics class while studying at the university. She did, however, have a circle of friends that were certainly on the fringe of political thinking. Calida was surprised to find that a few of them belonged to the Montoneros—a radical group that wanted a return to Peron socialism. Between work and school, she didn't have much time for Imelda's crowd. And after the last few years in Chile, she didn't think it was such a good idea to be hanging out with extremists anyway; she kept her distance.

Life for Calida in Buenos Aires gradually settled into a pleasant routine. Her prison days and the months of fear in Chile were behind her, and she enjoyed the normal day-to-day life she was carving out in her new home. Going to work, making new friends, socializing over dinners—it reminded her of life in Santiago with Roberto before the Junta. She stayed in touch with her parents and Felipe, always anxious for news about what was happening at home. The situation in Chile was essentially unchanged—economic austerity measures and repression of political freedoms. But her father's steel wire business was doing okay. Production was actually up, according to Felipe.

As the months wore on, Calida became aware that she was gradually forgetting Roberto. When she joined her fellow students for a coffee after class, she no longer searched the space of the student union in hopes of spotting Roberto. In the beginning, she would cry at nights, still missing him. Now she spent more time thinking about her new life in Buenos Aires. The photo of her and her former friend and lover in a park in Santiago, resting by itself on the nightstand next to her bed, was the only object that kept his memory and their life together in Santiago alive within her.

Economic life in Buenos Aires also reminded her eerily of Santiago in 1973—high inflation with little economic growth and growing deficits. But the violent clashes between competing groups within Argentina were different from Chile and they were increasing—bombings of police stations and killings of politicians and business executives. Isabel Peron was obviously not the leader her husband was. She was losing the support of the people because of the inflation and the violence throughout the country. And her numerous attempts at changing advisors made no difference to the political or economic landscape.

As Christmas approached, Calida barely thought about where she was one year ago—just released from Pinochet's prison, determined to go to Argentina to find Roberto. She spent the holiday with Imelda and her mother, exchanging small gifts and having a lamb roast for dinner.

New Year's Eve of '75 was a warm summer night. Calida and Imelda went out with some of Imelda's friends to a small jazz club filled with younger people their age, drinking, smoking, and keeping the beat to the live music. Even with the fans and open windows, the club was hot and stuffy, and the music so loud that they could talk only when the musicians took a break.

A young man at the table next to hers caught her eye. Calida recognized him from a party about a month ago, perhaps one of Imelda's friends. Yes, she recalled, his name was Vasco Madero, but a number of his male friends called him *El Cuervo.*

Emboldened by a cocktail and the party spirit around her, she waited for the band to take a break and then leaned over toward his table.

"Why do they call you the crow?"

"Ah, you have not heard the legend?" he replied with a smile and seemed eager to engage her in conversation.

"Sorry, my mother and father told me fairy tales as a child, but I do not know any legends. Tell me the legend, *El Cuervo.*"

Vasco leaned in close to her. "Well," he said, "there once was a man who was very much in love with his wife and his only child, a girl. Their love for each other was so strong that it bloomed like an aura around them. The man worked hard at a factory, trying to make a meager living for his family. Every afternoon at the end of work, his wife would come to the plant with their young daughter to walk him home. One-day the boss of the factory noticed his wife—she was quite beautiful. Very much like you I would imagine." He smiled at her with his deep dark eyes.

Calida felt herself blushing.

"After the first time seeing the wife, the boss began to covet her, his desire growing each day when she came to walk her husband home. Finally one day while the man was at work, the boss left the plant and went to the man's house and raped his beautiful wife. She screamed, and told him she would report him to the police. The man laughed. 'The police work for me. It will do you no good.' Then the woman said, 'I will tell my husband, and he will kill you.' The boss told the woman that was a pity, and proceeded to kill her, and when the child walked into the room, he stabbed her, too."

Calida listened with her mouth open, appalled at how casually he recounted such violence.

Vasco continued, closely watching Calida's reaction to the story. "The man could not figure out where his wife and daughter were at the end of work, so he hurried home as quickly as he could. When he got home his wife was dead, but his daughter still breathed life. He bent over his daughter. 'It was your boss,' she said as she took her last breath.

The man was enraged. He went back to the plant to kill his boss. But the boss was prepared. He had his thugs waiting for the man. They beat him to death.

The boss just laughed, but the man would have the last laugh. The desire to avenge his wife and daughter's deaths was so strong that he was reincarnated as a crow. Alive again the crow caught the boss as he was arriving to work the next morning. The crow attacked him, clawed his face and plucked out his eyes with his beak. The boss bled to death in the parking lot of the plant."

Calida got the drift of Vasco's horrific story. But did he think it might be a bit too gruesome to tell a woman, especially one he had just met? Then again there was something in his directness that Calida found appealing. Who was Vasco Madero? But he had still not answered her question.

"I still do not understand. Why do your friends call you by this legend?"

"Because, my sweet Calida," he said with warm smile, "I am the avenger."

All of the gruesomeness of Vasco's story was overcome by his smile and the way he called her "sweet Calida." She imagined a deep and caring spirit, a man who knew what to do in the face of violence, a man who would be strong, who could protect her. Calida started to ask what he avenged when the jazz band began playing a new set.

JUST A WEEK into the New Year, Calida was spending a lazy Saturday afternoon lost in a novel. She could not remember the last time she had just laid around on a Saturday since she arrived in Buenos Aires, much less read a book. A sort of peace had filled her being or, maybe better, an inner satisfaction that permitted her to just be for awhile, to drift, without the pressure of finding Roberto or starting a new life in a country, so near yet so far in many ways from her home.

The summer sunlight, bright and hot, streamed through the northwestern window of her small apartment, sneaking gradually up the legs of the sofa like a cat until it caught the open page of her book. Just as she shifted slightly to recast the page in shadow the buzzer to the apartment startled her. Dropping her book in surprise, she hurried to the intercom at the door.

"Hello," she said, speaking into the intercom.

"Hi there, it is Vasco. Vasco Madero."

Surprised and a little giddy, Calida answered, "Oh, is it Vasco or *El Cuervo*?"

"Whichever you prefer, but I think Vasco would be best. Would you like to go for a coffee?"

She recalled their last encounter on New Year's Eve. Of course, she would go out with him. "Can you give me a few minutes?" She smiled at the intercom.

"I will wait right here for you, sweet Calida."

She blushed, remembering how he had called her that night at the club. "I'll be down soon."

After running a brush through her hair and putting on a fresh pale yellow blouse, which she knew always made her eyes look even darker, Calida took a breath and, not wanting to appear too eager, forced herself to walk slowly down the apartment building stairs. After a short walk filled with polite conversation the two settled into a soft sofa at the coffee house in front of a low table, sitting in awkward silence, wondering how to begin a conversation. When the waitress finally delivered their espressos and the slice of cheesecake Vasco had ordered with "Two forks, if you please," Calida began to feel more comfortable.

"Vasco, what do you do for work?" Calida delicately cut a small piece off the edge of the cheesecake.

"I have an inconsequential export/import business," he said. "Mostly arts and crafts made by Argentine artisans. It provides enough to support me. I do not have or need much."

"And the imports?"

"Not much on that side really. Occasionally I arrange the import of unusual, hard to get things for people. I have the government license so people use me. I get things through customs and do the necessary paperwork for them. And you? Imelda tells me you work for a bank."

"Yes, Chase Manhattan of Argentina. Mostly I analyze their loan portfolios for risk. At quarter's end, I help prepare financial statements. The work is not as interesting as working for the Development Corporation in Chile, but it is okay."

She regretted it as soon as she mentioned her old job. How did she know whether or not it was safe to discuss her role at Corfo, even now, here? She had spent months in a dank prison cell, fed barely enough to keep her alive. She had put that behind her, and yet here she was, talking about how interesting her job used to be.

"You worked for Corfo?"

"Yes, as an analyst. Not a top level position or even close to it."

"Corfo was key to your county's economic program. It was at the heart of creating new businesses and taking back your natural resources from the exploiting capitalists."

Exploiting capitalists. Those words told her a lot about this man's political views.

"Yes, Vasco, I think Corfo made a big difference in the direction of Chile. God knows what has become of it."

He sipped his espresso and shifted slightly into a more comfortable position on the couch. "Well, I can tell you, it is not good. Corfo is now responsible for selling off Chilean nationalized assets to private companies and investors, including their public assets like the trains and the utilities."

How would her former work associates feel about using their company that had done so many good things, to now reverse and do the opposite? Just one more sadness in her country, she thought. Her decision to leave it was the right one.

"Your cousin told me you moved here from Santiago and that you are looking for your boyfriend," Vasco continued. "Why do you think he is here?"

"He made a plan to leave about this time last year. But I really do not believe he made it. Otherwise, I would have heard from him."

"Are you still looking for him?"

Calida had to face the truth. She looked directly at Vasco. "I think I have given up."

"What did he do in Chile?"

"He was an economist for the Central Bank of Chile. Under the Allende government."

"And they did not get him in the coup? I thought they rounded up all of Allende's economists, first thing."

"The bank is in a separate building from the president's palace. With all of the chaos of the coup, he got away. He went into hiding at my parents' until somehow the security forces found me. They believed I knew where his was, but I told them nothing, so they kept me in prison for eight months."

"Prison! Eight months!" Vasco shifted forward and leaned slightly toward her. "I have never been in jail myself, but I have heard the stories from acquaintances. You are very brave." He reached out to gently stroke her hair. She wished she could just curl up under his arm and let him console her.

"It was not so bad after they quit interrogating me," she admitted. "That is funny, thinking about it. They quit the interrogation after only a few weeks of my arrest."

"Calida, surely you must know what that means—they found what they were looking for. You are probably right that he did not make it across the border to Argentina." He put his hand, large and warm, over hers.

She looked away from him, fixing her gaze instead on a point in the distance.

"Do you think they have him in prison?"

"He was a senior policy maker for the Chilean economy. From what I hear, the Junta is trying to eliminate all Marxist thinking in your country. To do that they have to get rid of the leaders and the thinkers who espouse progressive thinking of any kind. It is no wonder they held you in jail. It was not just Roberto, I suspect. They probably wanted to make sure you were not part of the communist plague infesting your country."

"Right. Like I was really dangerous. But seriously, do you think they have murdered Roberto?"

Vasco hesitated. "I have heard stories from my sources. They are not pleasant. If they captured Roberto, his death may be a blessing."

Tears welled up in Calida's eyes. Vasco put his arm around her and drew her closer to him.

"Calida, I am so sorry. I may be wrong."

"I loved him so much. It is hard to let go."

So much that she had been holding within now threatened to spill out; here, in a public place, with a man she had just met.

"It is the cruelest thing a man can do against another," Vasco continued. "Make people disappear and not give their loved ones a body and a grave to morn over. Leave them forever to wonder without a closure."

Calida pulled herself together. "Do you think they do that to protect themselves from their crimes or just to express the ultimate cruelty in their hearts?"

Vasco looked down at the table and shook his head. "I do not know."

They talked for at least an hour about the politics of Argentina, the climate and the foods of the two neighboring countries, noting the many similarities and differences. And she could not help but notice the similarities and differences between Vasco and Roberto. Yes, both of them were handsome, but Roberto was shorter and lean, while Vasco was muscular. Certainly, both men were very intelligent. But with Roberto she always felt his equal; that decisions would be taken jointly. She was not so sure Vasco had the same inclination. Still, she could tell Vasco was a caring person, and her initial impression from their first encounter at the jazz club that he was a man who could protect her was reaffirmed. Yes, she felt at peace, and now she was beginning to feel more secure as well.

"I would like to see you again, Calida," he said, grabbing her hand as they reached her apartment door after their walk back.

"And I you. I feel very comfortable talking with you."

"It has been too long since I have had a warm conversation with an intelligent woman. May we go out for dinner next Saturday?"

"Yes, I would like that . . . but, Vasco, I would rather cook a dinner for you. I cannot say I am the best cook, but I am not that bad either." She smiled.

"That would be all the better. I will bring the wine. Is 20:00 too early?"

"20:00 is perfect. See you then, *El Cuervo*."

25

Washington, D.C.

I REALLY WANTED Fallon and Anton to meet, but I was beginning to have second thoughts about the dinner plans tonight. It had been snowing off and on all day, and now it was coming down pretty heavy. I carefully drove the toll road to Dulles Airport in my rental car and noted the Saturday night traffic was much lighter than usual.

I pulled into the short-term lot at Dulles and looked at my watch—Anton's plane wouldn't land for another 15 minutes. Before going to meet him in baggage claim I lit up another smoke. The snow was still falling in big flakes on my windshield, and at least four inches had accumulated on the asphalt of the parking lot. The radio station announced the upcoming Led Zeppelin concert later this month before playing *Stairway to Heaven*. I loved that song but didn't want to miss Anton by sitting in the car listening to the whole thing. I slipped the rubbers over the leather soles of my black wingtips and headed for the terminal, flicking the last of my cigarette in the snow before reaching the underground entrance to the terminal baggage claim.

Anton's flight was listed on the black and white arrivals monitor. I stood there glaring at the monitor. Crap. Delayed another forty-five minutes.

"Jude, there you are," a voice pierced from behind through the drone of arriving passengers.

I turned around and saw Anton standing there in a dark blue cashmere overcoat, luggage in hand. I was happy to see him—happier that I didn't have to wait another hour while the weather got worse.

149

"You're not supposed to land for another forty-five minutes."

"Got an earlier flight, my man. With all the snow, I figured there would be delays. And I did not want to miss my first meeting with this woman you have talked about so much."

"Well, my man," I retorted, "looks like you were right." I pointed to his flight on the monitor. "I see you've got your luggage. Let's go."

"So where are we going to have dinner?" Anton asked as we walked to my car. "I hope it is somewhere as good as the Old Ebbitt."

"Actually, we're going to Fallon's place in the burbs. She's cooking. I was going to drop you off at your hotel first, but the way the snow's coming down, I think we should just go to Fal's." I popped the trunk and lifted his suitcase in for him.

"We may have to stay the night, if this doesn't let up." Anton stood in the falling snow with his hands out, as though he had never seen such a thing before in Canada.

"You might like that." I winked at him. "I mean with Fallon."

"Surely you do not believe I would sleep with one of your work associates. That really would be tacky." Anton climbed into the car, tapping his shoes lightly on the doorframe to knock the snow off.

"Yeah, right. You haven't seen her yet. You might change your mind."

The drive was slow and tedious, but it gave Anton and I plenty of time to catch up. His export/import business was growing steadily, helped along by the changes in Indonesia, Brazil, and Chile. I cringed several times when the discussion turned to privatizing several of the state-owned assets of those countries, but held my tongue. Although Anton no longer went out of his way with me to champion unencumbered free-market economies, he certainly benefited. And though I was certain we both knew that, he and I seemed to have come to some unspoken agreement—a neutral zone where our differences on economic approaches was avoided at all costs. By the time we finally reached Fallon's house, the snow had all but stopped.

"Come in," Fallon said. "Give me your coats. So this is Anton."

"It is very nice to meet you, Miss Connelly," Anton replied, offering her his hand. Anton was so suave you would have thought he was greeting the Queen of England. I almost choked.

"Please call me Fallon." She had that girlish grin that comes over a woman when a new guy takes an interest. "I would have thought some of your friend's manners would have rubbed off on you, Jude."

"I brought the wine, Fal, doesn't that count?" What did she expect from a lower-middle class guy? Comparing me with Anton, who grew up in the rarified atmosphere of sophistication, wasn't fair at all.

We moved into the kitchen where Fallon was still preparing the *coq au vin*. I pulled out the single malt scotch from the cabinet, while Anton decanted the cabernet I had brought for dinner. Fallon was already on her second glass of Chablis, and had made up a plate of stuffed mushroom caps and cheese balls that sat on the island counter. Anton and I dug in, scotch already in hand.

"Well, you ought to be in a good mood, Jude. They convicted your boys," Fallon started in as I took a stool at the island.

Anton had a quizzical look.

"She means Haldeman, Ehrlichman, and Mitchell—you know, Nixon's henchmen in the Watergate scandal," I said.

"Ah, yes, I read about that. But your president let Nixon off; he gave him a full pardon."

Fallon lifted the lid from the simmering pot of chicken and mushrooms and stirred, releasing a fragrant cloud of garlic that filled the room. "The guys at the top always get off."

"Yeah, just like Allende," I quipped. "Too bad the military didn't bomb the White House when Nixon was still in it."

"But that is something unique about the United States, and Canada as well," Anton jumped in. "The military is constitutionally in the hands of the civilian government. They would not seize power in direct contradiction of our constitutions."

"It goes much deeper than that, Anton." I had thought about this more than once. "If you think about it, the military has enough manpower and firepower to take over the government. But in our country we have a long tradition of the military staying out of civilian affairs. It's part of our culture. Maybe that is why we had the draft. I can't imagine that a general would give the order to kill one of our elected officials. And if they did, what draftee would obey it?"

"Gee, Jude," Fallon interjected, "I guess you've forgotten Kent State. Besides now the soldiers are paid volunteers."

I was suddenly drawn back to those days on the Quad. One general from the Ohio National Guard gave the orders and the soldiers complied, killing four students. Could the military take over our government? Sure, I guess they could, but would they? What if Nixon had used his emergency powers, like he did with the oil crisis, when he saw that he would lose everything because of the Watergate scandal and be forced from office? Would he have suspended Congress and declared martial law like Pinochet? Would U.S. soldiers enforce a state of emergency on the American people?

I shared my thoughts, but they were dismissed as being a little paranoid. We enjoyed the dinner and the wine, and I watched Anton and Fallon flirt with each other like two teenagers. While they talked and actually giggled occasionally, I kept thinking about the emergency powers Nixon had used during the oil embargo. Where did he get them? I certainly wasn't a constitutional scholar, but couldn't think of anywhere in our founding document that gave the president that kind of authority.

26

March 24, 1976
Buenos Aires, Argentina

SATURDAY NIGHT CAME, along with Calida's date with Vasco. Vasco did not leave the apartment until Monday morning when they both left for work together. January and February were hot and sunny with occasional thunderstorms, not unlike the relationship developing between Calida and Vasco. By the beginning of March, Vasco had several changes of clothes and toiletries in the apartment, staying with her a couple of nights during the week and usually on the weekends. It was a small place for two people, but they just laughed when they bumped into each other in the bathroom and kitchen. In the bedroom they fit together very well.

When Vasco stayed with Calida, they often went out for dinner, and took long walks through the parks, feeding the pigeons as they held hands, deep in conversation. On weekends, they took in many of the festivals that were held in the parks and on the streets of Buenos Aires during the summer months. But when Vasco was not with her, they rarely spoke by phone. According to Vasco, he often had dinner meetings with clients that lasted late into the night. Calida was not always pleased by his absence, but she did not want Vasco to think she was clinging to him and forcing him into something that he was not ready to accept. Vasco had always lived alone. Living with someone else full-time would be a big step for him.

On a warm March morning, Calida went to her office at the normal time. It was an increasingly rare day—such as today—that she had not kissed Vasco goodbye. She was surprised when he called her at work just before lunch.

"Calida, it is Vasco."

"Hello, my dear, did you sleep well last night without me?" She was looking forward to the trip they had planned for the coming weekend, a drive to the country, perhaps overnight in a small inn.

"Calida, listen to me carefully. There is a *coup d'état* underway. General Videla and his military henchmen have taken over the government."

"What?" Calida felt like she had been punched in the stomach. How well she remembered that day in Chile three and a half years earlier.

"Yes. Now listen to me. I do not know what to tell you to do—stay at your office or go to your apartment. No one will be looking for you . . . yet. The military will protect U.S. businesses, so you should be safe in your office. But when you go home tonight I am sure the military will be everywhere and maybe checking papers. Being an expatriate from Chile, you might be detained. So maybe you should go home now." There was a pause; Calida could tell he was considering something. "But then, that may arouse suspicion with your superiors at work. Damn, I do not know how to advise you."

Calida considered what Vasco had said. Even though he sounded uncertain, he was right. Either choice could be bad. She decided to stay at work.

"I must act the truth. I have done nothing wrong. Nothing to anger the Junta. Nothing here in Argentina, and nothing in Chile, either."

"I understand. It is just . . ."

"Where are you?" Calida interrupted. There was one thing she knew about being caught in separate places in the middle of a coup. She was not going to let it happen again.

"I am at my office. I, too, am trying to figure out what to do. Why?"

"Could you go to my apartment now? You have a key. Then I can be assured we will be together tonight. At least we will have each other."

"That is a good idea. I will see you there tonight. Call me at your apartment before you leave work, so if you do not get home on time . . ."

"Please do not worry, Vasco. I will see you tonight. I love you."

She hung up the phone and slowly began cleaning off her desk, methodically filing papers and replacing folders in the cabinet. Not this time, she vowed.

SAFE IN HER apartment, Calida and Vasco sat up in the bed, drinking wine and watching the news on their small TV. To Calida, the reasons for the coup sounded all too familiar. But for Vasco, the coup would ratchet up a new level of resistance.

"Since the founding of the Republic we have mostly been a praetorian state," Vasco said, muting the sound of the endless news reports. "It is the way of this country. But now enemies of yesterday will become allies tonight and tomorrow. The Junta knows this, and it is my guess that they already know who their supporters and enemies will be. This will not be a passive takeover with a quick return to civilian control of the government like in the past. No. Not this time. As in your country, they will attempt to stamp out all leftist thinking. And they will do so brutally."

"But we will be okay. We are not extremists. We can go about our lives."

Calida's words sounded hollow even to herself. Who was she kidding? She poured them each a little more wine.

"We will try. But we must be careful. The Junta will cast a wide swath of blame for what is wrong with my country—unionists, leftists, Marxists, Peronists, and foreign influence. In spite of what you think, the security forces between Chile and Argentina will likely be collaborating. Your name may be on a list. If it is, hopefully, it will be at the bottom."

Calida turned and stared at him. She had suddenly become suspicious about his apparent knowledge of what was happening behind the scenes of the coup.

"How do you know all of this?"

He did not meet her eyes. "I do not for sure. But I do have some information about the cooperation between our military and DIDA—your security police. We must both be cautious."

"Where did you get this information? I can understand my situation here in your country, but why must you be cautious? You are a reputable businessman."

Her heart beat in her throat; she could barely swallow. Memories of prison, of hiding Roberto, of her father's broken spirit, rose to the surface.

"Because I have friends and acquaintances who may well be on the Junta's lists. And maybe I am not so reputable, Calida. I am a Montonero."

27

June 1978
Washington, D.C.

"YOU HAVE STUDIED the loan requests from the government of Argentina?" he asked even before he offered me a chair. I elected to stay standing. He was several grades above my own boss, and it was rare for any on my team to be called in here.

"Yes, Director."

"And their economic and debt analysis?"

"Yes."

"Please take a seat." He gestured again to the chair. "Listen, Mr. Anders, we rarely ask our economists to travel to a, you know, less than hospitable place, but we need some face-to-face discussions with the Minister of Economy in Argentina and his staff. What is his name?" He looked at a document on his desk. "Mr. Fernandez de Salis. We have been requested by State to take a hard look at their requests—the human rights issues in Argentina run counter to the policies of our new administration. But frankly, we have some serious questions of our own about doling out more money when they are reluctant to implement necessary reforms."

"I understand."

I had reviewed the prospectus for an interim loan from the Central Bank of Argentina. It had been six years, but it looked strikingly familiar—just like Chile's request in 1972. But this time it was for a loan to prop up the military government of Argentina, which had taken over in a coup two years earlier. When the Junta took over the Argentine government, I was once again reminded of the project Fallon and I had worked on many years before. The day after the coup, I marched first thing into her office. "I told you, Jude, pawns," was all she said.

"There is a broader problem at work here." The director put his elbows on the desk, his hands forming a steeple in front of his face. "There are several commercial lending institutions that are carrying a considerable liability in loans to the Argentine government. Frankly, they are becoming quite nervous. They fear the government may default or try to renegotiate the terms of the loans to something less favorable. Given Argentina's current economic situation, you can understand their concerns."

Ever since my first assignment with Fallon, I had become increasingly skeptical of the IMF's objectives in working with many of their member countries. In Chile, we could smell Nixon's henchmen and the U.S. intelligence agencies. While I suspected the IMF in their own way also helped support the coup in Argentina, this request was obviously more directed at the interests of the large commercial bankers in the U.S. and Europe. I waited for the director to get to the final point.

"The IMF has informally been requested to discuss the debt issues with the Ministry of the Economy in Argentina—get the specifics of their plan to deal with their sovereign debt, and certainly suggest face-to-face the measures they must take to bring their fiscal situation under control."

Of course, I thought, an informal request from . . . well, over the years I had learned to look beyond the specifics of such requests. As Fallon always asked, who and why? I knew I would never be given the specific names. I could only surmise.

"We know you have very deep knowledge of their economic and political history, as well as their current situation. That will be extremely valuable."

He looked at me pointedly. What else was he not saying?

"Thank you, sir." I knew more than the director could ever imagine, and certainly more than he did on some levels.

"We have made arrangements with the U.S. government to ensure your safety and protection while you are in Buenos Aires. In spite of what you have heard in the news, I have been assured that the streets are peaceful, and that you will have no problems."

"Sir, then why do I need protection from our government?"

"It is just an insurance policy, Mr. Anders. You are too valuable to the IMF for even a minor incident to distract you from this important assignment."

An alarm bell went off in my head. Protection? Minor incident?

"When do I go?"

"Next week. Monday."

THE NEXT EVENING I got a call from Anton. He was going to be in town tomorrow, but wasn't staying over night. He said he just wanted to catch a drink together before his late night flight. "Better than sitting alone in Dulles," he said. Over the years, he had made frequent visits to D.C., and we often got together over lunch or dinner. Our conversations rarely touched on my work or his anymore, and when they did, they were theoretical or personal. When I asked Anton about his job he would shrug it off. "Export-import. Pretty basic and boring."

That morning Fallon stopped by my office with a wide smile on her face and closed the door. She perched on the corner of my desk, her red hair piled up on top of her head like the day we first met.

"Wow, orders from the deputy director himself. Aren't we getting important?"

"It's just that I have more working knowledge of the account than anyone else." I tried to downplay the importance of the mission, but secretly I admit I was quite pleased.

"Well, thanks a lot."

"Fallon, I know you know as much as I do, well, maybe not quite as much when it comes to South America. But you're working on . . ."

"I know, I know, I'm not hurt. But how do you feel about going down there? I'd be scared shitless." She reached up to pin up a stray lock of hair.

"Honestly? I am a little scared. The director is arranging a security detail from State while I am there."

"Really. I thought the marines weren't allowed out of the U.S. Embassy."

"Something tells me it won't be guys in uniform."

Fallon smiled. "Suits from the Agency?"

"Or something like that."

Fallon stood and smoothed her skirt. Turning to go, she stopped at the door and looked back at me.

"Oh, when you get back I have a girl I want you to meet."

She smiled and flippantly tossed "later" over her shoulder as she left my office.

THAT NIGHT I met Anton in a small bar off the lobby of the Mayflower Hotel. He was sipping a Macallan when I arrived.

"Hey, buddy, what's up?" I asked as shook hands.

"Same shit, different day."

I looked at him quizzically.

"What? I am learning to talk like you Yanks."

We both laughed.

"What are you drinking?" the bartender asked.

"I'll have the same," pointing to Anton's single malt with the efficient two cubes—no more, no less.

"I knew when they made you a senior economist, you would get off the beer and cheap wine. Very good, my man."

I shot him a harsh look and then smiled. "My man" had become a teasing sign of affection between us. I pulled up the stool next to him.

"Jude, I know this is going to piss you off, but I understand you are making a little trip down south."

"What the fuck, Anton. Is your father spying on me again? What is he, a personal friend of the director?"

"No, no, certainly not . . . the director."

I shook my head and took a sip of my scotch. "Will you ever tell me how you know what is going on in my life all the time?"

"I do not know what is going on in your life. But I occasionally know what is going on at the IMF. And no, I will not tell you."

"Why not?"

The bartender had moved down the bar to make our drinks, but even so, Anton had lowered his voice. "Because there are some things it is best you do not know."

"Give me a break."

"Anyway, while you are in Buenos Aires, there is a favor you could do for me."

"A favor? And I thought you wanted my company before your boring flight back to Toronto. Still, Anton Tomasin asking Jude Anders for a favor? That's a first. What is it?" I pulled out a pack of smokes from my jacket pocket.

"There is a gentleman there I would like you to meet. Actually, a close work associate. I would like for him to meet you as well. I think the two of you have much in common."

He was watching me carefully, so I decided to play his game for a while.

"Sure. What's his name and how do I get in touch with him?"

I knew that would surprise him, but he didn't quibble.

"His name is Vasco Madero. He is our age or thereabout. He is in the export-import business in Argentina. I think it easier if he contacts you while you are there. Do you know where you will be staying?"

I gave him the name of the hotel and the specific dates I would be in Buenos Aires, and wondered again who was feeding Anton information about my work at the IMF.

"Oh, one more thing." He reached into his suit coat pocket and pulled out a white envelope. "Would you give him this when you see him?"

"Now I am feeling like a spy. Really, Anton, what is this?" I lit a cigarette and did not touch the envelope.

"Let us just say it is some very sensitive financial information on a mutual business deal. I understand the government down there is quite nosy these days, even going through people's mail. Disgusting. Since you are going anyway, this is just . . . simpler."

I smoked, gazing into the mirror behind the bar and searching in the reflection for anyone who might be standing or sitting near Anton and paying attention to our conversation. I nudged the envelope like it was a dead thing and finally picked it up. No name, nothing written on it. I put in my inside coat pocket.

"Done."

MY FLIGHT ARRIVED in Buenos Aires at 7:20 on Tuesday morning at a new, modern airport south of the city. Going through customs took forever, but I wasn't hassled by the custom agents or any of the military guards who were standing everywhere throughout the customs staging area. I retrieved my bags and endured detailed questioning by agents who were checking every piece of luggage, including briefcases. It was a good thing I had moved Anton's envelope from my briefcase to my suit coat pocket before disembarking the plane. Finally through the entry process, I walked out of one of several frosted glass doors and into the terminal. There were dozens of people waiting to greet the new arrivals to Argentina.

I was told someone would meet me and drive me to the hotel, but how was I supposed to find him in this crowd? I knew the name of the hotel; I decided to just skip the formality and take a cab. Once I got past the initial throng, however, I saw a smaller group of suits standing together at the end of the long line of greeters, each holding a small sign with a name on it. Nice going, guys; who wouldn't guess these were government or VIP drivers? Sure enough, there was a guy in trench coat with "Anders" on his little sign.

"I am Jude Anders."

"Jim Jones," he replied. "May I take your bag?"

Jones, how more of an American name can you get. Was that really his name or the one he used in Argentina? Is he just my driver or my bodyguard as well? I handed him my bag and followed him out of the terminal to the parking lot. We got into the small Fiat and headed out of the parking lot.

"It will be a slow go into the city, Mr. Anders. Rush hour."

"Not a problem. I don't have any meetings until tomorrow. How far is it?"

He shifted expertly through the noisy traffic. There was a cloud of pollution in the distance, in the direction we were headed. "Many kilometers, but I'll get you to your hotel as soon as possible. Did you have a nice flight?"

"Sitting in a seat for seventeen hours is not pleasant. Do you mind if I smoke?"

"Not at all. Mind if I join you, Mr. Anders?"

"Please do. And call me Jude."

"Thank you, Jude."

We both lit up and cracked the windows of the car to let out the smoke.

"Too much wind, Jude?"

"No, it's fine. Are you going to be with me during my stay in Buenos Aires?"

"Yes, sir. I will drive you wherever you need to go."

That answered one question: bodyguard, definitely.

"You're not going to sleep with me, then?"

We both chuckled. I was about to ask Jim whom he worked for, but thought better of it. At least for now.

We got to the hotel about an hour later. Along the highway into the city, there were periodic signs of the military—trucks, jeeps, and soldiers, but no tanks. We were not stopped or hindered in any way. I began to feel a bit more comfortable. When we got to the hotel, Jim carried my bag to the front desk and handed me his card with his telephone number.

"I'll be here at 9:00 in the morning to take you to the Ministry. If you want to go out before that, just call me. And if you do go out, even for a short walk, please carry your passport with you. You never know when you may be stopped and asked for your papers."

Stopped? Asked for papers? Maybe I should feel a little concerned.

"Okay, but right now I'm going to get some sleep. I probably won't go out today or tonight, but if I do, I'll call you. Thanks for your help." I offered him a tip but he waved it away.

In my room, I unpacked, smoked another cigarette, and then laid down on the bed for a short nap. It was 16:00 local time when I woke up. It took me a few seconds to realize where I was. I turned on the TV, but that was useless—everything was in Spanish and I hadn't spoke any since high school. I dragged myself into the shower, which helped me wake up, and had just finished shaving when the phone rang.

"Jude Anders?" the voice on the other end asked.

"Yes, this is Jude Anders."

"Hello, my name is Vasco Madero. I am an acquaintance of Anton Tomasin."

Wow, that was quick. "Yes, Anton said you would be in touch."

"I was wondering if you could join me for a drink? Unless this is a bad time."

"No, no. It will be okay. I just got up from a nap and am still a bit groggy. But if we could meet in half an hour, that would be good for me."

"That would be fine. How about the bar in your hotel?"

"Okay, although I'm not sure I can drink much right now."

"Then we can have an espresso."

"How will I know you?"

"Just come to the bar. There will be very few people there at this time of day. I would tell you I have dark hair, but then in Buenos Aires I am not sure that would be of much help."

I hadn't thought about that. "See you in thirty minutes then."

I hung up the phone and smoked a couple of cigarettes, before throwing on a leather jacket, hoping for a more casual look rather than something that screamed U.S. Business Man . . . or Government Flunky. Just when I was about to close the door to my room I remembered the envelope. I didn't know what was in it, but its secrecy in this environment made me feel very nervous. I retrieved the envelope from my suit coat pocket and slipped it in the inside pocket of my jacket.

The bar was empty except for one man my age sitting at a table along the wall of the bar. When I walked in he got up immediately and walked over to me with his hand out.

"Jude," he said, smiling as he shook my hand.

"Vasco?" It was somewhere between a question and an affirmation.

"Sure, sure. Sit down." He spoke Spanish to the bartender. "I hope you still wanted an espresso."

"Yes, thank you." I took off my jacket and laid it on the empty stool between us.

"I know the flights from the States and Europe arrive early. Quite the long flight is it not?"

"Seventeen hours."

"Did you have any problems coming from our new international airport?"

"None. My government provided me with a driver."

I could see the wheels turn in Vasco's mind.

"Really?"

"Before I left they told me it would be someone from our State Department, but frankly he could just as well be CIA."

He looked quickly over at the bartender who was at the far end of the bar brewing the espressos. "I would not say that too loudly. It raises eyebrows."

The obvious truth of that hit me. "Yes, I suppose you are right. I'll watch it from now on." I had made my first *faux pas*. I had to be more careful.

"Even before the coup that word was vile to most people in my country. Since the coup . . . well, many think they were involved."

"So do I. One more disgrace upon my country."

Vasco shook his head. "With or without them, the outcome would have been the same." He paused. "Anton tells me you are here as a representative of the IMF."

"Yes. It is not uncommon for economists to visit their counterparts in member countries."

The bartender brought our espressos and some sugar to our table. Vasco said thank you and something else to him in Spanish.

"I hope you enjoy the espresso. This is one thing we do as well as in Italy or France."

"It will be a treat. Thank you. Anton tells me you also are in the export-import business like him. I assume that is how you know him."

"Yes. We go back a few years. We have put together a couple of deals that were fairly lucrative to both of us. We spent some time together here in Buenos Aires a few years ago, before the coup."

He was being cautious, I could tell.

"Anton is a very charming person."

"That's an understatement," I concurred.

I didn't know why Anton wanted me to meet this man, but I was here and so was he. This could be my chance to learn a little more about what I was getting into.

"Vasco, I would be interested in your impressions and opinions about Argentina's economy." It came out a little more formally than I had intended, but considering that Anton had set this up and I really had no idea what Vasco knew about me, I decided to just wait and see what he would tell me.

"Well, I am not an economist. I do not understand all these things about growth, inflation, debt. What I know is what the people feel and see. Prices keep going up, the poor people suffer, and the lives of those in the middle are being pushed in the direction of the poor. We used to have good services in my country. The trains ran on time, the electricity remained on, public education was good and available to everyone. Now with the new regime, they have begun to, how do you say it in English . . . privatize a lot of what the government used to provide. Already, the quality of the services is getting worse, not better."

I hadn't expected him to be so direct. "So much for free-market efficiencies."

"Yes. Yes. That is exactly how the government puts it. But you know, in this country there is always the back and forth of who controls the money. Land owners to farm laborers, industrialists to unionized factory workers, and now back again. But through all of this back-and-forth, the generals get their share. And now that they are completely in power, they will take even more."

"I am not sure I understand." I lit a cigarette and sipped the espresso. I was definitely awake now.

Vasco leaned in toward me and spoke quietly. "Well, instead of taking what money the government has to improve the lives of the people or to make our streets without potholes or complete the railway to the south of my country, they will use more and more on military weapons, more soldiers and police. And they will do this because they tell themselves, and the rest of us, that these things are necessary to control the Marxists and Peronistas—the ones destroying the country. But maybe the real reason is to protect what they have. The military is an institution in this country, Jude. It is part of the fabric, not only of government, but also of society in general. There are thousands of jobs that are controlled and handed out by the military. Officers in the upper echelons have financial interests in government programs, and even in private businesses that benefit from public programs. The military in this country has become an economic class unto itself and will do what it needs to protect its interests. So, who will benefit from the coup? The generals, admirals, colonels, and the like. The companies that make the weapons. And the companies in this country that will reduce wages and eliminate government restraints on what they do."

"So when your government wants to borrow money from, say, the U.S. or even the IMF, you're saying the money will go toward repression, the benefit of the wealthy, and the perpetuation of a military class?"

"Of course, not all of it, but yes, much of it."

I remembered my conversations with the deputy director when he gave me this assignment. Whose interests was I really here to protect—the IMF, the Argentine military, or a laundry list of big name creditors? Certainly not the citizens of Argentina. "So you would not recommend the IMF make a loan to your government?"

"Like I said, I am not an economist. But you are. You ask me for my opinion."

"I did. Your perspective is one I don't normally get." I stubbed out the butt. I wished Fallon could be here; she would be all over this information.

"Listen, Jude, I am afraid I must leave soon. I promised my girlfriend to take her to a movie tonight. Let me get the bill." Vasco made a signal to the bartender.

"Thank you very much for the coffee. It was nice to meet you," I said, still unsure of why Anton wanted me to meet Vasco.

"Oh, we will see each other again. You are returning to the U.S. on a flight Saturday night?"

"How did you know that?"

"I am sorry. It is not hard. Anton told me. But anyway, I want to show you around B's A's on Friday afternoon and then have dinner."

"That sounds good." I was uncomfortable with how much he knew. What were he and Anton up to, and why the hell was I involved? We were just starting to get up when I remembered Anton's envelope.

"Oh, I almost forgot. Anton sent an envelope to give you."

Vasco quickly put his hand on top of mine as I was reaching in my jacket pocket for the envelope. He looked around. There was no one in the bar and the bartender was arranging liquor bottles on the shelves behind the bar with his back turned to us. Vasco smiled.

"Allow me." He quickly reached into my jacket pocket, grabbed the envelope and stuck it under his coat. It couldn't have been smoother if he had been a professional pickpocket, and I patted my wallet in my back pocket just to be sure. We said goodbye and I went up to my room, wondering what was in that envelope.

28

JIM JONES MET me at the hotel at 9:00 the next morning and drove me to the Ministry of the Economy. My meetings would last until lunchtime.

"I will pick you up right here at 13:00 unless you call me with a different time."

"Okay, Jim. Got it."

The first of several meetings over the next few days started with two senior economists at the Ministry. I had no reason to doubt that that's who they were, but what did I really know? They could have just as well have been colonels in the Argentine military dressed up as bureaucrats, just like the suits in the "fish bowls" at the IMF. My conversation with Vasco had rumbled through my mind all night, coloring my dreams and leaving me unsettled when I woke. On Thursday I would meet with officials of the Central Bank of Argentina, and on Friday morning I had a concluding meeting with the Minister of Economy himself, Señor Fernandez de Salis.

The opening of the first meeting was flanked by pleasantries and discussions of the geological and climate similarities between Argentina and the U.S., economic differences and similarities, and the general political climates in each country. The officials were very curious about our newly elected president, Jimmy Carter, and how his presidency might change U.S. foreign policy toward South America. I told them that I did not know, but as an American I would hope the U.S. would present a more hands-off position than it had historically. I couldn't gauge their reaction, but quickly added that I was not here as an American but as a representative of the IMF. I emphasized the word "International."

After about thirty minutes, we got down to the specifics of their loan request. They were most interested in the time it would take to get the loan approved. I was more interested in how this added to Argentina's overall debt. They presented specific measures they were taking to bring the country's accounts into balance. I presented specific economic data from the past two quarters that showed how far out of balance their accounts were. They claimed most of the measures they had adopted were just being implemented and expected the effects to be felt later in the year. I listened skeptically. On the one hand, just another loan request meeting; on the other, Anton and Vasco, military coups and the effects of so-called privatization.

The meeting ended at 12:45, so I stepped outside in the sun for a smoke while I waited for my ride.

"Have a good meeting?" Jim asked, arriving five minutes ahead of schedule.

"As good as could be expected." I knew Vasco was going to show me the city on Friday, but I decided to get a head start. "Jim, do you think there is a chance you could drive me around Buenos Aires a bit this afternoon? I'd like to get a feel for the city without walking."

I also wanted the protection of a driving tour; I was a little spooked by my experience here so far between Vasco and the Junta. The last thing I wanted was to stroll down a city street, a witless foreigner.

"Sure. You want to go now or a little later? Maybe change into something more casual?"

"Yes. I can make it quick. Can you wait for me in the hotel lobby?"

"*No hay problema.*"

Within fifteen minutes, I had changed clothes and shoes and put on my black leather jacket. The weather was on the warmish side even though it was still winter in the southern hemisphere. The sun was bright and made it feel warmer than it probably was.

I met Jim in the lobby.

"What would you like to see, Jude?"

"I don't know. We can cover some of the more touristy sites I guess, but I want to get a feel for the city."

He looked at me pointedly. "It's a big city, Jude. Lots of different feels. Some of them not so good."

"Well, just take me to the areas that feel good. Okay?"

"Sure thing."

We drove along a parkway not far from the La Plata river. It was a wide boulevard, lined on one side by a park that went on for miles. Occasionally there was a stately neo-classical building.

"That's part of the university," Jim pointed out as we whizzed by it.

The little cars didn't seem to obey any lanes. In fact, it was difficult for me to make out any lines demarking lanes at all. There were statues everywhere. Jim knew most of them and tried to give me a history lesson surrounding each one. Somehow I didn't believe most of what he said.

"There's the motherland," he shouted as he pointed to a large classical building on our left as we speeded down the boulevard. "The Embassy of the U.S. of A."

Everywhere there were trees along the boulevards and the smallest side streets, even though they had lost their leaves for the winter. This was a beautiful city and reminded me of the pictures I had seen of Paris.

"What about where the president works?" I asked. "Can we go by there?"

"It's pretty heavily guarded. Not such a good idea these days. But let me take you to La Boca. It's the old Italian immigrant section of the city. Lots of colorful buildings. I'll drive near the Pink House on the way. You can at least see it from a distance."

We passed by the president's house from the east side. It sat on a small hill on the other side of a large park and was difficult to see through the leafless trees. I could also see army jeeps and soldiers standing guard around the perimeter of the pink building. I wondered what they were protecting. Did they expect the people to rise up and take over the palace, or a terrorist to hurl a bomb at it?

Jim gunned his little car up the boulevard and turned sharply left onto a potholed side street that ran through a slummy area, dead-ending at a polluted river bordered by a little community of brightly painted buildings.

"This is La Boca. Kind of cool with all the colors, huh? Now it's a tourist destination filled with street artisans selling their wares and restaurants. I wouldn't go four blocks in any direction from here, though. You might get your throat slashed. Robbed for sure."

We headed back to the hotel; I thanked Jim for the tour and we agreed to meet again at 9:00 the next morning. Sure there were slums, but what city didn't have them? Over all Buenos Aires seemed like a charming city, full of parks and tree-lined streets, and monuments everywhere. But the police and the army were also everywhere, along with the potholes, just as Vasco had said.

MORE MEETINGS THE next day—this time with the central bankers. We talked endlessly about currency valuation and restriction of money supply to fight inflation, international market forces on current *peso* values and steps the government was taking to strengthen the *peso*, trade imbalances, lines of credit from New York and Paris commercial banks, the public debt and percentage of GDP. The entire day I could hear the chanting of the Chicago School mantra. I remembered the analysis Fallon and I had done several years earlier. We thought we understood why we were doing the analysis and for whom. Now I could see firsthand that our naiveté only assisted the forces underway here in Argentina.

I got back to my hotel room about 18:00 that night. My mind was fried. I went to the bar and had a couple of scotches then returned to my room for a long night's sleep. Tomorrow I had to meet with the big dog—The Minister of the Economy.

"MR. ANDERS, I trust you have seen the good work we are doing in Argentina to purge our economy from the disastrous plague of socialism that has dominated us for the last fifteen years." Fernandez de Salis was a tall, thin man with slick black hair, slightly receding. His black suit and matching narrow tie looked like he had just stepped out of the 1960s. We were seated at the end of the long conference table in a room with a private entrance to his office in the Ministry of the Economy.

"As you can imagine, it will be a long and difficult struggle. But with the help of the IMF and your government—you are from the United States, I believe?—we will bring Argentina back in line with the international economic community." The minister sat back in his chair and smoothed his buttoned suit coat. I remembered Vasco's words and wondered if Fernandez de Salis was also a part of the military class of the country. What role did he have in the coup—was he a part of it or brought in afterwards by the military hacks? How much of an IMF loan would line his pockets, even if indirectly?

"It is obvious the you are taking action on many fronts to deal with your economic issues. I have discussed many of the them at length with your colleagues." I took a measured pause. "Argentina is in a very difficult situation, and the IMF is committed to taking appropriate measures to assist your country."

I had slept well and enjoyed an espresso and a pastry in the hotel's café before Jim drove me to the Ministry. Now I steadied myself for the delicate discussions that I expected from my meeting with the minister.

"Surely, the IMF knows that we are not looking for long-term financial aid," the minister said. "We think of our request more as a . . . what you call a 'bridge loan' to see us through our short-term financial difficulties."

"Yes, Señor Fernandez. We understand what your country is proposing. It will be given due consideration."

He paused, in thought, and looked at the papers in front of him, then turned away from me to look outside through the windows of the conference room—an interesting choice, I thought.

"Señor Anders, you know, of course, that we are under very restrictive time constraints. We would like an answer in a reasonable period, let us say by the end of the month."

He turned to look at me. Surely he did not expect me to make any commitments right now. His attitude toward timing led me to believe he thought the loan a foregone conclusion. I thought about who was behind my visit to Argentina, and their agendas, some of them obviously in conflict; of those interested parties who had the most clout with the management of the IMF? Perhaps Fernandez de Salis already knew the answer.

"I understand, and from my perspective, that time frame is reasonable. I will be back in Washington on Monday and provide a complete report with recommendations early in the week. It is, however, up to the Board of Governors to make a final decision."

"Yes, yes. That is understood." The minister paused again. I wondered where he would take our meeting next. "Thank you for visiting here to see and hear for yourself the progress of our country." He got up from his chair and offered me his hand; his grip was firm but not overly so. I guessed he had made the points he intended; he had no reason to overdo it.

"And thank you and your colleagues for the hospitality and cordiality they have shown me." I gathered up my reports and placed them in my briefcase. We were obviously done here.

"Very well, Señor Anders. Good day."

The minister left the conference room while I was still gathering my things. De Salis obviously believed he had the upper hand in any negotiations with the Fund. Whether he was right or not, my job was to let him believe it. I called Jim Jones then put on my coat and left the Ministry. It was still early in the day. Jim was surprised by my earlier than expected phone call. The meeting was so short he had just gotten back to his office, wherever that was.

Back at the hotel, I reviewed some of the data provided by the Central Bank and Ministry of the Economy while eating a salad in my room. My eyes burned and my nerves were shot. I climbed on the bed with another file. Unlike Chile's loan request in the early '70s all the projections of Argentina's economic success were based on assumptions with little probability they would happen. Who were these guys kidding, and why did the IMF send me down here anyway? I could just as well analyze their request from the comfort of my D.C. office. I must have dozed off while reading and jumped when the phone rang.

"Hello," I answered, a bit groggy. The sunlight coming through my window had that yellow glow of late afternoon.

"Jude, this is Vasco."

"Oh, Vasco." My mind cleared quickly, remembering our planned dinner meeting tonight. "*Hola, como te va?*"

"Wow, I am impressed. Do you learn Spanish because you are going to move to Argentina?"

"No, sorry, I just didn't want to sound like an American."

"But, Jude, we are both Americans. You are from the North and I am from the South. Even Anton is an American."

"I suppose we in the United States are a bit self-centered, even with how we call ourselves." I winced at his words as well as my own.

"Sure you are, a little. But, are you ready to go now? I would like to take you for a little drive to show you something before it gets dark. Then we can go to the apartment for some dinner."

"Yes, I would like that. It has been a long, painful three days." I rubbed my eyes and wondered if I had any aspirin in my kit. Certainly an espresso would help.

"Are you saying that economists are painful?"

"Just your economists."

We both laughed.

"I will pick you up in ten minutes?"

"I'll be in the lobby. This time I'd like to see the real Buenos Aires."

We hopped into Vasco's black sedan parked out front. He gunned it before I could fasten my seatbelt.

"Do you people always drive this way?" I asked, clutching the handle above the doorframe as he sped around a corner.

"Only for you Americans." I smiled and looked ahead as Vasco deftly maneuvered around traffic.

"Where are we going?"

"Sightseeing, as I promised you."

The car raced north to the wide boulevard I had been on with Jim Jones, then turned left and headed west. We drove for several miles, the dimming sun in our faces, finally exiting onto a street headed north toward the Rio de La Plata.

"I want you to see where your IMF funds will go." Vasco slowed his car to the speed limit. "Coming up on our left is the Escuela de Mecánica de la Armada."

"The what?"

"The Mechanics School of the Navy. It is a place where they train naval men how to maintain their ships. But that is not what it is used for today."

As we approached the large building there were numerous military trucks and jeeps. Several soldiers moved between the trucks and the entrance to the building.

"Look quick and if a soldier is looking at us, turn away."

"So what is it used for today?"

"Torture and imprisonment—of anyone expected to be a Marxist."

I stared at the brick and stone edifice partially covered in ivy. The soldiers were busy moving boxes from the trucks and dollying them into the building. It covered at least half a city block.

"Wow, it's a big place."

"Not that big, really."

We drove on until we got to a wide boulevard near the Rio de La Plata, turned right and headed back toward the downtown area as the sky turned to dusk.

"So, it is true? The rumors."

"Yes, quite true. Many places throughout Argentina are used for the same purpose. People go in and are never heard from again." He kept his eyes on the road.

"How many?"

"I do not know. But we are still in the early days of the Junta's rule."

"But it's not big enough to hold a lot of people for a long time."

"Yes, as I said, not that big. So where do they take them?"

"To bigger prisons?"

We were speeding down the wide boulevard with the river to our left.

"Up ahead. See the airport?" I looked ahead to the left and could see a large airfield running between the boulevard and the Rio de La Plata.

"Yes. I didn't know Buenos Aires had a second airport."

"This one is for domestic flights and some to neighboring countries. But it also used by the military."

We were nearing the far end of the airport when Vasco suddenly turned right into the park that paralleled the airport. He maneuvered his little black car into one of several small streets that wound their way throughout the park, finally parking in a quiet spot with a good view of the tarmac in the distance. I knew Vasco was telling me something I wasn't supposed to know, not as a representative of the IMF, not as an American, not even just as a concerned human being. I pulled out a smoke, my brain buzzing with all this new information that was hidden between the lines of the data I had been digesting the last few days.

"See those planes?"

There were several C-130 transports parked to the side of the tarmac.

"Yes. Made in the USA. Lockheed Corporation." They were huge.

"I will tell you what others have told me. What they have seen. Late in the afternoon many trucks—the kinds you saw that are used to transport troops and supplies—leave the Escuela de Mecánica de la Armada. They travel the same route as we just did, but get off at the airport entrance. The trucks drive to where those planes are parked." Vasco pointed at the C-130s. "The soldiers get out and begin to drag and push people inside of a plane. When the trucks are empty, the plane takes off in the direction of the Atlantic. In an hour or so, the plane returns by night. Only the soldiers get off. Now, Jude, where have the people gone?"

"Were they flying them to another prison to the east side of Argentina?"

"That is what we thought at first. But there are no prisons of any size in that direction. Why always the same time of day? And we asked: How could they fly, land, off-load the prisoners, take off and fly back to Buenos Aires in only an hour or so?"

"You're right. That doesn't make any sense."

"But then another thing happened. About a month ago several dead bodies were found on the shore near to where the Rio de La Plata flows into the Atlantic. They were drowned—with their clothes and shoes on."

I thought about what Vasco was hinting at; it was too brutal to believe. "Maybe they were on a boat which capsized."

"Maybe, but yesterday there were more bodies—fully clothed. Another boat accident?"

We sat in silence, Vasco allowing the full scene he was directing to sink in while I stared ahead at the location where his unfathomable movie scene began. Two troop transport trucks suddenly appeared on the scene and drove to C-130s.

"Look," Vasco said excitedly, as though he too could not believe it was happening, right before our own eyes. "I told you, Jude. Watch. See for yourself."

Several military jumped out and proceeded to the rear of the truck, some with their machine guns at the ready while other soldiers climbed into the back of the trucks. People staggered out as though they were drugged or just woken from a deep sleep.

Vasco suddenly turned the ignition, slammed the car in gear, and sped away. "We need to go now. Look in your side view mirror." The lights of a small car were following and gaining on us.

I had been so entranced by the scene that I never noticed the lights coming up behind us. "Who are they?"

"Security forces."

"How do you know?"

"I know the cars they drive. Hang on; we need to lose them."

Vasco maneuvered his little black sedan through the evening rush hour traffic, then deftly turned onto several narrow streets and finally back onto the boulevard filled with traffic. I looked back—no evidence of the car that had been tailing us.

"Do you think we lost them?"

"I think so, but I am going drive out of our way for a while until I am sure." He turned again off the busy boulevard onto several streets—right for three blocks, right again for two, then left for several more blocks, then left again down a four lane street—all the time checking the rear view mirror and looking up and down the side streets as we went through the many intersections. "I think they are no longer following us. We can go to the apartment now."

175

He turned up a narrow street near the port area and found a parking space. "Here we are. I want you to meet Calida, my girlfriend."

I didn't move. The normalcy of his comment made me wonder what just happened; it was almost as though the last thirty minutes had been a hallucination . . . or a dream. I just sat there thinking about what Vasco had told me, the trucks and the people moving like zombies, and our little brush with the Argentine security forces chasing us through the streets of Buenos Aires.

"What you told me at the airport—these are suspicions. You don't have any hard facts?"

"What we have is a loosely connected string of events and dead bodies in the river. You just witnessed the beginning of the story. I know these people in charge of the Junta. They are brutal."

We got out of the car without another word and walked down the block and across the street to Vasco's apartment building, both of us looking anxiously at the cars passing on the street. We went into a small lobby and walked up two flights of stairs. The apartment was at the end of the hall at the rear of the building.

"Listen, Jude, please, not a word of our little sightseeing adventure to my girlfriend. She does not know what I know, and it is best that we spare her—she wrestles with her own demons from her past."

It was more of a command than a request. But I now had another piece of information—this time about his girlfriend and her past. What had I gotten into here in this beautiful city of parks and statues, and security forces chasing citizens through its streets and dumping them into the La Plata River? And Anton—how did he fit into the movie that Vasco was directing, for that is exactly what it felt like?

"Calida," Vasco called as we entered the apartment. "*Estamos aquí.*"

I could hear the clatter of bowls and water running.

"*Un segundo. Estoy acabando para arriba algunos platos.*"

A petite woman with long, wavy brown hair walked out of the kitchen as we were taking off our jackets.

"Calida, this is Jude Anders. Jude, this is my girlfriend, Calida."

"Very nice to meet you," I said, reaching out my hand. "Calida, that is a beautiful name."

"*Gracias*, I mean, thank you. I am sorry but my English is not good."

She was so charming, I believe I saw her blush. "I am sure your English is better than my Spanish."

"Trust me, Calida, he is telling the truth," Vasco asserted. "Would you like a glass of wine, Jude?"

"Love one, thank you."

Vasco went to the kitchen for the wine. Calida ushered me nervously into the living room and told me to sit.

"I hope you like Malbec," Vasco said, returning with three glasses and a bottle in his hands. "It is our famous grape in Argentina."

"I've never had it."

He poured the wine then offered a toast. "To new friends."

We all toasted. I took a sip of the red wine. "Very good," I said. "Rich and very smooth, no tannins."

Calida told me a bit about herself and her job at Chase Manhattan. I was surprised to hear that she had come from Chile two and a half years ago. Did her demons follow her from there?

"Wow, you have been through two coups. What was it like in Chile?"

She gave me her take on life before and after the coup, and told me of the time she had spent in prison. I was shocked by what she told me—her demons, yes, they were real. Again, I wished Fallon was here to hear this first-hand. When I recounted all this information to her after returning to the States she would never believe half of it. I considered telling Calida and Vasco of our role in their coups, but could not bring myself to do it.

"What did you do before the coup in Chile?"

"I worked for Corfo as an analyst." She poured more wine.

"Corfo?"

"Oh, I am sorry. Corfo is the Production Development Corporation. It was the organization responsible for making companies part of the government and making investments in new Chilean companies."

"So Corfo was in charge of nationalizing foreign businesses?" I was trying to figure out how Vasco, an obvious resistor of the Junta, had wound up with this lovely woman who had worked in banking and economics, both in Chile and Argentina. Luck? Or something else? And where did Anton fit into this cozy little picture?

"More or less, I guess. The president and his staff mostly made those decisions. We at Corfo made it happen."

"Were the Chilean military as aggressive with the left in your country as they seem to be here?" I sipped the delicious Malbec. I had long forgotten about Jim Jones and Anton's envelope, but I was very keen to hear about daily life in Argentina.

"Much the same thing, Jude," Vasco replied. "Torture, imprisonment, murders, disappearance. We heard the story that their army rounded up anyone on the street the day of the coup and detained them at the National Stadium for weeks. We think they got Calida's boyfriend trying to cross the border into Argentina. There is no word of him—just disappeared."

"Vasco says you work for the Monetary Fund," Calida interrupted, perhaps eager to change the conversion.

"The IMF, yes."

"I remember Roberto saying that they had made a loan application to the IMF."

"Really, when was that?"

"Let me see." Calida paused. "It would have been in early 1972."

"Wow, I worked on a loan request from the Chilean Central Bank in April of 1972." I carefully set down my wine glass; I did not want to get a buzz on while I tried to dissect the coincidences that seemed to be mounting.

"Yes, yes. That would have been the request Roberto submitted." She was getting excited. We were both connecting the dots, like points on a line.

"The request was signed by a Señor Baca . . ."

"That was Roberto's boss." She jumped up from the sofa and began pacing. Vasco watched her with concern.

"And a Roberto Me . . ."

"Menendez!" She nearly shrieked.

"Yeah, I think that was it."

"That was my Beto. He was an economist with the Central Bank."

"This is a very small world," I said, now thoroughly suspicious of all these connections.

"Roberto told me the loan was not approved." She sat down again, deflated. Vasco moved closer, protectively.

"Calida, I recommended that the loan go through. But I heard later that it was pigeonholed. Given all that happened in your country back then, I think there was pressure on the IMF to deny or defer the loan."

Calida got up suddenly, saying she had to stir the paella. My heart ached for her. I didn't know what I was doing here, how I had found myself in the middle of all this. Anton. This had something to do with Anton, but I couldn't imagine how. Or why.

"CIA," Vasco said.

"Maybe, but I think the whole executive branch of the U.S. government was in on it. U.S. politicians fear communism more than anything else."

"That is stupid."

"I know, but that's the way it was and probably still is. It is our bogeyman."

We sat around the small kitchen table eating Calida's delicious paella. I was overwhelmed by its saffron fragrance. She told me it was her specialty. Whatever our discussion of her former boyfriend had meant to her, she had done a courageous job of hiding it. Calida was the consummate hostess, filling and refilling the plates, pouring wine. Vasco was a lucky man; I didn't need to look far to see that.

Vasco cracked open a second bottle of Malbec, and we discussed actions the military was taking against the civilians of Argentina. In any other circumstance, I would have thought that would hardly be appropriate dinner conversation, but here we were. The reality of Argentina and Chile weighed heavily over our table. Vasco was privy to a lot of information about what was happening all over the country—in Santa Fe, in Cordoba, even in the far south land of Patagonia. I wondered how he came by all of his information.

At one time I had wanted to talk with Señor Baca and Roberto Menendez about how they were shaping the economy of Chile. I wanted to know what was working and what wasn't, and what decisions they had taken that led to its failure. Now, by a strange twist of fate, I was talking about those issues with Roberto's girlfriend. While she couldn't answer all of my questions, she certainly provided enough information to give me a better sense of what had gone wrong.

Why didn't I have friends like this in D.C.? Vasco and Calida reminded me of Sasha and Mark, my fellow protesters during our college years. I missed the intensity of our conversations back then and the warmth of our comradeship. Did that happen to everyone—go to work, become isolated and dull, cease to grow?

Vasco was first to hear it. The quick step of boots on the stairs. Then down the hall. He jumped from his chair and ran to the living room window. Calida was getting up from the table when the door exploded off its hinges, splinters of wood flying through the air as though in slow motion. Military police rushed through the narrow door, pointing automatics and handguns at Vasco and then at Calida and me.

"*¡Abajo en el suelo!*" shouted one of the men.

"*Tú también. En la planta,*" another shouted at Calida and me.

Vasco dropped to the floor. "*Él no habla español. Él es de los Estados Unidos,*" he yelled.

"*¡Cállate!*" The soldier kicked him in his ribs. I saw Vasco slump to a prone position on the floor.

Following Calida's lead, I dropped to my knees on the floor. One of the soldiers pushed me down on my face with his boot on my back. I turned my head toward the living room. There were six of them.

"*Usted está bajo detención,*" one of the men shouted.

They tied our hands behind our back with a hard plastic binding, pulled us to our feet, and shoved us down the hall and stairs. Outside there were three light green sedans with drivers seated in front. Each of us were pushed into a separate car and flanked by two of the soldiers who had broken into the apartment. A fourth car pulled in behind us. Three men in suits got out and went into the apartment building as our cars sped off through the night of Buenos Aires.

29

I LOOKED OUT through a tiny window in the door of a filthy brick-walled cell. Sit on the floor or stand, those were my options; there was no chair, no bed. I could barely see a row of similar doors opposite mine. Moans sometimes broke the silence. In the distance there was slamming of doors, then screams—soul-wrenching screams. I moved away from the door, away from the moans and screams, and crouched in a corner of the tiny cell. All I knew was what had happened so far; I had no idea what would happen next.

They came for me finally. Was it night or day? I had fallen asleep amid the intermittent screams, waking up on the cold stone floor. I was jerked by my arms to a plain room. Four walls, one door, no windows. I was shoved into a hard wooden chair with my hands bound behind my back. A man walked in, a piece of paper and my passport in hand.

"Señor Anders?"

"Yes, I am Jude Anders."

"Tell me, Señor Anders, how do you know *El Cuervo*?"

"*El* who?"

"The man you may know as Vasco Madero?" He paced the room in front of me, his uniform wrinkled, his boots scuffed. Low-level functionary? Or master of my fate?

"I met Vasco when I came to Buenos Aires four days ago."

"How did you meet Señor Madero?"

I forced myself to be as calm as I could. "I have a friend who knew Vasco. He suggested we meet while I was in Buenos Aires."

"And did you contact Señor Madero when you came to Argentina?"

"No, he contacted me."

"And how did he know how to contact you?"

"Our mutual friend told him what hotel I would be staying at." I decided that if I got out of here with all my teeth and bones intact, I would probably have to kill Anton Tomasin. I did not relish the thought.

"I see. Who is this mutual friend, Señor Anders?"

"A Canadian."

"I do not care about his nationality. His name!"

I stopped answering his questions.

"His name!"

"What difference does it make?"

"That is not for you to decide. Give me his name."

I sat without answering.

The man walked toward me and slapped me with an open hand. I felt its sting on my left cheek.

"Señor Anders. This is just the beginning of my questions. I suggest you answer me, now!"

I said nothing. He paced back and forth in front of me.

"Okay, we will try another tact. We know that you are employed by the International Monetary Fund. What is your business in Argentina?" I had begun asking myself that very question. Fuck Anton.

"I have been meeting with Mr. Fernandez de Salis and his staff."

The man went quiet. He left the room suddenly. My wrists had gone numb. I thought of Calida in prison in Chile; did they beat her? Starve her? Rape her? She never said. It was at least thirty minutes before the officer returned.

He paraded around my chair, behind me where I could not see him.

"Most unusual. An American from the IMF, meeting with Señor Fernandez. And involved with . . . well, a treasonous enemy of Argentina."

"I can assure you I do not know anything about treason. I know Vasco Madero as a business man."

"And what do you know of his business?"

"Exports and imports."

"Do you know what kind of exports?"

"He told me art."

"And the imports?"

"We never discussed that."

"I see. So you engage a man here in Buenos Aires you have never met on the advice of a mutual friend, who remains unnamed?"

"Yes."

He moved in front of me, staring hard into my eyes. "Surely, Señor Anders, you can see how ridiculous this story sounds." He folded his arms across his chest.

"Sometimes the truth sounds a little strange, especially when you are not looking for the truth."

The officer slapped me again, and I nearly fell off the chair, the sting lasting longer than the first.

"You can lie to me, Señor Anders, but you will show respect."

I remained silent. The door to the room was partially open to a larger room where there were more military personnel. I glimpsed who I thought to be Jim Jones pass through the room.

Oh, please, be Jim. Get me out of here, I screamed inside my head, hoping he could hear.

"And what were you doing at Señor Madero's apartment last night?"

"Having dinner with him and his girlfriend."

"And how long have you known Señorita Iposa."

"I just met her for the first time at the apartment last night."

"And did you know her previous lover from Chile?"

How did they get that information so quickly? "What? What lover?"

"Come on, Señor Anders, you did not know a Roberto Menendez from the Chilean Central Bank?"

"Never met him." I answered truthfully.

A soldier came to the door and said something in Spanish to my interrogator. The officer left the room again, saying something to the soldier as he left. The soldier stayed, guarding the door.

I sat in the hard chair, my right leg starting to numb, wondering where this was going to lead. I didn't know much about either Vasco or Calida. Who were they really? And what was their connection to Anton? Fuck you, Anton, I thought again. You got me into this mess.

I sat and sat. It must have been about noon. I just wanted to get back inside the States. And then I thought about my drive with Vasco yesterday. I was sure I was in the Escuela de Mecánica. Would they put me in a truck, carry me to the airport and dump me in the Rio de La Plata? Fully clothed, just one more body washing up on the shores of Argentina?

A man in a suit spoke to the guard at the door, and he entered the room and removed the bindings on my hands. Jim Jones appeared in the doorway with my passport in hand. All I could think of was how badly I wanted to get home.

"Jude, get your jacket and let's go."

I grabbed my coat and followed Jim through the room, down a hallway, out the front door, and into the parking lot of the Escuela de Mecánica. I saw his little Fiat and hurried toward it.

"Get in, now!" Jones commanded, now intensely serious. Of course he was in charge; he had been in charge the whole time, and I had really fucked up by going off with Vasco. Man, I was way out of my league here.

We drove off, followed by a light green Ford Falcon.

"Okay, Jude. Here's the deal. We're going back to your hotel. You have thirty minutes to pack. Then we're going to the airport. The Argentine security police will escort us. When we get to the airport, they and I will escort you to your gate. We will wait with you until you board your plane. You will fly back to D.C. and you will never come back. You got that?"

Oh, I got it, all right. "What will happen to them, Vasco and Calida?"

"Jesus Christ! You come to Argentina and make friends with Montoneros." He stared straight ahead at the road. "One more thing, Jude, what you may have seen yesterday . . . it never happened. You hear me—never happened." He looked over at me. Was it anger, desperation?

I nodded.

I ARRIVED AT Dulles at 9:40 on Sunday morning, my head still aching, my eyes still burning. Though I had tried, I hadn't slept the entire trip back. In the cab on the way to my apartment, I kept rolling the events of the week around in my mind. I felt like I had been used, but how? Anton, you motherfucker!

After a shower I poured a cup of coffee, lit up a cigarette and called Anton.

"How is your morning going?" I asked as he politely answered his phone.

"Fine, Jude. Just get back?"

"No thanks to you, buddy."

There was a long pause. I smoked.

"What are you talking about?"

"Vasco Madero."

"Vasco? What do you mean?" I thought I detected a slight note of panic in his voice. I wanted to wring his neck.

"You mean to tell me, that for a man who knows everything about my life, you didn't know your friend, Vasco, was a Montonero?

"A what?"

"A left-wing revolutionary."

Another pause.

"Jude, I can assure you I only know Vasco from our business deals. He seemed quite ordinary to me. A true capitalist as far as I could tell. You sound really upset. What happened down there?"

I told Anton the whole story—except for the parts that Jim Jones admonished me from repeating. When I had finished he had only one comment.

"Holy shit!"

In all the years I had known Anton I had never heard him utter a single curse word.

"How did your meetings go?" he asked finally. I stubbed out my smoke. Jet lag was beginning to overtake me; I sat on the couch and leaned my head back.

"After what I heard from those right-winged sons o' bitches, I would never recommend approval of their loan request. Chile didn't get it when they could have been saved. Let their Junta go to hell."

"Of course, I understand. But your superiors might think you a bit biased after your . . . your run-in with the *gendarmes*."

"Nice word for thugs."

"Perhaps. But who helped them to power? Listen, Jude, you should carefully consider your recommendation. Make sure it can be justified beyond reproach. The director will get a lot of pressure from Argentina, who will claim foul if their loan request is not approved."

"I know what I have to do. I'm no fool." I closed my eyes.

"Of course, you're not, Jude."

I SPENT MONDAY and Tuesday on my recommendations and written summary for the deputy director. I never discussed what happened in Buenos Aires with Fallon, but did seek her objective review of my recommendations and her opinion. She agreed with my position. On Wednesday morning I submitted my report and spent the next day pushing paper around in my office. The jet lag was a bitch; it took me most of the week to get myself back on track. More than anything, I tried to keep my focus on the reports, and off of everything that happened in Buenos Aires outside the Ministry office. On Friday the deputy director called me into his office.

"Mr. Anders, I have read your recommendations on Argentina's request. Your conclusions are very well substantiated. I am inclined to agree and take them to the Board for their approval."

He pointed to a chair in his office and indicated I should sit. That could only mean that his so-called inclination to agree had some strings attached. I sat down with a sigh I hoped wasn't audible.

"That being said, the little incident of last week, will . . . well, it puts us in a difficult position. Do not misunderstand me, Mr. Anders. I believe you were an unfortunate victim of circumstance. We are sorry for your . . . experience. Still, Mr. Fernandez de Salis, will claim some sort of bias based on the incident. He will use it. I will have to give the IMF position on this matter some thought before I take it forward. When did the minister say they needed a response?"

"By the end of the month, sir."

"That gives us a little time. I need to discuss your recommendation with others. Thank you, Mr. Anders." He went back to the reports on his desk; I had been dismissed.

So apparently I had made the correct assessment of the Argentina request and the right recommendation, in spite of all that had happened there. It was all I could do. At the end of the month I received an internal memo from the director. It said Argentina's application for a loan from the IMF had been approved by the Board, but with some very strict conditions. And he thanked me for all my hard work. The next week I told Fallon the outcome.

"I told you, Jude. Pawns, just pawns." She sat on the edge of my desk, her usual perch, one leg across the other in her pencil-straight skirt. I was going to miss that.

"Not anymore," I said and showed her the letter I had drafted the night before.

She read through it quickly. "Jude, you can't resign."

"Yes, Fallon, I can. I have a choice. Now tell me about that woman you were going to fix me up with."

30

September 1978
Chicago, Illinois

THE TWO OF them were having lunch in a private room at the University Club on Michigan Avenue near downtown Chicago.

"Joseph, I thought the Argentina loan was going to be a no-go, especially with Carter and his human rights crap. This complicates things."

"Things don't always go according to plan. Sometimes there are unforeseen eventualities. We salvaged some restrictions which should make you more comfortable."

"They are not enough," Benjamin said softly. "You know that. The generals still control too much, just like Suharto."

"Yes, I agree. But have your boys carry their loans. They will be back for more. The next time we will not be so accommodating."

There was the sound of a dropped glass and they both looked in the direction of the sound.

"Goddamn Fascists," Benjamin said, picking up his whiskey.

Joseph pulled a Davidoff cigar from the leather case and smelled its fresh aroma. "I think it's time to end our preoccupation with that—fascism, Marxism, communism, socialism."

"What?"

"We're no longer fighting to control the means of production—traditional capitalist interests."

"I'm listening."

"The world is changing, Benjamin. Third-world economies will become developed economies. Yes, it will take time, but it will happen. And once people taste a little of the good life, they will want more—much more. And the leaders of those countries will be pressed by their people to open their doors to what free-market economies can provide. That will take money. Or maybe, a better word would be credit."

"Interesting. We would be well positioned. Is there a plan?"

He pulled his cutter from his pocket and made a clean slice at the tip of his Davidoff. "In the formative stages. And I think the IMF and the World Bank could be useful."

"I understand we lost our man at the IMF."

He sighed and methodically twirled the cigar an inch above the flame of his gold Dunhill lighter. Joseph snapped the lighter closed and blew a small smoke ring into the air. "I heard that. It is difficult to find someone with the right pedigree. Still, he may yet prove useful, and we have others."

"The woman?"

He took another drag on his cigar and exhaled a perfect ring of smoke that hovered above their table. "Yes, she has been quite helpful."

PART THREE
The Sacking

31

Present Time
Aegean Sea

"DAD, JUST SHOOT him!" she pleaded.

I looked around at the dead bodies in navy blue suits and rep ties lying on the dirt floor of the grass hut.

"I can't, Lex, I don't know how to kill."

She stood in the doorway of the hut, the sand beach and blue ocean framing her lithe silhouette.

"You're crazy. You just killed *them*," she insisted, pointing to the bodies that lay around us. "He's the last one. Kill him, kill him, now!" This time she pointed to the old man in a black trench coat who stood in front of us, a mocking smile spreading across his wrinkled face.

"Come on, Anders, do as your daughter beckons," the black coat said. "End it finally . . . for all eternity."

Who was he? His features were so familiar . . . and his voice . . .

"Dad!" Lex pleaded again.

I could feel the hilt of the gun in my right hand, hanging at my side. I raised the weapon to my waist and gazed at it. Where did I get this? I looked back at Lex, then to the gun again, then up to the old man. Why must I kill him?

As though she could read my mind, Lex answered. "Because he will destroy our world and force me to live in his. I've seen it; the trees stand with no leaves and the rivers run dry. And there are others . . . like *him*. Dad, please!"

I pointed the barrel somewhere at his chest, and looked into his cold, grey eyes. What was there about those eyes? They were like a mirror. My index finger was already wrapped around the trigger. I could feel it contract and begin to squeeze the flat metal. Who was this man I am going to kill? No. No. Not this man. My finger relaxed.

"I can't do it, Lex."

"Of course, you cannot, Anders, and we both know why." His laughter held a sardonic tone. "Now your world dies and your daughter follows me."

The old man opened his trench coat, exposing only a skeleton beneath. He grabbed the right side of the open coat and twirled it over Lex like a large cape and they both disappeared into blackness.

"Dad!" Her voice trailed into oblivion.

"Lex!"

My eyes flew open, squared on the back of the dark blue seat in front of me. I was sucking in air. It was the *Albion*, on my way to Amorgos. The woman seated next to me was leaning from her seat halfway into the aisle. I quickly tried to retrace the steps of the nightmare, but it had already retreated and left me only with the sick feeling of losing my daughter—at my hand.

My breathing slowed. What did it mean? I felt like Pandora—opening the box and unleashing chaos. I was still waiting and watching to see what would happen. A part of me said I should have stayed in D.C. But I couldn't; I just couldn't stay any longer. For me, it didn't matter anymore, but for Lex . . . what would happen to her? Had I left her with a nightmare where each day she would watch a piece of her world fall to the ground like leaves in autumn? I'll be gone, leaving Lex to step upon the fallen leaves alone.

I leaned back in my seat, my mind racing. Alone. If it had been up to me, that's what I would be. That would have been better; at least my guilt would be less if things didn't work out.

Lex was so real in the dream, I felt as though she were sitting next to me. There were so many things I wanted to tell her but never did. Here I was far out to sea and thousands of miles away from her. Was this the time to have the conversation we never had? I turned to gaze out the small window of the *Albion*.

I never wanted you, Lex. I thought I would be too busy with my career to give you the time I never got from my mother or the father who never knew me. That was no way for a child to grow up. Trust me; I should know. But I loved your mother, and in the end could not say "no" when she insisted on having you. And here you are—the most important thing in my life.

My eyes welled and a tear from my right eye trickled down my cheek. Lex, I'm sorry it didn't work out between your mother and me. I truly am. You missed so many years of a normal childhood, shuffling in between the addresses and emotions of two divorced parents. Maybe I could have chosen better, or not at all, like Fallon. But then there would be no Lex.

My throat started to tighten, but I resisted the urge to give in to the flurry of long-buried emotions I could feel rising to the surface. I looked down at my book, open on my lap at page 215—not even half way through it. I gazed out the window again. The *Albion* was still making headway in the open sea along its path to Amorgos, but I wasn't making much progress with the book. Once again I tried to concentrate on reading, forcing myself to silently mouth the words on the page, but my past kept intruding.

After my ever-growing misgivings about some of the questionable missions of the IMF, capped by my nerve-racking trip to Argentina, I had to resign. Staying would have been equivalent to letting myself be drafted and sent to fight in a war I didn't believe in. I didn't move to Toronto to save my life and my principles just to acquiesce later when my material well-being was cemented. The moment I finished crafting my letter of resignation I felt a sense of freedom—maybe the first real freedom since my undergraduate years at the University of Missouri. Even before I graduated I could feel the noose tightening—dead-ends in a maze that were forcing me forward in a predictable direction. To some extent I even felt free of the influence and control of Anton and Jack. After Argentina I wanted a life that was more on the "normal" side of interesting, without spooks and spies, military generals dressed up like business leaders, or clandestine plots cooked up by . . . by whoever. Of course there were options, especially for someone with my experience—think tanks, lobbying firms, and the like—each accompanied by a paycheck substantially greater than I had been accustomed to. But who would be my clients—people like Jack Tomasin or some of the same creditors I had surreptitiously worked for at the IMF?

Instead of jumping into something new right away, I took some time off; more than a dozen books I had wanted to read had been collecting dust on the shelves for far too long. Not since college had I let myself take long, leisurely afternoons with a good book. After a couple months of that, however, I was ready for a new challenge. I applied and was accepted to the Federal Reserve Board—a junior economist position—basically a lateral pay transfer but with much more emphasis on economic analysis and policy. Within two years, I married Fallon's friend, Gillian—a beautiful and spunky woman, optimistic and full of life. We bought a nice house in the suburbs; I even bought a car, a 280Z. It was an effort that, for the most part, succeeded. I just wanted to go to work each day and come home to the warm embrace of the woman I loved, and after Lex was born, to her enthusiastic spirit and openness to the world. Most of all, I wanted peace, and for many years, I found it.

Regardless of the chaos of my life up to that point, I never wanted to bury my years at the university, my time in Toronto avoiding the draft, my work at the IMF. And whether I wanted to or not, I could never forget Vasco and Calida, or Roberto and Señor Baca in Chile—for me, names on a document. Over time my memories of each of them faded, but I held on to their threads. What I did, I did as much to honor their hope for their countries as to save our own. Was that true, or was I just trying to put a fancy bow on the package I put together? Now, instead of memories there was a question—one cutting to the core of my motivation.

I had heard the stories of the Great Depression and its hard times from my mother and grandparents. Lex grew up so far removed from those times that the Depression was no more than a chapter in one of her history books. Although I didn't experience it firsthand, I never wanted that to happen again—not to Lex or anyone else. Since the time harsh austerity measures were instituted on the people of Chile, I imagined a world that didn't require periodic hard times along with the good—the ups and downs of the economic cycle. There had to be another way. Now, we all waited to see if there was.

I looked at my book and chuckled. My plan to finish it on the journey to Amorgos was obviously not working. I stole a glance at the woman in the seat next to mine, working intently on her needlepoint. What did she think of the world now? Did she even know what was happening out there—beyond the serenity of these islands so remote from my world?

After politely excusing my way past her, I strolled down the long aisle toward the bar in the rear of the *Albion* to buy a coke, examining the faces of the passengers on the way. How many of them really understood the world of global economics? What would they think if they knew I had a hand in the chaos they now faced? I sipped my Coke, wishing I could smoke in the ferry, and stared at the backs of their heads from my seat in the bar. Maybe none of their lives had changed at all—just continued on their day-to-day routines like their parents before them.

I thought back to my early days at the Federal Reserve Board. In the late 1970s, we were attempting to hold inflation in check while at the same time stimulate growth—to put people back to work so they could get on with their "normal" lives. As an economist, I understood that was an intractable problem, if not an oxymoron, because attacking one side of the economic problem made the other worse.

Like the Depression, those days provided tough economic challenges. This time, I saw them firsthand—definitely one of the down cycles. Many people were unemployed, and though we didn't have the soup lines of the Great Depression, there were large numbers of people without homes living on the streets, begging for money. State and local governments slashed their budgets and struggled to provide basic services. Even in D.C., trash piled up on the streets because the city could only afford to pick it up every other week. People were desperate.

In 1980 Reagan came to office, promising to slash the size and role of government by cutting social programs, eliminating regulations on the private sector, and lowering taxes. I had heard that before—from the new regimes that controlled Chile and Argentina. Reagan convinced Americans that his program would spur economic growth, and he was supported by a number of influential economists at the time who argued that those actions would stimulate businesses to grow and create more employment and corresponding wealth for everyone. It was the hope people wanted to hear. Even then I could hear the mantra whispering in my ear. The government implemented Reagan's vision; the economy went into recession and more jobs were lost.

But Reagan kept his promise to cut social programs, including clearing out the indigent mentally ill from the hospitals and throwing them all out on the streets. At the same time he oversaw the greatest increase in defense spending since WWII. Government got bigger, not smaller; it just got bigger in a different area. Maybe Reagan was more preoccupied with fighting communism than with his promise for prosperity. As a result, our federal deficit soared, and we at the Fed had to do all we could to hold inflation in check once again until the president and Congress raised taxes. But in spite of these facts, the mantra gained its voice.

What was Reagan's legacy? Hastening the fall of communism? It was already happening. Sure, he got the credit for killing the bogeyman we had lived with most of our lives, but it seemed our country still needed a bogeyman—maybe it always has—and it took us some time to finally find a new one. No, Reagan's legacy would be that he lent his voice to the mantra. I saw it at the IMF almost from day one. The Chicago-style economic theory, implemented in Indonesia and carried to the Southern Cone of South America, had finally reached the shores of the United States. But unlike Chile, Argentina, Uruguay, and Brazil, the majority of U.S. citizens embraced the mantra with little resistance. By the time they understood what it really meant, it was too late.

32

May 1997
Washington D.C.

IT COULD HAVE been anywhere; I could have been any place. Was I staring at the screen of my new computer monitor filled with colored charts and graphs, or at the silver-green birch leaves outside the window, twirling in the spring breeze like pinwheels stuck in a canvas of brilliant blue sky? Being a senior economist at the Fed would now put me in direct contact with members of the Board of Governors, including the Chairman of the Federal Reserve. They would no longer just read my reports, but engage me in direct questions and discussions. The news of my promotion earlier that morning was gradually sinking in as I sat there blankly, imagining debriefing the Fed Open Markets Committee about the dangers of unregulated financial markets. The phone jarred me out of my reverie.

"Jude, it's Fallon."

"Hey, Fallon, what's up?" I wondered if she called about my promotion. Surely Marie, one of my new team members, had called to tell her. She and Fallon had gotten close from our frequent happy hours after work, but she never did take over Fallon's job of sitting on the edge of my desk. Marie was a junior economist who transferred to D.C. from the Dallas Federal Reserve about two years ago. I loved to hear her talk with that deep New Orleans accent, which she claimed she did not have. When I told her she tended to drop the r's in her words, she insisted I was wrong, then proceeded to pronounce "quahtah" for "quarter"—for her a perfect example of not dropping them. It was my problem—I just couldn't hear them.

"Have you guys been tracking activity on the Thai *baht*?" Fallon asked, her voice tense.

"And I thought you were calling to congratulate me."

"For what?"

"My promotion to senior economist."

"Really? Well, that is news and well deserved. Good thing you went back to Georgetown for your master's degree—they wouldn't have promoted you without it. But back to my question."

I admit her lack of enthusiasm kind of bothered me, but I could tell her interest in the *baht* said this was urgent. "We heard there's been some speculation recently. Why?"

"Do you think someone's trying to drive down the value of the *baht*?"

"Why would they do that? Who owns enough *bahts* to do that kind of manipulation?"

"I don't know and agree it seems unlikely. But fear can create panic and do some real damage."

"Is the IMF involved?" Now I was puzzled. The IMF usually didn't jump in until there was a full-blown crisis, or serious threat of one; certainly not until they were asked by a member country to get involved. Or by someone who stood to lose a lot. Still, Fallon always had such a sharp eye; she was often a couple steps ahead of me. That's probably why I liked her so much.

"We're just doing a preliminary inquiry and analysis." Her tone shifted just enough to let me know she thought she had already said too much. We weren't co-workers anymore, after all. "But like the flu, it could spread."

"Ah, you still have the Indonesia account," I kidded, remembering our numerous conversations about her primary client.

"So astute, my friend. But the Fed interest rate policy won't help the situation if the Thai *baht* loses significant value."

"It's the Fed's job to keep inflation in check. You know that." The Fed had raised interest rates by over a percentage point during the past year to dampen speculation in technology companies, which otherwise had the potential to create an economic bubble.

Fallon pressed on. "But with a stronger dollar and a currency crisis in Southeast Asia, we could see significant capital flight from those countries."

"And end your Asian economic miracle?"

"Just cut the crap, Jude. We may have a real problem."

Yeah, I was ticked off a little for Fallon's tepid response to my promotion. The IMF was not my problem anyway. Still, she would not be discussing this with me if there were not some real concerns beyond the pockets of a few creditors. I opened up the Forex site on my computer while we were talking. Either this was just the foreign exchange market sorting out the relative values of global currencies, or there really was something going on there.

"I understand, but seriously, the Asian governments have allowed their economies to get a little too hot over the past few years—too much capital speculation without any real growth in output. Don't you think this is just a normal correction? Anyway, from our perspective more investment money will move back to the U.S. in the longer-term."

"What you consider a normal correction can create a lot of pain and suffering, not to mention spreading political and economic chaos," Fallon said, her voice starting to rise. "If Southeast Asian exports decline because of your strong dollar, and the countries don't have enough capital to get through a crisis, their GDP goes to hell and they tumble into recession. Recession begets political unrest, Jude. It could spread to the entire region. You don't think that might eventually impact the great U.S. of A."

"I'm kidding, Fallon. Jesus, you don't have to get all serious on me." I scanned the trading trends and volumes that appeared on my computer screen. Christ, there was a lot of activity on the Thai *baht*. "I'll get Marie to pull some data. Let's see what it tells us before we set off the fire alarm."

Of course, she was right. Higher interest rates on U.S. Treasury Bonds would attract more foreign investment to the U.S., and much of that money would come from investors who had their money in Southeast Asia. A capital flight from those countries would only create greater economic difficulties for them at a time when they needed the capital to re-stimulate their economies.

After hanging up with Fallon, I got on the phone to Marie. "Marie, I need you to pull some data."

"After lunch?

"The celebration will have to wait. There maybe trouble brewing in Thailand."

"Thailand? Really? What do you need?" Marie's honeyed Southern voice was a perfect antidote to Fallon's matter-of-fact tone.

"A three-month trend on the Thai *baht*, current account balance, capital account balance, exports trends—the usual stuff."

"That may take a little time. It's not like U.S. data."

"Get Josh to help you. Have him look at the recent currency trades; you focus on the economic stats."

"On it, Jude."

"COME IN," JOSH called out when Marie knocked on the partially open conference room door.

She laid a stack of computer printouts on the already cluttered conference table. It had taken two days, but my team had gathered all the data and statistics we needed.

"Here's the last batch, Jude."

"Thanks, Marie. Josh and I were just getting started on the currency trades. Have a seat."

Josh was a senior analyst assigned to my team. He started at the Fed right out of college from Michigan State. A Midwesterner who looked kind of geeky with his frizzy, disheveled sandy-blond hair and shirt sleeves that were an inch too short for his arms, Josh was a whiz-kid when it came to numbers.

"Jude, on the surface these numbers look innocuous," Josh started in. "A slow build-up of *baht* buys several months before the currency crisis, then a quick sell-off leading up to the panic. But look at this: the buys were done in relatively equal increments once you strip out the normal transactions—50 million, then 75 million, then 50, then 75, and then the sales were in similarly equal increments, but done over a much shorter time frame. Look." Josh showed the graph and corresponding numbers to Marie and I. "Patterned buys three months before; patterned sells right up to two weeks before the panic started."

"Who was doing the buys and sells?" I asked.

"It's Thailand. No records, no transparency."

"We don't know if it was one individual or many?" Marie asked.

"Nope. But the pattern and amounts of the buys-sells would be a coincidence if it were multiple speculators. This is where the panic set in." Again, he pointed to the data. "Now the sells became erratic, lots of volume, no pattern. Typical herd sell-off."

"If it was a few speculators, they could have buried the remaining divestitures in the sell-off panic," I inserted.

"With the volume, of course."

It was obvious. Someone had manipulated the currency through speculative trading. Score another one for Fallon Connelly.

"Josh, I want you to go farther back than three months. Pull data for the full year before the collapse. See if there was patterned buying earlier and how much earlier."

"I'll see if those numbers exist. Remember, it's Thailand."

"Okay, Marie, what have you got?"

She pulled several typed sheets from the top of the stack of printouts and tossed one to Josh and me. "Thailand had eleven years of growth averaging 9% per year—better than any other economy during the period. Inflation was reasonable given the growth rate: 3.4-5.5%. Strong export growth over a sustained period like the other players in Southeast Asia—textiles, autos, semi-conductors, consumer electronics. Large inflows of investment capital. Higher than average interest rates drew in the money initially. Recently a boom in commercial and residential real estate. Heavy commercial borrowing to keep up with demand. Pretty much of a bubble.

Now they have excess real estate capacity and declining prices. Current account trade deficits are way out of balance. Unserviceable debt burden will likely spread to their financial institutions. Planned interest rate hikes by their central bank will only exacerbate the weakness in their economy. Once you look under the cover, it's clear the country is overextended without enough foreign currency reserves to back up a crisis."

She tapped the sheet with the tip of her pencil. This Cajun was one sharp cookie. I was lucky to have her as one of my team.

"If the currency depreciates substantially, defaults will go through the roof. The government bonds will be junk," I said, pondering our next steps. Fallon was right. This could be trouble . . . for all of us. "Josh, where's the *baht* now?"

"Floating and way down against the dollar—in the toilet."

"Guys, let's look at the surrounding territory."

"Which countries?" Josh asked.

"All of them. I need talk to the boss and then call Connelly."

"FALLON, YOUR FEARS were justified. The Thai *baht* is in free-fall," I said that afternoon as we walked through one of our favorite parks. It was in between two one-way sections of E Street and canopied by old Sycamore trees. "The spill-over is likely to be wide and deep. The fundamentals ailing Thailand also apply to Malaysia, Indonesia, even South Korea."

Fallon stopped. "Christ. What are their reserves like?"

"If this goes the way we think, not near enough."

Fallon looked up into the cascade of greenery above us. "The *ringgit*, *rupiah*, and Singapore dollar are under pressure. Who's in the best shape to weather a crisis?"

"China. Most of their investments have been in factories and infrastructure. Much less speculation. Maybe Singapore—they've had stronger monetary controls. Indonesia has strong foreign currency reserves; that might help them . . . up to a point." The afternoon sun was getting hot, even for May. I pulled off my suit coat and threw it over my shoulder as we walked.

"Malaysia, Indonesia, and Singapore intend to float their currencies. We're preparing to back them up. The Thai government has just requested an emergency loan of $17B. What's the Fed going to do?"

"It's in policy now," I said, raising my voice to counter the increase in traffic on E Street. "The Fed has some funds, but not enough to cover the potential damage. They're working with other commercial banks and will likely request the IMF to assist the countries."

We continued down the walk to one of the usual places we went to and sat down on a bench. I pulled a pack of cigarettes from my suit coat and lit up a smoke with my grandfather's old Zippo.

"Got one for me?"

I handed her mine and held the Zippo in my hand for a moment, enjoying its familiar weight. When my grandfather gave it to me at nineteen, realizing I was already a smoker, I had stuffed it in my pocket without a second thought. Now it had almost become a part of me. I lit another cigarette for myself.

Fallon took a long drag and cocked her head toward the sky as she exhaled the smoke. "A loan package will come with severe strings," she said. "Indonesia is used to it. But the medicine will be unfamiliar to the others."

"So what's new? If I didn't know any better, I'd say there's some secret group of Chicago Boys pulling your strings."

"My strings? What the hell do mean by that?"

"The IMF, Fallon, you know what I mean."

"It's just that the Fund has its own prescription for solving crises. It doesn't line up completely with Friedman's elixir, but speaking of pulling strings, any evidence of manipulation?"

"Josh is pulling more data to be certain, but yes, there was some patterned currency trading before the run up to the crisis."

"And that led to this mess?" She looked at me square on.

"Hardly. There was as much speculation in their real estate markets as with their currency, but it certainly triggered the crisis."

"Who would do that, I mean, a planned currency manipulation?"

"Good question, and why."

We both thought about that one for a few minutes as we sat on the bench, smoking. It was just like old times at the IMF, when we spent hours trying to figure out the assorted agendas behind our analysis of the economies of Chile, Uruguay, and Argentina.

"Well, the Fund is lining up some private entities to help too—corporations and commercial banks. A few targeted takeover deals will help to stabilize some of the weakest corporations and banks." Fallon took another drag of her smoke.

"Acquisitions at bargain basement prices. I've seen that before." Of course there would be a group of entrepreneurial wolves seeking to benefit from the IMF's austerity measures—just like in Chile and Argentina in the 1970s. "Have you seen Anton in the neighborhood?"

Fallon glared at me. "Got any better solutions?"

I knew it was a sore spot, but I couldn't help needling her. He and Fallon had dated on and off for about a year after I first introduced them. The affair had ended amicably—according to Fallon—but I always wondered. Since that time, the fingerprints of Anton's brokerage business always seemed to be found somewhere near those countries forced to drink Friedman's elixir.

"Not for Asia, my dear. It's too late to do anything else," I said after a moment. "Certainly, prevention would have been the best policy, but as we both know, even if we eventually understand how we got into this mess, somehow we'll forget it over time. I think we can assume we'll face this kind of crisis again."

"In Asia?"

"Anywhere in the world, Fallon. Even here, in the United States."

"Yeah, and what would your solution be, Mr. Senior Economist?" She smiled; it was her first real acknowledgement of the significance of my promotion.

I tossed my finished butt on the path and stamped it out with my foot. "I don't know, but this little episode should teach us one thing: We're no longer isolated from global economic events. And with American corporations going international, anything that happens in one part of the world can affect us here. We used to own the economic pie. No one else was big enough to affect us here. Now we're becoming just a slice. That changes the economic framework we've been operating under for the past fifty years. I guess that's worth thinking about."

Even more compelling to me at the moment, however, was Fallon's question: "Got any better solutions?" That was particularly worth thinking about. I watched Fallon head back to the IMF a few short blocks away. I lit another smoke, deciding to sit for a while longer.

33

June 1997
Darien, Connecticut

"IS THE PRIME Minister holding firm?"

"He refuses to devalue his Thai *baht.*" Thomas took off his coat and seated himself in the opposite chair.

"Can they defend it?"

"Of course not. They don't have the reserves, and false hope keeps him from taking the necessary actions."

The wrinkles around Joseph's mouth became pronounced with the familiar mocking smile. "Do we have our funds out?" He sipped his whiskey and shifted his weight in the overstuffed chair in his paneled study.

"We sold off the last of our *bahts* a month ago. It will be difficult to track our activities. Our transactions came from many sources. Mind if I join you?" Thomas grabbed a glass, reached for the decanter, and poured two fingers worth of whiskey.

"I congratulate you on a good plan," Joseph said as he lifted his glass in salute. "How far will the contagion spread?"

"Throughout the region, most likely. Except for China and Japan, most countries were pursuing the same growth policies."

Joseph was silent, staring at the empty fireplace in front of him, his mind wrapped around something. "Tell me about China."

"They can control the contagion better than the others."

Of course they can, Joseph thought. We prepared them for that. "Good. It improves their position."

"If they play it right. But you know, it is the Chinese. Hopefully, we will have enough influence in the . . . what do they call it?

"The Development and Reform Commission."

"Yes, that is it. I hear the Fund is getting involved."

"They will, eventually. Things will boil for a while, and when they get bad enough, the Fund will use its power of persuasion."

"And our debt position?" Thomas loosened his tie and unbuttoned his collar.

"Large enough to insist on our own prescriptions. We can use the IMF's program to reinforce them."

"Do you think this little event will convince those governments to keep their hands out of the cookie jar?" He chuckled.

That was part of what stood in their way. It wasn't part of their plan, but a welcomed consequence. "Cronyism has gotten out of control," Joseph answered. "I am afraid some politicians have become too entrenched in their own interests—forgot how they got where they are—just like our military friends down south. They will have to go, even that flabby drunk that pretends to be the president of the former Soviet Union. Let's see how he reacts when oil prices plummet like a rock." He smiled and sipped at his drink. "A little austerity does wonders for the political process."

"A good reminder for their next leaders." Thomas smiled. "I hear the Fed is getting involved."

"Just lip service, my friend. They will work through the IMF and assist with the consolidation of the weaker financial institutions."

"How many more of them will we control?"

"Before too long, enough to achieve our ends."

34

January 1998
Washington D.C.

IN THE MORNING, I took the Red Line to Metro Station, bought my usual copy of the *Washington Post* from the street vendor a block from the Federal Reserve building, and finished my walk to the office. As was my usual routine, I sipped at a cup of coffee from the break room, waiting for my computer to boot.

The headline caught my attention straight off: *Clinton Denies Sexual Relationship*. At the top of the article the by-line was even more interesting: Sasha Drecovich, contributing reporter. "Sasha." I said aloud. "So that's where you've been?"

I quickly skimmed the article; apparently, the president was being accused of having sex with a White House intern, and his staff had transferred her to a job at the Pentagon in 1996 because they thought Clinton was a little too "close" to her at the White House. But it wasn't just the sex with this intern—allegedly Clinton told her he lied to the FBI about having sex with another woman while he was governor of Arkansas. I sighed. Nothing surprised me anymore. Hillary might care, but why should we? I was much more interested in the sudden reappearance of my old protest buddy, who hovered around the edges of my memories like a wisp of patchouli oil, dirty jeans, and leather halter-tops. Marie knocked on my open door and the image disappeared as quickly as it had risen.

"Jude, I have preliminary data on the proposed bank merger."

I took another sip of my coffee, folded the paper and tossed it on the credenza behind my desk. "What have we got?"

"Well, you were right. This will be the largest bank combination in U.S. history."

"How big?"

"The combined bank would have almost 15% of the country's deposit assets."

"Really. And just how does that benefit our financial system?" I leaned back in my chair, getting comfortable. This was not going to be a quick visit, I could tell.

"The banks claim greater efficiency and cost reduction with economies of scale, freeing up more operating capital for loans."

I motioned Marie to have a seat. "That's *their* benefit. It's the same line of argument as the other mergers. Did any of them ever achieve those objectives?"

Marie smiled. It was clear she had anticipated that question. "No, but they did get some benefit from geographic expansion. If one part of the country has an economic slump, another geographic area can keep the profits coming in."

I had seen this before over the past ten years, and I had a theory that covered the real reasons for the mergers. "Let's not forget the increased deposit base, which means more money for loans," I said. "If they have a larger capital base to lend from, then they need to bring fewer parties to the table on the *big* deals."

"Makes sense. One stop shopping for their customers, especially with merger and acquisition and IPO deals. That would increase their market share." She put her reports on my desk.

"And decrease the competition. I'm not so sure *that's* good for our financial system."

"A financial monopoly?" She was quickly getting the picture.

Since the passage of the Interstate Banking Act, permitting nationally chartered banks to operate across state lines without following state laws and regulations, there had been a flurry of bank acquisitions and mergers. If this one was approved, only twelve financial institutions would own 60% of deposits.

"Does the FDIC have enough capital to cover the big banks in case of a failure?"

"I'll have to get that from the FDIC."

"And what would happen if the FDIC was not appropriately funded?" I pressed my line of reasoning.

"Well, I guess we could look at Continental Illinois. In 1984 Continental was deemed too big to fail, so the government came to the rescue, which they also did in the late '80s with the savings and loans."

Of course, the S&L Crisis. "What if these banks think that at some point they will also be too big to fail if anything goes wrong, and the government will just have to bail them out with taxpayer dollars?"

"But, Jude, they aren't like the savings and loans—there are regulatory controls over what banks can do with their deposits and assets. And there are stringent capital and reserve requirements."

"For now, Marie." For now.

35

June 1998
New York City

JONATHAN PETERS POKED at his salad. Well-toned from 22 years of daily workouts, Peters, head of USA National Bancorp, rarely deviated from the "lite" side of the club menu. His colleagues, on the other hand—like himself, titans of the financial industry who often met at the private club for luncheon meetings—were still meat-and-potatoes men.

"Stephen, I know you said I'd recognize the play when I saw it, but don't you think this is a bit over the top?" He tried to control the tone of hostility creeping into his voice as he finished his salad.

"The plan was to embarrass and weaken him, not get him impeached, Jonathan," Russell replied. "Just enough to put him on his heels—pressure him to go along with the program."

Seven years Peters' junior, Russell was CEO of a well-known investment house on Wall Street. Slim and not quite as grey yet as Peters, he favored Armani suits and Italian loafers. Both men had attended Princeton and both still proudly wore their Alpha Tau Omega rings.

"Then what's this shit Starr is doing?" Peters asked.

"Starr's a loose cannon," Jack Henquist jumped in. "We didn't put him in the job, our friends in the Congress did. All we did was get some information out there." He speared a chunk of his filet.

Henquist was the CEO of Fannie Mae, a government-sponsored corporation responsible for expanding the secondary mortgage market by securitizing mortgage loans. All three men were influential members of the Financial Services Interest Group at the U.S. Chamber of Commerce.

"Well, now he's hell bent on impeaching the president," Peters continued quietly but sternly while leaning toward the two men across the table. "Have you thought about who is next in line if that were to happen?"

Russell and Henquist looked at each other.

Russell sighed. "I hadn't thought of that. We might have to start all over."

"I have no stomach for starting from scratch again. This thing has gone too far." Peters no longer tried to hide his anger.

"Okay, okay," interrupted Russell. "We need to find a way to pull Starr back."

"Like I said, Starr's a rogue." Henquist laid his fork to the side of his plate. "He's on his own mission. If we tried to corral him, he'd find a way to go after us. No, we have to get to some of our guys in the House. Tell them to avoid the hearings and give the president a slap on the wrist. You know, a reprimand or censure."

"Good luck with that," Peters chided them. "The House Speaker and his thugs are still fuming over the shutdown. Clinton made them look like fools. Now they smell raw meat. Hungry wolves don't back off a kill." He paused, considering the options. "I think we can stop this in the Senate if it gets that far. Gannon's been pushing our agenda and needs to understand what this might do to the repeal of Glass-Steagall."

Peters and his colleagues needed that repeal in order to expand into the booming investment and insurance businesses. Glass-Steagall, enacted after the financial crisis that led to the Great Depression, had effectively locked banks out of the far more lucrative money-machine that Wall Street had become; he wanted some of the action and he wanted it now.

"While I agree, this isn't the only thing on our plate right now," Russell insisted. "The Commodity Futures Trading Commission is pressuring Clinton and Congress to regulate the over-the-counter stuff. If that happens, it will make doing business a lot more difficult for us, even if we get Glass repealed."

"Come on, Stephen," Henquist responded. "The CFTC has no clue what's going on in the derivatives market."

"Right. And that's why they're clamoring for more transparency."

"I've been assured our guys on the inside will keep them in check." Henquist sipped his water.

"I wish I felt as confident as you. If they get what they want, it will expose everything, and that will lead to regulating the only free market we have left. We can't let that happen." Russell pushed his plate away and downed the last of his Manhattan. "Once we get the banking act repealed, we're going to make sure government stays out of our other business entirely."

36

Present Time
Paros, Greece

THE ALBION PUT into port at Parakia on the island of Paros, our last stop before landing at Amorgos. Anxious to stretch my legs and have another cigarette, I put the "reserved" sign on my seat and went on deck. There was smoke billowing up in thick clouds from a building in Parakia, maybe a house fire? I couldn't tell. The shape and movement of the rising gray smoke reminded me of the puffy cumulus clouds in Missouri, marching across the summer sky like an invading army.

Leaning over the railing, I let the sea air and sunshine wash over me. I took a drag and followed its smoke as it drifted out to sea. All these years later, I was still looking for the shape of the invaders who triggered the Asian financial crisis, and intended or not, the Russian financial crisis and then the pop of the dot-com bubble a year later. Years of working with Fallon at the IMF had taught me well—always ask the who and why. I could understand the speculative behavior of investors in the real estate markets in Southeast Asia—they were always interested in making a quick buck. Certainly, the reluctance of the political leaders of those countries to intervene to hold the bubble in check was predictable—their citizens hungered for the good life that came with the commerce surrounding the boom. We had seen both before in the twentieth century. But who would deliberately manipulate the Thai currency and for what end?

In the midst of the Asian crisis, Fallon had asked me if I had a better solution to the ups and downs of economic events fueled by speculation and resulting bubbles, which were always followed by collapse, fear and debt. At that time I didn't, but the Asian Flu set my thinking on a very different line from the economic theories we had labored under for almost two centuries.

I paced the deck of the Albion, stretching my legs before I had to return to my seat below. Maybe it was my own lower-middle class background that led me to my conclusions; maybe it was the values and principles that were cemented for me during my college years. What I believed then—and still believe today—is that until we found a different way, ordinary people would pay the steepest price from the inevitable bust side of the economic cycle—plummeting home values and stock markets, lost jobs and reduced wages and benefits, and staggering debt that had to be paid to the creditors on the backs of weakened economies. Those who had the money to gamble on speculative investments also lost, but most could bear the consequences. The average citizen, on the other hand, could not. They wanted a way out of their endless economic stagnation, and when they saw a bet that gave them the opportunity to move up, they leaped into the frenzy of the bubble, ready to cash in. But just when they finally grabbed hold of the next rung, they were thrown back pitifully into the same conditions their families had lived in for generations. And with the debt they now shouldered, it would take a generation before they had another chance to crawl back out of the ditch. No, there had to be a better way.

I was trained in economics. But what was the purpose of economy? No one ever asked that question in my college courses. Did my professors just believe that the answer was obvious—as innate to our thinking as the language that shapes it? I thought about the book I was reading . . . or trying to read, anyway. People came together, formed societies for a reason. There had to be a benefit or they wouldn't have done it, anymore than they would have made their migrations across the continents. Why was an economy any different? If it didn't benefit people—and not just a few—then why participate, unless forced to by warlords and tyrants? I finished my smoke and tossed it in the harbor. And just why did the creditors always come out ahead? Investments weren't supposed to be risk-free. The smoke hovering over the island was beginning to dissipate and blow out to sea. I lit another cigarette with my Zippo, impervious to the wind.

The late '90s were turbulent, and many, including myself, were glad to see them pass like the smoke from Parakia's fire. With the end of the twentieth century also came the end of Clinton's second term, and a final conclusion to all the scandals and impeachment threats. Most of us were relieved, and even somewhat happy, about the prospect of a steady, calmer life without the daily rancor of Washington politics. At the time, I mused over the deals that were likely struck to keep Clinton from being impeached—secret, behind the scenes machinations of politicians and the moneyed interests that placed and kept them in power.

I gazed out over the harbor, my mind a blank. The points appeared on the line of my thinking—they were obvious to me now, but certainly not then. And I was in the middle of them, only dimly aware that they could create an event as significant as the crash of the stock market in 1929. Three points lead to the crisis: the megabanks that were spawned by the passage of the Interstate Banking Act; the repeal of the Glass-Steagall Act, which gave those banks access to investment banking, tearing down the wall built after the Depression between those who safeguarded the assets of everyday people and those who speculated in securities; and the grand deal, occurring in the final days of Clinton's term—the Commodity Futures Modernization Act. That was an obscure piece of legislation covering the trading of derivatives, which were complex financial instruments that no one seemed to understand except—perhaps—those behind the deals, who managed to make huge amounts of money gambling with little personal risk. With the passage of each of these pieces of legislation, the mantra grew louder. It was poised to drown out the voices of caution and reason that grew out of the Great Depression.

At the time, most Americans had never heard of the term "derivative." Some of the more earnest people in Clinton's administration questioned what was going on in that market, but those who tried to look under its dark covers were quickly discredited or dismissed. At the Fed, we discussed the effect of derivatives on the financial system of the country, but there was no serious interest in understanding their potential impact. Even the Fed Chairman signaled his tacit approval for privately traded derivatives—secret contracts between dealmakers, investors, and counterparties.

It was hard to argue against something that had such great potential for infusing a huge amount of capital into our economy, especially with the downturn in the dot-com market. Incomes were at an all-time high and demand was beginning to pick up. The other ingredient to economic growth was capital. And the additional capital from the derivatives market had the potential to generate economic expansion at levels we had never seen. A large amount of money was out there seeking a home, as was the promise of making more—a whole lot more.

As an economist at the Federal Reserve, I should have seen what was coming. With this single piece of legislation the financial giants of America gained access to the biggest casino the global economy had ever seen, and a shadow banking system not under control of the Federal Reserve. Sure, I eventually connected the dots—after it was too late to silence the voice of the beast.

37

June 1999
Newport, Rhode Island

"G.P. SAYS HE'S our boy," James insisted, as the three men strolled across the lawn to the edge of the estate overlooking the ocean.

"I respected his father's opinions—a lot more than G.P.'s. I'm old enough to remember his father," Joseph asserted. "And this boy, as G.P. calls him, has the sense of a teenager and the IQ of a gorilla."

"My, my, Joseph, you are getting old," Benjamin chided. "Do you have anyone better in mind?"

Joseph grumbled. "Well, at least his family has been very accommodating over the years. Maybe the father could keep him under control. Give him advice at the appropriate times."

"We have thought of that. And look at the alternatives. Right now we need someone we can trust to do the right thing at the right time."

"His opponent has a real chance, you know," James chimed in. "This is not a done deal. The ordinary people like a populist."

"We have the means to change that." Benjamin was unperturbed by the prospect. "Still, a number of us would feel more comfortable with someone on the inside—next to the new president, day-to-day."

"Yes, that would make sense," Joseph agreed. He gazed out over the ocean. "Can you field some candidates?"

"Probably," James agreed.

"Good." Joseph returned his eyes to his companions. "Speaking of candidates, we have a new one for our little group."

"I heard." Benjamin smiled. "I know him somewhat, and of course we all know his father."

"Which one?" James asked.

All three men laughed heartily at the inside joke as they continued their walk across the estate grounds.

"This young man has the right stuff. He certainly has the right views and family background," Benjamin asserted.

"We need to be cautious," Joseph insisted. "Admission is a big step for us . . . and for him."

"Certainly that is true, but he would be coming in at the bottom layer. He would be told only enough to carry out his assignments."

"How much more vetting needs to be done?" James asked.

"We have reviewed his activities since he took over Jack's business. They are straightforward, as far as we can tell, and he has some very good international connections. Those could be useful to us." Benjamin stopped walking and relit the butt of his cigar. "He seems to have pretty much adopted Jack's political views, and I have seen some of the business deals he put together after Chile, Argentina, and our little Asian adventure. They displayed a certain . . . ruthlessness. His father, of course, believes he would fit in well."

"He is still young." A scowl crossed Joseph's face. "Some more years under his belt could not hurt."

"He is in his fifties, Joseph, for god's sake. That is not young unless you are comparing him to yourself." Again the three of them chuckled. "Most of us are well beyond retirement age, except for James here," he said, pointing to his compatriot with the tip of his cigar. "We need younger blood, new ways of looking at opportunities. Each of us was younger than he when we joined." Benjamin paused, taking a final puff on the cigar and tossing it over the cliff that edged his estate. "The Deep has been around a long time. It survives only because we bring in new members from time to time—you know that."

"You failed to mention his acquaintanceship with Anders. If we bring him in, we must be cautious until we know we can trust him," Joseph insisted. "Will his father go along with that?"

"Yes. I've already discussed that with Thomas. Of course, we must still test him over time . . . to make sure. Besides, his relationship with Anders might prove useful as well."

"Or a problem if Anton ever discovers the truth." Joseph huffed.

"That is quite unlikely. You know that."

"And if we are wrong?"

"Like we were with Anders? If he becomes a problem, we will deal with the situation, as we have before." Benjamin affirmed.

"Which side of the equation?"

Benjamin smiled. "Both if necessary."

Joseph kicked a small stone from the well-groomed walkway into the grass. "Okay, let us proceed then, but cautiously."

The three men made their way slowly back to the stone mansion that overlooked the ocean from its perch high atop the cliffs.

"How about your son, Joseph?" Benjamin asked as they reached the front steps. "Why haven't you brought his name forward?"

"I would not trust him to turn out the lights, much less with our deliberations. All he cares about is his wealth." Joseph scowled again. "He would be in prison if it were not for that cop in Buffalo."

"All in all that turned out quite well, even if your son didn't. You helped the policeman's daughter through college. At least you left a legacy you can be proud of. Did she ever find out?"

"About who paid her college? She knows nothing. If she did, I would know. We maintain contact through the Harvard Alumni Association. I am quite proud of her success."

"And she has been useful," James asserted.

"She has helped in small ways," Joseph agreed. "There may be a bigger role for her in the future somewhere in the pyramid. We will see. How about your daughter, Benjamin? Times are changing. We could use a female member."

"It's a pity really. She is quite bright. Threw away a promising career in law just to have babies. What a waste of my money." Benjamin shook his head. "We could use another attorney, but she cares too much about raising a family. And if she knew what we do . . . well, she'd disown me. Looks like we will all have to wait for our grandchildren to grow up."

38

January 2001
Silver Spring, Maryland

"I HOPE YOU bought some snacks for this movie," Fallon called to me from the living room. My suburban Maryland house, with its spacious sprawl, was a far cry from my tiny apartment those first years in D.C. before I was married.

"Movie?" I called back from the kitchen where I was rounding up some drinks. "It's an inauguration, Fallon."

"Looks like a movie set to me." American flags were draped around every square foot of the Capitol grounds, including the podium where the new president would be sworn in.

"To use your metaphor, a new set of actors. That'll make things interesting for a while," I said as I walked into the living room. "I'm almost finished with the food. You want a beer now?"

"Sure thing . . . might as well get drunk." She had made herself comfortable on the sofa with her feet tucked underneath her like a school kid. I wondered how she managed that feat of flexibility in her tight-fitting jeans. How many years had I known Fallon, and yet it was as if she had hardly aged a day.

"Yeah, right, Fallon Connelly drunk. You can out-drink me—your Irish ancestry."

"That's bullshit, and you know it!" She insisted as I made my way back to the kitchen.

Fallon always got testy when I brought up her Irish immigrant roots. I probably shouldn't needle her about it so much; it's not as if I was Mayflower stock, after all. We had a few conversations about her family and background, but she really didn't like to talk about it. I didn't get it; my mom worked her butt off in a factory so I could be where I was today and I would never forget that. Fallon, on the other hand, equally successful with equally blue-collar roots, seemed to have nothing but disdain for where she came from. I opened a couple bottles of Heineken and walked them and a tray of cheese, chips, and sandwiches back into the living room.

"Here you go. Need a glass?"

"No thank you. I'm a bottle-baby. Wow." She tipped the bottle towards me in a toast. "That's a spread."

"I figured we needed some comfort food to make ourselves happy today."

"Boy, that's the truth. When's Gillian getting home?"

"Not till 6:00, probably." I picked up a handful of chips.

"How are you two doing?"

There was nothing casual in her question, and that was a conversation I really didn't want to have.

"Okay." I avoided her eyes, preferring to fiddle with the remote.

"Just okay?"

"She has her work; I have mine." I looked out the window to the house across the street where my neighbor was still picking up leaves from last fall. They were soggy by now, and he needed a shovel to get them out from beneath his shrubs. The joys of home ownership.

"Uh-huh, I've heard that before." She took a swig of her beer. "And the chemistry?"

Here it was—where Fallon was headed. Over the years I had learned that tact was not one of her attributes. "That doesn't last, Fallon. You know that. It's never lasted for you."

"True enough, but I never married, did I?" She turned that smug little smile on me like she always did when she thought she had won a debating point. "So what are you two going to do?"

"We've been through some rough patches before and come out of them." I plopped down in the overstuffed chair next to Fallon and ran the cheese slicer over a hunk of cheddar. "We'll get through this one. Besides, we have Lex. It's best if she has two parents . . . together."

"Not if they're unhappy together."

The dignitaries were filling the stands. There were cut-away shots showing Bill and Hillary leaving the White House and getting into the presidential limo for the short ride to the Capitol Building.

"So, what have you been working on at the IMF?" I asked, hoping to change the subject.

"Still screwing with Southeast Asia. I think they're turning the corner." She seemed fine with letting my relationship with Gillian go. Maybe she figured she had made her point. She reached for a sandwich and nibbled an edge. "And I have a new account, one you might recognize."

"Really, who?"

"Argentina. They've been messing around with their currency valuation again, and they're in debt up to their you-know-what. They might default on part of their debt if they don't get some concessions from their creditors. Did you ever find out what happened to those people you met there?"

I hadn't thought about Argentina in years, nor about Anton's friend Vasco and his lovely girlfriend. I wondered if they had been imprisoned or tortured in the Escuela Mechanica. Would they have been released? Able to resume a normal life? Were they still together?

"Not really. The job and the family have kept me busy, if you know what I mean." I flashed back to that night with Vasco and Calida in Buenos Aires. Over the past twenty years I hadn't had any friends or acquaintances that stimulated me as much as they did that single evening over dinner. Maybe it was my age at the time, or the exotic environment. Maybe it was just the circles I've run in since—professional colleagues, neighbors, and other parents. Fallon's comments brought back a host of memories, not all of them pleasant.

"Argentina will get creamed if they default. They'll be back for more money sooner rather than later. And the terms will be harsh."

"How deep is the Fund in?"

"The member states will cover the IMF tab, you know that. The other creditors won't be so happy though."

I lit a cigarette and put my feet up on the coffee table. Gillian would chide me for smoking in the house when she got home. She had a good nose for stale cigarette smoke even with the open window I had cracked an hour ago. My smoking had been banished to the back deck or my makeshift office in the basement.

"So tell me, how are things at the Fed?" Fallon asked.

"Mostly Open Markets Committee work, trying to engineer a soft landing to the latest recessionary cycle."

"Interest rates . . . how boring." She leaned back in the couch, taking another bite of her sandwich.

"At least we're not debt collectors—the stooges of the big global banks."

Fallon swallowed hard. I had hit another sore spot. These days, the IMF was a lot less the savior of struggling Third World economies and a lot more a strong-arm for the banks, who demanded loans structured to protect their own bottom lines rather than what might actually be good for the people in those countries.

"Oh really, you think so. Now tell me, Mr. Anders, just who do you think controls all those regional Federal Reserve Banks?"

"The Federal Reserve, Fallon." She couldn't win, but I liked to play just the same—one of our bantering games that we used to play when I was with the IMF.

"Well, let's see. Who's on the boards of governors of those Fed banks? The officers of the banks the Fed is supposed to police. A bit of a conflict of interest, don't you think?"

"They're only one voice."

"Uh-huh. And given the size of those upstanding institutions after all the mergers and acquisitions, which *you* sanctioned, that's a pretty big, powerful voice, my friend." She tipped her beer bottle at me to make her point.

"Some of us agree that's a problem." I ceded her that one. "Unfortunately, the chairman doesn't share our reservations."

"I think you should have more than reservations."

I had to hand it to her. We both had exactly the same concerns about the larger banking system, but she didn't hesitate to give the knife a little twist. I could have fought harder against the biggest mergers, the repeal of Glass-Steagall, the unfettered investment instruments that were being developed by our financial institutions. But I didn't.

Clinton and the president-elect moved their way through the Capitol on their way to the outdoor grandstand. The Clintons were ceremoniously seated, effectively passing the torch to the new guy and marking the end of an era. Now the forty-third President of the United States was walking down the steps past the applause and handshakes from the well-wishers.

"And see that guy." Fallon pointed to the newly elected president on the TV screen. "You don't think he's going to cut into the regulations that are left, or at least, turn his back on enforcing them? He's a Republican, for god sake. And look who controls the Congress—Republicans." She took a drink of her beer. "And who controls all of them? The money, Jude, the money."

"What can we do about that?" I thought about Vietnam, the conviction that we could and should do something about the injustice of it . . . and we did.

"You have to be kidding. There's nothing *we* can do."

I felt a hollowness in my stomach. She was right, but what was I going to do, arrange a protest?

"There's always the next election."

"Jude, you are so naive. It won't matter. The money that owns the Republicans owns the other party too. This is no longer the country of *We the People*. The corporations own the government. The financial institutions own the government. Special interests with lots of bucks." She took the last bite of her sandwich and delicately licked away the dab of mayonnaise left on her fingers.

"We still have laws . . . to keep them in check." My voice sounded empty even to me. What had happened to that guy with the megaphone on the steps of Jesse Hall?

"Ha, who makes the laws? Congress."

The new president had taken the oath of office and was moving to the podium to deliver his inaugural address. The Republicans already controlled Congress. Where were the checks and balances?

"Thank god there's the Supreme Court."

"Really? Look at the composition of the court. This guy," she said, pointing again to the new president on the TV, "is going to have the best opportunity in thirty years to change that. It's over, Jude. Keep your nose clean. Don't make any waves. Make as much money as you can and live the good life." She sat back on the sofa and finished the last of her beer. Her voice had taken on an edge I hadn't heard before. When had Fallon become so hardened?

"I've tried that, Fallon. It hasn't worked out so great, as you so aptly pointed out. And I don't want a small group of wealthy and powerful people controlling the rest of my life. If it's come to that, I'll find another place to live." It was the first time in a very long while that I had given thought to escaping, leaving it all behind to make a new life somewhere far away.

"Oh, yeah, and just where will that be? Sudan? These guys are global, and they are gaining control of every place in the world where the word 'economy' has some meaning. They got their way in South America and Southeast Asia. At least in the U.S. you don't have the secret police pulling you out of your house in the middle of the night. You've been through that. You want some more?"

I shook my head, thinking again of that night in Buenos Aires. Fallon had a point—was there any country I could live in that didn't have negatives just as bad as, if not worse than, the United States? I stared at the TV. Maybe the only choice left was a distant island, hard to get to, but self-sustaining; somewhere that hadn't been caught up in the global economy. Where on earth was that?

"The American people elected this guy because they were worried that government was taking over their lives," I said. "You know, the government is too damn big. Taxes are too high." I thought about my grandfather. Americans today were nothing like him. His values were different; they made more sense. "Americans these days refuse to recognize that it takes government institutions and money to run a country as complex as ours. It's not like this is still the unexplored country of rugged individualism."

The majority of people who voted this guy into office had little to gain from his election and a lot to lose. The middle-class and the under-privileged, even the NASCAR set, with their American flags all over the place and their junk food and big TVs, would likely be worse off as a result of Republican economic policies. Yet it was their votes that put him in office. It was government—not the private sector—that invested in things that didn't turn a quick profit but were required to support a functioning society and economy for all the citizens. And it was taxes that paid for them. Why couldn't they see that?

"Remember, Jude, democracy assumes an educated electorate. If people can't understand the issues and aren't capable of reaching intelligent decisions, you can make them believe anything." She munched on an olive that she had speared from the tray with a toothpick. "Make the average Joe hate the government; tell them to go out and buy, and give them more credit to consume more stuff. De-fund public education; dumb us down even further. Make college so expensive only the wealthy can afford it. The corporations already own the news media, so they can give us the headlines of their choosing and distractions to cover up what's really going on."

The new President of the United States was in the middle of his inaugural address.

"Jesus, Fallon, you're depressing the hell out of me. We can't just give up."

"There is no *we*. I've resigned myself to the situation, and you'd better stay out of their way, too, if you know what's good for you. But there is something you can do. Go buy a new car—that Z is getting pretty old. Enjoy Lex; she'll be leaving for college before you know it. And do what I do when I get in your state of mind."

"What's that?"

"Get laid."

39

Present Time
Paros, Greece

A SMALL SINGLE-ENGINE plane flew overhead just as the boat blew its horn, signaling its departure from Parakia. Startled, I dropped my cigarette into the water below. Shit! No time to light another one. I watched the plane continue out to sea before I went back downstairs. The woman who was seated next to me had either gotten off the ferry or found another seat. I couldn't blame her. She probably thought I was just another American on drugs, what with my bad dreams and tears. But that meant I had the rest of the trip to Amorgos by myself.

The sounds of police car sirens began blaring loudly outside the ferry, echoing through the narrow streets of Parakia. My body shuddered, and the memory gripped me, even in the security of the *Albion* and the serenity of the Greek islands.

It was a Tuesday I will never forget. Marie Turbeau and I were getting ready for an Open Markets meeting of the Fed later that week when Josh Williams anxiously burst into my office without knocking. We had to turn on the TV in my office, he insisted—a plane had just hit one of the World Trade Center towers.

Reluctantly I agreed to the interruption, but once we—the three of us, along with a host of other Fed employees who had heard the news and rushed into my office to watch it on TV—saw the replay of the first plane knifing through the building, or the flames from the second one exploding out like hot breath from the South Tower, or the rattled windows of the Federal Reserve when another airliner dove mercilessly into the Pentagon . . . or finally when we watched the two towers crumble beneath their own weight, crushing the thousands of souls that would not be home for dinner, we knew there would be no returning to our work that day, or to business as usual in the days and weeks that followed.

I remembered thinking that day that we were at war—the first real war since Vietnam. My grandparents and my mother had told me their personal stories about where they were when they heard the news of Pearl Harbor. We knew who attacked us then, and we knew who our enemies were. But it took us a while to figure out who attacked us this time—the new bogeyman.

I looked out the window of the *Albion*. We were now well away from the dock and moving out of the harbor and into open sea. I picked up *Guns, Germs and Steel* once again, but turned back to look out the window at the smoke starting to rise again above Parakia. I guess they didn't put out the fire after all.

September 11 had shaken me to my core; this was much worse than the fear of being drafted and sent to Vietnam to die in the jungle. Like the war in Vietnam, flying commercial airliners into buildings was no game—not like the chess being played at the White House or on Capitol Hill, or even at the Fed for that matter. Thousands of people were killed by one single event, as two giant symbols of American economic and military power collapsed with people inside. We were all scared and no longer confident of our power, superiority or safety, much less our future.

While many thought 9/11 caused the economy to enter a recession, we at the Fed knew the economy had already contracted for the first three quarters of the year. The dot-com bubble had already burst, and our monetary policy during the first half of the year eased credit to stimulate demand, but such policies took many months to ripple through the economy. When 9/11 hit, we took further immediate action to avert a financial panic and provide additional liquidity to the financial system. At my suggestion, the Fed enlisted the major central banks from around the world to shore up the dollar in global financial markets. Although the stock market reacted with a quick and substantial sell-off, our actions staved off a severe panic and the markets quickly recovered.

Fallon was the first one to tell me 9/11 would give the president the excuse to invade Afghanistan and Iraq. Now, even after our involvement in those wars was over, they still went on—just like they had before our invasions. I was reminded of something I read in a Joseph Kanon novel. It was a long time ago, but here it was rushing to the front of my thoughts as insightful as the first reading. "Be careful when you fight monsters. Be careful of what you become."

Fallon had also predicted the economic actions the new president would take with extraordinary prescience. There were few financial regulations remaining after Clinton's term, and the new president would look the other way when it came to enforcing those that were left. The mantra had gained control of the voices in Washington, D.C., including the voice of the Fed. Still, after the breakup of the Soviet Union and the fall of communism, America did not have a bogeyman—until September 11, 2001. Now we had a distraction big enough to dominate the news cycles, one that put fear in the hearts and minds of all of us. Maybe more important, that single event destroyed the belief that we carried with us out of the depths of the Great Depression—that the world would get better, that somehow we would eventually perfect all that ailed it. Now, all was complete. The sacking could begin.

I shifted in my seat and laid my book on the empty seat next to me. A year before the president was re-elected in 2004, Gillian and I separated. Shortly after his second inauguration we divorced. Funny, I hadn't connected those points before. But I had gotten to have the "normal" life I wanted—cutting grass on the weekends, going to Lex's dance recitals and soccer games, BBQs on the deck. It lasted sixteen years. Near the end, all I felt was its emptiness—a wasteland of dead love, arguments, and boring conversation. It was time to pick up the pieces and move on to a new life, which would be anything but normal.

40

May 2006
Washington D.C.

MY CELL PHONE rang. I pulled it from my suit coat hanging on the back of my office chair and looked at the number on the display. Now what does she want?

"Yes, Gillian."

"I have an important conference call late this afternoon. Can you pick up Lex from track practice?"

"What time does she finish?" I looked at my watch. It was 3:10 pm.

"Oh, come on, you can't even remember your daughter's schedule."

"If you remember, it's not my week to have Lex, and frankly, I have a lot to think about these days myself." A stack of reports sat on my desk; two computer screens both showed charts and graphs.

"Well, I can't help it I have to work."

"And I don't?"

She huffed. "You're just as self-centered as ever. I hope sometime in your life you realize it's not always about you. Can you pick her up or not?"

I stared out the window of my office, tuning her out. How much longer would I have to put up with these conversations?

"I asked you what time. Do you think you could just answer me without a lecture about my perceived personal failings? We don't live together anymore and you're not my friend, so I don't need to listen to you go off on me." I wondered why I hadn't been that direct sooner; we probably could have avoided a lot of the drama over the past few years.

"Five o'clock."

"I'll have her at my apartment. You can pick her up when you've finished."

"Can you bring her to my office? Your place is in the opposite direction."

"No. Why should I fight the traffic when my place is closer to her school?"

I hung up the phone, satisfied with myself for not giving in to Gillian's rant and standing my ground. How had I lived with this woman for so long and put up with her constant criticism? She insisted I was selfish and narcissistic. What about her? She got everything she wanted, including attention and understanding. All I asked for was a little appreciation for who I was and some occasional support when things got rough at work. As it turned out, that was way too much for me to expect.

I arrived at Lex's school about fifteen minutes before track practice was scheduled to end and began the long trek through the parking lot to the field. Most of the students had left for the day, but there were still many vehicles in the lot. Some had a driver sitting patiently inside—the parents who had come to pick up their kids. But I knew that most of the empty cars belonged to the students themselves. When I was in high school, we drove cars that were at least ten years old, many of them clunkers by today's standards. In this lot were late model Lexus's, Volvo's, and Beemer's, with only an occasional older model car. Lex would be driving in a couple of years, and I hadn't thought about what kind of vehicle I would buy her, if any. Here I was, still driving my old Z. I shook my head. Maybe I'd give her the Z and buy a new car for myself.

By the time I reached the track, Lex was standing in line with her teammates, getting ready to run the 100-meter hurdles. Tough race, I thought, as I took a seat on the metal bleachers.

I was happy Lex had finally found a sport she was committed to. All the sports she tried—soccer, gymnastics, softball—she quit after a year or two. It was the same thing with music—piano, guitar. Maybe she was too young. Finally she fell in love with the violin while trying various instruments at a weeklong music camp with her friends. She wasn't going to be a virtuoso, but she played it occasionally. She said it soothed her when she was stressed or upset. When she played her violin, hidden away in her bedroom, it was my clue to find out what was up.

Only a freshman in high school, Lex had already decided what she's going to be when she grows up—an author. But she loved painting too, so some days she was both an author and an artist, figuring out how she could live a life that let her do both. She'd written several short stories, was working on a novel, and occasionally painted several pictures in a single day. I did what I could to encourage her aspirations, discussing the stories she wrote and keeping her well supplied with a new Mac, painting easel, brushes, and paints. I took her aspirations seriously; they'd lasted for more than a year. Maybe she really had found her calling.

The runners were just setting up in their starting blocks for the race when a dog ran onto the track and up to the runners, it's tail wagging. The dog's owner jumped from the bleachers and ran out to the track to retrieve her animal.

Lex was now a full-fledged teenager, complete with mood swings and insistence on her independence. At least we still spent time together like we did when she was younger, watching and discussing the news over dinner. Today her knowledge of current events far outstripped the average adult in this country; that made me very proud.

One of the mothers and her young son scooted past me in the bleachers just as the runners were returning to their starting blocks. I moved my legs to the side to let them pass. She smiled as she dragged the boy past me. Lex was in the third lane and was shaking her arms, trying to keep herself loose. They took their starting positions again. The pistol sounded and the runners raced down the track, approaching the first hurdle.

I knew that deep down Lex had always hated school, maybe because she had been frequently ostracized over the years by her classmates, and had very few real friends. Who knew why; maybe she was too brainy or just too independent. And when those few friends eventually moved away, as they typically did in Washington, I could feel her sadness that would last for months.

I remembered how it felt when I was shunned in school, called a bastard; it's a feeling that stays with you your entire life. It caused Lex to delve inward just as it had me. I kept telling myself in the long term that a self-reflective bent would serve her well. But regardless of her attitude toward school, she understood that to get into Princeton and subsequently into graduate school at Oxford—both schools of her choice—she needed top-notch grades. She was determined and had a lot of practical and common sense and, most of all, an innate ability to figure things out, including how to ace her classes. I wasn't sure I had it in me to be a dad, but if I could have guaranteed this kind of turnout, maybe I would have taken the leap a lot sooner.

Lex came in third in the scrimmage race. She saw me when she finished and came running up to me.

"Where's Mom?" she said, giving me a quick hug.

"Had a conference call."

She rolled her eyes. "That's all she cares about—her job."

"That's not true, Lex." We had had this conversation before. According to the divorce decree, I couldn't say anything negative about Gillian to her. So I lied. We got her stuff into the car and drove to my apartment.

We were halfway home when I noticed it. One of the cars parked in Lex's school parking lot—or one that looked just like it—was just behind me. Why should that be strange? Other kids that went to the same school probably lived in Chevy Chase; it probably wasn't the same car anyway. I was reminded of Buenos Aires with Vasco, being chased by a little green Falcon. I pulled into the driveway of my condo and looked through the rear view mirror. The car drove by, but slowly.

"Any of your teammates' parents drive a silver BMW?"

"Not that I can think of. Why?"

"Just curious. Hungry?" I asked as we were hiking up the stairs to the main floor of the condo.

"Starved. Whatcha got?" She slid her backpack to its familiar home in the corner next to the kitchen refrigerator.

"Oranges, plums, yogurt . . . Cheezits." Lex opened the refrigerator door and looked inside. "Want a sandwich?" I suggested.

"Muenster?"

"I think so. You make it."

This was her favorite—Muenster cheese on buttered bread broiled in the oven. She turned the oven to broil. I remembered the eight-year-old who always delighted in eating "monster cheese."

"How did I look, you know, at track?"

To me, this was akin to asking if her jeans made her look fat. I chose my words carefully. "I'm not a track guy, but it looks like you need a little more height and extension on the hurdles."

"Dad, the coach says not to worry about that yet. You need to be able to jump in control before you work on your extension." She gave me one of those teenage looks, the ones that mean, you know, how could you

233

be so stupid? I knew this was a fruitless discussion. God forbid I should disagree with the guru of track.

"That makes sense." The best part about these kinds of discussions was that she always considered my input later, while making her own decisions. It was a pattern she had developed early on.

"When's Mom picking me up?"

"I assume when she gets done with work."

"Yeah, when's that?" She helped herself to a plate and napkin, well acquainted with my bachelor-pad kitchen.

"She said her con call would probably go until 5:00 or a little later. Thirty minutes to get here when she's done unless traffic is bad."

"Hmm, so six."

"That's a good guess." I sat at the kitchen counter and watched her, wondering what it would be like if she lived with me full-time instead of this back-and-forth nonsense the divorce lawyers cooked up.

"What's on TV?"

"News. Want to watch it?"

"Sure. How about *Hardball*?" It had become her favorite news program and told me a lot about her political persuasion.

Lex put her sandwich in the oven while I turned on the TV and poured myself a glass of Chardonnay.

"How's school?"

"As."

Did she think that was all I cared about? "That's good. What else?"

"Dad, I don't want to talk about it."

"Okay," I said matter-of-factly. It was such a simple tactic; I couldn't believe how well it worked. Let them know you're interested, but just don't push; they'll tell you everything you want—or need—to know in their own time.

We both sat silently watching *Hardball* from the island counter. Chris Matthews was in attack mode, as he often was. Lex got up, pulled her toasted cheese from the oven, and slid the two slices onto a plate.

I didn't have to wait long. After only two bites, she started. "Alisa's a real bitch."

Bingo! "Alisa again, what this time?"

"She's got Cassy making fun of me too. They're calling me a nerd."

"Why, because you make good grades?"

"Because I hang around with Brent."

I tried to place the kid but drew a blank. "Is he . . . a nerd?"

"Dad, Alisa thinks anyone who doesn't go along with what she wants to do is a nerd."

"And what do you think?"

"I think that's bullshit."

I flinched. "I hope you don't cuss at school, or around your mother."

"Don't worry, Dad, I know when I can and can't."

"Good." Apparently, she had told me all I needed to know; it was up to me to figure out what it all meant.

Lex had finished her toasted cheese and was eating an orange when the buzzer rang.

"Is she ready?" her mother snapped over the intercom.

I looked at Lex. She vaulted off the stool and grabbed her backpack popping the last of the orange into her mouth.

"Love you, Dad."

I gave her a hug. I could smell the fresh orange and the toasted cheese and a bit of the track in her hair.

"Love you too, Lex. See you next week."

These days when Gillian needed a favor were a huge bonus for me. I just had to be careful never to let her know.

41

July 2006

THE REAL ESTATE market—a pretty good indicator of just how robust the American economy was—had begun to contract during the long, hot summer, and D.C. was starting to feel the pressure. The President of the New York Federal Reserve Bank was called to Capitol Hill to give testimony on the economic impact of the looming housing crisis. Marie and I accompanied him, since we had led his team in analyzing the most recent housing data and impact on the economy. Residential real estate had definitely slowed in most major metropolitan cities in the country, and the inventory of unsold units was growing. Permits for new construction were down, but the demand for rental units was increasing. The only good news in the housing market was that demand for commercial properties was on the uptick.

The New York Fed President gave testimony to the House first and finished before lunch. Marie offered to take him back to the office until he testified before the Senate committee later in the day. I told them to go on without me; I'd be back in an hour.

Walking out the west doors of the Capitol, I planned to sit on a step in the sunshine and have a smoke before I went for a walk along the Mall. It wasn't that I was fat, but I did think that loosing five pounds would make buttoning my suit pants a little easier. As I lit up I noticed an attractive, slender woman leaning up against a column base, also taking a smoke break. It was the familiar color of her auburn hair that drew my attention. Instead of sitting, I casually strolled toward her. Sasha, could it be? It had

236

been so many years since I last saw her. I moved closer, taking another drag on my smoke. She turned to look at me. I could see her struggling for recognition, then awareness.

"Hello, Sasha. What are you doing on the Hill? The Clinton thing was over years ago," I said, referring to her frequent by-lines in the *Washington Post* in the late '90s.

"I'll be damned. Jude Anders. Where have you been hiding all these years?" Her voice was calm with overtones of sarcasm.

"I quit hiding when the draft was over. But you haven't answered my question."

Sasha gave me that same flirtatious smile that immediately brought back the memories of her at college. She was still quite fetching, especially with her short auburn hair and green eyes. She obviously worked out.

"What are you, a lawyer now?" This time her tone was almost mocking.

"No. Are you still a reporter? I haven't seen your name in print for years."

She dropped her cigarette on the stone and crushed it with the ball of her high-heeled shoe, reached into the bag draped over her shoulder and pulled out another. I moved next to her with my lighter in hand.

"Here." I struck the wheel on my Zippo.

"That looks familiar. Same one?"

"The same, Sash. Quality products don't wear out if you take care of them." She hadn't worn out either for a woman in her fifties. "Seriously, what are you doing up here on the Hill?"

"What most people do here—lobbying."

I wondered why I had never run into her before. D.C. really wasn't that big, and government, well, sometimes it felt a like fishbowl, all the same faces all the time. "Lobbying, now that's a change from reporting. For whom?"

"The Chamber of Commerce. And you, what are you doing here?"

I wanted to say, "Leading the revolution against the insanity of our time," but of course, I wasn't. "Assisting with testimony to the House this morning."

"Really? Covering what?"

"Recession, depression, bubbles, downturns, cycles. The usual economic du jour."

"So you followed your career in economics?"

"More or less. I'm surprised you remembered. I work for the Federal Reserve."

"Now that's cool. What do you do for them?"

"Economic analysis."

"Sounds important." Her voice was sensual, almost flirtatious. I wondered if she talked to her male clients at the Chamber in the same way. Same old Sasha; I'd bet she could turn an economic hearing into something sexy and exciting.

"In some ways."

Sasha smiled. "So how long have you been in D. C.?"

"Since 1972." It felt like forever. "And you?"

"About eight and a half years.

"I saw your name on the by-lines of the *Post*. How did you end up here?"

"That's a long story, Jude. Listen, the hearings resume in fifteen minutes, and I need to get back in there." She pointed to the Capitol, then reached into her bag and pulled out a business card. "This seems weird, a long way from our protest days, but here's my card. I'd really like to get together and catch up"

"Me too. It's been a long time."

I pulled my business card out of my wallet and handed it to her. "Lunch later this week?"

"As long as you're flexible on time. You know, these hearing times are unpredictable."

"Sure no problem. I'll call you."

"Sounds good," she said, walking away toward the capitol while finishing the remainder of her cigarette.

I watched her walk back toward the Capitol building. For a minute we were back on the steps of Jesse Hall. This would definitely not be one of those "let's do lunch sometime" encounters that never happen. I should have asked her if she was seeing someone; I knew what I wanted her answer to be.

IT HAD BEEN a long time since I had dated; after my divorce with Gillian I had lost interest in pursuing another relationship. Falling in love had taken me a long time, and when it gradually faded away I quit believing it would ever happen again. Those last few years with Gil were tortuous, filled with fights and boredom and a sick feeling in my gut as I watched the life we had built together come unglued. I'm sure my growing cynicism about American politics had spread to my views on the viability of lasting, loving relationships, for better or worse. I thought I could be content with my daughter and my friendships with Anton and Fallon. But Sasha had been a person who appealed to me in college; she was not only attractive but also smart and passionate. If there was to be another relationship in my life, she would certainly be a strong candidate.

Two days later when I called her for that lunch, I felt like a pimply-faced teenager asking for his first date. When she declined, citing her busy work schedule, I might as well have just been turned down by the popular girl in high school; the pain of the rejection was so swift. Her suggestion for dinner Friday night instead not only surprised me, I was sure it saved me from the hermit life I figured I was destined to lead from now on.

Right up to Friday night I couldn't take my mind off her. Even Marie had asked me why I seemed in a good mood. By the time I was ready to pick up Sasha for dinner, I noticed I had burned through two packs of cigarettes in two days—at least one pack more than I normally smoked.

Even with a last-minute frenzy around wearing a tie, I arrived at Sasha's apartment right on time; I remembered the rules about not keeping a woman waiting. She wore a short black cocktail dress with a low back and a delicate strand of pearls around her neck—a classic look that was always in style, especially in D.C. Her deep auburn hair was cut short in the back with a side-swept bang across her forehead.

"Wow, Sash, you look stunning." She had looked great in her suit that afternoon; I have to say I wasn't expecting her to go all out, but I was pleased just the same.

"Thank you. You act surprised."

"No, no, it's just that I've never seen you in a dress before. When we were in college you just wore jeans. I mean you wore a top, too."

Sasha laughed.

"And then at the Capitol, you wore a pant suit."

"I understood what you meant. If I remember, I liked halter-tops back then. It just sounds funny now. You look dapper too—a black silk T-shirt with the sports coat, Calvin Klein I bet." She patted the lapels of my coat; I could smell perfume. "It's a nice change from the white shirts and rep ties that blanket D.C. This look fits the Jude Anders I remember from college. By the way, where are we going for dinner?"

"It's a cozy place I haven't been to in years—a good place to get reacquainted."

Traffic was heavy, especially as we entered Georgetown where the college kids were out to party. I made a right turn off the main drag. The 1789 was a small place in a residential section of Georgetown, complete with valet parking. After I was promoted to junior economist at the IMF I could afford to take my dates out for a nice dinner. The 1789 always helped me score points on the first date. We pulled to the valet stand and made our way up the walk to the restaurant, talking about those pivotal years—'69, '70—and the people we knew in common back then.

"Before I left for Toronto, Paul and I went out one night for a couple of beers," I told her, recalling a story I hadn't given thought to in decades. "After my pre-induction physical, I tipped him off that he might be able to fail the physical by flunking the hearing test. It turns out that's what he did. He was re-tested several times and managed to fail the test the same way each time. Amazing."

"Well, I haven't seen or talked with Bill or Doug since I graduated," Sasha said, ticking through the list of our friends. "I talked with Mark once after our graduation, and heard he went on to grad school after he found out his lottery number was high enough not to be drafted. Ah, those were the good old days. We were all on a mission to end the Vietnam War."

"Or as a friend of mine once told me, a mission to end the draft."

She stopped and grabbed my arm just outside the door to the restaurant. "But, Jude, we shut down the university. That was quite the coup, and you led it."

"And what good did it do? The war went on for years." I remembered Bill's penchant for a violent solution; maybe he was right.

"I guess we were a bit idealistic. Certainly we were naïve." I could hear the slightest edge of cynicism in her voice.

"Yeah, maybe so."

"But those days are gone." She sighed. "Sometimes I miss them, especially when compared to how jaded everyone is these days. Especially here in D.C."

I hadn't really thought about it in quite those terms. Even with the intractable positions held by the politicians at that time to keep the war going, we still believed we had the power to bring it to an end. And when it did end, finally, we believed that our concerted, consistent pressure was the cause of its demise. Did we really help to end the war? Was it my age, or working and living in D.C. that made me doubt it now?

We took our table along the far wall of the main room. The lights were dim but bright enough to cast Sasha's face in a warm glow. I wondered why I never tried going out with her in college—maybe I thought I couldn't compete with her other lovers, who knows? But here I was staring at her delicate nose with soft angles that blended in with her high cheekbones. And those amazing deep-set green eyes. She looked fantastic; it hardly seemed as though thirty-five years had passed. She was conscious of my staring, and it made me feel a little awkward. But I couldn't stop looking at her face. She seemed to enjoy it.

"How did you end up as a lobbyist?"

She was about to answer when our waiter ask if we wanted a cocktail.

"I'll have a Cosmo." Sasha answered in a way that said it was what she normally drank.

"Macallan rocks, two cubes for me. Thank you." After all our nights out, Anton had finally gotten me into single malt scotch on the rocks.

"Will you be having wine with your dinner tonight?" the waiter asked.

"Yes, we will." The waiter handed me a wine list that was three times as thick as the menus on the table and left to place our drink orders.

"Anyway, I thought you majored in psychology in college. How did you get into the newspaper business?"

"I did major in psych, and when I graduated, I went to work for Youth Services, counseling disturbed kids. At first it was challenging and I loved it. But then I started getting some really tough cases. There were kids who were badly abused physically and sexually. A number of them were so fucked up they ended up in a residential treatment center. After that there was nothing anyone could do for them. They went deeper into their psychosis and were gone—just gone." She paused. "After two years or so I decided I needed a different path. There weren't many options available back then in my field. There are a lot more choices available today. Hell, now I could go to work for a large corporation working in their human resources department."

"Would you want to do that?"

"Not really." She smiled. Her fingers played idly with the strand of pearls at her neck. So Washington, those pearls, and yet I could see that leather halter-top she used to wear plain as day.

The waiter gently set our cocktails on the pewter plates that sat in front of us and departed. Sasha picked up her Cosmo martini glass and lifted it toward me. "To reunions."

"And fond memories," I toasted back and sipped my scotch. Her bright green eyes sparkled in the soft light of the room just above the rim of her glass. "So what did you decide to do?"

"Oh, right," she said, setting her glass on the plate. "I decided to go to journalism school. It would take another two years, but I had gotten over being sick of school. I had enough money to do it with the help of some student loans. I even thought that my psychology degree would make me a better interviewer."

"You mean interrogator, don't you?"

"Journalism has kind of turned into that, hasn't it?" It was more of a statement than a question. I could tell it wasn't the first time she had considered it. "If you think about it, that 'in your face' style of questioning we use today may have started with Watergate."

"That could be true." I hadn't thought about that before, but it made some sense. I watched as she delicately sipped the Cosmo, her lip poised gracefully on the edge of the martini glass. "I bet you had to do time in some small towns before getting the gig at the *Washington Post*. That's a big fish to land, isn't it?"

"Exactly right. I worked for the *Journal Star* in Peoria for a few years. Later I got a job with the *Sun Times* in Chicago where I got my start in the gossip column business—cheesy local stuff, mainly with up-and-comers in Chicago society. Do you know what it's like to follow the little scandals of the rich and famous?" She made a face, as though she had just smelled bad milk. "I was good at it, but it really got old. Then about ten years ago I met this guy at a newspaper editors and writers conference in Chicago. We had an interesting night together," she said with a mischievous eye. "Turns out he was an editor with the *Post*. We had an occasional fling for a year or so when he came to Chicago on business. Then one day I got a call from him, wanting to know if I would consider a job in D.C. Frankly, I thought he just wanted a mistress in town."

"Is that what he wanted?" I recalled the days at the university. There were plenty of rumors about her prowess in the sack back then, and most us believed them. But that was the era of free love. Did she just continue on while the rest of us settled into a more conventional lifestyle?

Sasha took another sip of her Cosmo. "I don't know, maybe. I never found out. But the paper offered me the job and I needed a change, so I took it. At least I was moving out of gossip although I had to start on the entertainment pages before I got into real news, like the Clinton stuff. Getting into D.C. and the *Post*—that was a good change and one that would only help my resume."

"What do you mean, you never found out? What happened?"

"Nothing ever happened." She shrugged. "We saw each other in the office occasionally, but never even went to lunch. I think he got cold feet." She leaned toward me and spoke softly. "Allegedly, his wife is a real bitch."

I imagined how good a mistress Sasha would be. Certainly there were plenty of men, and men with money and power, who would like to have her on the string. "So I guess somewhere along the way, a plum job at the *Post* turned into a job with the Chamber?"

"I met this guy at a charity ball here in D.C. about a year ago. Jesus, I'm starting to sound like a hooker." She laughed, nibbling ever so slightly on the swizzle stick from her cocktail. "Anyway he was interesting, the CEO of some company in New York. I told him I was sick of being a news reporter. He said he knew some people that might be interested in a person with my skills. I gave him my business card. Two weeks later I got a call from the Chamber. The rest is history."

Sasha took another sip and set her drink back on the plate. She reached forward and touched the back of my left hand with her slender fingers. "Enough of me, Jude. How did you get here?"

I could feel her warmth enter my hand and run up my arm. My body tingled. I took a drink of my scotch and told her the tale of my days in Toronto and hanging out with Anton. Anton led to my IMF stories about Chile and Argentina.

"You're joking. You were really in Buenos Aires during the coup?" she asked wide-eyed.

"No, not during the coup; a little over two years after the coup. But it was still a military state at the time. Army, security forces, military trucks and jeeps, and little green Ford Falcons that came to take people away in the dead of night."

"And you were thrown into jail and interrogated?"

"I wasn't in jail long enough for them to put me under the rack. The CIA bailed me out the day after my arrest. But I can tell you, I was scared shitless."

"CIA!"

"Shhh," I said, pushing the palms of my hands down toward the table. I was reminded suddenly of Vasco doing the same thing the afternoon I met him at the hotel bar. "Not so loud."

"Sorry." We both looked around at the tables nearest ours. "Really?"

"Yes, Sash, really." Here I was recanting a story from over twenty-five years ago—one I was reminded to forget by a CIA operative. At least that's what I thought he was. And I hated to even think it, but it appeared I had just succeeded at using a terrible experience to score a point with a date.

"Wow. That would make a great story."

"Buenos Aires?"

"Sure, what a thriller. A paper could break it up over multiple weeks, you know, installments. It might even be a book or a novel."

The thought was intriguing, but what would that do to Fallon, Anton, or the former Deputy Director of the IMF? I certainly didn't need to drag them into the middle of the Dirty War scandal that went on in Argentina.

"No, thanks," I told her, shaking my head. "Some things need to remain quiet. Too many people are involved who could get hurt, even if I made them fictional characters. Not only that, a story like that might not help my career with the Fed much." I wondered what would have happened to me if I had told the story when I got back from Argentina. Up to now no one knew about Vasco's story or the troop trucks at the airport dragging bodies into the C-130—not Fallon, or Gillian; not even Anton. It was so long ago. Who would have believed me back then anyway?

"So, I guess the Jude Anders I knew hasn't changed that much." She leaned back in her chair and gazed at me over the rim of her glass.

"What do you mean?"

"Still a little too cautious, my friend."

I smiled. She was obviously referring to my reluctance to implement Plan B after Cambodia and Kent State. "And I thought I was just getting older." I raised my glass to her in a slight toast. But maybe she was right; maybe I had been too cautious most of my life.

"Okay, so you came back from Argentina. Then what did you do?"

"I quit my job at the IMF and went to work for the Fed."

"Why did you quit the IMF? I hear it's hard to get hired there."

Not when you have connections, I thought to myself. Anton had all but admitted that Jack had pulled strings to get me hired. "There was a lot shit that went on there. Things I didn't like. You could feel Nixon and his cronies' hands on many deals going on between the Fund and other countries. The U.S. government, the banks, and a number of corporations were manipulating the IMF to affect the politics and economies in other countries. My trip to Buenos Aires brought that home firsthand. I didn't want to be a part of it." So the scotch may have loosened my tongue a little, but I didn't think there was any harm in sharing my feelings about my work. After all, this was Sasha, my comrade-in-arms, agitator and protestor extraordinaire.

"That's also part of the Jude Anders I used to know—your penchant for doing the right thing. So how are you different?"

"Did I say I was?" I swirled the ice cubes in my glass.

"I thought you did when we first met at the Capitol."

I traced our conversation that morning, but couldn't remember saying that. Maybe Sasha just thought I was different.

"Hmm, well if I said that, I must have meant going from being a hippie to part of the establishment." I took another drink.

"But that's happened to all of us, Jude. Well, maybe a few of us dropped out permanently. But you can't live comfortably in this society without having a real job. It's not like the '60s and '70s when it took virtually nothing to live on."

"I guess you're right. It's just that sometimes I feel that I sold out. Here I am in D.C., well off, working for the most powerful economic institution in the world, surrounded by all the pressure and machinations of the leisure class. Sometimes I think I should have used my education to help people instead." I thought again of Vasco and Calida, and her disappeared boyfriend Roberto, caught by the junta in Chile.

"You don't think you're helping people with the work you do?" Her fingers were at her throat again, twisting that pearl necklace. I had to pull my gaze away, wanting to linger at her long white neck but instead looked straight into her eyes.

"Not when I see what we did in Chile, Argentina, Indonesia, and other countries around the world. Even here, I suspect we're doing more to protect the wealthy than the people who really need a break. I'd like to see a little economic justice for a change."

We sat there silently, finishing our drinks. The waiter came back to the table to take our orders. While I was confirming my wine selection, Sasha took our conversation in another direction.

"Okay, Jude. Tell me about your love life." The waiter took his cue and hurried off, tossing a wink at me over his shoulder.

"That's a long story. It's your turn." Was I ready to talk about Gillian? About Lex? I wasn't so sure. But she seemed more than willing to continue talking.

"Well, there's not much to tell I guess. I've had a number of lovers. No different than the good old college days. You remember how it was then. And I've had a couple of long-term relationships. You know, living together. One for three years, another for a year and a half."

"Never married?"

Sasha laughed. "I never believed in it."

"Never?" She was as rare as some stone-age bird in D.C.; a woman who had heeded the call of liberated free love in the '60s and never looked back. God, I was so happy to have found her again.

"It's funny you bring that up. I have thought about it lately. Maybe it's something I've missed, but it's little late for that now."

"What do you mean, too late?"

"In case you hadn't noticed, I'm—that is *we're*—old."

"My dear, Sasha, the way you look, I think you have a lot of good years ahead of you."

She smiled as she looked into my eyes and put her hand on top of mine again. "How about you. Were you . . . or are you married?"

"Was. For sixteen years." Could she really think I was still married and only out with her for a fling? I wondered about her clients at the Chamber; most were probably married.

"What happened?"

"The usual. It was good to start with when the love thing was strong. Then the chemistry gradually faded. That was okay; I never thought the chemistry was meant to last anyway." I poured the last of my drink down my throat. Even now, talking about it was painful. "She believed it should last forever. It died for her, too. After the chemistry was gone, I guess we didn't have enough to keep us together."

"Does she live here, in D.C?"

"Yes, in Alexandria. She also has a job with a lobbying firm."

"Ha, ha. And kids?"

"One. A fourteen-year-old girl. Elexus. She goes by Lex."

"Wow. I really like that name. Does it have a meaning?"

"I think it is Latin for 'outside the law" or 'truth teller'—something like that."

"Still, you a father. It's hard to imagine you . . . then, I guess there's a lot about you I don't know. Does she live with her mother?"

"Fifty/fifty. Two weeks on, two weeks off. A textbook divorce."

"Well, I hope Lex has her father's looks."

I smiled. "Her genes definitely come from my side of the family; she looks a lot like my mother."

"Is she with her mother tonight?" Sasha looked up at me through lowered lashes.

"We did the hand-off today, every other Friday. How about you? Are you dating anyone?"

"Umm, no one special right now. A date now and again. You?"

I suppose I could make up a story. What would she think of me if she knew the truth? Only one way to find out. "I haven't had a date in over a year."

The waiter delivered our dinner salads and meticulously ground pepper across the top of them. After he decanted and poured the wine, we had another toast.

"To a renewed friendship," Sasha said.

"Thank you." I looked into those eyes again. "That means a lot to me."

We ate our salads and then dinner, remembering the days of the big protests back in April and May of 1970, and talked about Lex and some of the details of our jobs. By the time we ordered coffee after lingering over a shared dessert, it was close to midnight. The restaurant had grown quiet with only a few couples left, deep in conversation just like we were. When we finally stood, she let me put her wrap over her shoulders and linger there for just a moment. But it wasn't until we were halfway back to her apartment when she asked, "Where do you live?"

"I have a townhouse in Chevy Chase."

"I'd like to see it."

"I think we can arrange that sometime." I kept my eyes on the road, although I could tell she was edging closer to me.

"How about now, Jude?"

"Tonight? It's getting pretty late," I said, having foolishly not picked up on the signals for where this might be headed.

"It's Friday. Do you have to work tomorrow?"

"No. And you?" I asked, warming up to the idea.

"I'm done for the weekend. Remember the old days? We stayed up late a lot."

"Yeah, but we were tripping then."

We both laughed as I quickly made a left turn onto Connecticut Avenue to make our way to Chevy Chase. In less than twenty minutes we pulled into the driveway of my condo.

"Well, here it is," I said as I automatically reached to turn on the lights to the foyer. But they were already on. Did I leave them on? As we climbed the stairs to the living area above the garages on the ground level I mentally retraced my steps before I left to pick up Sasha earlier that evening.

"This is beautiful, Jude," Sasha said as we reached the top. "It's a lot bigger than the postage stamp I live in. How long have you lived here?"

"I bought it after the divorce. Can I make you a drink?" I gently lifted her wrap from her shoulders, standing as close to her as I dared for a moment. After all these years . . .

"Sure, how about a martini? Do you have Bombay Sapphire?" She stepped back just enough to let me know I was on the right track.

"It's the house gin, Sash. I bet you expected the gin version of Ripple."

"Wow, I forgot about Ripple. What was the other swill we used to drink?"

"Thunderbird," I said, making my way to the kitchen.

"Yeah, that's it."

She had followed me into the kitchen and hovered next to me as I pulled the shaker and the liquor from the cabinet. "How do you want your martini? Extra dry, shaken, not stirred?"

"Yes, Mr. Bond. That will do nicely."

I shook and poured the martini with her standing next to me. She took a sip.

"Yummy," she said, as she set the glass on the counter and moved next to me.

We were inches apart and I could feel her warmth without her touching an inch of my body. She reached to the back of my head and gently drew me to her mouth—her lips to mine, moist, exploring every part of each other. I could smell her scent mixing with her perfume. I pulled her toned body closer, pressing my growing erection against her thighs, as my kisses moved irresistibly from her mouth to her neck. She pulled away and looked into my face.

"Jude, I always wondered—back then in the good old days—what you'd be like. But you never seemed interested. Finally, I think I'm going to find out."

42

I WOKE UP on Saturday morning alone in my bed. I could still smell Sasha on the sheets and pillows.

Did she leave? I looked over to the bathroom—empty.

I got up, put on pajama bottoms, and headed for the kitchen. I needed coffee. Sasha was in my silk robe, fiddling with the coffee maker and trying to figure out how to use it. In typical male fashion, I tried to help her.

"It's a Moka Brew, Sash. A little more complicated than your normal coffee maker. It steams the coffee."

"I expected something simpler; you're a guy." She kissed me gently. "Good morning, Mr. Anders. Sleep well?"

Her kiss gave me the same tingle as the night before. "Yes, I did. And you?"

She sighed. "As good as it gets. Now show me how to use this damn thing."

We laughed together as I showed her how to use the machine. Water here, coffee there, special filter. It was the perfect kitchen gadget for a guy, just complicated enough to make it interesting, and it made great coffee. When the coffee had brewed I poured it and set two cups on the counter.

"Well? What do you think?" I asked as she took her first sips.

"Robust, just like you said. I like it. Where do you get your coffee?"

"I order it. Whole beans. Grind them myself. But it's not just the coffee; it's the machine." I knew I sounded like a geek but the coffee maker was one of the few things I enjoyed anymore. Everything else about my life was work, work, work. Starting the day with this simple gizmo and a good cuppa joe gave me at least the illusion that I had some control over my life—something I rarely felt once my workday got going.

"Wow, isn't that a Pink Floyd song: *Welcome to the Machine*? She leaned over and kissed me again.

This time I pulled Sasha close to me and felt her body through my silk robe she had stolen from the bathroom. Her perfume had vanished. This smell was just Sasha. I licked her neck and ear with the tip of my tongue. I ran my hands down her back to her ass, and from her ass to the back of her thighs.

"You like what you feel, Jude?"

I kissed her gently, picked her up and carried her back to the bedroom.

I DROVE SASHA home on Sunday afternoon. We said goodbye with a long, lingering kiss on the doorstep to her apartment before we made plans for the following weekend. Maybe it was the entire weekend of unexpected sex or maybe the prospect of a relationship with Sasha that made it impossible for me to go back home. The noise and congestion of the city made me feel cramped; I wanted the wind through my hair and wide-open spaces. I maneuvered the Z out of D.C. traffic and opened it up to 80 mph as I climbed to the top of the Shenandoahs where I could feel the wind and look over the countryside. I was happy for the first time in years. I knew this feeling and had no faith that it would last. Still, maybe with Sasha there was something more than infatuation.

I was headed back down the mountain when my cell phone played its musical ringtone. I glanced at the screen. Anton. I hadn't heard from him in months. I quickly pulled into a scenic overlook and answered. He was boarding a plane for D.C. for meetings he had tomorrow. We agreed to meet at my condo when he finished, then figure out where to go to dinner.

AT 7:00 PM the next evening Anton called. He was on his way over to my place. Thirty minutes later I buzzed him in the front door from upstairs in the kitchen.

"Come on up."

Anton appeared at the top of the stairs as I was coming out of the kitchen. I shook his hand and gave him a big hug.

"Brother, how are you?" he asked as we made our way back into the kitchen.

"I'm good. Scotch?" I reached for two rocks glasses from the cabinet.

"A single malt, I presume?" He shrugged out of his Armani double-breasted suit coat and tossed it on the counter, undid his tie, and began rolling it neatly.

"Of course, Springbank though. The liquor store was out of Macallan."

"That will do nicely. Thank you."

"Nice tie. Mind if I see it?"

He carefully unrolled it. "Certainly, my man."

I handed him a scotch and took the tie with a quick dirty look. When would he stop this snobbish reference, even though I knew this was Anton's form of teasing? The tie was definitely not the typical ones seen in D.C.—little olive-green teardrops in burgundy and beige squares positioned diagonally. It reminded me of Cubism.

"It's been a long time, Anton. What have you been up to? Picking up the pieces of decimated economies?" I handed back his tie, and Anton pulled up the chair he always sat in when we talked in the kitchen around the counter island, again rolling his tie neatly into a ball and leaving it on the counter.

"Jude, I have told you before, I do not buy anything. I am merely a broker." He set his drink on the counter and picked up a watercolor Lex had finished before she left for her mother's.

"Isn't that the same thing as a lobbyist, especially in this town?"

"Why do you suspect that? Dirty business, really." There was a tone of resignation in his voice—a tone unfamiliar coming from Anton. He put Lex's picture back on the counter and gave me a blank look.

"Your trips to D.C., meetings with . . . well, who with this time?"

"I did meet with some people from your Chamber of Commerce today. That is hardly lobbying."

"The Chamber?" This was too much of a coincidence. First Sasha, and now Anton. I remembered that Anton had met with them at least one time before.

"Yes, Jude, the Chamber, as you call it. Some of my brokerage deals are with U.S. companies that are members." He took a sip of his scotch and set the glass back on the counter.

"Yeah, right. The Chamber is one of the biggest lobbying organizations in this country. That's their primary purpose. Surely you know that."

"Well, that may be, but I can assure you I am not in town to lobby anyone or have anyone lobby for me."

Of course, I didn't believe him. Anton was at the Chamber. That meant only one thing—he was cooking up a deal and he needed somebody's backing to pull it off, or someone needed him to pull it off. We'd been around this block many times before, with him never giving a straight answer.

"Okay, okay. I give." I pulled a cigarette from the pack on the counter and offered one to Anton. "How have you been?"

He waved his hand to decline. "How do you Americans put it: same shit, different day." He picked a piece of lint from his suit pants and dropped it into my ashtray. "Really, my life is quite boring most of the time."

"Unless you're dealing with revolutionaries in Argentina." I cocked an eyebrow at him. Sure, it had been a long time, decades even, but I couldn't let it go. There were some things you just didn't do to a friend. Anton crossed the line with me once. Would it happen again?

"That really is not fair, Jude, but, speaking of that, I do have something you will want to see."

Anton reached over for his suit coat and pulled out an envelope from its inner pocket. I was reminded of that night at the bar in the Mayflower Hotel before I left for Buenos Aires. Even from a distance I could see that it was sent airmail from outside the U.S. or Canada.

"Here," he said as he handed me the envelope.

I looked at the front—it was from the Argentina Ministry of Justice. What now? I looked back at Anton. His head was bowed and he slumped slightly. I pulled out the document. Although it was in Spanish, I got the gist of most of it: deceased, Vasco Madero, body found in mass gravesite, bullet to head. The memories of my last night with Vasco and Calida flashed through my mind.

"How did you get this?" I asked, tossing the letter across the counter back to Anton.

"Overall, the government in Argentina has been quite cooperative about these matters. I submitted an official inquiry on Vasco's whereabouts over a year ago. The government has thousands of such inquiries, as you might expect." He took a sip of his scotch. "I am sure it will take a long time to find all the missing people who have just disappeared. But Vasco has been found, and I wanted you to know what happened to him."

I felt my stomach knot. Every time I pretended that none of it had happened, that it was just a bad dream, I was reminded of the corporal reality. People got picked up and were dumped into prisons and left to rot, drugged and dumped in the Rio de La Plata, or they took a bullet to the head, like Vasco, and were tossed into a big hole with other nameless bodies. What the hell did Anton have to do with all that, anyway?

"And Calida? Did you inquire about her?"

"No, I did not know her, remember, nor her name. But look, Jude, I will show you how to make these type of inquiries on your own. Finding people is not that difficult." He took another sip of his scotch and looked at me curiously. "You could even find your father if you wanted to."

Anton's comment had come totally out of left field; talk about switching tracks. I stood at the counter island drinking my scotch. I was not certain I wanted to find out what happened to either Calida or my father—the news was more likely to be bad than good. Besides, I had lived my entire life without my father, not knowing who he was. And unlike Anton's father, he was not curious enough to ever find me. But there was one thing I had been curious about.

"Anton, what was in the envelope you had me hand-carry to Vasco?"

He seemed surprised by the question. Surely he knew I had always wondered.

"Just a detailed bill."

"Mind if I ask for what?"

"That was so long ago, I am not sure I remember."

Once again it was obvious I would not get an answer, so I made no attempt to follow up. Was that a guy thing or something between Anton and me—not pushing across some line the other had drawn in the sand? Anton was quick to change the subject, asking me how things were gong with my job.

"Really busy lately . . . with the housing crisis. This whole thing could blow up and send the economy into a tailspin."

"I recall reading about that back home. You may be correct, Jude. It is your job to bring your crisis to a . . . how do you say it? A soft landing."

"Trust me, I feel the pressure." I pulled a brick of cheddar and some goat cheese out of the fridge and rummaged in the cabinet for some crackers. Pressure was an understatement. Everyone was looking for an answer to prevent a collapse—the Fed Chairman and the Board of Governors, the president and Treasury Secretary, and every politician on the Hill.

"There are a number of players in the real estate market with a lot at stake—the banks, obviously, who hold the mortgages," he insisted.

"I'm not sure how many mortgage loans they actually hold." I put the cheese and crackers on a platter, including a knife for the cheese, and set it on the island, helping myself to a bite of cheddar.

"Another?" he asked, holding up the bottle of scotch. Anton walked to the refrigerator, got two cubes from the freezer, and refilled his glass.

"Sure, why not."

"Well, if not your banks, then who holds the mortgages?"

"It turns out the banks have been bundling them into pools of securities and then selling the pools to various investors. The banks don't keep the loans they write, they just service the loan payments." It was definitely not the way banks used to do business.

"Really? And who are these investors?"

I pushed the platter towards Anton. "Other banks, equity funds, pension funds, private investors. These mortgage-backed securities, as they call them, became very attractive during the rise in the housing market."

"Well, I hope you figure it out. If anyone can deal with a crisis, I am sure it is you."

I was glad Anton had confidence in me. I wondered if anyone could save the economy from this housing bubble. We were teetering on the edge of a severe collapse.

"Thanks, but I'm not that influential."

"But you are, Jude. Why else would people be watching you, or better put, watching how you conclude on certain issues." His spirits seemed to pick up. He sliced a hunk of cheddar and placed it on a cracker, nibbling on its edge.

"Watching me? What issues?" I stared at him. Anton was full of surprises tonight.

"Please do not be naïve. People know what you have been working on as senior economist for your Federal Reserve, and you have a very positive reputation after your suggestions following September 11. People know your advice was key to averting a crisis in the stock markets. I am quite certain there is a lot of money at stake in the current crisis. The outcome of your recommendations could significantly affect a number of balance sheets."

He was so matter-of-fact about it, I wasn't sure what shocked me more, what he was saying or that he acted as though it was no big deal, just business as usual.

"I'm not the goddamn Fed Chairman. I only do the analysis and make recommendations. There are plenty of instances where the boss or the Board of Governors has gone against them." I watched him spread goat cheese on a cracker like he didn't have a care in the world—so different from his mood just five minutes ago.

"I am certain that is correct. But your recommendations are not buried at the Federal Reserve. There are others who get their hands on them—congressmen, senators, and people at your Treasury, even the media. And in certain hands, your views could provide some very useful ammunition."

Sure, I had thought of that—a lesson learned from my early days at the IMF when Fallon and I had been used to support Nixon's agenda, American economic interests, and those of the big banks. Now I quickly traced the reports I had written during the past few months and who might have access to them. Maybe I needed to be more careful in how I stated my conclusions. Why was Anton telling me this? Why now?

"I'm not sure I can stop that."

"Of course, you cannot. And I am not suggesting that you begin modifying your positions based on what you think someone wants you to conclude. You would never be able to figure it out anyway." He paused. "Listen, Jude, there are many people with influence, different people with conflicting agendas. What I am telling you is that there are powerful men who are determined to get their way. And they are watching and manipulating. So be alert."

"Christ, Anton, it sounds like some hit man is going to take me out if I say or do the wrong thing." I laughed, but even I could hear the nervousness in my voice. Once again, Anton brought high intrigue with him. You'd think I'd be used to it by now.

"My friend, do not be paranoid over being shot or having your car explode when you turn on the ignition. Still, there are other ways someone could take you out of the game—eliminating your job position or transferring you somewhere else, discrediting you in some way, even an attractive job offer . . . or an attractive woman." He cocked an eyebrow ever so slightly.

Jim Jones had told me to keep my mouth shut and I had—until last night with Sasha. She had said I had a penchant for being overly cautious. Now I felt like I wasn't being cautious enough. Surely the CIA, NSA, or whatever national intelligence agency existed these days would no longer have an interest in what I saw that late afternoon in Buenos Aires. Most of what went on back then was already out in the open. So who might be watching me and why? Who had anything to lose from what I witnessed then . . . or the economic recommendations I make now?

"I'll keep my eyes open, okay, but I'm starving. You think we can get some real food?"

He grabbed his suit coat and slung it over his shoulder.

"Don't forget your tie."

"Keep it—not really my style anyway."

Anton and I drove to a trendy Southwest-style restaurant nearby. We had our scotch; now it was time for Margaritas. I was preoccupied by what Anton had told me and, frankly, a little paranoid. The light I didn't remember leaving on Friday night; the silver BMW following me home from Lex's school.

The hostess ushered us to the bar while we waited for a table. The place was loaded with Santa Fe Style—cow skulls, Indian blankets, what have you—even though that stuff had been passé for some years now.

"Hey, I wanted to tell you, I met this woman," I started. "Well, actually, she's someone I knew back in college. We had a fantastic weekend together, if you get my drift." I sipped my Margarita, licking some salt from the edge of the glass.

"I am sure it is past time for you to get laid, my friend. Did you know her from your economic classes at the university?"

"No, she majored in psychology. She was a protest organizer back then and was part of a group I hung with."

"So this is a rekindling of an old thing?" A basket of chips and salsa appeared on the bar.

"No, no. We weren't together back then. I had another girl, and she . . . well, Sasha had a number of different guys."

"Ah, free love from the '60s. How did you re-establish your connection with . . . what was her name?"

"Sasha. Actually, I ran into her at the Capitol. She's a lobbyist, with the Chamber." As soon as the words came out, I regretted saying them.

"A lobbyist with your Chamber of Commerce? Really, tell me all about her." He smiled.

43

August 2006

"JONATHAN, HERE'S SOMETHING I bet you didn't know. President Taft was the guy who developed the initial blueprint for the Chamber of Commerce." Stephen Russell sat in an overstuffed chair, drinking a cup of coffee in a private lounge in the Chamber's headquarters.

Jonathan Peters pulled a bottle of sparkling water from a small refrigerator. "Really? Didn't Taft follow Teddy Roosevelt into office?"

Russell took a sip of his black coffee. "Come to think of it, he did. Roosevelt went after big business. Many of us believe he was a traitor to the party. I heard Taft was incensed by Roosevelt's policies and wanted to make sure big business could never be steam-rolled again. Although I think we've taken it beyond Taft's vision."

Both men chuckled, recognizing their success and that of their predecessors.

"The Chamber is now a major force in shaping policy and legislation that protects our interests," Russell continued, pride coloring his voice. "We funnel more dollars into legislative affairs than any single organization in this country. The Chamber has membership in every major city of the country, even in larger towns in every state. And that spreads our influence into every legislature of every state, a number of mayor and governor's offices, right down to the state regulatory agencies controlling financial, utility and insurance regulations. Hell, we're even beginning to elect state judges that can control those liberal trial lawyers that waste our corporations' profits defending frivolous lawsuits. There won't be another Teddy Roosevelt, we've made sure of that."

"Roosevelt and Taft both Republicans," Peters mused. "That's a big tent . . . maybe a little too big, Stephen. The party needs more focus and a clear direction. Roosevelt is just an example of what goes wrong when we don't have it."

Peters finished pouring his bottle of mineral water in his glass and sat down in the chair next to Russell.

"Stephen, we're getting a little concerned with the drop in the real estate market."

"We've been watching it, too. My guys are looking into some new instruments that would hedge our risks if the market seriously goes south. Our portfolio is fairly clean, but there is some toxic stuff." He paused. "We are not in the business of holding assets anyway. It's time to reduce our position."

"Toxic?"

"Sub-prime stuff mingled in with AA rated assets. How about you?"

"I guess we ought to review our portfolio more thoroughly. We were supposed to be buying AAA pools, but I'm sure there's *some* bad stuff mingled in. Any recommendations?"

"Reduce your positions in the mortgage shit," Russell concluded. "But I saw your quarterlies. Your balance sheet looks pretty strong."

"Thanks to the Fed's securitization policies. We're in much better shape than we would be if we had to hold the loans. But it's getting harder to sell off our pools. Like I said, most of the stuff we have is AAA rated. Still, if the housing market takes a dive, even the good stuff is going to lose value, and we'd be stuck with a whole lot of securities on our books whose value would be questionable." Peters leaned forward in his chair and tugged at his crisply pressed slacks to smooth out the wrinkles.

Russell took a drink of his coffee and considered how those ratings were given to the pools of securities that were bought and sold. His firm put many of the deals together. He and members of his board had applied a lot of pressure to the ratings agencies to get their deals properly rated. And that pressure had cost his firm a few bucks and a number of expensive lunches and dinners along the way.

"We don't think it's coming to that, Jonathan. You've purchased credit default swap protection haven't you?"

"We started doing that about a year ago when we began seeing some weakness in the market. Hell, we sold some of the insurance ourselves on the smaller deals and made a bundle off the premiums, but IAFI seems like they will insure anything." Peters refastened the left cufflink on his shirtsleeve.

"You're covered for a downside," Russell said. "If the pools you still own fall below the guaranteed return, the insurance covers your losses. You have solid asset pools; you're making money for your shareholders. Your investment guys are happy with their bonuses. Life's good. What's not to love?"

True, things were still good and they were making money, but the pace wasn't as strong as it had been a couple years ago. "I hear some rumblings at our Fed board meetings. Some of them are getting nervous," Peters noted.

"About what?"

"Liquidity—whether we are appropriately capitalized given the downturn in real estate."

"The Fed and Treasury set the reserve and capital requirements. They encouraged you to sell off your loans. Your board supported it. They didn't balk at you getting into the credit default business. Hell, the Fed even lowered your cap requirements if you bought mortgage-backed securities," Russell pointed out. "What can they do?"

"I'm not sure they will do anything. But they could change our capital and reserve requirements or increase our FDIC premiums. Even worse they could change policy and make us hold onto the loans we write going forward."

"They won't do that because they know you'll quit making loans." Russell helped himself to more coffee from the carafe on the table. "We're the engine that drives this economy. They know that. Besides, the Federal Reserve is not as independent as it used to be. Our people are on the Regional Boards of the Fed and have a direct line into the Board of Governors. We control most of members of Congress that would nip any severe restrictions from Treasury in the bud. Even the president is inclined to look the other way. When was the last time you had a serious SEC audit?"

"But, Stephen, what if things really turn south?"

"Two things to keep in mind, Jonathan." Russell leaned forward in his chair to make his point. "The first is that you collect fees for every loan you service, including fees on processing foreclosures. The second is that your bank is too big to fail. The government can't let any of us go out of business. If they did, the entire financial system would collapse. The Fed and Treasury have no alternative but to let this thing ride itself out." He paused. "Listen, we've had bubbles and downturns before. We tighten the belt for a while until things turn around. It will work out. Quit worrying."

"I don't know. The word on the street is that the Fed is asking questions about our loans, residential and commercial. They're looking at our approval practices. I even hear they are going to review our derivatives portfolio. The FDIC is concerned that we are not appropriately capitalized for a downturn. That can mean only one thing—capitalization and reserves."

"How do you know that?" Russell's voice was sharp.

"Henquist from Fannie Mae. One of the Fed stooges has been meeting with them and Freddie. What did Henquist say his name was?" Peters paused, trying to recall the name Jack had mentioned. "Yea, Anders, Jude Anders."

Russell wrote down the name in a little black notebook he kept in his suit coat pocket.

"Okay, I'll look into it. In the meantime, take a long weekend on your yacht with that lovely little thing you've been seeing lately."

"How did you know about her?"

"New York is really a small place, Jonathan. But as long as your wife doesn't know, who cares?"

Russell took the elevator to the second floor of the Chamber of Commerce. When he got off he paused, trying to remember where her office was. Turning right he walked down a long hallway to a small office about half way down. The door to the office was open, and he could hear a woman talking as he got closer. Sasha sat behind her desk, ear to the phone. She saw Stephen Russell immediately and waved him in, pointing to the chair opposite her desk.

She place her hand over the mouthpiece of the phone. "Almost done. Just a minute." She continued with a few "Oh, reallys" and "I appreciate thats" until she finally found an excuse to end the conversation.

"Stephen, how are you? I didn't know you were in town."

"Still like your job at the Chamber, Sasha?"

"Love it. I really . . ."

Stephen Russell put his hands in the air, palms facing her. "No need. You're great for the job." She wore a fetching green blouse that showcased her ample gifts, not to mention those remarkable green eyes.

"What are you doing here?"

"Meetings, my dear. I just thought I'd check in with you since I was here. How are you doing?"

"Good." She smiled at him; a slight glint of mischief in her eyes. "I've made a contact . . . inside the Fed."

"Really." He enjoyed the view of her curves as she stepped around him in the small space to close her office door. "Who is it?"

"You're not going to believe me, but he's actually an old friend from college days. He's an economist with the Fed Board here in D.C."

"Well, that is quite a coincidence. How did you . . . reconnect?"

"Purely by accident, actually. On the steps of the Capitol."

"How close have you gotten to this economist?"

"As close as two people can get. You know." She parked on the edge of the desk directly in front of his chair, her legs brushing lightly against his.

"How long have you been, uh, seeing him?" Russell asked, quoting the word "seeing" with his fingers.

"For a few weeks."

"Is this something more than a fling?" His fingers itched to reach for his black notebook in his suit pocket. All information was good information, he knew.

"Why, Stephen, are you jealous?" She winked at him and smiled again. "I don't want to spend the rest of my life with him. It's been kind of fun though."

"Does the mystery man have a name, Sasha?" He tried to keep his voice casual.

"Jude Anders."

The coincidences were mounting up. Russell worked hard to keep his face a mask. "And what does Mr. Anders do at the Fed?"

"Senior economist. He says he reports directly to the chairman and sometimes to the Fed bank presidents." She shifted her position on the desk, her tight skirt hiking up a little higher.

This time he couldn't help but smile. "I bet that makes some interesting bedtime conversation."

"Actually, he hasn't talked much about work—yet anyway."

"Do you think you can get him to open up a little?"

"Probably. I haven't pressed him. Sometimes he seems preoccupied, distant." She pouted just the littlest bit; oh, she was good, Russell thought.

"Maybe he's had a lot on his mind. You know, with his job. There's a lot going on at these days at the Fed." He reached out a finger and gently stroked her ankle, hanging so tantalizingly right in front of him.

"I don't know. It could be that. Or maybe he's losing interest. It happens." She shifted again on the desk, moving her leg ever so slightly closer to him, while otherwise ignoring him. He drew his finger a little further up her calf. "I know he's had some meetings with the Fed Chairman recently."

"Knowing some of the details of those conversations could certainly be valuable."

"I'll try." She flexed her ankle, loosening her shoe. "But if I get too pushy, he might clam up, maybe even end it."

"Take your time." Russell dragged his finger back down her calf, along her ankle and along the sole of her foot. He could hear her breathing change. "I'm sure you'll find the right opportunity."

"I'll do what I can."

Russell carefully fitted her dangerously high-heeled shoe back on her slender foot and stood, smoothing his trousers and suit coat. There was a reason they were called stilettos.

"I have to go, Sasha. My private jet leaves in an hour."

"When will we find our right opportunity again, Stephen?" Her cheeks were flushed.

"Soon. But the goings on inside the Fed are very important right now—plans on capital and reserve requirements, and any talk about derivatives. Anything at all could be useful. Do your best. There will be a little extra in it for you. You know what I mean." Russell looked at his Rolex. "Got to go, love. Call me when you get something." He winked at her as he walked out.

44

September 2006

A PHONE CALL from Fallon on Thursday morning rearranged my day's plans. Instead of sitting at my desk with my second cup of coffee, I grabbed my jacket and headed out to meet her, just a few minutes shy of 10:30. I had never heard or seen Fallon cry before. I wasn't sure how I would handle our meeting. This was not something I was very good at.

The clouds cut into the normal heat of an August day in D.C. but it was still humid. I carried my suit coat over my shoulder as I walked the few blocks to the park. Fallon and I often got a sandwich to go and lunched in Rawlins Park because it was more or less halfway between the IMF and the Fed. When we both worked at the IMF, we would take a break and walk through the park, often discussing our mutual clients or economic issues in general. It wasn't the quietest place, surrounded on each side by busy one-way branches of E Street, but it was big enough for some seclusion. Fallon was seated on one of several benches that we often used near the center of the park under tall, old sycamore trees. She saw me approaching, and got up from the bench. I put my arms around her and hugged her gently while she sobbed into my shirt.

"Fallon, I am so sorry. How did your father die?"

She pulled away and held my hand as we sat down together on the bench.

"Heart attack. He'd been sick a lot lately. Had pneumonia last year, and never really recovered."

I squeezed her hand. "How old was he?"

"Eighty-two. We thought he had more years." Her voice trailed off into an outburst of tears.

"That's a long life, Fallon."

"I know, I know. It's just I cannot imagine him . . . gone." She began crying again. We sat in silence for a couple of minutes.

"How's your mom taking it?" I asked when she finished wiping the tears from her cheeks. She had a white handkerchief embroidered with a large blue C, an elegant touch for someone who came from a blue-collar background.

"She's a mess. I need to go home to Buffalo. She'll need my help."

"What about your brothers?"

"They're men, Jude. They'll deal with the arrangements, but they can't be there for Mom. I'm her only daughter."

"When are you going?"

"There's a 5:30 plane this afternoon. The viewing will probably be on Sunday afternoon."

"I'll fly up on Sunday morning."

"You don't need to do that."

"You're my friend, Fallon. I'll be there."

She touched my arm. "Thank you."

My mother had passed eight years ago. I made the funeral arrangements and flew home for the burial. Unlike Fallon, I wasn't close to my mother. As a kid growing up she worked a full-time job to support us. By the time I was eight, I was letting myself into our rented house after school. At ten I was cooking the dinners so they would be ready when Mom got home from work. When I was fourteen I was working a part-time job after school and on weekends. Sure, I loved my mother as most children do, but we rarely talked about anything significant. After taking the job with the IMF, I made it a point to get home at least once a year, and Mom and I would talk on the phone a couple a times each month. I thought when she died, I would be sad, but I felt nothing, not even loss.

FALLON CALLED EARLY in the afternoon with the details of her father's funeral—viewing on Sunday afternoon and Monday morning at Fitzgerald's Funeral Home and burial on Monday afternoon. I made my flight arrangements, no small feat at such short notice, and called Gillian to make sure she could take care of Lex on Saturday night through Monday—it was my weekend to have her. On Sunday morning, I dressed in my navy blue suit and flew to Buffalo. I grabbed a quick burger and cup of coffee at the airport and caught a cab to Fitzgerald's.

The funeral home was a single-story brick building on a corner in the old Irish neighborhood where Fallon and her brothers had grown up. It was a patchwork of two and three story brick and frame shotgun houses crowding the narrow streets of the neighborhood. The trees lining the streets were tall and old like the buildings they shaded. A yellow taxi dropped me off in front of the funeral home where small children were jumping up and down the front steps while younger men stood around talking and smoking. I had never met any of Fallon's family. These men were too young to be her brothers, but maybe nieces and nephews. Or maybe they were family members of another dead person lying in a casket in one of the rooms inside.

I walked through the front doors of the funeral parlor and checked the sign in the entranceway assigning names to parlors. Connelly, Parlor B, Viewing 2:00. The perfume of flowers overpowered me as I made my way to the room where Fallon's father lay—a fragrance I hated when I went to my grandparent's funerals, and then again at my mother's. It was always the same.

Fallon and two men, all three in somber suits, were standing just inside the open double doors to the parlor. She greeted me with a gentle hug before I could even get through the doorway and introduced me to her brothers, Patrick and Michael. I gave my customary sympathies to her brothers as we shook hands. The two of them couldn't have been more different. Patrick was stocky with reddish-blond hair, while Michael was lanky, his hair coal black. Which parent was the redhead, I wondered? We made polite conversation for several minutes. Other people were coming in, and Patrick and Mike excused themselves to greet them.

Fallon gently took hold of my arm and ushered me into the room and up to an elderly woman with white hair in a black dress seated in a chair near the casket. People dressed in dark suits and white shirts, black dresses, or pantsuits surrounded her. These viewings were always the same. Nothing but sadness. When we should have been celebrating their life, instead we mourned their death. And I did no better with my own mother's funeral; I just gave into to convention to make things easier for me.

"Excuse me, Mom, this is my friend, Jude Anders."

I reached down to the seated frail woman and took her hand. "I'm very sorry, Mrs. Connelly."

"Oh, Mr. Anders, thank you for coming. I have heard so much about you over the years."

"I hope good things."

"Well, of course, Mr. Anders . . ."

"Jude," I insisted.

". . . you are my daughter's friend." She was so gracious even during such a difficult time. I thought about Fallon's childhood and wondered why I hadn't made the effort to meet her family sooner.

"And she is mine. A very good friend."

Just then two more people came up to Mrs. Connelly to offer their condolences. Fallon excused us and whisked me away to view her father in his open casket. He was short, unlike Fallon, and looked as though he had been ill for some time.

"He was such a good man. He was always there for me."

"That's what fathers are supposed to be for their daughters," I said.

I never had a father and with my mother working I had pretty much raised myself, so what did I really know about parenting a child? And Lex was a girl; I might have had a better chance with a boy. At least then, my personal experience would have given me some guidance. So with Lex, I just felt my way through it, being there when she needed me, hoping I was doing the right thing.

"I'll miss him, Jude." She started to sob.

I took hold of her hand as we stood over her dead father. When she had regained her composure, Fallon walked me around the room, introducing me to other family and friends, including her sister-in-law, Jean. So many names, I couldn't begin to remember them. It was obvious Fallon would be busy with the well-wishers who came to pay their respects. I engaged in several small conversations with Fallon's friends, most of them from college, and finally excused myself to join the smokers and impatient kids on the steps outside.

Fallon's brother Patrick was standing to right side of the front doors smoking a cigarette and laughing with a fat older man when I went outside.

"Hey, Jude," Patrick said as I approached, "this is my uncle, Seamus. Seamus, this is Jude, Fallon's friend."

"Ah, a smoker, too?" Seamus said as I lit one up.

"I enjoy it too much to quit."

"Life is too short." Seamus chuckled. "May as well enjoy it."

"You can say that again."

"Listen, Patrick," Seamus said as he stomped out his butt, "I had better be gettin' back to the morgue, if you know what I mean. We'll go tip a few to celebrate the partin' of my dear, beloved brother when this show is over." He winked. "Nice to meet you, Jude." He turned to go inside.

Maybe all funerals weren't the same. It sounded like there would be a celebration later, and it sounded like a place I would prefer to the funeral home. Too bad I had to get back to D.C. I took a deep drag on the cigarette and blew the exhaled smoke away from Patrick.

"What did your father do for a living?"

He chuckled. "It's Buffalo, and he's, I mean he was, Irish. Whatta you think?"

"Cop?"

"There you go. Until they forced him to retire. Even up to last year he still walked to the station and hung around a lot."

That would explain the growing number of mourners coming to the funeral home. At first it was just a trickle, but by now quite a crowd had shown up to pay their respects, something the legendary brotherhood was known for.

"And you, did you follow in his footsteps?"

"Nope, but close. I'm a firefighter."

"In Buffalo?"

"No, in Toledo where my wife's from. She wanted to be near her family."

"And your brother, Michael, right?"

"Yeah. Mikey lives here."

Patrick paused to shake hands with a couple of cops in dress uniform. He seemed to know them by their first names, and he didn't even live here anymore. He turned back to me. "Mikey's a businessman. Owns a small electrical manufacturing company. He's been working on this surge protector thing. Says it could save our electric grid from being wiped out some day."

The electrical grid, that was a bit further afield than I expected. Instead of pieces of Fallon's life falling in to place for me, I just got more curious. We both took drags on our cigarettes. I wondered what they thought of their Harvard-educated sister and her D.C. job.

"And you, Jude, Fallon says you work in economics like her."

"Yes, for the Federal Reserve."

"Wow, now that's up there, ain't it? Fallon's the one in our family who's really made it—Harvard and all. Kind of hard to imagine her at the IMF, not that I understand what they do."

There was a long pause as we smoked.

"Growing up she was quite the tomboy," he went on, rocking back and forth, heel to toe. "Bet you'd of never figured that one. Played ball with us guys, not with dolls. And if you pissed her off, look out. She'd lay one in your gut. No guys ever screwed with Fallon, if you get my meaning." He had a funny sideways kind of smile.

"A tomboy. I guess I can see that. And, Patrick I can tell you the guys still don't screw with her," I said with a smile. "Did you or Mike go to college?"

"Na, Pop couldn't afford it. Neither Mike or me was very good in school anyway. Mikey went to trade school. That's where he learned electronics."

That seemed a bit odd—the youngest child and a female getting to college over her brothers. "How did Fallon get to go? Harvard isn't cheap."

"You know, that's still a bit of a mystery." He paused to stub out his butt on the steps, which included carefully picking it back up and dropping it in a small can filled with sand on the edge of the porch. "She had good grades in school but not top of her high school class. Dad said she got a scholarship, but none of us really believed that story. Maybe she got something, but come on, not enough to go to Harvard."

I could hear just the tiniest edge in his voice. Obviously this was more than just family lore; if he wasn't carrying a full-blown grudge, Patrick was at the very least still unsettled over his sister's advantage.

"Where do you think she got the money?" Another piece of the puzzle that had no place to go. I was intrigued; who was Fallon Connelly, really?

"Like I said, I don't know for sure." Patrick slid his finger into his too-tight collar. A firefighter stuck in a suit and tie; maybe that the was the only reason he seemed uncomfortable.

"Did your father ever tell you anything that gave you a clue?" I asked.

"There you are," Fallon said, coming out the front door of the funeral home. Patrick went mum and shot me a look that clearly said, zip it. "What time is your flight back to D.C.?"

I instinctively looked at my watch as though it would give me the answer to her question. "Eight." It was close to 4:00 now.

269

"Good. Then we have some time to get a bite before you leave. I've been here for too long as it is. I really need a break. Mikey said he'd stay with Mom."

"Sounds good. Patrick, you want to come?" I asked.

"Na, the wife's coming at 6:00 with the kids. We'll get something then."

Fallon and I left after goodbyes to her mother, Mike and a few of her friends that I had met earlier, and had a light dinner at her favorite Italian restaurant a couple of miles away. I didn't ask Fallon about her secret benefactor, but I intended to . . . someday.

"Fallon Connelly, a tomboy," I said as I elbowed her lightly in her side as we entered the restaurant.

"Fuck off, Jude." She smiled for the first time since I arrived.

Fallon shared some tales of her childhood as we tipped a beer. She told me they were having a traditional Irish wake at her parents' house after the funeral home closed, and she expected it to continue after the burial tomorrow. I wished I could stay, especially after she told me someone would invariably be singing "Danny Boy" before the night was over. There was sure to be plenty of good Irish whiskey to go around too. I got a cab back to the airport, thinking about my meeting tomorrow with the Chairman of the Federal Reserve. I had to recheck my data when I got home tonight. Thoughts of work were overcome by a picture of Sasha in my mind. I could almost smell her scent and wondered if she had been sleeping with my dark blue suit. Sasha. Maybe tomorrow night. What better way to unwind after a hard day's work?

45

ON MONDAY I went to work earlier than usual. The new Fed Chairman was anxious to see the latest housing numbers from each of the Fed Districts that Marie and I had pulled together at the end of last week. The news was anything but good. I was hoping he could see a positive sign that I couldn't. Besides, who wanted to give their boss bad news? I was experienced enough to see the signs of what was likely coming—the bubble would burst. Now the question was, when? And what we could do to soften the blow?

I reviewed the data again just before our meeting, even though I had spent over an hour going through it last night. Housing markets and residential construction were weak in most areas of the country. Sales of existing homes were off substantially, and permits for new home construction had dipped slightly, especially in California, Arizona, and Nevada. The inventory of unsold homes was up significantly over last quarter, most likely from a substantial increase in home foreclosures. Home prices were flat or declining in the northeast, mid-Atlantic, and mid-west. On the upside, commercial real estate, especially office and retail construction, still showed strong signs of growth in most districts. I suspected that wouldn't last much longer.

The banks were reporting slowing trends in lending activity during the summer, especially for home mortgages. Demand for residential mortgages was softening. Some districts reported a strong uptick in demand for refinancing that was attributed to homeowners looking to lock in fixed rates instead of their adjustable-rate mortgages. There were several districts that reported declines in general commercial loans as well. Overall, it wasn't a pretty picture.

I met with the Fed Chairman at 3:00 that afternoon to go over the data. He had arranged to have our meeting in the Board of Governors Room—a very large and impressive room where the key leaders of the Fed met to shape monetary policy for the country, policy that would also affect the economies of most of the world. When I walked in, the chairman was seated alone at the end of the enormous wooden conference room table.

"Come in, Mr. Anders. Coffee, water, soda?" he asked graciously, in contrast to his usual subdued demeanor.

"No thank you, Mr. Chairman."

"Please be seated then," he said, pointing to the chair next to his. "It's an intimidating room, isn't it?"

"Especially when you know the kinds of decisions that are made here." I put the reports on the big table and settled in. I kept my suit coat on; this room was no place for rolled-up shirtsleeves.

"I suspect you are right. Are you ready? Let's get down to it, shall we."

We spent the next thirty minutes discussing the details of the housing market data district by district. The news was not disastrous but clearly demonstrated a continuous downward trend in the real estate market since late last year.

"Okay, Mr. Anders. The news is as I suspected." He took off his glasses and rubbed his eyes for a moment. I did not envy him his job, especially these days. "Are there any data points that suggest a flattening or upward trend in the near or longer term?"

"No, sir. The trend projects continued decline. It will be exacerbated by tightening mortgage credit, which we see already, and of course, by any significant downturn in the broader economy if that were to occur."

"Panic could exacerbate a downturn—fear of a bursting real estate bubble—a downturn not just in residential and commercial real estate, but one that could ripple throughout the entire economy." He leaned back in his chair.

"That remains a possibility, sir."

The chairman remained silent, obviously thinking. He looked up at me, peering over the top of his black reading glasses. "We have seen economic bubbles before, Mr. Anders. Some of our fellow economists believe that they are inconsequential in the long term—simply a matter of wealth redistribution without any net increase or decrease in the overall wealth of the economy. Those who buy before the bubble and sell before it bursts gain wealth; those who get in late and wait until after the bubble bursts lose. Wealth merely changes hands."

I tried to keep my thinking as clinical and theoretical as he did, but I was too well acquainted with the reality of this scenario: real consequences for real people.

"From my perspective it depends on who gains and who loses, sir." I said, choosing my words carefully. "If those who can afford it lose some of their wealth while those who have the least gain, I would be less interested in the effects of the bubble. But just the opposite usually occurs. By the time those with the less wealth got into the real estate market prices were already peaking. And these people have the least resources to weather a downturn in the market."

"So wealth redistribution is acceptable as long as it moves wealth from the 'haves' to the 'have-nots'?" the chairman asked. He raised an eyebrow but waited for my answer.

I rarely had a chance to clarify both my personal and professional opinion on the work I did and the policies that resulted. He left me an open window and I was going to go ahead and take the leap.

"Sir, what are the long-term economic and social impacts of redistributing wealth to a fewer rather than greater number of people? The larger the number of people who consume, the greater the demand for goods and services, and the greater the need for people to work to provide them. This results in lower unemployment and even larger economic growth. Fewer people with greater wealth do not provide the same level of demand. In fact, as fewer individuals amass a greater percentage of the pie, demand falls off and jobs are lost, resulting in even less demand. More jobs are lost, poverty rates increase, and government must spend more revenue on social safety nets."

The chairman leaned back in his chair again, clasping his hands behind his head. He looked to the ceiling of the great room. Exhaled and looked back to me.

"Are you married, Mr. Anders?"

I was somewhat taken aback by his abrupt change in topic and tone. "Divorced," I replied.

"Another statistic. Children?"

"One, a daughter, fifteen."

"Started late in life. My girls are gone with their own families. What is it like having a teenager at your age?"

"Very rewarding, actually. She is bright and creative." I shuffled my reports a bit. I was unprepared for the shift in our discussion, and a little unsure of how candid to be. "And with my years I have some knowledge and a little wisdom to share with her."

The chairman smiled, digesting my words. "I suspect you are right. I will have to wait for my grandchildren to grow up a bit before I have the same opportunity."

"It is worth looking forward to, sir."

"You mean, as opposed to what's waiting for us around the corner?" He paused. Unlike his recent predecessor, this Fed Chairman actually seemed to show some understanding of what was real in the lives of most people.

He continued. "Sometimes I think . . . if they knew what was really going on . . . the people would most likely lynch us."

That was the last thing I expected the Chairman of the Federal Reserve to say.

"Why is that, sir?"

"Because they trusted us to safeguard their assets and keep the economy on a steady keel. The vast majority of our people want certainty, consistency around which to build their lives. They are not speculators. They prefer stability to wealth." He took off his glasses again and pinched the bridge of his nose.

"I have always thought that severe swings in the economic cycle most harm those who can least afford it. Those working on the factory floor or in a restaurant—you know who I mean. What happens to them when the speculation goes wrong? They lose their jobs and insurance, their houses, and their life savings."

"And possibly their hope, Mr. Anders." The chairman picked up his reading glasses from the table and twirled them between his fingers. "If things get bad enough and stay that way for a prolonged period, people without hope either become slaves or they eventually revolt. I am not sure which way Americans would go. Let's hope we don't have to find out."

46

January 2007

HEAD POUNDING, I gently cracked one eye open, grateful to find the bedroom still dark. My throat felt like I had not only smoked a whole pack but also licked the ashtray. I rolled over gingerly to check the digital clock on my nightstand; how could it be close to noon? Thank god for well-made window blinds.

I got up, stumbled into the bathroom and struggled with the safety cap on the bottle of Advil. Shit, when you really needed drugs, the packaging made it impossible to get at them. In the kitchen I picked off the pink sticky attached to the full Mocha Brew. *Went for my jog. Back in an hour. Fallon's at 3:00.* Another party at Fallon's—her annual Hair of the Dog gathering—and New Year's Day or not, Sasha was going to keep that fine bod in shape. At least she took the time to put on a pot of coffee before she left. Lately she'd been acting like an aggrieved spouse. I washed down the Advil with my coffee, found the remote, and turned on the kitchen TV with the sound off.

I tried to recall the details of last night's party. It wasn't a huge crowd, but there were plenty of people I didn't know, in addition to Fallon and her date, a couple of people from the IMF, and one from the Chamber. Vignettes of conversations crawled to the surface. I remembered one about skiing; and Fallon and I also talked about clandestine IMF plots. I think Fallon started that one. No, I did; I told her IMF aliens had taken over the Fed. Christ, where did that conversation end up? And there was some work stuff at dinner. I was beginning to feel a little uneasy about how drunk I had gotten. I hoped I hadn't said anything *really* stupid, beyond, of course, that there were aliens at the Fed.

The networks had the New Year's Day parades, and MSNBC had *Lock-Up Raw*. Gak. I switched the channel again to CNN and finished my coffee. News at last. I turned the volume up.

An airplane with 102 passengers on board had disappeared somewhere over Indonesia. Civil unions among same sex couples were approved in Switzerland. Bulgaria and Romania were admitted to the European Union. And Gaelic became the Union's twenty-first official language. "Who gives a shit?" I muttered as I muted the TV again. Hangovers and mute buttons, a perfect match.

I finished a second cup of coffee and took a shower, and had just finished shaving when Sasha returned.

"You look better." She poked her head into the bathroom. "My turn."

She stripped off her running tights and top and walked into the shower.

"How much did I drink last night?" I asked her over the noise of the shower.

She yelled back. "A scotch before dinner, several glasses of wine with dinner, and who knows how much champagne after midnight. I drove us home."

"Yeah, I remember that part." I rubbed the steam off the mirror and looked closely at my bloodshot eyes. "How did I get undressed?"

"Boy, were you drunk."

By the time we headed over to Fallon's, coffee and Advil had cleared my head—somewhat. She met us at her door with hugs and New Year's wishes, took our coats, and ushered us into her living room with the rest of her guests. Sasha found a couple that were at the party the night before and started talking with them, while Fallon grabbed my hand and led me dutifully into the kitchen, where she handcrafted a marvelous Bloody Mary in a tall narrow glass topped with a stalk of fresh celery.

"Drink this before you die. And don't get drunk today, okay?"

"What?"

"You talk too much when you drink heavily."

"What do you mean, talk too much?" I swirled the celery in the glass.

"A little too much detail over dinner about your work at the Fed, my friend." She patted my hand as though I was a child. "Thankfully, most people had no clue what you were talking about, and those who might have gotten it were too drunk to remember anything you said."

I strained to remember the dinner conversation, but drew a blank. "What did I say?"

"Oh, your analysis of our economic troubles, prescriptions for solving them, private conversations with the Fed Chair. Not your usual party talk in D.C. Know what I mean?"

"Really, that's not like me." I took a tentative sip of the drink. "I don't typically talk business outside of work, you know that. I have to stay away from the champagne."

"You got started before the champagne, Jude."

With the help of some food and the Bloody Marie, I gradually regained enough consciousness to carry on a light conversation at dinner. I was relieved there was no discussion of world events or economic disasters and looked forward to getting home and a good night sleep before work the next day. Thank god this holiday season was finally coming to an end.

Sasha and I barely spoke as we made our way back to her apartment. After the long holiday week of parties, maybe both of us were relieved by the silence. I was still operating more or less on autopilot. But about halfway there Sasha began peppering me with questions.

"Why do you believe the banks are trying to take over the country?"

I cringed. My drunken ramblings from the night before were coming back to haunt me.

"I just meant there isn't enough oversight of the banks by the federal government."

"Is that why you think the banks are in bed with the president?"

Oh, Christ, had I really said that? There was something steely underneath her nonchalant demeanor. I tried to sidestep the issue.

"No, no, I meant that the president believes the banks can regulate themselves, that market forces would force them to make the right decisions."

Thank god, it was New Year's Day and the traffic light so it didn't take long to wind our way to her part of town. I was in no state of mind to grind through a series of serious economic issues, especially with Sasha. But she turned off the radio and continued, this time asking about capitalization requirements and FDIC premiums. Allegedly, I had insisted that they be raised. I was surprised that I even brought up those topics, but now I had to find a way back out of this whole conversation. It was one thing to be asking for clarification and another thing entirely to be looking for an argument. I was strongly feeling the latter from Sasha.

I told her those issues required a wonkish, highly technical explanation, but that just started another argument about her intelligence. And so I was forced to explain that capital requirements essentially required a bank to have enough cash, property, and other assets on hand to cover its outstanding debts and liabilities like, for example, a loan that someone cannot pay back.

"And you don't think the banks have enough of that . . . in the bank?" she asked.

"The Federal Reserve and the FDIC set those requirements and determine how they are calculated." I pulled into her neighborhood. This could only go on so much longer.

"So you haven't set them high enough?"

"I didn't say that."

Sasha was quiet. I hoped this would be enough to satisfy her. One more turn took me to her street. I could hardly wait to deposit her on her doorstep and drive away.

"And FDI . . . whatever you called it?"

I found a spot on the street in front of her apartment building and parked. She didn't make a move to get out of the car.

"FDIC," I said. "It's insurance the banks buy from the federal government to cover any shortages if they get into trouble. They pay premiums for the insurance just like we do for our car insurance."

"I don't have a car, remember?" Her voice changed to a kidding tone.

"Give me a break. You know what I mean."

Sasha laughed. "Got you. But what does the insurance cover?"

"It covers the deposits you and I have at the bank. It started after the Depression to make sure that when people wanted to withdraw their money, there would be enough to cover what they had in the bank."

"That makes sense. Why do you want to raise the premiums?"

"If a bank becomes insolvent, the FDIC steps in and takes over the bank. Some people think that the FDIC doesn't have enough money to cover the deposits if a number of large banks go insolvent at the same time."

"Is that going to happen?" she asked, suddenly becoming very serious.

"No, Sasha, that's not likely to happen."

At least I hoped it wouldn't. I gazed out the windshield as she finally gathered her things and let herself out of the car.

47

Summer, 2007

THE DAYS HAD been long and humid, even though I saw the sun only on my way to work and through the window of my office. My social life had dwindled from minimal to nothing, and my relationship with Sasha had become erratic. She either peppered me with questions about my work or took days to return phone calls. Our relationship had just hit a plateau—or it was heading for that valley where all of my relationships had ended. I found myself not caring much.

The housing market and economy in general were as sultry as the weather. Many nights I took the last metro home after long hours looking at the data for any scrap of positive news. Was it the lack of encouraging news or the oppressive weather that weighed me down? By the time I walked the six blocks from the station to my condo, my starched shirt could no longer absorb the streams of sweat snaking down my back.

Alone in my kitchen watching TV, I picked at the salad I bought at McDonalds on the walk home. A tall, tan-skinned politician was standing at a podium outside of the state capitol in Denver surrounded by several hundred people. I reached for the remote to turn up the volume.

"Today where the Great Plains meet the Rocky Mountains, tying the vast lands to the east and west together into one country, one people, I have come to announce my candidacy for President of the United States of America . . ."

The banner at the bottom of the screen read: "Mitchell Nez Taylor announces his candidacy for president."

He was the U.S. Senator from Colorado. I had seen him on a few Sunday morning talk shows, and he seemed to be a reasoned progressive. But he had only been in the Senate for four years—a virtual newcomer to Washington. Wow, I thought, an American Indian, running for president. We have come a long way. Still, I remembered he was half British on his father's side. What did they call them in the old western movies? Half-breeds.

The candidate was outlining the basic principles he would run on: new programs to improve the condition of the middle class, lower taxes on middle-income families, restore taxes on the wealthy among us who can afford them, cut health care costs and make health care coverage available to everyone, energy independence, improve our schools, and an end to the wars that are sucking up our nations "blood and treasure." Standard Democrat stuff. There was no mention of reforming our financial system. Did he avoid that because he didn't know what was going on or because he was already in the industry's pocket?

"We need leadership, and we need to roll up our sleeves and tackle the difficult issues facing this country. The way we do business in Washington must change. I've only been in Washington a short time. I know what you know—it's broken. Together we can fix it."

The crowds surrounding the capitol yelled in unison: "Mitchell! Mitchell! Mitchell! Mitchell!"

I got goose bumps listening to the chants of the crowd. I had heard that same optimism and idealistic spirit some thirty-six years ago when I was the one firing up the crowd. My practical side regained control and the goose bumps disappeared. This guy doesn't stand a chance. He's wasting his time and somebody's money. A Native American and a Washington outsider—it won't happen. I listened to my own thoughts as they tumbled through my mind. I really had come a long way since my college days. I had finally become just as cynical as Fallon and the rest of D.C.

I STARED AT the tall birch tree outside the window of my office, thankful for a slight cold snap and cooling northern breezes. Its silvery leaves, shimmering in the light summer breeze, sounded like a whisper through the closed window. I tried to decipher its muffled code.

"Jude, Bear Stearns suspended redemptions on one of its sub-prime bond funds!" Marie didn't even knock before she burst into my office. It took me a few seconds to come out of my trance and put her comment—it came out *sub-prahm* in her New Orleans accent—into context.

"That makes one-hundred and one," I replied.

"What do you mean?"

"It's the one-hundred and first of those kind of funds to get in trouble in the last week." I immediately turned to my computer and began typing in keywords. At the end of last week, Moody's and Standard and Poor downgraded 100 bond funds backed by second-lien sub-prime mortgages.

"Is it just the sub-prime funds finally getting into trouble?"

"I don't know, Marie." I really didn't. Was this just the bottom of the barrel taking their lumps? Or was this the beginning of something more widespread? The real estate bubble had been slowly collapsing. Too much bad news too quickly might cause the bubble to explode, with nasty rippling effects through the entire economy. "But those funds will be worthless."

"That's a lot of money taken out of the economy, Jude. State pensions are heavily invested in those funds."

"Right now we need to stay focused on the banks' portfolios. Their solvency is the Fed's responsibility. We can't worry about institutions we don't control." I looked at the stock market ticker on-line. The Dow was down 220 points.

"But the banks have AAA and AA rated mortgage-backed securities pools in their portfolios. They should be okay." She came around to my side of the desk and looked at the screen over my shoulder.

"Come on, Marie. We don't know what's in those pools anymore than most of the banks do, and we don't know how they were rated, do we? Do you really trust Moody's and Standard and Poor?" There was such frenzy during the real estate bubble to repackage the mortgages into pools and sell them, who knew what got into those pools.

"You're saying the value of the banks' portfolios isn't what they think they are?" She leaned against my desk and crossed her arms.

"That's very possible. But more important, if this causes a general downturn in the economy, then there will be more foreclosures, and even the AAA rated securities will take a hit."

"Then the banks would lose their capital base and ability to lend. Businesses won't be able to borrow. That could cause a recession. What will the Open Markets Committee do?"

I had analyzed the possibilities to death over the past year, as well as actions the Fed could take to avert a meltdown. I switched to a real time feed of CNBC.

"Probably maintain the Fed Fund Rate steady—5.25%." The last thing they wanted to do was create panic in the market place. That would be the worst thing that could happen at this point. It could lead to a general market sell-off, leaving many viable businesses without capital to operate. I listened to the reporter at CNBC. Shit! Nothing looked good.

"And a run on the banks. The FDIC doesn't have enough reserves to cover the deposits."

As she spoke I had an absurd vision: the bank run scene in that maudlin Jimmy Stewart movie that always plays at Christmastime.

"Not enough for the megabanks. They're just too big. We didn't raise FDIC premiums or cap requirements when we had the chance to."

"Jude, that's people's life savings."

This is one of the exact reasons I loved working with Marie. For all her years in the banking industry, she still remembered who supported it: individual people depositing their paychecks and expecting it to be taken care of properly. I remembered the Fed Chairman's words: "If the people knew what was really going on . . ."

"If the market crashes, there goes the rest of their savings . . . and the market value of their homes may sink below the value of their mortgage. The assets on the balance sheets of the big banks would be next to worthless, and there won't be enough collateral to back up their deposits."

I looked at Marie. Her mouth stood open, her eyes bulged; the office was so silent I could hear the birch leaves rustle through the closed window.

Over the next several weeks, tracking the American economy was like watching a horror film. Nearly three weeks after my conversation with Marie, Standard and Poor placed 612 securities backed by sub-prime mortgage funds on credit watch. Two weeks after that, Countrywide

Financial, a major sub-prime mortgage company, announced they were having financial difficulties, and by the end of the month Bear Stearns liquidated two hedge funds that invested heavily in mortgage-backed securities. One week later, in early August, American Home Mortgage Investment filed for bankruptcy, but the Fed held its Fund Rate steady. With each collapse I hoped this was the bottom, but two days later the largest bank in France stopped redemption on three of its investment funds, and my fear that our financial system and the entire economy could collapse became almost surrealistic—like Dali's twisted timepieces dangling from a dead tree. The question was when and how hard.

Going to work became alternately a depressing slog and an exhausting sprint. Like everyone else, I had begun to lose sleep and eat more than my share of junk food while I rushed between meetings. During the next twelve months, we took what we thought were prudent steps to avert a financial meltdown unseen since The Great Depression, cutting the Fed Funds Rate from 5.25% to 2.0% and the Primary Credit Rate to 2.25%. The Fed negotiated the purchase of failing financial institutions, including Merrill Lynch, Bear Stearns, Countrywide Financial, and Indy Mac Bank, and took conservatorship of Freddie Mac and Fannie Mae.

But when Lehman Brothers failed, it was over. The Fed quietly intervened, employing rarely used facilities to provide temporary loans and liquidity to the nation's banks to keep them from failing and sending our financial system into complete chaos—loans in the trillions of dollars. At the same time, the CEOs of those giant institutions insisted publically they were sound. Meanwhile, the U.S. Treasury raised FDIC protection on deposits from $100,000 to $250,000 to prevent a run on the banks. We all held our breath, waiting for the bottom.

Most Americans read the headlines and watched the nightly news programs as the financial and economic crisis unfolded and their life savings disappeared. But I couldn't bear the endless nightly replays of my workdays. When Lex turned on the news, I usually found an excuse to leave the room. What could we have done to prevent this crisis or least contain it? I kept coming to the same answers: bank mergers, capital requirements, and privately-traded derivatives by the banks. God knows how many times I brought those up to the Fed Chair and his predecessor. Each time, I got the same response: any one or all would severely constrain economic growth. Politics had thoroughly permeated the halls of the Federal Reserve with the free-markets mantra. Now, all we could do was to try to prevent a complete collapse of our financial system and economy with the tools that were left. But when all those tools were exhausted and the nation's financial system remained in free-fall, the president and Secretary of the Treasury drafted and submitted to Congress the Troubled Asset Relief Program to bail out the banks and capital investment firms that comprised the American financial system.

I remembered the financial crisis in Southeast Asia ten years previous. I had told Fallon it would likely happen again, and here we were. But in spite of my predictions, what had I done to prevent it from happening here?

48

September 2008

JONATHAN PETERS WAS anxious to end the meeting so he could use the phone in a reserved visitors office at the Chamber of Commerce. He had an important call to make, but Wingate seemed determine to drag out the conversation as long as possible.

"I'm glad we knew what options the Fed and Treasury were considering," Wingate said as he deleted the emails on his Blackberry.

He and ten other CEOs from the nation's largest financial institutions had just finished their formal meeting and were talking as they packed up their briefcases and checked their cell phone emails.

"Yes," Peters responded, "very useful information. A few calls, and the secretary suddenly appears to be on-board. TARP is back on track, but it's not a done deal. The Dems control the House."

"The Democrats aren't the problem, Jonathan, it's the Republicans. Idiots. We need to remind them who funds their re-elections."

"Marshall is on it. He's been making calls all day to both sides of the aisle."

"When are you going to call the secretary?"

"As soon as we're done here." Peters put the last papers in his briefcase.

Peters had listened carefully to the leaders of the Financial Services Industry Group. Most insisted that it was in their interest to hold on to their securitized mortgage assets. The market would eventually turn around and they'd be worth a lot more than what the government would pay for them. He snapped his briefcase closed. The Treasury Secretary would listen to their proposal; at least, that was their hope.

Finally escaping the conference room, Peters headed into the visitor's office, closed the door and dialed the secretary's direct line. "Mr. Secretary, Jonathan Peters."

"Afternoon, Jonathan, what can I do for you today?"

"The Financial Services Industry Committee was wondering if there is any new information on TARP." He reached into his briefcase and pulled out his folder.

"Our colleagues seem to be warming to it. Some version will likely pass. As you told me a month ago, we have no choice. How are you guys holding up?"

Peters marveled at the sudden change in commitment to the proposed legislation. Just a couple of weeks ago, the Administration had been dragging its feet on any kind of government interference, perhaps not recognizing the magnitude of the situation. More likely, they were all just trying to figure out how to best position themselves in the event of fallout.

"The Fed lending facilities have been helpful. But with the real estate market still declining, our balance sheets are a moving target. We don't know where the bottom is." He idly doodled a bulls-eye on the manila folder in front of him.

"Well, now, that's the benefit of TARP," the secretary continued. "It passes, and we purchase those assets from you."

"Do you have any idea what their discount value will be?" He drew some dollar signs. Peters knew this issue would come up sooner or later. He might as well get the lay of the land now.

"It won't be your initial purchase value, Jonathan, if that's where you're heading. The whole idea here is we buy your troubled assets at or below market. You get the cash to improve your balance sheet and liquidity, and they won't count against your capital and reserve requirements anymore."

Peters cautiously broached the topic, trying to spin it in a way that would be attractive. "Mr. Secretary, a number of us have been discussing that part of the legislation. We believe there may be a better option than Treasury buying those assets."

"What? You guys told me you had to get the mortgage pools off your books. Now you're proposing something else?"

Peters could almost feel the heat from the secretary's anger. It was well-known he had a short fuse.

"I'm out on a goddamn limb with this program, Jonathan, and so is the president. It goes against almost everything we believe. And you know the Congress—they're skittish in this political environment. Any change now could derail the whole deal."

Peters remained calm, hoping he could cool the secretary's anger. "Please, Mr. Secretary, just hear me out."

"I don't have a lot of time right now, Jonathan." His voice was clipped. Peters drew a little explosion around his dollar sign doodles.

"I understand, sir. I will try to be brief."

The Treasury Secretary seemed to cool. After all, Peters reasoned, he'd be hearing the same thing from the Hill tomorrow. Surely the secretary knew that. He'd be stupid not to take advantage of some advance information that might make his job easier?

"Okay, but give it to me quickly."

"A number of us in the industry believe it quicker and less risky for us to issue the Treasury shares of preferred stock or equity warrants," he began, referring to the notes in his folder. "This infuses the capital we need much more quickly in the near-term and eliminates the need for the government to work through these assets on a case-by-case basis like it did with the Savings and Loans in the '80s. That would take you years. We could buy the stock or warrants back in a much shorter time with interest once things stabilize and turn around. Both the banks and the government would be better served."

There was a long pause. Peters knew their plan would have some appeal to the secretary, an avid free-marketer.

"I like the idea of a quicker return on our investment, but you're asking the government to take an equity stake in your banks," he said finally. "I'm not sure that is attractive for a variety of reasons, especially having the federal government sitting on your boards of directors."

The secretary paused again and Peters let him think it through. He and the other bank CEOs had already hashed out all the possible objections and come up with spin-worthy responses. He checked his notes again, willing himself to be patient.

"And we wouldn't have any control over your business decisions with equity warrants."

"But like you said, Mr. Secretary, you don't want the government in our boardrooms. The equity warrants avoid the appearance of the U.S. Government nationalizing our banks." He drew some little houses like the ones in the Monopoly game he played as a kid. It was his favorite game; he even had one of the little houses in his desk drawer at the office.

"That might have some appeal to the president. I'll give it some thought and talk it over with him, but frankly, I think we are too far down the line on our current plan."

"We appreciate you bringing it up to him, but, Mr. Secretary. As we read the proposed TARP legislation it gives you a lot flexibility. You could decide on our proposal after it passes. But just one more thing." Peters chose his words carefully. "Our financial institutions also hold a number of securitized assets beyond the mortgage-backed crap. They have been very useful in hedging our risk associated with various commercial loans and credit card debt."

"Now what are you suggesting, Jonathan?" Peters could hear the suspicion in his voice.

"We think it might be in the economy's interest if you consider extending the proposed TARP program to shore up the securitization market in general. If we are going to grow out of this downturn, we will need capital infusion from the derivatives market." There, he said it. He closed his eyes, waiting for the secretary to blast him.

"Infusion from the market that put us in this mess! You guys have to be nuts."

"But you know the estimates—before the crash it was over $600 trillion. It's still a prime source of capital needed for our future growth." Don't beg, he could hear the others saying at the meeting earlier, coaching him. Don't grovel!

"That one rubs me the wrong way, Jonathan, and I'm sure it will give the president heartburn."

Peters held his breath. There was no way the secretary could ignore the fact that it would take a long time for the banks and the economy to get back on their feet, even with TARP. The derivatives market could start pumping capital back into the economy a lot quicker.

"I'll consider it. I've got to go. We'll talk later."

Peters hung up the phone with a smile. The secretary was a smart man—and a man with his back against the wall. Peters had just given him an easier way out, one he would take. Not only that, Peters would be a hero to his board and the industry. Things were looking up, and he was starting to rethink his bonus position for the year.

49

October 2008

"SENATOR TAYLOR, WE need to prep for the debate next week." David Milestone, the candidate's campaign manager, stood just outside the closed bathroom door of the senator's Milwaukee hotel room.

Taylor splashed cold water on his face and reached for a hand towel on the rack next to the counter. "I'll be with you shortly," he called out. *Jesus, not a moment's peace, even in the damn bathroom.*

The senator had won his party's nomination and was locked in a tough race with his unpredictable counterpart from the other side of the aisle in the Senate. The latest polls gave Taylor a four-point lead, but with a little over a month to go before the election, anything could happen.

Senator Taylor walked into the living room. "Okay, David, I'm ready."

"Senator, we're pretty weak on economic policy with respect to the financial crisis." Milestone launched into his pitch without pause. "None of our team has enough expertise in this area to create a saleable position on the issues. We could look weak in the debate."

The senator gazed out the hotel window. His campaign manager was right. Meeting after meeting, this discussion had been non-stop for weeks and now it was crunch time. The economic crisis had created a landscape of unchartered territory. It had been too many years since the Great Depression to follow that lead, although it had provided some lessons. This crisis was more akin to what happened in Southeast Asia in the late '90s.

"Do you think my opponent will do much better?" Taylor asked, sarcasm edging in to his normally placid voice.

"No, but if you demonstrate strong knowledge of the issue and a reasonable path forward, it could make him look incompetent. Whether your solution is right or wrong won't matter."

Taylor knew Milestone had correctly assessed the situation; sounding reasonable often wins out over actually making the right decisions. But he didn't just want to win the debate; he wanted to win the election, and he wanted to get America back on track. They needed someone who'd seen this kind of thing before. But who? Taylor considered the question. He was shocked at how quickly the idea came to him.

"How about someone from the IMF?" He looked directly at Milestone. It was either a brilliant idea or a foolish impossibility.

"I don't believe we can get the Deputy Director of the IMF to assist you with your campaign, Senator. But you're on the right path." Milestone smiled.

"Not the deputy director, but I do have a contact there who may be able to recommend someone. Where's my cell phone?"

"OKAY, GEORGE, I'LL get back to you when I get an answer." Fallon hung up the phone and went back to her keyboard. The phone rang again just as she was about to click open a file. "Now what?" she said out loud, her frustration getting the better of her. This day was not going well—too much to do and too many interruptions. She looked at phone caller ID.

Mitchell Taylor. Wow, there's a flash from the past. She had watched his rise in the Senate the last few years but was stunned when he threw his hat into the presidential campaign ring.

"Fallon Connelly," she answered, no trace in her voice of her previous irritation.

"Fallon, Mitch Taylor."

"Mitchell, I haven't talked with you since . . ."

"Ten years ago at the Harvard reunion." She could hear the smile in his voice.

"You've made some changes in your life since then, Senator." She knew that was an understatement, but it made her point. Taylor was always on the fast track to somewhere even in college, and he always knew when to play his hand.

"Yeah, just a few," Taylor replied with a small laugh. "And how about you? It's obvious you're still at the IMF. How about the other things?"

Like that night at the reunion, she thought. "Still single, if that's what you mean, Mitch."

"Pros and cons with that, Fallon. Are you happy?"

"I don't know. I don't think about it. I have my job and friends." That was too personal a question to ask someone you hadn't seen in ten years, especially given the nature of their last encounter. "So what's up, just calling me up out of the blue?"

"I need a favor."

"I should have guessed. No one calls me unless they want something." That was certainly true at the IMF and definitely true with Mitch Taylor. "Kidding. What do you need?"

"I'm a little behind the curve on our financial crisis. None of my economic advisors to the campaign are deep enough in this kind of thing. I thought you might be able to recommend someone."

Ah, she thought, he's run into some muck on his fast path to the presidency. Maybe now he'll realize that it takes more than a law degree to solve the problems of the country.

"Well, it's not going to be me, Mitch, conflict of interest, and I'm not giving up my day job to take a run at some golden ring."

Fallon heard his laugh and remembered how he had laughed at the reunion. It was uniquely his.

"I get it, Fallon. I'm not asking for you, although you would be perfect. My take is that our crisis is similar to the Asian financial crisis in the '90s. Do you know anyone who understands what really went on then?"

"Well, you're right. They are similar. And most of the people that were involved in that little crisis are at the IMF, including myself." Or at the Fed, Fallon thought. Would Jude be interested? She grabbed a pen and a piece of notepaper on her desk.

"Mitch, you know, I might just know someone who could help you, but he is also employed in a governmental position and has a kid to support. Are you willing to put him on salary to come on board with your campaign?" She started jotting some notes.

"I've already considered that. This is a pivotal issue in the campaign. My positions on this mess could make the difference between winning and losing. Yes, I'm prepared to put him on salary."

"I'm not saying he'd take it, but I know he's a little frustrated in his current position."

"What's that?"

"Senior economist to the Fed Board. He worked closely with the Fund during the Asian crisis. The Fed had significant involvement in that one, too."

"Wow, that is a heavyweight. Sounds like the right guy, but I bet he's a little busy right now. What would he need to quit?"

"We're government employees. How much do you think we make?"

"I hear you, Fallon. If I'm elected, maybe we can do something about that, not that I could affect your salary at the IMF. What's his name?"

"Judas Anders."

There was a long silence. "Not to be superstitious, but I can trust him can't I?"

"What? Of course you can. Why did you ask that?"

"You know, Judas, a traitor."

"Give me a break, Mitchell. He goes by Jude." That was the last thing anyone would think of Jude Anders, she thought.

"Just kidding, Fallon. How do I get in touch with him?"

LEX GOT STARTED on her homework at the kitchen island while I finished up the dinner dishes. She had iTunes playing loudly on her Mac; some new kind of rock she called indie music. I was looking forward to a quiet evening watching *Crime Scene Investigation* when the ringing phone interrupted my plans.

"Jude Anders?" The voice was familiar but I couldn't quite place it.

"Yes." Lex's music was making it hard to hear.

"This is Senator Mitchell Taylor. Do have a couple of minutes?"

Right, the guy running for president. If this was Fed business, I wondered why he was calling me at home in the evening.

"Just a minute, Senator," I said and covered the receiver. "Lex, could you finish your work in your room? I've got an important call I need to take."

"Sure, Dad. Let me know when you're done. I have some math questions."

Lex packed up her Mac and books, and headed for her room.

I lit a cigarette and reached for my glass of Chardonnay. This was going to be interesting. "Yes, Senator, how may I help you?"

I WALKED DOWN the long hall to the chairman's office at the end, still thinking of the confrontational conversation I had just had with Gillian. Nothing had changed between us after four years of divorce. I expected her to be happy that I had an offer to work on Mitch Taylor's campaign, but all she cared about was collecting the child support payments. When had she become so self-centered and materialistic? Or was she always that way and I just didn't see it? She'd get her payments; all I wanted was for her to take care of Lex full-time until the election was over. It was only a few more weeks, after all. I tried to clear my head of our conversation and hoped the notice I was about to give the Fed Chairman would end up on a more positive note.

I had drafted a letter of resignation yesterday and made an appointment with the chairman. This resignation wasn't like the one with the IMF. It had been a bit of a struggle. I really respected and liked the chairman, and I felt that my resignation was a betrayal, especially in light of the condition of our financial system. Still, after meeting with Taylor in person, I knew I had to accept his offer.

"Sir, I understand this is short notice, and normally I would give enough time to find a replacement. But I'm sure you can understand the need for immediacy." I stood in front of his desk, waiting for permission to sit.

"Yes, Mr. Anders, I can," the chairman said as he laid his glasses on his oversized desk and looked directly at me. After a moment, he waved me towards the chair to sit down. "Frankly, the timing of your resignation is less than optimal. We need your expertise right now. We are not sure how this crisis will play out."

"I understand, but I believe, my colleague Marie Turbeau can fill in for me until you find a replacement. She's been with me every step of the way during the collapse."

The chairman leaned back in his chair. "Why do you think we would fill your position, Mr. Anders?"

That caught me by surprise. "As you said, sir, we are in the midst of the crisis."

He picked up his glasses from his desk and twisted them back and forth between his right thumb and forefinger. "Even with that, I would rather put you on a temporary leave of absence until the election is over. It's less than a month away. In the meantime, as you say, Ms. Turbeau can fill in for you."

I hadn't considered this option. The chairman knew I had a teenager to take care of, and college was looming on the horizon. Was he protecting me financially in case Taylor lost the election? Or was he trying to make sure I didn't get so involved with Taylor that I wound up taking a White House position?

"Thank you, Mr. Chairman, but if Senator Taylor wins the election, there will likely be other opportunities in his administration. Some may be very enticing."

"Do you think he will win?" His voice was noncommittal. I had stayed awake the last few nights trying to answer that question myself.

"Yes, sir, I do. I wouldn't be doing this if I didn't think so."

"Between you and me, I agree with you, and should the senator win, I would expect you to take a position in the new administration, assuming of course, they are good offers. Perhaps in the president's office or, at a minimum, in Treasury."

"Thank you, sir." His gentle tone was so unlike his public persona, I almost blushed. I had never thought of him as paternal, and yet, even in middle age, I realized how much his fatherly praise meant to me.

"Don't thank me, Jude. You're a first-rate economist. You will be useful to a new president; and you may be more help to us there than here given our current situation."

"IT ALMOST LOOKS like a conspiracy," Senator Taylor mused as I took him through the long history leading up to our financial crisis—the Interstate Banking Act, the repeal of Glass-Steagall, and the Commodity Futures Modernization Act—and the key players along the way.

"Kind of does, or maybe better, a methodical plan to gradually eliminate the financial constraints that grew out of the Great Depression."

"Still sounds like greed to me. Who are all these guys?"

That was a good question, and one I had thought about for many years. I connected the dots for him—some of the players were obvious.

"If they are interested in amassing wealth, they're easy to identify—bankers, investment and hedge fund managers, investment capitalists, derivative brokers and dealers, corporate CEOs, real estate speculators—until recently—and of course, the politicians who get their campaign contributions."

The senator gave me harsh look.

"Just kidding, Senator."

"That's a long list. You said 'if they want to amass wealth'. What else would drive them?"

That was the other piece of the equation. Still, something was missing; there was more to it, but that was harder to articulate than sheer greed. I considered how best to layout the larger framework of my thinking. "There's been a consistent railing against the size, role, and cost of government; government regulation, unions, public schools, public employees, entitlements, and the like. And advocating for limited government, privatization, free markets, and free trade."

"Jude, that's just standard far-right ideology." Taylor stood, stretched, and poured a glass of water.

"True, but more important, it's been a growing ideology for the last forty-five years or so. It has been very popular in academic circles since the Depression, but seemed to gain more support in the '60s and '70s. It was the underlying justification for taking down the regimes in South America," I pointed out. "In the '80s you could hear it in Reagan's smaller government, anti-regulation, anti-union messages. It got quieter during Clinton's tenure in office, although that's where most of the current damage originated. But since the current administration came to power, it's gotten louder again. It's been around a lot longer than you or me. I suspect there's more than greed and right-wing ideology at work, Senator."

After a long silence, the senator continued. "Okay, I got an answer to my question—at least for now. But back to the current mess were in. The debate is next week. I need a position on TARP."

I smiled. I guess he did need a little history. He couldn't be too narrowly focused on this stuff; he had to look at the bigger picture. "It's not just TARP. You have to understand the proposed legislation in context."

"I'm ready; give it to me."

"Over the past nine months the Federal Reserve has had two primary objectives: provide liquidity to the banks and avoid creating panic in the economy. The Fed has lowered Fed Fund Rates, but it has also created several instruments that helped to collateralize the bad assets held by the banks."

"You mean the mortgage-backed securities and other CDOs?"

"Mostly, yes. Backing them with Fed funds improved the banks' balance sheets. These moves stabilized the banks and reduced the fear that they would become insolvent. But these measures have only partially worked. The banks are still reluctant to make interbank loans and loans to the commercial businesses. Without those loans, the economy grinds to a halt."

We had been in his stuffy office for hours; a plate with some breakfast rolls and toast had long since lost its freshness and we had forgotten about ordering lunch. I reached over for a wilted croissant and tore off a piece.

"How does TARP fit in?" Taylor asked.

"TARP would buy up the non-performing securities currently held by the banks, eliminating them from their balance sheets—help them to recapitalize and put them on a sound footing."

"And so TARP is a good thing."

"I guess you have to look at the alternative," I said. "If we don't implement it, there would be a strong possibility that the major banks would become insolvent, because they don't have enough capital reserves to back up the losses on their balance sheets."

"That sounds like the same thing that happened in the Depression."

"Very similar. And there would likely be a run on the banks by depositors."

"But we have FDIC to cover deposits."

"Not with the megabanks controlling such a large percentage of deposit assets. The FDIC premiums have not kept up with the potential loss liability. So the federal government would have to step in with taxpayer money to cover the deposits. With TARP or without it, either way the taxpayers will pay. The good thing about TARP is that it keeps our financial system, and that of the rest of the world, from tumbling into complete chaos."

Taylor leaned forward in his chair digesting my points. "If the banks are stabilized, will that solve the financial crisis?"

"The financial crisis, probably, but not the broader economic crisis," I said, struggling to separate the two. There was a pivotal—and often overlooked—distinction. "Over the past ten years, the country has put most of its capital into speculative ventures and consumption—just like in Southeast Asia in the late '90s. And we did it without creating any growth in real economic output or by investing in the kinds of things that would position us for real growth down the line—roads, bridges, schools, alternative energy, or factories. And a lot of ordinary people got into the speculation by borrowing against their assets—mostly their homes, expecting the markets to continue to skyrocket. When the bubble burst most of what they had left was their debt."

I washed down the stale croissant with some cold coffee and tried to provide Taylor with some context. "There's a lot of psychology at work.

Banks have to feel confident that any loans they make will be fully repaid with interest. But just as important, there has to be consumer demand and corresponding business demand. Small businesses won't expand or invest in new equipment if they don't see demand for their products or services. If the demand is weak because whatever disposable income people have is being used to pay off their debt, the economy will weaken even further. Without demand, businesses will not grow and will have little need to borrow."

Surely, the senator was getting this, but to be absolutely certain I made the point another way. "Like I said, consumers have pretty well shut down their borrowing entirely with the amount of debt they already own, not to mention the fear that they might lose their jobs. But here's the kicker: the rich and well-off are not a large enough percentage of the population to create enough demand to add jobs, even if we reduce their tax rates to zero. No consumption, no demand, no need for loans. Businesses lay off their workers. Depression."

Taylor leaned back in his office chair and looked up at the ceiling. For a Harvard Law guy, he was sure taking his time comprehending the big picture here.

"But if the wealthy have more available resources, they will invest them and that will create jobs."

Had he also been listening to the mantra too long? Was he just as brainwashed by this line of economic thinking as the majority of the American people?

"With respect, Senator, those with enough wealth will invest their excess money, but not to create jobs. They invest to make more money, and they will invest in those corporations and countries that give them the greatest return on investment. That's why corporations are primarily interested in profit—with it they pay greater dividends and show the potential for growth, attracting more investment. They will go wherever they can maximize their profits and the return to their shareholders."

"You mean like China."

"Yes, like China, India, Brazil. Like any country that has the ingredients for generating more profit—lower wages and healthcare costs, and fewer regulations that inhibit what they do or cost them too much to comply. That's what happens in a free-market economy."

"So the investments made by the wealthy will generate jobs, just not here." Taylor seemed like he was finally getting it.

"So we might as well raise taxes on those with the excess wealth and invest those revenues in things like rebuilding our infrastructure. Those kinds of investments will create jobs in this country and provide the structure for future economic expansion. When people go back to work they will spend more, creating demand. If we get the demand up, it will unclog the plumbing so to speak."

Taylor leaned forward and poured another cup of coffee, by now probably cold and stale. "I can see why TARP *won't* solve our economic problems."

"It won't, but it will make the banks solvent and put our financial system on a sounder footing for eventual economic growth—when demand picks up."

"Are there alternatives to TARP?"

"There are always alternatives, Senator," I said, "but unrealistic in this political environment."

"Do we need to discuss them now?"

"Not now, but down the road we will need to discuss other issues like the size of our banks and the types of business they're in—the kind of things that got us into this mess in the first place. Politically, for now I think you should strongly support TARP. Let's see how it unwinds. If you're elected, there will be time to discuss alternatives."

"Jude, what do you mean 'if'?"

Before I could respond, one of Taylor's aides cracked open the door to his office.

"Yes, Jeremy, what's up?"

"The House has just defeated the TARP legislation, Senator. The president is asking to meet with you, your opponent and the leaders of the House and Senate tomorrow."

"What time?"

"Eleven."

"Tell the president I'll be there. Check my calendar and make whatever adjustments are necessary." He waved Jeremy away and looked me in the eye. His focus was unnerving, to say the least. "Jude, be available here tomorrow afternoon. We need to discuss what we can do to kick this economy in the ass. The election will be here before we know it. I want to figure out how we're going to fix this mess *before* I take office."

SEVERAL SENIOR CAMPAIGN advisors and I watched the third and final presidential debate from a hotel room in the Four Seasons Resort of

New Orleans. If I were still in D.C., I'd be watching the debate with Fallon over a pizza and some beers. Sasha didn't like Taylor and would only make snide comments about him the whole night if we were together. We'd go to bed mad at each other, and it would take days for us to start talking again. The relationship had worn thin some months ago. My new job wasn't helping, but if I had to choose today, I didn't have any question about where I'd be: exactly where I was right now.

This debate focused on economic issues with some cultural issues interspersed. I listened intently to what the senator said, trusting that he had absorbed at least the most salient points of our many discussions on the topic. And he didn't disappoint. Taylor was spot-on with his response to each question on the economy, while his opponent offered the same old right-wing prescriptions. There wasn't much hope in his opponent's message—austerity, austerity, austerity. I thought back to Reagan. Just as in Reagan's time, people needed to hear a positive message and Senator Taylor was delivering one—a calm, measured message of intelligent action and optimism.

I was the first to react when the two candidates shook hands and smiled for the cameras at the end.

"He nailed it! Yes," I said with a fist pump.

"Well, if you're happy, Jude, I guess we should be too. I didn't understand half of what he said," David Milestone said as he hugged me.

50

November 2008

I ROLLED OVER in bed and put my arm around the woman next to me. All night long I had been shifting in and out of quick intense dreams. Just as I was slowly waking, I was in a hut on a Tahitian beach with Fallon, wrapping my arms around her. I finally left the dream behind and realized with momentary surprise that this was Sasha in bed with me, not Fallon.

I quickly got my bearings. It had been a long night. Senator Mitchell Nez Taylor won the election, and we spent the evening celebrating with the senator, his wife, and the senior campaign staff. I lay in bed, remembering my dream. Fallon.

At the senator's invitation Fallon showed up at the celebration. She and the senator were old acquaintances from college. How funny that I was with my old college friend, too. I got up quietly, not wanting to wake Sasha, and went to the kitchen to make coffee and watch the news.

The senator had won by 5 percentage points—a landslide. That boded well for his ability to push through his legislative agenda. But the Democrats still didn't have enough seats to override a filibuster in the Senate, and there were too many conservative Democrats in the House who might side with their Republican colleagues on certain issues. If they wanted, the Republicans could block every major piece of legislation the president submitted. But surely they would recognize that he had a mandate from the people for his agenda? That had to count for something.

"Good morning," Sasha said. She stood in the kitchen doorway in her panties, my white shirt thrown quite casually over her otherwise naked body.

I kissed her softly on her cheek. "Sleep well?"

"Yeah, I did. Are you going to work today?"

"No. Everyone's taking off. We meet tomorrow to begin planning the transition."

Sasha poured herself a cup of coffee and sat down at the island. "Did the senator talk with you anymore about a job in his administration?"

"A little. He's still thinking about a position in Treasury." I wasn't sure what position would be right for me at the moment; admittedly, I was still digesting the significance of Taylor's truly historic win. A half-Native American, half-British Senator who had only been in Washington four years walked away with an election on the solid liberal principles that had been mercilessly trampled on over the last fifty years or so. It was more than surprising; it was miraculous.

"Secretary?"

"I doubt that. He'll be looking for someone with more operational experience for that job." I rubbed my stubbled chin, considering. "Whoever he chooses though, it's going to be someone who'll play hardball with Wall Street and the big banks."

"And where will Jude Anders fit in?" She smiled at me but there was something cold behind her eyes. I couldn't name what had gone wrong between us, but I found myself bristling at her question.

"Maybe Economic Policy within the Treasury. It would fit my skills better. What are you going to do today?"

"I have to go into the office this afternoon. There are a few things that I need to get done today, and I don't want to miss the election scuttlebutt at the Chamber. Taylor's election is going to give a number of those guys some real heartburn." Sasha lifted the mug to her lips. "I can't wait to hear what they're planning next."

"Please let me know," I quipped as I kissed her again. "The Chamber poured in tons of money against the senator's election. Do you think they'll try to find ways to work with him as president?"

"It depends on the president, I guess . . . how well he listens to their concerns; his position on taxes."

I poured myself another cup of coffee and sat next to Sasha at the island counter. She nuzzled her head on my shoulder and put her arms around me.

"I'm proud of you, Jude." She pointed to the TV replaying parts of Taylor's victory speech the night before. "You helped to make that possible."

STEPHEN RUSSELL PICKED up the receiver and muted the speakerphone. "Good afternoon, Sasha. I didn't expect you to be at work today. Enjoy the celebration?"

"What's not to like except the results? It was free food and booze. A lot of drunk people in the room with loose lips and the chance to mingle with our next president."

"I can imagine. Did our boy get drunk, too?" Russell took his small black notebook out of his jacket pocket, ready to take notes.

"No, Stephen, he kept himself under control this time." He heard disappointment in her voice. "But I did get a tidbit or two over coffee this morning. Jude says the senator is talking to him about heading up Economic Policy at Treasury."

Russell knew that position. It had considerable influence on the president's fiscal and monetary policies. He jotted it down. "That's not good. How about the secretary, any idea who the senator's thinking about?"

"No specific name, if that's what you mean, but Jude said it would be someone who'll play tough with the Street and the banks."

"Really? Well, we will have to work on that one." Russell was quiet. That was not good news and could be dangerous. He began thinking of a strategy to control whoever got that position.

"When will I see you next, Stephen?" There was just the slightest hint of a plea in her tone. She had done well for him over the last year, certainly exceeding expectations in many ways. Perhaps she deserved a bonus. Russell pulled himself out of his thoughts and looked at the calendar on his PC.

"I'll be in town next week, my dear. Are you free, say, Tuesday night?"

"I think I can make myself available. Call me with your plans."

"STEPHEN, I ONLY have about an hour," Peters said as he took his seat in the lounge of the Core Club.

"I just wanted to pass on some information." Russell sipped at his Manhattan. "We may have a problem."

"From our source?" Peters confirmed with a wry smile on his lips. Russell wasn't the only one who had blackmail material if it was ever needed. And he wanted Russell to know it.

"Yes," he said, getting the point of Peters' little smirk. "She says the president-elect intends to appoint a Treasury Secretary who's going to be tough on the financial companies. Any idea who fits that profile?"

"No one from the Street. Certainly no one from the banks or investment firms."

"That's obvious." Russell snickered. "How about from the Fed or someone buried deeper in Treasury?"

"He'll be looking for someone very familiar with the crisis, so either of those make some sense. But he won't want a Republican, so someone higher up from Treasury is probably not an option. He'll be replacing all the top jobs there." Peters raised a finger towards the bartender and nodded. His customary Perrier with lime would be on its way momentarily.

Russell consulted his little notebook. "Speaking of Treasury, I also heard that Anders might be a candidate to head Economic Policy. We won't have a welcomed ear if that happens."

Peters considered Russell's intel. "It depends on who gets the secretary's job—he'll be the real policy maker. The secretary and the Fed Chairman will make future decisions on capitalization and reserves, not to mention the financial regulatory reform promised by our new president. But if Anders is in a position to have the president's ear, he could still be a problem."

"I'm not sure there's much we can do about that, at least for now. As you say, we need to focus on the secretary position—block Ander's influence as much as possible. If that son-of-a-bitch got his way, he'd kill our private derivative deals. No, we need to come up with names for the Secretary of Treasury position and float them quickly, before Taylor gets too involved in the process."

Peters drank from his glass of Perrier. "We can come up with some names. Getting one of them in the position is quite another matter."

"I've already considered that. We have a trump card—the president-elect won't have enough votes in the Senate to block a nomination filibuster. And we have senators on the string who are beholden to us. Let's see if we can find someone whose views are closer to ours but still acceptable to the new president. I know how to get names in front of the Minority Leader, and I am sure Taylor already understands the filibuster threat. He comes from the Senate, after all. It will be one of his first appointments. He won't want a fight."

Peters agreed with the logic of Russell's thinking, but had something else on his mind. "The current secretary is making the TARP changes we wanted. They give us the funds; we keep the securities. In the long run, we'll make a bundle when the economy gets on its feet again."

"Are they going to insist on voting power for the shares we'd be giving them in exchange?" Russell fished the cherry out of his Manhattan and stuck it in his mouth, pulling out the stem and depositing it on the bar napkin.

"Non-voting, so it keeps the government out of our boardrooms," Peters replied. "But there will be limits on executive compensation. Personally that one is quite disagreeable. Political pressure. It was our compromise."

"Until we pay them back, then all of us can continue to live life as we've become accustomed, my friend. At least they won't have the power to walk your ass out of your office," Russell said with a smile. "Any word on what Justice might do? My lawyers tell me there are some grounds for prosecution."

"I have my lawyers looking into that as we speak. We don't know who the Attorney General's going to be. For now, our guy inside is protecting us. He's told the FBI and SEC to back off. It's likely to be just like the Nixon pardon—the new administration will want to put what happened behind them and move forward."

Russell looked at his empty glass and considered ordering another. "And if they want their pound of flesh, my legal guys say they'll tie the whole thing up in the courts forever. We know which judges are on our side." Stephen Russell looked around the mostly empty tables of the club. A year ago each would be full with a waiting line at the bar. Now there was no boisterous laughter—just the quiet of glum faces.

51

December 2008
Darien, Connecticut

"ARE YOU GOING to host our holiday party this year?" Benjamin asked, warming his hands at the fire.

"Actually, no." Joseph was smiling and in a good mood. "I was planning to, but our new associate agreed to host it instead."

"In Toronto? It's cold there in December." He frowned and turned his backside to the flames.

"Please, it is probably no worse there than here in Connecticut. It will give a few of our associates a good opportunity to meet him face-to-face, on his turf."

"And our friends across the pond?"

"I have two confirmations. Not bad. We don't want too big an affair." Joseph got up from overstuffed chair and joined his friend at the fire.

"Make sure he knows what kind of whiskey to have in stock."

They both chuckled.

"What is he working on?" Benjamin asked.

"He is traveling abroad planting seeds."

"Seeds?"

Joseph had a glint of mischief in his aging eyes. "The seeds of revolt." An ember jumped over the grate in front of the fire and landed on the hardwood floor.

"Where this time?" Benjamin stamped at the glowing bit of fire.

"Our friends, the cartels, have outlived their usefulness, and stand in the way of our larger agenda. We intend to break them, for good this time."

"Like Suharto?"

"Same result, different approach." He turned away from the large fireplace and returned to his chair. "There is something else I need to discuss with you. If we are to have an impact on the new president's cabinet positions, we need to move quickly."

"He is from the other side. Why do you think that is possible?"

"We did it before in the last Democratic administration. Actually, having a Democrat in the office may work to our advantage. We can fairly predict what prescriptions Taylor will offer to the current crisis, and they can produce results that position us down the line."

"Well, I know we cannot influence the Attorney General choice. The president will fill that one with his college buddy who he roomed with at Harvard." He took a long draw on his whiskey. "Our friends on Wall Street are not going to like that."

Joseph adjusted his seating position to something more comfortable. His familiar bout of sciatica had flared up again. "Their boards encouraged them, Benjamin."

"You mean we did."

"That is splitting hairs, don't you think? Either way, they, too, have been quite helpful, but they dug their own hole with their egos and greed. They can climb out on their own. Each one is a survivor." It was more of a statement of fact than an opinion. "I am most concerned about Treasury, for obvious reasons. There are few candidates from the left who could manage the job, especially with our little crisis. We need someone we can count on to take the responsible position when the truth of their situation eventually tumbles down upon them."

"Taylor won't go for someone from Wall Street," Benjamin asserted.

"Certainly. But he needs someone competent and credible. He is not stupid."

"Surely you do not mean Anders?"

"Too much policy and not enough operational experience. No, not Anders."

"He's become somewhat of a wild card in our plan. We should have removed him from the game-board after Argentina—look where that has led. When we heard Taylor offered him a position in his campaign, we should have done it then. Now he's going to be on the inside."

"You may be right, old friend, but some of our group believe that he may yet play a useful role. And we may be better off with him on the inside. But Taylor still needs a better alternative for Treasury."

"Who do you have in mind?"

"I'm thinking about our friend at the IMF. They are old acquaintances, and in these times with the president's progressive background, a female would be attractive to him. At least she could direct the National Economic Council. As much as the treasury secretary that position holds the ear of the president."

"Would she do either?"

"It may take a little persuasion, but in the end, I think I can convince her."

Benjamin grabbed the poker and stoked the dwindling fire, still cold from the long drive. "But Anders, he may still be a problem. He will be placed somewhere in the administration."

"Maybe," Joseph acknowledged, "but it depends on where he ends up. In the short-term, he will encourage our new president towards a Keynesian solution to the crisis—more than Connelly ever would."

"I can see how that fits into our plan, but what about the long-term?"

A wry smile covered Joseph's wrinkled face. "If he stays that long—if he becomes a problem—we have other assets to neutralize him."

52

Washington D.C.

"SENATOR, PLEASE COME in," Mitch Taylor said to the Minority Leader of the Senate, as he escorted him into his temporary office at the Executive Office Building.

Jimmy Wilkerson strode into the office with confidence. Taylor won big, but so what. Wilkerson knew who really ran the show.

"Mr. President-elect, congratulations on your stunning victory," the Minority Leader said as he shook Taylor's hand.

"Thank you. Are we ready to get down to business?" Taylor pointed to a chair next to the couch in his office.

"That is why I am here. Let's get to it."

The Minority Leader of the Senate had caucused with the Senate and House minority leadership team, trying to anticipate the newly elected president's agenda and how they would choose to respond. They knew he would propose some form of economic stimulus program, but how much and the specific contents, they could only speculate.

Wilkerson's party had lost control of both houses of Congress two years ago and now the presidency as well. He knew the people wanted a different approach to that of eight years of Republican control. Their job was to give the people just enough to make it look like Republicans were concerned about the economic crisis, but not enough to help a Democrat plan succeed. He and his counterpart in the House had their eyes on the mid-term election in two years, and they knew how to dampen economic growth just enough to claim the president's policies had failed. They had a preliminary plan and would adjust it as events unfolded.

"I'll come right to the point, Senator," Taylor began. "We intend to put forth a stimulus plan as soon as Congress convenes after the inauguration."

Wilkerson had anticipated that. Now he needed the details. "How big and in what form? We hope there will be some sizeable tax cuts in your package. It's the only way to stimulate growth."

Taylor smiled slightly. "Let's not play games, Senator. This is not a public conversation. You know there are a number of ways to stimulate growth, and there is little evidence that your tax cuts did anything to grow the economy over the last eight years—just a housing bubble and the wealth of the already rich. But yes, we will consider some tax cuts, as long as they are targeted."

"Targeted how?" Wilkerson was perfectly aware of the result of tax cuts over the years and how they fit within their long-term plans.

"At those people who have been hit hardest by the recession and the economic policies of the last eight years. And at those businesses that offer the greatest opportunity for job growth and are willing to take some risks. And that does not include major corporations or oil companies, Senator." Taylor paused for a response but Wilkerson remained stoic; the president-elect was traveling on thin ice here. "In fact, we're looking at legislation that would take away some of the tax breaks they've benefited from over the past decades."

"Of course, you know we believe that broadly-based tax cuts are the most effective means of stimulating the economy and creating jobs," the Minority Leader responded, remembering to stay on the message he and his colleagues had agreed to. "And with all due respect, I am sure you do not want to create another oil shortage or have the price of gas spike in the middle of the recession. That would only make things worse."

"One of the benefits of the recession is that oil demand is down and so are prices at the pump." Taylor said, deftly avoiding Wilkerson's jab. "But we need to increase the tax incentives for alternative energy. We cannot continue our dependence on fossil fuels; it's a matter of national security. At current consumption levels, we will exhaust most of the world's known oil reserves by 2045. Then what?"

"That's known reserves," Wilkerson replied. Taylor sounded like he was still in campaign mode, what was it going to take to get this guy down to brass tacks? "There are a number of unexplored areas of the globe. Why, just look at Brazil . . ."

"You want to count on that?" Taylor scoffed. "Maybe we could find more oil. How long would that extend the inevitable—another ten or twenty years? And at what price to our people or our economy? No, it's time to get serious about an energy policy that does not make oil and coal its centerpiece."

The senator's oil and gas constituency had supported Republican candidates and expected Wilkerson and his colleagues to hold the line. They needed their tax breaks to keep their dividends high, while making investments to gain control of natural gas leases—the fuel that would power America for the next hundred years. In the meantime, they would advertise their initiatives to develop alternative fuels as the price of gas gradually rose and increased their profits. Hell, he even had support from the coal miner unions.

"We understand there's a potential short-term energy issue," Wilkerson said calmly. "But I think we disagree on how to deal with it. You will get a lot of opposition from a number of our industries if you try to make a major switch from traditional energy sources and find it difficult to get that through Congress. I can tell you now that any kind of cap and trade legislation will be dead on arrival. My colleagues will filibuster it to death."

Wilkerson had made his first salvo and he hoped Taylor got the message loud and clear. The Minority Leader continued. "Besides targeted tax cuts, what else will your administration include in a stimulus package?"

"Infrastructure projects, from roads and bridges to rail. We've let our highway system deteriorate for years in order to pay for your tax cuts and our wars. It's time to reinvest. In order to reduce our energy dependence, we need alternative forms of transportation like regional high-speed rail in the heavily populated parts of our country. And we need to look at our electric grid. It was designed and built in the 1940s. We need to move electricity from source to consumer quickly and efficiently, especially with the advent of wind and solar farms that must be placed in supportable areas of the country."

Taylor didn't flinch. Instead he continued to roll out the same tired New Deal notions he blathered about during the campaign. "There may be an appetite for some of that, but it will be a question of how much of an outlay we would be talking about," Wilkerson responded, knowing that none of his constituents gave a rat's ass about rail. "With the recession, we are going to be constrained by a lack of tax revenue. Everyone, including the government, will have to tighten his belt. We have to keep the deficit and our debt within reasonable bounds," he said, rehearsing another part of the message they had already planned to role out over the next two years. "And the other components of a stimulus program?"

"State and local governments are going to be hit hard by the recession. They have a bigger revenue issue than the federal government because they have to balance their budgets each year. We need to make sure that they can continue essential services: police, fire, education and the like."

"Would that support come in the form of block grants to the states?" The majority of Republican governors also supported assistance from the Federal government to help balance their budgets, but they wanted control over how it was spent. They had their own constituents to worry about.

"Unsure at this point."

"Well, we will need to look your program." Part of their strategy for the next two years was to regain control of several key governorships. Putting economic pressure on Democratic-controlled states would help that agenda. "A number of states have been over-taxing and over-spending for years. It's time they learn to live within their means like the rest of us. We would not look favorably on using federal funds to pay for their negligence."

Another salvo; Wilkerson knew his words only thinly disguised the austerity program his side planned to implement to hinder any real economic growth over the next four years.

"Except some of you have larger means, Senator. The Republicans controlled all branches of government for six of the past eight years. I didn't see you living within your means then."

Of course, he knew this was coming. The new president had used it many times during the campaign. But they had developed a talking point to rebut the accusation.

"The economy was growing then, Mr. President-elect."

"And so was our budget deficit and debt, Senator."

"But not like it is going to grow with the kind of program you're talking about," Wilkerson asserted.

"And giving deep tax cuts to businesses and wealthy individuals won't grow the deficit?"

"For every dollar in tax cuts to business or the upper 2% of income, almost $2 is generated back into the economy."

"Even if that were true, how much of that $2 comes back in revenues for the government, Senator?"

"The government will just have to get smaller. It's the only way." They had four years before the tax cuts would expire and they had to find some way to make them permanent. It was the only way to take away the power of the Federal government. He stood firm.

"So no new roads, bridges, rail systems, electric grids?" Taylor asked. His voice was casual, but his gaze was pure steel. "Police, firefighters, school teachers? Make unemployment worse than it is already?"

"I'm not saying that," Wilkerson pushed back with a smirk. "We'll have to look at your specific proposals."

Taylor stood and strolled to his desk. "I was hoping that with the magnitude of our crisis, your party would find a way to work with me to pull us out of it. It's your mess, too."

"Well, of course we will, but we have our principles and beliefs in what works and what doesn't. Surely you didn't expect a blank check."

"No, just a commitment to work together to get through this." Taylor sat down at his desk, effectively dismissing him before the meeting was even over.

"You've heard all I have to say on the matter at this time, Mr. President-elect."

Wilkerson was furious. He had a good fifteen years on this half-breed punk, not to mention a lifetime strolling the halls of Capitol Hill, and yet here Taylor was, insisting his campaign promises were some kind of real strategy. He'd learn soon enough, Wilkerson thought. The arrows he launched—no cap and trade, no tax increases on the wealthy, an austerity program sure to break the back of Big Government state by state—had hit home.

"Thank you, Senator. We'll be talking again soon," Taylor said. He did not extend his hand.

The Minority Leader strode to the door, but stopped and turned back to the president-elect. "There is one more thing. How is your selection for Cabinet secretaries proceeding?"

Taylor looked up from the files on his desk. "We're being thorough, as I'm sure you would expect."

"Oh, I'm quite sure you are. You just need to understand that there are some positions that concern us."

"Like?" The president-elect raised an eyebrow.

"Secretary of Treasury. We would not look favorably upon someone in that position who is out of the mainstream."

"Meaning what, Senator?"

"Well, to be frank, someone like Jude Anders. His views are far too left of center and could make matters worse. If we are to get out of this crisis, we need someone at the helm of Treasury who can appreciate the positions of all segments of the economy. I'm sure you don't want a fight over your nominations—not at the beginning of your term."

"And who might you suggest I consider, Senator?" Taylor shuffled the files and placed them neatly in a stack.

"Of course there are some eminently qualified people associated with our financial institutions . . ."

"Wall Street is out, Senator." Taylor was curt. "The American people would come unglued after the mess they got us into, and frankly, I wouldn't blame them."

"Well there are a couple of people from the Federal Reserve—New York, Kansas City—both qualified. Given the nature of our crisis, maybe someone from the IMF."

"Thank you again, Senator. I'll consider what you've told me. If you have a specific name, please give me a call." He turned back to his files.

By all accounts, Wilkerson knew he had succeeded in his mission. All he really had to do was plant a seed, but he could see it take root before his eyes. Taylor would now think twice about Anders . . . and anyone else he wanted to appoint.

"HOW DID YOUR discussion with the Senate Minority Leader go this morning?" David Milestone, now on tap to be Chief of Staff in the new administration sat on the floor of the president-elect's temporary office, sorting through boxes of files sent over by the current administration.

"As expected." Taylor sighed and rubbed his eyes. His desk was still covered with stacks of folders, and he tried to shuffle a few off to make room for the armload Milestone had just brought in. "They'll block attempts to change the tax credit redistribution from oil and gas to alternative fuels."

"And the larger stimulus plan?"

"I sensed some willingness to work with us. But who knows. Outside of trying to regain power in two years, I'm unclear what their agenda will be. And I'm not sure the Minority Leader completely controls his caucus." He leaned back in his desk chair, his fingers laced behind his head.

"It's not like we control ours, either. We have oil and gas senators in our party too, not to mention the other Democratic senators who are scared to take a shit without a poll."

The president-elect laughed. "I like that. Make it up on your own?"

"Actually, Mr. President, I can't remember." Milestone smiled slightly.

"Let's not get ahead of ourselves, David. We still have a month and half to go before the inauguration." Taylor paused. "You know what was most disconcerting. The Senator told me not to nominate Anders for Secretary of Treasury."

Milestone looked up from the file boxes he was browsing through. "He wasn't on the list anyway. What's up with that?"

"I don't know, but it tells me those guys are afraid of him."

"Should we cut him loose?"

"No, on the contrary. We were considering him for the head of Economic Policy at Treasury. Maybe we should consider him for Director of the National Economic Council. I'm curious what he knows and why he scares the hell out of Wilkerson."

"It's essentially an economic policy role anyway," Milestone said, a smile spreading across his face. He knew what an asset Anders was; he could see Anders' work all over the last debate, not to mention several of the final campaign speeches.

"And he would be in the West Wing, not across the street." Taylor smiled.

PART FOUR
Voices of Babel

53

Present Time
Katapola, Amorgos, Greece

THERE WAS A slight thud as the *Albion* docked in the harbor. The town of Katapola surrounded it on three sides. In unison, the passengers quickly got out of their seats, and began gathering their suitcases and bags filled with packages from the mainland that they had stuffed beneath the seat in front of them. It was always the same, whether on planes, trains or boats, passengers would get up and stand in packed aisles long before there was anywhere to move. I remained in my seat, watching them—my new neighbors for the next three months. The rental agency where I was to pick up the keys to my small house in Lagada was not far from the ferry terminal, and my new home was on the other side of the island. I would have to stay the night in Katapola anyway.

As the traffic behind me cleared, I dragged my large roller bag into the aisle of the ferry and threw my backpack over my left shoulder, following the end of the line of impatient travelers to the door. A long wooden ramp led us to the terminal building, where we passed through a single room packed with people waiting to board the *Albion's* for its return trip to the Greek mainland. In a sunny spot just outside the entrance, I pulled out my pack of cigarettes along with directions to the rental agency from my backpack. I looked at the familiar pack of Marlboro Lights in my left hand; it was a last vestige of the life I had left behind. I brought four cartons with me; maybe when they were gone I'd end this stupid habit that I've had since I was nineteen.

The hike to the rental agency took me up a steep grade over cobblestone pavers that kept tipping my awkward roller bag onto its side. Bending over to right the suitcase, I could feel the strain in my lower back. After years of desk jobs, I was badly out of shape, and my age wasn't helping either. Walking at least a mile each day while I was here might help. I huffed as I climbed the hill and tossed the half-smoked cigarette into the street. It was 17:00, and I was a little nervous the agency might be closed, but luck was with me.

"Hello," I said as I poked my head through the open door of the tiny office.

A dark-haired woman sat behind a single desk close to the door in the small room; she looked at me without surprise and said something unintelligible. I handed her my rental agreement.

"Ah, Anders. Yes, yes," she said with a deep accent as she looked at the contract. "My English no so good. Sit, sit."

I took the chair in front of the desk as she pulled some paperwork out of a file drawer in the desk. An old-fashioned key with two notches and a *fleur de lis* at the top was taped to the front of the manila folder that she laid on top the desk.

"You sign," she said pointing to a yellow-highlighted line on a paper she had pulled from the folder.

"Sure." I replied, and signed dutifully on the marked line—a copy of the agreement I had brought with me.

"Three month?" she asked, holding up her thumb and first two fingers.

"Yes, three months." I did the same, smiling at her.

She peeled off the tape, handed the key to me and smiled for the first time. "Welcome Amorgos." I had waited a long time to hear those words.

I rechecked the map to find the best way to my hotel, and once again began dragging my bag through the narrow cobblestone streets, but this time laterally across the top of the hill.

"At least these are still good," the hotel clerk commented as he took an imprint of my AmEx card using a manual imprinter. It had been years since I had seen one of those old, bulky machines. "Only one night, Mr. Anders?"

"Only one. I've rented a house in Lagada for a few months."

"Will you need transport to Lagada?" His English was pretty good, but I shouldn't have been surprised. A number of Europeans start learning English in grade school.

"Yes, to drop off my luggage, and after that to Chora, where I've rented a motor bike." This journey was endless; I had to wait yet another day before I could get fully settled in to whatever life had in store for me.

"I can arrange both for you. What time will you leave?"

"Around 10:00."

The clerk wrote down my name and the time I would need transport on a slip of paper. "I will have a car waiting for you in front of the hotel at 10:00."

"Thank you. That is very helpful."

After so many years of pushing through obstacles and fighting the clock, patience was not one of my strong points. Then again, that's one reason I was in the Greece in the first place. I didn't have any choice but to be patient. For now, I would clean up, get some food, and then sleep.

The clerk handed me my room key and gave me directions to my room. "It has a small balcony overlooking the harbor. Very nice. One of our best."

Not far off the lobby, the smallish room was on the top level of the hotel that cascaded three stories down the hillside toward the harbor—a good thing since there was no elevator. The simple furniture, whitewashed walls, and terracotta tiled floor gave the room a crisp, clean look—the epitome of "Spartan." It had a window facing east and French doors that opened to a small balcony looking north out to the harbor.

I immediately opened both doors and strode onto the balcony where I could feel the sea breeze. I looked around at the panorama of the harbor, hands resting on the iron rail, taking in as much of the town and island as I could see. How many times I had visualized this moment, gazing out to sea from my perch on a Greek island far away from the commercial world. It was amazing how close to the real thing my visions had been. But as good as my intuition had been most of my life, it did not always match the reality I trusted it to predict.

There were many times during my career that I had imagined having the power to shape the future of the economy, maybe even create a new kind of economy—something I had frequently thought about since my first conversations with Jack Tomasin so long ago in Toronto. But at the pinnacle of my profession, and finally in a position to make a difference,

I found another reality. Any progress I thought I could bring about came in inches when miles were needed. What power I thought I had was diluted, not only by the contentious sides engaging in constant debate, but by political strategies and power plays that, to me at least, bordered on subversion.

Politicians had become so addicted to money and power that they were willing to destroy the very thing that made this country great—the belief that hard-work and fairness would improve one's lot in life—all the while hiding behind the empty rhetoric of "small government" and "free markets." Even the American people were weary of how both sides had become so entrenched that it was impossible to take significant action in any direction.

There was more to it than that. A standoff was one thing, but what we got was caused by a conscious decision to bring everything to a grinding halt—and for what? Principle? Money? Power?—without care or concern for the very real damage they were causing to millions of ordinary hard-working folks.

54

January 2009
Washington D.C.

"IT DIDN'T TAKE you long to get here," I said, getting up from the conference table when Fallon walked into the room at Treasury. "I guess the new president didn't have to twist your arm too hard, Madame Secretary."

"God, I have to work with you again," Fallon replied, her smile as mischievous as ever. She took off her navy-blue Burberry trench coat and carefully folded it over one of the conference room chairs. "The Senate still has to confirm me, so don't get too excited—yet."

"It's fate, my dear. The confirmation's a shoe-in."

"You don't believe in predestination, Jude, so cut the crap. You've been here longer than me, bring me up to speed." She put her Gucci briefcase on the table and pulled out a legal pad.

"Have you signed your confidentiality agreement?" I quipped as we both took our chairs at the corner of the long table. God, it was good to be able to work with her again. I didn't realize how much I had missed our day-to-banter on the job.

Fallon rolled her eyes. She got the point—our first encounter at the IMF. I couldn't resist, although I was as ready as she was to get down to business.

"Current events first." I pushed a pile of file folders over to her side of the table. "TARP funds have been delivered to the big boys. We're looking at smaller institutions around the country that have the largest liquidity problems. Freddie and Fannie are in receivership to the government; we already guaranteed their loans anyway—might as well just own them. But another problem has surfaced."

"And it is?"

"IAFI."

"Insurance. What do they have to do with this mess?"

"They've insured a large number of pooled assets that our friends in the banks and investment firms put together through Credit Default Swaps." Discovering this part of the puzzle had kept me up for too many long nights. Unraveling the pieces of our economic mess was complex. Figuring out how to fix it was even more so.

"I thought the Fed intervened in that last fall."

"Yes, the Fed took shares in exchange for an $85 billion capital infusion to cover their swap lines with the counter-parties. But it turns out that was just the tip of the iceberg."

"How big is their liability?"

"At least $200 billion, but we don't know if that's the bottom or not. The current secretary and his staff are meeting with them today. And they insure globally."

For a first day on the job, this one probably ranked up there with the worst. I felt bad for Fallon. It was a hornet's nest, but surely she understood the basics of what had been going on the past several months.

"So if they go under, the balance sheets of the banks get creamed. How many banks are affected?"

"All the big ones, investment houses, even some of the big European banks."

Fallon shook her head in disbelief. "Can this mess get any more complicated? What's the effect of letting IAFI become insolvent?"

"Our financial institutions would take another hit—a big one. Not a good thing at this point; it could throw us over the edge." I drummed my fingers on the stack of folders. We had considered every option and then gone back and looked at them again. The alternatives were not good. "Europe can't deal with it any better than us. If either of us goes down, so does the global economy."

"Okay, you're telling me we're going to backup IAFI so they can pay off the banks for their wild-ass derivative speculation?" Fallon was incredulous. I was reminded of the IMF's role in protecting the loans commercial banks made to countries that were teetering on the verge of default.

"Looks like it. Any better ideas?"

"Let the current administration deal with this one," she said with finality. "We have a few more weeks before it's our liability. Where are we with the stimulus package the president-elect wants me to focus on?"

"The Fed has about run out of its monetary tools." There was a large bowl on the table filled with ice that held bottles of water, juice, and soda. I pulled a couple of waters out and handed one to Fallon. "Hell, interest rates are at .4%. They've stabilized the financial system, but the banks are still over-leveraged and the true value of their balance sheets is unknown. Without economic growth, we'll likely tumble into a depression. All the Fed's monetary policy to date hasn't been able to save us. I recognize that your IMF bent makes that a little hard to swallow, Fallon."

She glared at me; if there was one thing Fallon hated, it was being perceived as a company man.

"Okay, I get it; I never said monetary policy was the answer to every economic problem. So we need some government spending to stimulate the economy. But we have to be careful—too much too quick will create a big debt burden relative to GDP. We already had a debt problem before this mess. Too much out of the gates will make creditors nervous." She tapped her pen pointedly on the legal pad. "We've seen what happens to those governments that take that path."

"You're not at the IMF anymore, Fallon." I leaned forward across the table. "Yes, we understand the risks, but we have a much bigger economy than Chile, Argentina, Thailand, or South Korea. We can afford a bigger government investment without crowding out private-sector borrowing or giving our creditors cause for alarm."

I knew she'd find merit in my position. After a few minutes in which she appeared to doodle aimlessly on her legal pad but was probably furiously number crunching in her head, she asked me for details.

"Broadly, tax cuts to individuals who are hit hardest by the recession; a smaller set of targeted cuts to business to incent them to invest and hire. Second, infrastructure construction to put people back to work—transportation, water and sewage, government buildings, communications, and energy. Finally, unemployment compensation, job training, education, and assistance to the states to cover their essential public services—fire, police, teachers." I ticked off the items like a grocery list. I had gone over it so many times with Taylor and the rest of his advisors that I knew it all by heart anyway.

"The dollars are adding up quickly, Jude. How much are we talking about?"

"My first estimate given the magnitude of the recession—$1.5 trillion."

Fallon remained silent for a moment. "Surely, you've made a math error. You have one too many commas in your number."

"I was always better at math than you, Fallon, and that is a reasonable number." I had managed to convince every one of Taylor's advisors, his entire inner circle. The last thing I wanted right now was pushback from my oldest colleague.

"U.S. debt is already at least 60% of GDP. That would bring it to what, 85% or a little more? That's not sustainable, especially if the recession gets worse or recovery is anemic."

This was our first day of working together in twenty-five years. All the teasing throughout the years over our unique economic prescriptions for solving the world's problems had just turned into a serious debate. I looked at her for a moment before pressing my case, just long enough to let her know this was not some policy discussion about far-away places. This was a real-world scenario, and it was our world, America and everything it stood for, that we were talking about.

"Whose side are you on, Fallon?"

"I'm on the side of fiscal responsibility, one you had better be on, too," she shot back crisply. "All of us pay our debts, Jude. Were you brought up any differently?" She cocked her eyebrows; I was sure I detected a smirk.

"I believe in paying what I owe when I make the decision to borrow. But did the American people make the decision to lose $14 trillion in housing values, wages, and retirement savings? And that's about equal to our annual GDP." I could hear the tone of my voice rising. "Did they make the decision to take the economy over the cliff, killing economic growth and revenues, and requiring the government to spend even more to keep us out of a depression? What does debt as a percent of GDP mean to them? They created their own debt with the help of the lending practices of our fine, upstanding financial institutions—which they bailed out with taxpayer dollars—and they're tightening their belts to pay off what *they* borrowed. But they didn't create the federal government's debt. Why should they pay for it? They've paid enough."

"Is this really the time for a philosophical debate on economic justice?"

"And when is it a good time for that debate?" My anger rose again to the surface; I almost whacked the table for emphasis. "What's wrong with now when we're trying to find solutions to the mess a small group of greedy motherfuckers got us into? Let's find solutions that help the people who lost the most. Anyway, we're making debt into a bogyman. We already have one thanks to 9/11, we don't need another one." I stood at the table and loosened my tie. The room felt stuffy suddenly.

"Debt can be devastating. It could destroy the economy, just as easily as a depression." Fallon kept her cool, which I had to admire. Even so, she was missing the point.

"It's not like debt wipes out our GDP." I tried to control the passion in my voice. "And remember, Japan has carried debt almost twice the size of its GDP for how many years? We can carry it over a number of years. The U.S. has a strong economic engine—we're the largest economy in the world. It's our job to find ways to create good-paying jobs for the majority of Americans without artificial bubbles. If we put the money in the hands of the many rather than the top 1%, the people of this country will generate enough demand to make the economy grow at a sustained 3% to 4% a year. If the economy grows at that rate, it would generate enough to contain the debt and start paying it down."

"That's the economy. How do you get that money into the federal coffers to pay down that debt?" She stabbed her pad several times with the tip of her pen. She had a point.

"As the economy recovers so would tax revenues." My words sounded hollow even to me; I sounded like the supply-siders of the Reagan years.

"Not enough at current tax rates."

"You're right, Fallon, and if debt were your biggest concern, a modest tax increase targeted to those who could afford it would wipe it out much quicker. Before Reagan, the wealthiest Americans paid at a 60% tax rate. What is it now—36% for those who are too stupid to hire an expensive accountant to find the loopholes? A modest rate increase on the top tier, up to, say, 45% for a short period of time would take care of the problem without slowing economic growth."

Fallon looked at me for a long moment, and then began reviewing her notes she had scribbled on the pad.

"There are two things I know, Jude." She stared at her notes. "One, you'll never get a tax increase past this Congress, even if you call it a debt reduction tax. And the Republicans will never stomach your $1.5 trillion number."

55

February 2009

"SENATOR, YOUR CAUCUS meets in five minutes," Wilkerson's secretary announced at the open door to his office.

He put his hand over the mouthpiece of the phone receiver. "Thank you, Lois, I'm finishing up now."

James Norwood "Jimmy" Wilkerson hung up the phone, left his office, and walked the long hallway to his party's caucus room in the Capitol Building for a thirty-minute meeting of Republican senators. He would enjoy the reaction of his colleagues to the news he had just received.

"Gentlemen . . . and ladies," Wilkerson announced, almost forgetting they had a few female senators in his caucus as he entered the dark-paneled room in the Capitol. "Are we ready to begin?"

The other senators finished getting their coffee, sodas, and bottles of water as they took their seats.

The senator continued, a smirk playing across his lips. "I have it on good authority that the administration is going to submit a stimulus package next month for $1 to $1.5 trillion."

A combination of gasps and laughs filled the room. Wilkerson laughed too as he held up his hands to silence his caucus members.

"Really, Senator, the president has just taken office and is already setting a new bar for the tax-and-spend Democrats. Is this new president a socialist?" one of the senators asked from the back of the room.

"The president says he is a pragmatist. I take him at his word," Wilkerson responded. "But I have to say, this is unlike any pragmatism I have seen before." The caucus room was now quiet. "The question before us is what will our position be on a package of this size. Now, I haven't seen the details. We don't know how the funds are to be apportioned—how much of the package is tax cuts, how much direct spending and toward what. I have heard there will be significant requests for infrastructure spending, assistance to the states, and unemployment compensation, as you would expect from our liberal friends on the other side of the aisle."

"This is BS." Senator Ward from South Carolina, often outspoken about free-market principles was the first to react. "Any more government spending will crowd out private borrowing and investment. We were hoodwinked into TARP. We should have let the banks fail."

Several senators looked at him. Wilkerson tried to gauge their looks. Did they agree, or think him crazy?

"Anyway, we've spent enough," Ward continued. "It's time for the free-market to work the way it should. No more government programs to do what the private sector can do better."

"But Senator, surely you agree we should fund unemployment benefits while the economy recovers," Senator Elise Smith from New Hampshire interjected. "We have some moral obligation, and we get a return of 1.6 times the cost."

"My state is really taking its lumps, too. We have to provide them some assistance." It was Senator Ryan from Michigan. After five years Wilkerson had still not decided whether Ryan was a moderate or really a liberal who had disguised his views to get elected in a purple state. "Our unemployment level is already well above many other states. A modest infrastructure program would help create jobs. And I'm not too anxious to face my town halls next year, if we start firing teachers, cops, and firefighters."

"You're just concerned about being re-elected," Ward retorted. "Your state has been out of control for years with its public spending."

"I agree with Ward," asserted Senator Smeldly from Alabama. Typical Southern conservative, Wilkerson thought. You could always count on them to go after one of their colleagues from the North, even those from their own party. "It's time for states to take some harsh medicine and get their fiscal houses in order. Hell, they built a multi-million dollar commuter train from Birmingham to Mobile, and now they don't take in enough from ticket sales to keep it operating."

The Senate Minority Leader held his hands up again to regain order. "Any government spending, especially at these levels, is distasteful to all of us. But we have to be politically astute. If we drag our feet on the stimulus proposal and the economy gets worse, we will become the scapegoats."

Wilkerson suspected the corporations would be cutting their costs to keep the value of their stock up and drag their feet on any new hiring or capital investment until they were convinced the U.S. economy was under a robust recovery. Shareholder value was the only thing that motivated the CEOs of the global giants—that and getting rid of government regulations. What investments these corporations would make would be in other countries where the economies were growing faster and had fewer regulations that cost them profit. What the Republicans had to do was ensure the U.S. recovery was anemic enough to keep those corporations on the sidelines until after the next election.

"What kind of tax cuts are they talking about?" Senator Smeldly asked.

"We're not sure," Wilkerson replied, "but they're likely to be focused on the middle—and low-income people. That's who the liberals always help. There may be some targeted tax relief to small business—investment credits and the like—certainly none for corporations or Chapter S partnerships."

"Well, $1.5 trillion will never fly. I'd get killed in my state if I voted for that," Smeldly insisted.

Wilkerson could see the nods of the heads in the room, signaling general agreement among the caucus.

"I think we can all agree that the American people would never go along with that figure. At least, not if we explain to them why they shouldn't. We can negotiate that number down, but still demonstrate that we are willing to find some common ground without going against our principles."

"We need to focus on tax cuts!" Senator Ward yelled.

"Across the board," another senator said loudly from the back of the room. "They're still way too high. Want to get this economy booming? Just lower the top rate to 23%."

This wasn't the first time Wilkerson had trouble with Ward stirring things up in a caucus meeting. He didn't want the meeting to turn into a shouting match. Wilkerson raised his hands against the growing unrest in the room.

"While I agree with that direction, Senator, I'm not sure how palatable that would be at this time. We've already had significant tax cuts under the previous administration. Let's be honest about that. And obviously we have revenue issues with the downturn in the economy. Still, we can use that position in negotiations with the administration."

Ward persisted. "Then we need to lower the Corporation Tax rate; 35% is the highest in the world."

"Be careful what you ask for, Senator," Wilkerson quickly retorted, still trying to put Ward in his place. "Most of our corporations only pay an effective tax rate of 16-20% with various tax breaks and incentives." Wilkerson knew that many corporations didn't pay any corporate tax at all.

"You mean loopholes?" a senator remarked.

"Those too," Wilkerson quipped as the familiar smirk broke out across his mouth. "But if we move too hastily on Corporation Tax rates, we may end up giving our friends a larger tax liability than they already have. So let's proceed cautiously. I think we're going to have enough fights on our hands this session, like an attempt to reduce tax credits to oil and gas producers. The Dems will say we can't justify it, given the record earnings of these companies over the past ten years and the need for revenues. That's going to be hard enough to defend."

"Do we have any idea what kind of infrastructure projects they will be proposing?" asked Senator Smith.

Wilkerson was thankful for the opportunity to change the subject. "No specifics, but we've heard highways and bridges, electric grid modernization, energy efficiency."

"While I don't like government-funded programs, those projects would create some jobs."

"Maybe you should switch parties, Senator," Ward interjected once again. "We've been living beyond our means for years. That's why the people threw us out. Americans are sick of this runaway spending."

"Oh, please. You sound like a Fox News talking point," Smith retorted. "It's not like we've spent much on infrastructure during the past ten years. You replace the roof on your house when it starts leaking, and remember the bridge in Minneapolis. Who in the private sector is going fix those bridges?"

The Minority Leader held up his hands once more to end the ad hoc debate that was beginning. The thirty minutes allocated for the meeting was nearly up.

"Okay, I think I have the gist of your views. Remember, we are going to have to give somewhat on any stimulus proposal the administration brings us. I think we can all agree on unemployment extensions, at least for this year. Otherwise, we could be considered hard-hearted obstructionists. We can probably do some horse-trading on that one."

He chuckled, knowing that the only chance of winning the White House in four years was for them to block any legislation that might significantly move the economy forward.

"We have some tough negotiations ahead. If the administration insists on too much, then we'll dig in our heels. We have enough votes to prevent cloture. I think we can defend not going overboard. And remember, we have to convince the people that the debt we're piling up will kill economic growth and jobs. When we get the specific package and have some time to digest it, we'll meet again."

The Minority Leader strolled back to his office down the long hall of the Senate Wing of the Capitol. He and his party would show the American people just how ineffective government could be. They would lose hope in their government, too. He threw his suit jacket over the chair in front of desk and placed a call on his private line.

"Could I speak with the president at his earliest convenience?"

"JUDE, I'M AFRAID I've got some bad news for you," Fallon said, barging into my office and shutting the door behind her.

"Now what, Fallon?" I continued to read the Federal Reserve *Beige Book* that summarized the latest U.S. economic data, not bothering to look up.

"I've been doing a little of my own reconnaissance," she started, taking a seat in the chair opposite my desk, "since our meetings with David."

I suspected I knew the meetings she referred to—David Milestone had interviewed the entire economic team over the leak of the amount of the stimulus package to someone in Congress. I could offer little insight into who may have leaked the information, but I did know it affected our bargaining position on the Hill. The $1.5 trillion I was recommending to the president had now hit the press, and the right wing was having a field day leveling "tax and spend" accusations against the new administration.

"Yeah, so who's the mole?" I looked up from the *Beige Book*.

"You."

"Me? What?" I blinked, surely she was joking. "Okay, I get it, you've got my attention, what do you really want?"

Fallon played out a wry smile on her face and looked at her nails, a habit she frequently slipped into when she thought she had the upper hand in a debate.

"Tell me, Jude, has anyone ever told you that you talk in your sleep?"

Now where was she headed? Was this a conversation about the leak or something else? I briefly thought about her question, but I hadn't slept with that many women in my life, at least the same one for more than a few nights, besides Sasha, of course.

"Gillian never told me that I did, except when she woke me from a nightmare."

"And your occasional sleep-over these days?"

"Sasha? Never a word."

"Well, I guess that doesn't surprise me. Why would she?" She looked at me silently, tilting her head just slightly, as though she were waiting for something.

"Come on, Fallon, I'm busy. What's this about? Why would she what?" I threw the book on the table. The latest economic data was a pile of bad news; I needed a break, although Fallon's line of questioning was not exactly what I had in mind.

"Tell you that you talk in your sleep."

"As far as I know, I don't talk in my sleep. What does the leak have to do with Sasha?"

"Well," she said, sounding like a housewife about to tell a juicy piece of gossip, "I had an interesting dinner last night with . . . an acquaintance that works with her at the Chamber."

Now she had my attention. Sasha didn't talk much about her work or people she knew, even though she was always asking me questions about my job.

"And who is this acquaintance?" I heard the frost in my voice.

"Just someone I see off and on—he's not important. But what *is* important is that he works in the office next to Sasha's and talks with her almost every day."

"So what? You and I talk almost every day." I could feel something trying to rise to the surface, clawing its way up through a fog of distraction and misinformation.

"Yes, but we discuss economics mostly, and I don't see who you're meeting with each day."

Fallon was playing this out like a suspense novel, and it was getting tedious.

"Can you just get to the bottom line?"

Deliberately ignoring my plea, she continued. "You know, I was shocked to hear—from my acquaintance—how business is discussed at the Chamber. Unlike here, they often don't even completely shut the office door when they talk."

I rolled my eyes. "Maybe they don't talk about anything important?" I raced through every encounter and discussion I'd had recently with Sasha. Did she ever mention anything at all about her job?

"It turns out your friend meets with some very interesting people. I might even say powerful people."

"She's a lobbyist, for god sake. Of course, she would sometimes meet with important people."

"Well, I understand this guy is more than an occasional visitor, but more interesting, my acquaintance overheard them talking about the president's stimulus package, and a number—$1.5 trillion."

"But I haven't told her anything. Who's this guy she's meeting with?" My left knee started bobbing up and down suddenly, something so strange I had to put my hand on it to stop it.

"You never mentioned $1.5 trillion?" Again, she tilted her head and looked at me. I could feel a sweat break out on the back of my neck.

"No!"

I thought back to the last few times I had seen Sasha. We both were busy and we didn't see each other as regularly as we used to. God knows there were a few weekend evenings when we got a little inebriated. Work had its stresses. I tried to retrace our conversations over the past month, but couldn't recall any that hinted at the amount of the stimulus.

"She works for the Chamber, Jude." Her voice was quiet but firm. "And what you don't know is that she has contacts, contacts that run up the Hill and to the right side of the aisle. You might consider having her tongue cut out, or dumping her if you don't like a girlfriend without a tongue. David will insist anyway, if he finds out she's the source."

"Who's this guy she's allegedly blabbing to?" I asked, but I already knew it didn't matter. Sasha was not the problem here.

"You're just going to have to trust me on this one. You know my information is usually reliable."

Now I was nervous. If the leak came from me, at the very least I was in trouble with the president. I felt the same way when Jim Jones chastised me for associating with the Monteneros in Argentina some thirty years earlier, and I was always unsure whether the deputy director believed that was just a coincidence. My actions with Vasco back then may have blown the IMF's position on the Argentine loan request. If I had revealed the number to Sasha, it could blow any chance of getting the fiscal stimulus we needed, not to mention my credibility, my reputation, and my job.

"Sasha is not devious," I said finally, although I wasn't even sure I believed my own words. "Sure, she works for a conservative organization, but I've known her since college. She was a radical. If she was an . . ."

"Enemy of the State? People change."

Fallon was silent. This was huge, and we both knew it.

"Look, you have to talk with her about it," she said, placing her hand gently on my arm.

Yeah, right, I thought to myself. Just a casual conversation over a glass of wine.

"What if you're wrong?" I looked at her, hoping I didn't sound as pathetic as I felt.

"It's always possible, but the intel is pretty solid. Confront her and see how she reacts. You know her well enough to tell if she's lying."

"What are you going to tell David?" I know Fallon always had my back, but I wondered how I could face him or the president if they knew I was the source of the leak.

"Nothing. It wouldn't change things anyway. But talk to Sasha. If I'm right, I know you'll do the right thing." She got up to leave.

"And if I think you're wrong?"

"Then I'll find you somebody better, and you can dump her anyway. By the way, here's a name." She produced a yellow post-it note from the pocket of her jacket. "Have a look at her contacts in her cell phone. If this name is there, you can bet she's the informant. Mention his name and watch her reaction."

Even if Fallon was wrong, how could I ever trust Sasha again? I would always suspect her. Christ, I certainly couldn't sleep with her any more.

I LOOKED AROUND the bedroom for Sasha's cell phone while she was in the shower after her Saturday afternoon jog. I had waited hours to get to it. Spending the evening with her was tortuous; I couldn't get Fallon's words out of my head. We watched a movie on Netflix and I rolled over and started snoring before the movie was over. Even though I didn't have proof yet, I could barely stand to be in the same room with her, let alone in the same bed.

I took off in the morning while she slept, picking up some breakfast to bring back and planning what I would do next. When she left for her jog, I riffled nervously through her purse but she must have taken her phone with her. Now that she was in the shower, I had my chance. Finally I found it on the bed partially covered by her jogging tights. I felt like the NSA rooting around in people's personal mail while they were at work or picking up their kids from school. Quickly selecting the contacts list, I scrolled down: m, n, o, p, r. There it was—Stephen Russell—both work and cell phone numbers.

"Jude," Sasha yelled from the bathroom shower. "Will you bring me a fresh towel?"

I instinctively jumped and concealed the phone behind my back. She was still in the bathroom. I quickly placed the phone back under her tights.

"Yeah. Be there in a sec."

I didn't want to look at her, much less talk with her, but I got a towel from the linen closet and handed it to her.

"Thanks, sweetie," she said. I walked out of the bathroom without a word.

I went to the kitchen for a scotch, not my usual Saturday afternoon routine, but under the circumstances, completely understandable. A couple of sips and my jitters began to subside. Was Sasha, my friend from college who stood with me so many times at protests and marches, who planned the rallies with me and the others, an insider for the CEO of one the world's most powerful investment firms? Was she doing it just for the money? Even worse, was she sleeping with him, too?

"A little early to be drinking, don't you think?" Sasha snipped as she stood in the doorway to the kitchen wearing my bathrobe. "What do you want to do for dinner?"

"I needed a drink." I said abruptly. Any plan I had of being casual about all this flew out the window. I felt like choking her to death.

"Okay, suit yourself. Just don't get drunk. I'd like to go out for a nice dinner tonight." She flounced back into the bedroom to get dressed.

"I'll get drunk if I want," I snapped back, following her to the bedroom.

She turned on me as I stood in the doorway. "What the fuck is wrong with you? You've been acting distant since last night."

Sasha turned away to pick up her clothes on the bed. My stomach began to knot. I really had no appetite for this confrontation, but I had set the stage for our little talk and couldn't go back now.

"You know, Sasha, I thought we were friends. I thought you were someone I could trust."

"What are you talking about? Of course, you can trust me."

Funny how she said that without looking directly at me. I took another drink.

"Really?"

"Yes," she said as she walked to me, her arms curving in an embrace.

I turned away avoiding contact. "I have it on good authority that you have been telling a certain Chamber member information that I shared with you in confidence."

"What information? With who? You think I would blab things you told me in confidence?" She laughed, but I could hear a hard edge under her words.

"Did you?"

"Like what?" She crossed her arms defiantly.

"Like the size of the stimulus package we intended to recommend."

"What are you talking about? No way." She didn't move.

"Did I mention the size of the package to you, Sasha?"

"Yeah, I think so, but that was between you and me." Her voice faltered just a bit. I, on the other hand, was feeling stronger. I felt a knife twisting in my gut, but at least I was getting to the truth.

"Then how did your friend at the Chamber, Stephen Russell, find out?"

"Who? I don't know who you're talking about. It didn't come from me." She turned back to the bed and hastily began stuffing her running clothes into her overnight bag.

"You don't know Stephen Russell?"

"No. Well, yes, maybe. I think so—a guy from the Chamber. I've talked to him a couple of times." She collected her shoes from where she had kicked them off and made really quite a show of ignoring me. It was certainly an interesting way to handle my accusations.

"So you know him."

"Yes, I know him. I work at the Chamber. He's a member. But I never told him anything you've said to me."

Maybe she did only know of him casually through the Chamber despite what Fallon's friend had said. I held on to that little shred of hope. Still, in my gut, this was beginning to feel like quite the charade. Had I been played this whole time?

"I think you're lying, Sasha."

She turned to look at me square on, anger in her eyes. "How the fuck do you know who I talk to or what I tell them?" Score a point for me, I thought, as I took another sip of scotch.

"I hear things too, you know."

"What does that mean?"

"It means your friend has a big mouth." I knew this wasn't the truth, but I couldn't think of anything else to say.

Sasha's eyes darted from one side of the bedroom to the other.

"I don't believe you. Stephen would never tell your people anything. No one at the Chamber would say anything. They're not your friends, Mr. Director of whatever you call it."

There was a boatload of information in that little outburst. Obviously, everything Fallon had said was true. Worse, whatever I thought we had at the beginning of this little romance was probably my imagination. She'd been digging for intel the whole fucking time. What was it Anton had said to me that night? "There are powerful men who are determined to get their way. And they are watching and manipulating."

"I never said we found out from Russell."

"Fuck off, Jude. I'm tired of you and your cigarette smoke, and I don't need the fucking third degree from you. I'm bored with your progressive little elitism anyway."

I had to give her credit; she didn't miss a beat. Now that the game was over, she was all business. She dressed, packed up the remaining things she had in my townhouse, and left my bathrobe laying on the bathroom floor while I poured another scotch in the kitchen. The picture in the entrance way rattled against the wall as she slammed the door on her way out.

I lit a cigarette and threw the old Zippo on top of the near-empty pack on the kitchen counter. I stared at the lighter, and the memories of its former owner flooded my mind and my heart. I wondered what Grandpa would think of Sasha. What was it he used to say? "Only trust 'em as far as you can throw them." That was it. For a man who never graduated high school and ran a small independent hardware store his entire working life, he certainly had great insight to people.

I took a long drag on my smoke, remembering some of the other things my grandfather had told me as a kid. He was the closest thing I had to a father. What would he think about the economic mess our country was in now? He had always worked hard, played fair, and never let anyone down. At his funeral, his relatives and friends offered the same condolence: "He was a good man." Would he say the same of Sasha . . . or the people who got us into this mess?

56

Present Time
Kataploa, Amorgos, Greece

I LOOKED OUT over the harbor at Katapola, thinking about Sasha. The relationship had grown stale some time before I discovered her betrayal; maybe our blowout was just what I needed to focus my energy more fully on my work. The new administration still had a lot to do. And I was forever grateful to Fallon, not only for tipping me off to Sasha, but for not outing me to the team as the source of the leak. I didn't know anyone else in my life who would protect me that way, except for Anton.

By the end of February, a recovery bill had passed Congress, but the stimulus was only half the amount needed, in spite of my arguments that it should be bigger. It might be enough to keep things from getting worse, but not enough to get a substantial number of people back to work. I couldn't help wondering if my inadvertent leak killed any prospect for a larger package. Whether the president ever found out on his own about that, I couldn't tell. He had said he would go with the smaller package and more tax cuts to demonstrate he could work with Republicans. Regardless of his reasons, that wasn't good news for the mid-term elections; his supporters, disappointed by his actions, would fail to turn out to vote. The stimulus helped stave off the crash we all feared, but economic growth remained anemic. While the banks and Wall Street got back on their feet, unemployment stuck stubbornly to 10% well into the summer.

The banks were a big part of the problem, and I was often at loggerheads with my colleagues about why we needed to take additional action to save the banks when it was the poor and the middle-class who needed help. The banks had recapitalized themselves with the help of the TARP program, but consumer demand was far too low to spur enough growth to help the unemployed.

With sixteen million people out of work and millions more concerned about their jobs, people were only buying the basics and paying off the debt they had accumulated during the previous five years. Banks continued to make money off derivative speculation and the spread between their near-zero cost of money from the Fed and interest earned on safe investments like T Bills. Loans, on the other hand, which were supposed to be their primary business, were scarce.

They claimed there was little demand for bank loans, but I suspected they had other motives. Even people with high credit scores and good jobs were being turned down, and I wondered how the real estate market was going to improve if no one could get a mortgage.

Meanwhile, American corporations stood on the sidelines, not willing to take risks, obliged only to satisfy the demands of their shareholders to grow their bottom line. They weren't going to hire in the U.S. They were producing goods at a cheaper cost and selling them elsewhere around the globe—China, India, Brazil, and the like.

Every time I saw that ubiquitous "Made in China" label, my stomach tightened. American corporations had forgotten the country that made them. Millions of their fellow citizens were struggling to make their mortgage payments and put food on the table for their kids. Americans went without health insurance, hoping they would get by until they found a job with benefits. Many lost their homes and now lived in the streets and under the overpasses of the highways that blanketed the country. But the corporations turned away—they were global now.

The economy eventually stopped declining and began actually moving in an upward direction. But progress was slow—too slow. Without significant growth, the debt became a major focus. It started even before the president was inaugurated, but by summer the voice was growing, threatening to throw tea into the harbor. The mantra of the Southern Cone and Southeast Asia was murmuring throughout our country.

But today on Amorgos the only voices were those of the people who lived here and the gulls circling above the harbor in search of dinner. The only mantra was that of the sea and the wind. Why would I ever go back?

The sun was setting on the harbor at Katapola, shadowing the east side of the nearest islands of Kiros and Shinoossa in deep purple. After thirty-four hours of travel, I took a shower, shaved, and finally changed clothes. The desk clerk recommended a small restaurant a couple of blocks away. Tired and hungry, and not feeling particularly adventurous, I took his advice. I ordered dolmades and a local fish caught that day. The food was good, but I would miss the wine list at the Old Ebbitt Grill.

57

Spring 2009
Washington D.C.

ANOTHER WEEKLY MEETING on key economic indicators; another pile of fresh statistics to decipher and digest. This time the news was mixed—orders for durable goods were up as was the stock market, but unemployment barely budged. Although weekly jobless claims were down for the second month in a row, we knew that reflected the number of people who had run out of their unemployment compensation after 99 weeks of checks; they had reached the limit allowed under current law. I packed up my briefcase in the conference room at Treasury. The rest of the Economic Council had left, leaving Fallon and me alone in the room. She continued to check through the reports, even though the afternoon light was fading.

"How about dinner tonight, Fal?"

"Oh, Jude, I'd love to, but my brother, Mikey, is in town." She didn't look up from the files.

"Really, what for?"

"He's attending the International Conference on Solar Storms." I conjured up the faces of Fallon's brothers, one redhead, one with dark hair. And I was reminded of the conversation I had had with Patrick at their father's funeral. Fallon had managed a mysterious rise in academia and government positions, while her older brothers toiled in small business and public service. I had forgotten all about it until now.

"What? I thought Mike was a businessman, not a scientist."

"His surge protectors, idiot. Some big annual conference sponsored by the National Oceanic and . . ."

"NOAA. Oh, yeah." That's right, Fallon had told me he was looking for government funding to finish developing his product. And, of course, he didn't need to be a scientist to get a government contract.

"So if you can't join me, where's this woman you said you'd fix me up with?"

"Huh?" She finally looked up at me.

"You know, the someone better you'd find me if I broke up with Sasha."

"Still working on it, my friend," Fallon said, gathering up her things and shooting me a sly smile. "You are picky, and it's taking me a while to find just the right one."

"I'm beginning to think you lied just to get me away from her." I smiled back. "Is there any woman I can trust anymore?"

MICHAEL CONNELLY POURED a Coke in a glass of ice at the banquet table outside the large conference room at the Marriot Hotel in Alexandria. He fished through the bowl of snacks and pulled out a granola bar. The plenary session of the annual conference on solar activity was starting in ten minutes.

It was Mike's first government-sponsored conference. He had been to a few electrical engineering conventions during his career, but they were usually small affairs sponsored by the university in Buffalo. He stood outside the room, wondering who was attending this event—most likely scientists, government officials from the Department of Energy, NOAA, even FEMA. There were a few suits, but most were dressed like him in slacks and dress shirts without a tie.

He didn't expect to know anyone here; he came at the request of Dr. Rudolph Mengus from NOAA who was delivering the opening address. Mengus knew of his surge protection invention and had spent an hour or so talking to Mike about it on the phone. "Come to the conference," he had said. "There might be an opportunity to meet some people who could help you with funding."

He needed to move his prototype into a production-ready surge protector. In this sea of people, how was he going to find who could help him? Maybe he'd look for someone in the DOE, try to find out the status of any legislation that could provide his company some seed money. With the downturn in the economy, he was barely paying his business expenses. He had already laid off 20% of his employees. Without the seed money he didn't know how long he could keep his doors open.

Mike looked at his watch; he should probably go in. By the time he walked through the center doors to the room, most of the seats had been taken. He looked up and down the packed aisles and finally decided to stand with a few others in the back of the room. The lights dimmed and the huge screen on the stage flickered to life with the title of Mengus's address: *Is Armageddon Nearer Than You Think?* Dr. Mengus, tall and lean with a shock of prematurely white hair, hopped onto the stage amidst a rousing applause from the audience. He clipped a microphone to his shirt collar.

"Can you hear me in the back?" he asked, checking the volume of the microphone.

The guy next to Mike yelled "Just fine!" and Mengus continued.

"Welcome, ladies and gentlemen, to the Tenth Annual Conference on Solar Activity." Mengus took a long drag on the bottle of water he carried in his right hand. "Most of you have heard that our sun is beginning a cycle of increased solar activity. Certainly, this is not a new phenomenon; the sun periodically enters such cycles and then retreats to a more benign phase. The interesting thing about this cycle is that early predictions portend a fairly robust period of solar activity over the next three years—perhaps the most intense activity we have seen since scientists began studying and measuring the sun's cycles."

Mike thought back to the last period of intense solar activity some twenty years ago. That one had a big impact on Quebec, creating electrical outages throughout the city.

"You can predict by the title of my presentation that I have some concerns about this new solar cycle—some real concerns. So let's get on with it. First, some basics."

He clicked the small remote in his left hand. A slide of the sun erupting into bright orange bubbles appeared on the screen—a picture obviously taken by a satellite orbiting the sun. Mengus moved to the side of the stage with the ease of a cat.

"A solar flare is an explosion of the sun's magnetic energy. A coronal mass ejection, or CME as we call it, is a billion-ton cloud of matter and electromagnetic radiation exploding from the solar surface and beyond the sun's corona."

A new slide appeared, this time of a gelatinous orange blob extending well beyond the surface of the sun.

"While we do not understand a causal relationship between flares and CMEs, we believe they are related. Study on the cause of both solar flares and mass ejections continue. Why should we care? Because in the new period of solar activity, the likelihood of solar flares and mass ejections will increase exponentially. But the purpose of this discussion is the potential impact of these solar events on Earth."

Again a pronounced push on the remote and several more slides came to life on the giant screen, mostly of solar events. To Mike they were beautiful, but these were only pictures of something far off in space. Just how damaging could these flares be if they came into contact with Earth? Mengus paced back and forth across the stage, delivering his presentation with crafted precision.

"If an ejection moves in the direction of Earth, its solar particles can cause a geomagnetic storm that can disrupt Earth's magnetosphere. That storm can release terawatts of energy directed at the Earth's upper atmosphere. Most of the time these storms affect the magnetic poles and often produce an aurora borealis in the Northern Hemisphere or aurora australis in the Southern Hemisphere." A slide of the northern lights flickered across the screen.

"A number of us have seen these firsthand, especially if you've been to Alaska. But the intense radiation emanating from geomagnetic storms can cause radiation poisoning in humans and other animals on Earth. Fortunately, except for astronauts, our atmosphere and magnetosphere protect us from these severe effects, and generally leave us amazed as the northern lights twist and turn in the night sky. So why should we be concerned with solar flares and coronal mass ejections?" A slide divided into four quadrants appeared.

"A number of critical systems which we rely on as humans could be severely disrupted by a geomagnetic storm. Communications and navigation systems. Satellites. Pipelines. Electric grids."

Pictures of oceanic ships, cars, and a highway map appeared next on the screen.

"Communications that use the ionosphere to transmit radio waves over long distances could experience fluctuating signals, e.g., ship-to-shore, shortwave broadcasts, and amateur radio. Solar flares would disrupt GPS and LORAN signals, and for many of us, that means we would be lost." A chuckle spread through the room as Mengus punched his remote again. A picture of a giant satellite orbiting earth covered the screen.

"So far you say, 'So what'; there's nothing here that is absolutely critical to the functioning of our society. But what about satellites? Ah, you say, 'Now we're talking'."

"A geomagnetic storm can heat the upper atmosphere, causing it to expand. For satellites in low Earth orbit, this can produce drag on the satellite, causing its orbit to decay. If we don't correct the orbit, the satellite will eventually plummet to Earth. Remember Skylab?" Laughter arose from the audience. "Even more important, solar particles can destroy the microprocessors in a number of our satellites. Electrical discharges can completely disable a satellite. And what do we use satellites for? Telephones. Television. Radio. And yes, the Internet. Have I got your attention now?"

A picture of a pipeline coming out of and then going into the ground in a suburban neighborhood leapt on the screen.

"Pipelines crisscross our country carrying natural gas, gasoline and diesel fuel, oil, and water. A geomagnetic storm can produce currents in pipelines that affect the flow meters in the pipes, giving operators invalid flow information. Reacting to erroneous data could cause the operators to take actions that cause the pipes to explode. Not a pretty picture in a heavily populated city. And finally, there is the electric grid."

Now Mengus had Mike's attention as a slide of power transmission lines on huge steel towers popped onto the screen. This is the part where his invention came in.

"I will spare you all the technical details, but just let me say that geomagnetic storms can wipe out generators and transformers, especially for power grids that operate over very long transmission lines. Hey, Canada and the USA, that includes you." The audience laughed again. "Remember Quebec in 1989? That geomagnetic storm took out the transformers in their electric grid, cutting off power for 6 million people for over 9 hours."

The title of Mengus's presentation again appeared.

"Okay. I think you're beginning to get the picture of the potential damage a geomagnetic storm can create." Dr. Mengus paced from one side of the stage to the other. "In 1859 we had a major geomagnetic storm that effected a good portion of the Earth. Back then we didn't have satellites, few pipelines, and certainly not the complex electric grid of today. If that storm were to hit today near a major population area, it is estimated that over 130 million people would lose electric service, over 350 transformers would be destroyed, and it would cost over $2 trillion dollars and many months or years to repair the damage. One reason it would take so long is that transformers are in short supply. The waiting list is now three years." Mengus stood still, his arms in the air, as though appealing to a higher power.

"So think about how we use electricity today in order to fully appreciate the impact of a geomagnetic storm on our electric grid. Transportation, communications, financial systems, government operations—all would all be severely disrupted. For each of us, it would also mean the loss of refrigeration, leading to food spoilage, and the loss of potable water that we use to drink, take showers and flush our toilets. It would be quite the mess." This time the audience laughter was more muted.

"Can we prevent this kind of impact to our electric grid? Yes, we can. We protect our home electronics from electrical surges by using surge suppressors. We can employ the same principles to protect the transformers in our grid. Mind you, these surge suppressors are a little bigger than the ones we plug into our walls. How big did you say they were, Mike?"

Mengus gazed out over the audience looking for Mike. Mike raised his hand, startled to be singled out. "Ah, there you are." Mengus said. "How big is your surge protector, Mike?"

"About the size of a washing machine," Mike yelled from the back of the room, trying to demonstrate its size with his arms as the audience turned toward him.

"There you go. Ladies and gentlemen, this is Mike Connelly, who has successfully built and tested the type of surge suppressor we will need to protect our grid." Several people turned around in their seats and there was a quiet hum of approval.

"So what is the cost to insulate our electric grid in the U.S.? The math is simple: 5000 transformers that need protection at a projected cost of $40,000 to $50,000 per surge protector equal $250 million. Wow! That sounds like a lot of money, and it is. But let's look at some comparative numbers. How much did it cost us to bail out IAFI? $285 billion. What are the annual revenues of the electric industry? $385 billion. And as I have said earlier, a major geomagnetic storm hitting the U.S. could cost an estimated $2 *trillion* to repair, not to mention the costs associated with loss of economic activity." Mengus paused, gazing out into the audience, letting the magnitude of his words sink in.

Mike looked around the room. People were still turning and looking at him. Someone shoved a business card in his hand. He quickly reached into his pocket for his own.

58

Fall 2009

WHILE THE ANEMIC economy continued to fixate my attention over the summer, by fall it had become even further complicated. The debate over the president's progressive healthcare reform initiative—proposed as a way to protect consumers who were being bankrupted when serious illness struck and extend coverage for some thirty million individuals who lived without health insurance—was furious on both sides of the aisle, as well as throughout the country. I knew the banks were politically entrenched with members of Congress, but I had no idea how much control the health insurance and pharmaceutical companies had developed over the years. There were few in Congress willing to take them on, as these industries controlled the debate that dominated the airwaves and news cycles with advertisements against the initiative. Even medical care had become a political football. It looked like our healthcare initiative would fail, but the public debate at least gave my team cover while we worked on an equally important initiative—financial regulatory reform.

Both the House and Senate were crafting legislation that would try to rein in the abuses of the recent past that led to our financial crisis. Fallon and I had several meetings with the leadership and committee chairs of both houses of Congress, trying to influence their legislation, but we both quickly realized she and I had different opinions on how to regulate our financial institutions in the future. It was Fallon's idea that we block out an afternoon to try to end our impasse. Of course, Fallon insisted the debate be conducted on her turf at the Treasury Department, across the street from the White House.

After almost an hour of arguing the pros and cons of the risky trades the banks were doing that were more suitable to Wall Street investment firms, Fallon finally acquiesced to my position that the banks should be banned from derivative trading entirely. We settled on allowing derivative trading to be conducted on public exchanges by only those parties who had an interest in the trades they were making. That would make the deals transparent and drastically curtail speculation by investors and hedge funds that affected the wild swings in prices of commodities, like oil.

"Okay, I'm going to accept your position, Jude, and that will be our position to the legislative committees." She had put up a good fight, but she knew this was the right thing to do. "But don't get excited. I doubt we'll get the Senate and the House to go along with it. The investment bank lobbies have a strong hand in the halls."

I couldn't believe she was finally ready to go after the derivatives market. And she was right—it would be a hard sell.

Fallon knew my next argument only too well: there would be no meaningful reform of our banking system until we diversified the risks among a broader pool of smaller banks. After all, I should know—I was there when the Fed sanctioned the mergers and acquisitions that created the megabanks in the first place. Like I told Marie Turbeau at the time: "I'm not so sure that's good for our financial system." Although I cautioned the Fed Chair that there were risks with concentrating financial assets in a handful of very large institutions, he seemed less concerned. I should have pushed harder. Anton had warned me there were people watching how I decided on certain issues. I wondered what might have happened if I had more broadly asserted my reservations?

"What if we could limit the deposits a bank could hold?" Fallon asked. "At a minimum, it would prevent them from them getting any bigger. Over time we could lower the limit. Wouldn't that accomplish the same thing?"

A senator or two had mentioned the same option, but there was little appetite in the Congress to follow through. Anything that smacked of limits was *verboten*. It would corral the problem, but fundamentally wouldn't fix it.

"It keeps them at their current size, which is still too big to fail, Fallon, so we're still at risk," I pointed out. "And there's no guarantee we can get the limit lowered over time. Hell, it's more likely to be increased, given our history. Frankly, I think the banks are more interested in investment trading than deposit services and loans anyway. Let them become investment firms and get out of the regulated financial system."

"Good luck with that, Jude." She opened a bottle of water and took a long drink. "They still like the big M & A deals, and if we curtail what they can do on the investment side of their business, they can't fund mergers and acquisitions on their own without the deposit base."

"Are we going to capitulate to the financial services industry again? At least, let's do what we should have done three years ago—raise their FDIC premiums to cover any liquidation costs should they get into trouble again." At a minimum Fallon could agree to that, but I was losing patience. I felt like I was negotiating with the Republicans, not my own team. "Oh, and while we're at it, let's put some teeth into the legislation that makes the ratings agencies criminally responsible for the ratings they gave the assets of the derivative deals. Their negligence caused the crisis, too."

I was just getting ready to launch into the seamy underbelly of the ratings agencies when Fallon's office phone rang.

"Yes." she said as she picked up the phone.

"No, I'll take it." She looked at me with a nod, raising a "just a minute" finger.

Fallon punched the line 1 button. "Mikey, how are you?"

"What? How deep are you in? That's a lot."

I made a move to leave but she waved me back to my chair.

"What does the bank say? Well, how about private capital? I don't know; there are a number of sources. Are you sure the numbers don't work? We're seeing some improvement. It will just take a year or two. How much time do you have? Well, what are you going to do? The GRID bill, yeah, I remember you mentioned it over dinner the last time you were in D.C. I can get our legislative liaison to look into it. I believe you. You developed it. Of course it will work. It would save your business. I get it, but you have a family to support in the meantime. No, Mike, I'm not trying to make you feel guilty. Yes, I can help with the house payments for a while. Okay, let's talk tonight. I'll call you."

Fallon hung up the phone and had a vacant look on her face. Her end of the conversation had red flags all over it.

"Everything okay, Fal?" Of course it wasn't. She had kept her cool on the phone, but I could see distress on her face.

"Mikey is thinking about closing his business. He's in hock for over $250k with the bank, and orders are off over 50% with the recession. He's been counting on the passage of a bill called The GRID Act that's tied up in Congress, which would fund deployment of his line of surge protectors. It's supposed to pass the House, but the Senate's wrapped it up with other more controversial energy legislation."

I could see the dominos falling, another casualty. Collateral damage. "What is he going to do?"

"Look for a job."

"Good luck with that. Really, Fallon, there's no way to save his business without the R & D money?"

"I don't know. I'll talk with him tonight." She had run out of steam; our previous discussion would be tabled for another day. "Maybe he's not being creative enough, you know, there might be another source of private capital he's not looking at."

I knew Fallon meant well, but she'd never run a business before. We were both policy wonks; neither of us had enough knowledge of the options that might be available to her brother. The effects of the recession were hitting mighty close to home. It was a reality check we probably both needed.

"Who's in charge of legislative affairs these days?" she asked. "I need to check with them on the outlook of this bill Mikey's talking about." She turned to her computer and started typing.

"I don't know who's coordinating the energy legislation—David would. So is Mike still making a house payment?"

"They've lived there for fifteen years." She gazed at the monitor. "I don't know what's left on the mortgage, but after fifteen years I'm sure they have a big equity stake. Kind of hard to walk away from that." She turned her gaze from the computer and looked at me, her eyes watering. "Christ, they have to have food, pay the utilities. Let's hope no one gets seriously ill or hurt."

I left her office, stopped in at mine long enough to collect my stuff, and headed home early. Mike's call had opened up a big wrinkle in the whole situation, and I couldn't shake a feeling of despair. I wanted a drink, a smoke, and some time out.

Fallon called later that night; she had already spoken to Mike again and tried to keep things light, but I could tell she was deeply concerned.

The GRID bill had good prospects, she told me. "It's a national security necessity, but nothing is moving fast through Congress. The GOP is saying no to everything except tax cuts and defense spending, and even that is being scrutinized," she said. "I told him it would take time, Jude . . . but time is something he doesn't have."

"ANTON," I SAID, seeing his name and phone number displayed on my home phone and happy to hear from him again. It had been too long.

"Jude, my man, how are you?"

"Busy, and I'm not your man."

"Sorry, really, force of habit," he said with a laugh. "I just called to see what you are doing over Christmas."

"I don't know. I haven't thought that far in advance." It was still over two months away. Holidays with Gillian had meant the whole shebang—the tree, the packages, the big meals, the cocktail parties with other families. Since the split, we had some awkward visits over Christmas, with Lex bouncing back and forth between us. It had been pathetic on all fronts.

"Any chance you might like to spend it in Toronto?"

I remembered that big, old house from all those years ago; it was hardly a cozy place but it could be just the break in routine that I needed. "With you, in your mansion?"

"Hardly a mansion, but the place is a bit big for one person now that Jack and, I mean Dad and Mom are gone."

I fixed myself a scotch while we spoke. What would Lex think of Anton's place? I had told her about it, but that was ancient history. I wondered if she'd have any interest in seeing it.

"I don't know; Lex is with me this Christmas."

"Wonderful. She would come too. I haven't seen my goddaughter in over a year. Do you think she'd like to spend the holiday here? Of course, I would spoil her with gifts. You have to tell me everything she wants." He sounded genuinely delighted. I couldn't fault him for that; he doted on Lex.

"She's got enough stuff, and we don't make a big deal with gifts anymore. She is seventeen." My thoughts switched to Christmas gifts for Lex. It was just around the corner. "But I'm sure she would like some snow over Christmas. Do you think you can make that happen?"

"I know you think I am a god, Jude, but I will do what I can. After all, it will be December in Toronto. At least it will be cold enough for

Lex and I to go skating on the pond. We can have a turkey with all of the trimmings. Plenty of Macallan and good wine. What do you think?"

It did sound appealing to get out of D.C. for a while, not to mention spending more time than just a quick dinner with my friend. "Are you reliving your childhood?"

Anton chuckled. "Perhaps a little; I am regressing as I get older, but it would be fun. Anyway, it would give you and me some time to talk like we did when you were dodging the draft. We have not done that in a long time."

"Those weren't entirely good memories, but I guess we could as long as you're not doing the cooking." I lit a cigarette and flipped through the kitchen calendar. Lex had already marked off her school break. The "Daddy!" she had scrawled across the holiday weeks caught me by surprise. She hadn't called me Daddy in years. I rubbed my eyes. Memories tumbled through my mind: Lex as a little kid, running to meet me when I came home from work, the perfect symbol of that "normal" suburban life I had so craved so many years ago. I thought of Fallon's brother Mike, his own middle-class dreams torpedoed without warning.

"Listen, I have to clear it with Lex. And you know that things could happen in D.C. that might make it difficult to get out of town—a last minute crisis."

"I understand, of course. But for planning purposes, please come early on the 24th and stay through Christmas Day. Okay? Please, Jude, this would mean so much to me."

Anton pleading—how could I say no? "Okay, we'll plan on it."

I made a note on the calendar and was about to hang up the phone when the thought came to me. Jesus, why didn't I think of that? "Anton," I said as I put the receiver back to my mouth, "are you still there?"

"Yes, what is it?"

"You represent various investment capitalists, don't you?" My mind was racing.

"In a limited way, usually international acquisitions and investments. Why?"

"Do you remember the power black-out in Quebec in '89?"

"Of course, who here in Canada could forget that? Why do you ask?"

"I might have a very good investment opportunity for a product that could prevent that from happening again. There's some legislation pending here that would make it a good revenue opportunity."

"Do you know the return on investment?" Anton's voice shifted into business-mode. That guy, he didn't miss a trick. If there was a good deal to be made, he'd want to be the first to hear of it.

"I'm not a businessman, and I don't know those numbers, but it's got very large revenue potential. With the right investors who have manufacturing expertise, the right cost-to-revenue ratio could be achieved."

"Who has this investment opportunity?"

"Fallon's brother, Mike. In Buffalo. He has a commercial surge protector product that could save our electric grid from what I hear, but he needs funding to tide him over until the Congress appropriates the funds for further development and deployment." I stubbed out my smoke. Here I was, Jude Anders, dealmaker.

"Get me his number. I would be happy to talk with him about it."

"YOU'VE SEEMED DISTANT lately," Fallon insisted as we sat down for lunch in the White House cafeteria. It had been a week since my call with Anton. I wondered if he had had any luck with finding an investor for Mike's business. Surely, Mike would say something to Fallon if he had heard from Anton.

"I've just had a lot on my mind." It had become my standard reply.

"It looks like our financial reform measures are going to pass both houses, so what's going on?" She arranged her salad, fork, and paper napkin on the table and pushed the tray away.

"In spite of the restrictions, the banks will still be in the derivatives business and are still too big to fail. I'm aware of the political realities as you call them, but my instincts tell me that if we don't completely kill the beast, it will rise again, and then someone else will have to clean up its new mess." I unwrapped a cold tuna sandwich, sniffed it, and took a bite.

"This legislation will pretty much keep it locked up in its cage, to use your analogy," She dug into her salad.

"For how long? If we can't get this economy growing again, there'll be plenty of pressure to let it out." I had seen that political and economic reality a number of times during my career at the Fed. "I think this was our time, Fallon, and we missed it."

"You're just too wrapped up in this. Some progress is better than none." She took a bite of her salad. She seemed satisfied by the legislation that was crafted; I knew it did not go near far enough. "Why don't you take some time off? Go up into the Shenandoahs for a weekend to chill. I hear the leaves are gorgeous."

How could anybody *not* be wrapped up in it? Financial reform was the one thing I wanted to accomplish since I got my position in the administration. What we were agreeing to was only a partial victory.

"Yeah, maybe. There's a position paper I've been thinking of writing. Maybe a weekend away would help me clear my head and at least get a first draft." I couldn't let it linger any longer; some ideas had to get put on paper before they could become real.

"What position paper? Something for POTUS?"

"No, no, it's just something I've been thinking about off and on since . . . since the Asian crisis. I call it Plan B." Of course I had thought about another Plan B from long ago; we were going to blow up the ROTC building. I was glad cooler heads prevailed then. This time around, my Plan B was probably equally incendiary, but not in the literal sense. At least, I didn't expect it to be.

Fallon tried to cut a pale pink cherry tomato with her knife; the thing looked as hard as a golf ball. Finally she gave up.

"Plan B? What the hell is that?"

"I'll tell you when I finish it. Okay?"

"Jesus, Jude. You don't have to get snippy."

"I'm sorry. You're right. I guess I do need to get away."

When I went back to my office, I got on my PC and looked up resorts in the Shenandoah Mountains. A long weekend away from D.C. might help me put my thoughts into a coherent framework—one that the president would not dismiss out of hand as being crackpot, assuming I ever showed it to him. Even if he never did anything with it, at least he'd have a different vision than the one that is so ingrained in us from the time we learn how to balance checkbooks.

59

Christmas 2009
Toronto, Canada

"CRAP, CUSTOMS IN Canada," I said when I saw the line for non-Canadians. "It used to be easy coming here from the States. Where's your passport, Lex?"

"Right here, Dad. Just chill. You get yourself so uptight over the smallest things."

Lex carried her school backpack, stuffed to the gills with school books and the latest sequel to *Nightwatch* by an up and coming Russian author, and parked her duffle bag at her feet. Her parka was slung over her arm and she looked for all the world as though she were just hanging around in the mall, her skinny jeans tucked into her Uggs just like every other teenage girl in the airport.

"I know. It's just that traveling out of the country makes me anxious." Travel anywhere, even within the States, had become complicated and nerve-wracking. I chewed some gum and tried to stay calm. "Let's just get through customs. I hope Anton can find us."

"He's got a cell phone. You have a cell phone. Duh," she said as we inched our way through the line.

Lex and I finally walked through the opaque doors into the terminal building of Pearson International Airport and looked around for Anton. He was standing at the end of a long line of people greeting the foreigners coming into Canada. The image of Jim Jones standing at the end of the arrival line in the Buenos Aires airport over twenty years ago raced through my mind. Lex saw him first and ran up to him.

"Uncle Anton!" She threw her arms around him, somehow managing to be both the little girl we both adored and a young woman on the cusp of an independence I was sorry to see arriving so quickly.

"Elexus. My, look at you. You are almost a full-grown woman."

Lex shot him a look. "What do you mean almost? I'm seventeen."

A long underground tunnel took us to the airport-parking garage. Anton was driving a new bright red Audi A6. I was surprised; I had expected a black one. Maybe this was his version of a midlife crisis. After loading our luggage in the trunk, Anton gunned the Audi through the parking garage and headed out into the Toronto winter.

"Wow. It's snowing." Lex stared out the window as we drove toward the exit of the airport. "How much are we going to get?"

"A lot, and with the eight inches on the ground, there should be enough for a very fine snowman. What do you think, Lex?"

"Totally."

Anton shot me a look; he had already expressed confusion over his unfamiliarity with teen lingo. I resisted the urge to tell him to chill out.

With the snow coming down at a pretty good clip, it took us about forty-five minutes to reach Anton's house. Aside from a lot more tree growth, it looked pretty much the same as the first time I drove into the driveway in early '71. We trundled our luggage through the front door, which I had never used before. Anton and I had always entered through the rear door near the kitchen.

"Just leave your luggage." Anton closed the door and took our coats. "Anyone hungry?"

"Sure," Lex said, "I'm always hungry." She stood in the front foyer and stared at the high ceilings, the elegant stairway curving down from the second floor, the lush floral carpets, and enormous paintings on the walls.

"Fresh soup and sandwiches, Lex."

"What kind of soup?"

"Lex, come on."

"It is quite alright, Jude. I do not eat things that are distasteful either."

"The kitchen is this way, Lex. Follow me."

I looked into the formal dining room, remembering the meals I used to share with his family there, and was grateful Anton had kept things casual this afternoon. Even so, the small kitchen table was set, plates, bowls and flatware at the ready. The soup was hot, the sandwiches fresh; whatever staff he had attending to him were nowhere to be seen.

"Welcome to Toronto," Anton toasted, lifting his glass of chardonnay before he took his seat at the table next to the bay window, "and happy holidays."

"Happy holidays," Lex and I toasted back.

"Now, Lex, please tell me all about your school. What are you studying, what are your friends like, do you have a boyfriend? Well, of course you must, so tell me about him. Next year you will be going to college, so what are your plans?"

Lex would chew his ear off with that list of questions. She started in with the boyfriend. I guess we both could tell what was most important to her. I slowly sipped my soup and picked at my sandwich while I drank my glass of wine and looked out the window at the falling snow, thinking of the year and half I lived in Toronto. That was so long ago. I couldn't remember what I felt back then, other than fear of being drafted or worse. Had I just gotten older or had I buried any feelings I had back then to deal with my situation? And what were my feelings now? I had pretty much shut down since the last years with Gillian. I sat there thinking and watched the falling snow. I was angry when Gillian asked for the divorce, I was happy when I first met Sasha, and livid when I found out she was using me to gather information for her friends in the corporate elite and the political opposition. I was excited when I went to work on the president's campaign and later selected to serve in his administration. Beyond that, what have I felt besides love for the girl sitting across from me?

"Well, what universities would be the best fit for that?" Anton asked.

"Princeton. Where else?" She had wolfed down her sandwich in between filling Anton in, and reached for some grapes on a fruit platter in the center of the table.

"Wow. That is a very fine university. Have you submitted an application yet?"

"Jeez, you and Dad are just alike."

"And to Virginia and Maryland. Please tell her these are good state universities, will you?" I inserted while pouring myself another glass of wine.

"Well, of course they are, but Princeton would be at the top of the list, especially for her planned areas of study." Anton took the bottle from me and refilled his glass as well.

"And so will the price tag. I'm a public servant, not a CEO. Besides, who says Princeton will accept her?" I hated to phrase it that way but it was the truth; there were no guarantees and I hated for her to get her hopes up.

"Oh, come on, Jude. She says she has a 4.0 grade point average from a reputable high school, and her father is the Director of the National Economic Council. I think there will be no problem with her acceptance."

That made sense, but the cost would be a big hurdle. Lex would be devastated if she was accepted but I couldn't afford it. I had spent many a late evening scrolling through the financial aid forms, not to mention seeking out scholarship applications.

"We'll see what happens," I responded.

"Look, Lex," Anton said, pointing outside. "It has quit snowing. Would you do me a big favor?"

"What is it?" She had already begun removing the dirty dishes from the table, but Anton waved her away from the task.

"Oh, I can see you have grown up. You no longer agree to requests without first understanding what they are." Anton grinned. "I would like to have a giant snowman in the front lawn. It would not be Christmas without one. Would you mind making one?"

Lex smiled. "Sure, Uncle Anton." She actually sounded as though she were patronizing him; oh, they do grow up too fast.

"Good, let me show you to your room. I have some ski clothes that should fit you, hanging in your closet, and boots of course—size eight I believe."

That was just like Anton. They took the luggage upstairs, and I grabbed my glass and wandered through the grand foyer where I first met Laurel as she was coming down the staircase. The living room was pretty much the same, everything in its proper place, even after thirty-eight years, except for the Christmas tree hiding the front windows, complete with wrapped packages underneath. I gazed at the bar where Jack had poured my first beer in a chilled glass, and was reminded of my first conversation with him on the political realities of the world. I picked up a heavy glass paperweight from an end table. It was cut like a gemstone, and I remembered it from my very first visit when I dared not touch anything.

"Does it bring back memories?" Anton stood in the doorway to the room. "It has been a long time."

"Of course it does." I carefully returned the paperweight to its original position on the table. "You and your parents took me in, made me a part of your family when I needed to belong somewhere. You know, man without a country. I was remembering my first conversation with Jack right here in this room."

"I am sorry, I don't remember it. But you still had your mother—you were not completely alone in the world."

He was right I guess, but I wasn't with her during the one holiday that mattered to me.

"Jude, what did she look like, I mean do you resemble her?" Anton went to the bar and pulled out the Macallan.

"Yeah, I guess so. I've never seen my father, remember. So maybe I look like him." His question seemed oddly out of place, and why now after all the years between us? "Did you ever try to find your real mother? If, as you claim, I could find my father, you could find her."

"But I did try to find her, several years ago, about the same time I started my inquiry into Vasco." He held two highball glasses in his hands, two ice cubes in each glass.

"And?"

"Just her death certificate, I am afraid."

"Did you find out anything about her?"

"I guess I could have, but I did not see the point." He handed me a glass, somewhat generously poured. "What I really wanted was to meet her."

We both stood silently in the large living room of Anton's house. Words could not take away my friend's remorse, the same that I had felt over the years growing up without a father.

"But you still have your real father. It's not like you're alone. By the way, why haven't you invited him for Christmas? It would be interesting to meet the man who fathered you."

"You do not want to meet him, believe me."

I was about to ask why not, but held my tongue. Over the years with Anton, I had learned when not to press an issue based on how he responded and the tone in his voice. This was one of those times. I let it go and changed the subject instead.

"How's the export-import business?"

"Well, it is fine, but first I have to tell you that I have found some bridge funding for Fallon's brother. You were right—it is a good investment opportunity." Anton sounded like his usual self again. "We've had to move quickly on patents. GE will steal the idea."

I was surprised he had waited so long to tell me. "That's great, Anton. And the E-I business?"

"Oh, yes, well, I've launched a new career. My father has made me CEO of his media holding company." He tapped my glass with his in a toast.

"What?"

"Yes, he turned over the controlling interest in the business and pressured the board to make me CEO after six months of working directly with him in the day-to-day operation of the business."

"That's a shock. Why didn't you tell me sooner?" I sipped my drink, already feeling a comfortable buzz from the wine.

"I was not sure how it would turn out, and you know me, I love surprises."

Frankly, I was somewhat jealous. I worked hard for most of my career advancements; Anton had them handed to him. I guess privilege did have its benefits.

"So who's running the E-I business?"

"My Chief Operating Officer and the financial guys, but I am still the boss on major deals." Anton picked up the pack of Dunhill cigarettes from the bar. "Cigarette?"

"What's it like running newspapers and radio and TV stations . . . in how many countries?" I pulled a cigarette from his pack.

Anton lit our Dunhills with an ornate butane lighter he picked up from the corner of the bar. "Seven, to be precise," he said somewhat proudly as he exhaled his first drag toward the ceiling. "Challenging and exciting. It is good to do something new. But you already know that, Jude."

Lex came bounding down the stairs dressed in a purple and gold ski outfit.

"Dad, you should see my room. It's huge, and I have my own bathroom with a whirlpool."

"I'm happy for you, Lex. Don't get too used to it." That was part of our often-used light-hearted banter about getting preoccupied with material things. Actually, this time I was happy she got a chance to enjoy a little luxury for a change.

"Look what Anton bought me. Chic, don't you think." She twirled in a circle and skipped out the front door in her new ski garb.

"How about some dessert? I believe I have some pumpkin pie," Anton said as he led the way back to the kitchen. "You know Lex will likely get into Princeton, assuming she does well on her entrance exams. Is money really an issue?"

No matter how many times I reminded him, Anton always seemed to forget that White House positions were not that glamorous, and working in the White House had long lost its shine. My paychecks, while better than many people had these days, were hardly the sort that would lend themselves to large tuition payments over the next four years. And the divorce had not helped; even though Gillian and I split the proceeds on the Maryland house, I had private high school tuition for Lex and myriad expenses that come with city living. The recession certainly did not help.

"Sadly it is. Lex's college fund took a big hit in the market crash. The market won't recover in time to make up the loss by the time she goes to college. After all, I should know."

"I suppose you would know that, but please do not worry about the financing. If she is good enough to get in, I will take care of the rest."

I stared at him. Was this Anton just being a bit overblown with his new business or was he serious? "That's hard for me to accept, my friend, even though I suspect you can afford it."

"Nonsense. She is my goddaughter, and my heart melts when she calls me 'Uncle Anton'." He helped himself to a slice of pie and a generous dollop of whipped cream.

"I appreciate the offer, but let's wait until she gets accepted, okay?"

Anton did not respond. Instead he changed topics. "I have been following some interesting developments from our media outlets in your country. These people who call themselves the Tea Party. Are you concerned about them?"

"Me personally?"

"I was thinking more of your president." His tone had shifted just enough for me to notice. I picked at my piece of pie; it was delicious but I was running out of steam after a long day of traveling, and the last thing I wanted to do was get into anything with Anton. I tried to make a joke of it.

"Now that I know your new business enterprise, I'm not sure I should tell you anything the president might be thinking, and I'm still feeling a little stung from Sasha."

"Ah, the mole in Jude Anders' bed. That is as good as any spy novel," he said with his typical little chuckle. "I understand your reluctance. But, Jude, I would never use anything you ever told me in my media business."

"What do you think of the Tea Party movement, Anton?"

"Ah, a question as an answer to my question. You are learning." He smiled. Anton loved strategy, he loved political machination, and he loved philosophizing. "But to answer your question, I have a hard time understanding how a group of people can be protesting about how high their taxes are when under your president they are the lowest they have been in half a century. How do you Yanks put it: it's like cutting off your nose to spite your face."

"You're getting good at Yankee colloquialisms." I thought about the Tea Party and their sudden prominence in the media. It's rare a fringe movement gets so much press. "But it's not just the taxes. They also say they want smaller, more limited government."

"Yes, that too," Anton nodded. "Isn't it strange that the prior administration's reduced government and little enforcement of regulations got us all into this recession. Personally, I would be clamoring for more government intervention. But then you Yanks think we Canadians are socialists."

"America is just too polarized." I watched the snow, which had started falling again. Lex occasionally darted to the rear of the house in that silly purple snowsuit. It was beginning to get dark.

Anton took a sip of scotch. "Perhaps it would have been better if the Confederacy had won your Civil War."

Now that was one angle I hadn't thought of; it certainly seemed as though the country was torn in half. "It may come to that again. May I move to Toronto if that happens?"

He laughed. "Well, of course. Secretly I believe you are half Canadian anyway." He gave me a searching look, and I wondered what that was about. "But seriously, do you think these tea people will have any influence on your political elections next year?"

"Personally, yes. The polls indicate they are gaining popularity. I've heard that they intend to co-opt a number of Republican primaries and nominate their own candidates. I don't know how successful they will be. But if they are, that could mean two things: either the Democrats will win handily in the fall election because the tea baggers are too extreme or . . .

the extremists will win because people are fed up with the way things are going. If the latter happens, the administration will have a real problem."

"How can they change anything really, even if they get into power in your Congress?"

"Based on what I've heard from their mouthpieces, they would slash government spending at a time when it is needed to keep the economy afloat. They're more concerned about our short-term debt than growing our way out of the recession."

"Is the president concerned about your debt?"

Once bitten, twice shy; there was no way I was going to answer those kinds of questions ever again. "Would you be?" I smiled.

"I can see you still don't trust me, Jude. I understand. Let's go see how Lex is doing with the snowman."

IT WAS STILL snowing on Christmas morning, and I began to wonder about our travel plans the next day. Lex's snowman stood like a sentry guarding Anton's palace. I was pouring myself a cup of coffee when Anton entered the kitchen.

"Ah, coffee. Merry Christmas, Jude."

"I'm an atheist, remember? Want a cup?"

"Sure."

I pushed a clean cup across the counter to him. The little elves had been busy in the kitchen while we slept; it was spotless, with no trace of yesterday's meals. In its place, the table was freshly set with warm coffee cake and hot scrambled eggs and bacon on a silver platter with a lid.

"Is Lex still in bed?"

"She's a teenager, Anton. Would you expect something different?"

"I thought she'd be up looking for her packages under the tree."

Anton added sugar and cream to his coffee. He wore a royal blue robe over matching pajamas, looking like something out of a Cary Grant movie. I had on an old pair of sweats and a Missouri University fleece hoodie Lex had given me for my birthday.

"That's important when you're a kid. When you're a teenager, your beauty sleep is more important. I'm sure she'll be up soon. Have *you* checked *your* packages under the tree?"

"What do you think I was doing before I came to the kitchen?" He grinned.

"You're such a kid."

"Life has few joys; opening presents on Christmas Day is one of the last remaining."

"Now I understand why you wanted us to come." I laughed and wondered what he would think of the gifts we brought him.

"That too, of course, but I really wanted to spend some time with you and Lex. And talk through some things."

"Like what?"

"Like the Tea Party from yesterday."

I wondered why Anton was so curious about the Tea Party. Was he planning a piece in one of his newspapers and looking for angles to cover them?

"What about them?"

"I am sure it would not surprise you that there are groups pouring a lot of money into their organization or should I say organizations." Anton seated himself at the table and began heaping the steaming eggs onto his plate; he waved at me to join him.

"I think we all suspect that. It's not just a grassroots movement."

"My media operations are covering them extensively." He cut a piece of warm coffee cake and put it on my plate next to the eggs. There's one thing about Anton; we would never go unfed. "From what we've learned there will be a lot of money thrown into the primaries to ensure the Tea Party candidates are nominated, as you suggested yesterday. And since your Supreme Court will rule that corporations can contribute any amount to these third-party groups, you can imagine the amount of money that will be available to the candidates. I do not think you Democrats really appreciate how much money."

He was so nonchalant about it; I almost missed the biggest piece of intel he dropped. "What do you mean 'will rule'? The Citizens United case is still before the Court."

"Oh, yes. I apologize. Of course, I have gotten ahead of reality."

I put my fork down and looked at Anton. He never said anything that was not deliberate.

"However, if one looks at the composition of the court and the various influences with interests in the case, you can see that there is a very high probability your Supreme Court will rule in favor of the plaintiffs. In that case, corporations will be able to flood non-affiliated organizations with funds to promote their agendas."

"If that happens, we know it will be millions," I said finally. "The Democratic National Committee is working to raise funds to counter their efforts."

"Perhaps you are missing a few zeros, my friend. Can your DNC raise that kind of money in any one-election cycle? The opposition fully intends to take back your Congress next year. And the debt issue will be their rallying cry."

"So is that why you asked about the debt yesterday?" I nibbled on some bacon. Something was going on under the surface here, something I couldn't quite put my finger on.

"Actually, I was curious what your position was. But given the nature of the debate that is likely next year, if you do not have a defensible position, then perhaps you should develop one."

"We are working on that, but . . ."

"Merry Christmas," Lex announced as she stumbled sleepily into the kitchen. Hard as it was to let go of, the conversation was tabled for later.

It was late morning before we finished opening our gifts, telling stories of Christmases past and thanking each other for our gifts. Of course, Anton had spoiled Lex with a new iPod, several DVDs, and a substantial gift card for iTunes. I gave her a new set of paintbrushes and pallet knives. Lex was up the night before finishing the sketches of scenes from Washington, which were her gifts to Anton and me. Anton's praise for her artistic abilities went on and on through the morning, and I hoped that lavish praise would not dissuade her from her planned study of history and linguistics in college. My friend and I exchanged gifts at the same time—he gave me a rare bottle of 25-year-old scotch and a silly tie covered with tiny American flags; I gave him a three-volume edition of *Hume's Collected Philosophical Works*.

I thought of the many Christmas Days I spent with Gillian and Lex together; between neighbors, friends, colleagues, and Gillian's family, we often had a house full of people. Most of the day was spent in the kitchen, wrangling a huge turkey or gigantic rib roast into the oven, numerous side dishes scattered about on the stovetop and counter. It was always a nightmare of preparation, followed by a swift decimation of the prize and a kitchen full of dirty dishes, pots, and pans.

"What time is dinner, Anton," I asked as I gathered up the torn wrapping paper.

"About 3:00. Is that okay?"

"Sounds good. Shouldn't we start cooking?" Although I wondered about his invisible elves in the kitchen, I had yet to see any physical sign of a staff around the house. Surely he had given them the holiday off. And hell, I had done it enough times; it might be fun to try my hand at it again. It wouldn't really feel like Christmas without all that activity in the kitchen. Would it?

"Cooking? Surely you jest." He waved away any further comments about cooking, instead urging us to dress for a brisk walk in the snow, now sparkling in the sunshine.

At 2:30 a white van arrived at the back entrance to Anton's home. Promptly at 3:00 a full dinner of smoked turkey and all the trimmings was served by a butler in the formal dining room.

"YES, FATHER, THEY left this morning."

"Did you convince your friend of the merits of the opposition's position?"

"We discussed them, on and off, but I think I got my message across. Jude is his own man and keeps his opinions close to his vest, especially political ones. So I am not sure how he reacted to my arguments."

"We have started a huge tidal wave with these Tea people, and I doubt anyone can stop it. The broader issue will be, what actions the president and his administration will take once they begin to feel the pressure."

"What do our people think he will do?"

"They believe he will give in and ultimately follow the program, with your influence, of course."

"I can only do so much. And you, Father, what do you think will happen?"

"I think it depends on how persuasive your friend is, Anton, and how persuasive you are with him. He has the president's ear. But we have other pressures we can bring to bear."

"Like my work in the Middle East?"

"Perhaps, to create a distraction for the president, depending on when your efforts yield results. If there is too much on his plate, the more easily he might acquiesce. Each of us has his breaking point."

60

April 2010
Washington D.C.

"I DON'T THINK you can make it across the street, Fallon." I spoke to her on the phone as I looked out my office window at the crowd on Executive Avenue, which separated her office in the Treasury Department from mine in the White House. We were about to meet with the president to give him our recommendations on how to deal with the projected budget deficits for next year—and the debt the country had piled up since the Clinton era.

Today was April 15, a date that normally passed with much gnashing of teeth but little visible activity save for long lines at the post office. At this moment, however, there were huge crowds thronging the street outside the White House. On-line news reports suggested as many as three thousand people were out there protesting against high federal taxes, government debt and spending, and the size of the federal government. Chants of "We want our country back!" reverberated through the windows.

"Who the hell are these people anyway?" Fallon asked as she watched the crowd of protesters out her window.

"Read the signs—The Tea Party. Want to dress up like an Indian and join them?" The costumes had me confused; everything from tri-corner hats to giant teabags were parading out there. I thought it was patriots dressed up like Indians who threw the tea into the harbor.

"I prefer the makeup I am wearing to black and red paint under my eyes and on my forehead."

Like me, she seemed nonplussed by the whole display. Judging from media reports, it was hard to believe the Tea Party was anything more than a fringe element, but here they were in Washington. It was hard not to think about the Vietnam War protests; what a different world this was.

"Maybe I should change into a loin cloth and join them," I quipped.

"It's Tax Day; what else would you expect? Maybe after you pay your taxes this year, a loin cloth is all you'll have left."

Why they were protesting against taxes was beyond me. As Anton had suggested over Christmas, the stimulus package signed a little over a year ago reduced the tax burden on these folks to its lowest levels since the Eisenhower administration. Because of the recession, revenues were already in the tank, and the tax reductions only made the federal deficit worse. These people supposedly didn't want government debt, but were unwilling to pay to reduce it. Where were their protests during the previous administration, when a budget surplus was turned into the largest deficit in the history of the country? I wondered if they even understood what they were asking for.

"Fallon, please be careful. Why don't you get security to escort you?" I stood at the window. Was the crowd growing, or was that just my imagination?

"It's only a protest, not armed conflict. They have a walkway cordoned off between Treasury and the White House. I'll see you at the meeting."

I continued to watch the protestors in the street. They wanted jobs, but didn't want the government to do anything to create them. They wanted affordable healthcare, but didn't want to change the system in order to get it. They liked their interstates, but didn't want to pay to maintain them. They expected homeland security, but never thought about the cost of providing it. Was there any way to reason with these people? I looked at my watch—late again.

"Good morning, Mr. President, David," I said as I entered the Oval Office.

David Milestone, still the president's closest advisor, had his eyes glued to the protest outside the White House grounds. "Good morning, Jude, where's Fallon?"

"I talked with her on the phone about ten minutes ago," I said, unloading some files from my briefcase. "The protesters on Executive Avenue are probably slowing her down a bit."

"How many are there, David?" the president asked. He looked as though he hadn't slept well last night. Streaks of gray were beginning to highlight his jet-black hair.

"CNN is calling it around three thousand. It's tax day."

The president signed some paperwork on his desk. "Tea Partiers?"

"I think so, Mr. President," David replied.

I checked my watch. As soon as Fallon arrived, we could start. The door to the Oval Office suddenly opened. We all looked up, shocked. No one just barges into the Oval Office.

"Mr. President, there's been an incident!" The president's secretary was excited, panicked. "The protestors outside of Treasury have attacked Ms. Connelly. Our security detail got her free, but she's very shaken."

"Where is she?" the president asked.

"In the White House infirmary, sir."

The three of us quickly left the Oval Office for the infirmary one floor down.

"Are you alright?" President Taylor asked. Fallon sat on the edge of the gurney in the White House infirmary. "What is it with these people?"

"I'm okay, sir, just a little shaken up." The nurse applied a topical dressing to a scrape on her forehead.

"Why aren't the police breaking this up, David? It's gone too far this time. Get the head of security to coordinate with the D.C. Police."

"Mr. President, let's think this through," I said. "Sending in the police will only stir them up more and the news media will have a field day."

"Jude may have a point, sir," David interjected. "You know, interfering with their First Amendment rights. That's not a message we want them to have."

The nurse dabbed at Fallon's scraped knee through her stockings with a wad of tissue; Fallon waved her away and took over the job herself.

"Right now the media has footage of the Treasury Secretary, a woman, being attacked by middle-aged white men. The broader public will think the Tea Partiers have taken things too far this time," I added. "We'll have public opinion on our side."

The president fixed his eyes on me; his look focused, penetrating. "Maybe you're right. It sounds like you know a little about protests and media manipulation."

"Old history, Mr. President."

The president turned to Fallon. "Could you pick out any of them who did this?"

"No. It happened too fast." She pushed herself off the gurney and reached for her shoes, which had been kicked under a chair. "Really, I'm okay. I agree with Jude."

"Damn it, David, find out who's behind this demonstration—organizers, leaders, funding sources, web sites, and any blogs promoting their activity. It's time we find out everything we can about these people. Get Vance from NSA on it. Fallon, do you feel well enough to meet?"

"Yes, Mr. President."

"Okay, let's get on with it. I have a National Security briefing in two hours."

Once back in the Oval Office, Fallon was all business. She reminded the president of the risks of taking on too much debt with the stimulus program—if it didn't work and the economy remained anemic, the debt situation would only get worse. Now, Fallon insisted with the debt approaching a 100% of GDP, dramatic cutbacks in spending were the only alternative, and deepest of those cuts would have to be in the largest and fasted growing part of the budget—the social safety net. As she said, "that is where the money is."

She failed to mention the billions of dollars that were being siphoned off to Iraq and Afghanistan. There was no mention of the fact that the debt was largely the fault of the previous administration's cavalier raiding of the Social Security Trust Fund to pay for two wars without showing those costs in the official budget . . . or the popular Medicare drug program which was supposed to provide discount meds and instead lined the pockets of the pharmaceutical companies . . . or that the tax cuts for the wealthiest individuals in the country meant those who could most afford it didn't contribute their fair share. Fallon's approach left the middle-class and the elderly to bear the brunt of her recommended austerity.

When the meeting finally concluded, Fallon, David and I got up to leave. I thought I might offer to drive Fallon home, or at the very least walk her to her office. We were at the door to the Oval Office when the president called me back.

"Jude, I need to talk with you for a minute."

Fallon hesitated, but it was clear from President Taylor's face that he wanted to talk only with me. She stuck her folder under her arm and left the office with David, closing the door behind them.

The president stood at the window overlooking the White House lawn, his back to me. "Jude, you remember the conversation we had before the last debate of my campaign . . . the one about the motivations of certain conspirators?"

I was almost certain that after that conversation the president thought of me as a bit of a crackpot. All I had were threads of evidence, each with other plausible explanations.

"Yes, sir, I remember."

As he gazed out the window, I wondered if the protestors were still out there, beyond the placid gardens, the vast expanse of lawn, the eight-foot fence.

"In our country's past, anyone in their right mind would understand the situation we are in here. Reasonable people would say, okay, we have a problem, let's cut spending where it makes sense—you know, on those things that don't contribute to the growth of the economy, the security of the country, or that we can live without, at least for the short-term—and raise taxes on those who can afford them to cover our shortfalls until the economy gets back on its feet—as you say, it's not like paying a little more is going to wipe out their fortunes. But instead, we get this irrational entrenchment from our colleagues on the right." He turned back toward me. I waited for him to continue, but he just looked at me with a penetrating stare.

"Sir?"

"Is this part of the same conspiracy or something else?"

I was surprised by his question. Was the leader of the free world seriously entertaining a conspiracy theory? "I really don't know anything for sure, but a case could be made that we've been manipulated into this situation, with no way out other than drastic cuts to our social programs. It took a while to dismantle our financial regulations to where they were before the Great Depression. Maybe the social safety net is next."

Taylor turned to gaze out the window again and remained silent. I tried to imagine all the parties who might be behind a sustained effort to rollback the New Deal and the Great Society. Taylor hadn't been in Washington all that long. I doubted he fully appreciated—anymore than I did—who specifically might be capable of such a long-term strategy. On the other hand, he was savvy enough to appreciate the possibilities.

"If it's anything like the history of our financial mess, I can see how you might believe that. Our financial crisis didn't happen over night, and most of its players, which you have suggested, have come and gone over the years. Still, I get the gist of your thinking—some form of sustained collusion over time." He paused again. Was he imagining members of a secret society plotting out their strategy in some dark room? "Whether there's some conspiracy at play or not, austerity in the middle of an economic recession will only make the recession worse and lead to more job losses—as you have frequently lectured me—and then our friends will call for even greater austerity until we are in a full-blown depression. And that's exactly the course of Connelly's plan."

"It's Fallon's background. Getting debt under control is the IMF's primary focus. She has a hard time thinking about the situation from a different perspective." I sounded like I was defending her, when even I was uncomfortable listening to her proposals.

"Don't get me wrong, I respect Fallon Connelly, but I can't go along with the kind of cuts she's recommending." He turned and stared at me directly, his look determined. "This country can't live without its social safety net. Life, liberty and the pursuit of happiness doesn't mean everyone can focus on what's good only for them. We are all in this together. We have to ask ourselves a more fundamental question, Jude: what kind of country do we want? For that matter, what kind of people do we want to be?"

Taylor sighed. I wondered if any president had had such a rough entry into the job. It had been what, a year and a half since the historic election that put a half-Native American, half-Brit into the White House with only a few years of Congressional experience behind him? So far, he had held up well, but I could see the job taking its toll.

"I can accept belt-tightening at the right time," he continued, "but this isn't it. Christ, didn't we learn anything from the Depression? And I refuse to accept it at the expense of the poor and the middle-class."

"There's only one other element in the equation, Mr. President—taxes."

"Like I said in our meeting, I'll try, but this Congress will never go along with that. We can't get past a cloture vote in the Senate." He tapped his fingers on the stack of folders on his desk. We had had this conversation many times—his inability to get any traction on the tax issue was the source of a huge level of frustration around the offices in the White House.

"You can convince the American people, sir. They will listen to you. All the major economists from either side of the political spectrum agree—it's not time for draconian budget cuts, and selectively raising taxes on those who can afford it will not hurt economic growth. It's the lack of certainty and demand that is stifling business investment; not paying a few more percentages in taxes." I had been saying the same thing to the president for months, but his personal appeal with the citizens of the country seemed to be waning the longer the economic crisis continued.

"The people have quit listening to the truth, Jude, even when it comes from people with credentials. In fact, this Tea Party populism paints the educated and those in the know as effete intellectuals who are out of touch with the values that *they* claim are the foundation of this country. And our friends from the other side of the aisle have used that populism to convince the American people that our debt and deficit is the cause of our economic situation—that government spending is the core of our current financial problems. After the bank bailouts and the failure of the stimulus to adequately jump-start the economy, people don't trust government; they think it's too big and can't get anything done, and they want us to tighten our belts just like they're having to do. Facts and logic no longer matter."

"Like how the debt issue in the near-term is not the most important issue."

"It's too complex for the average Joe to comprehend. What they understand is that they got themselves in over their heads and now have to balance their books. They expect the government to do the same thing."

It was exactly the analogy the GOP and the Tea Party types were relying on, and it was working. The Republicans had successfully gained control of the message.

"So what will you do, Mr. President?"

"I don't know, Jude . . . I don't know." He turned again to look out the window. "We're at a stalemate and neither side wants to give. I know I can only give so much, and I'm nearing the end of that."

"A government shutdown?"

This was the latest threat coming from the other side; they would stonewall until everything came to a grinding halt and use that as an opportunity to blame President Taylor for mismanagement and a lack of leadership. All the while, they'd be covering their tracks, making sure they looked like fiscal saviors in their GOP-controlled media.

"I hope it doesn't come to that, or worse, if Congress doesn't vote to raise the debt ceiling—there have been some threats." He turned back to me again. "If that happens . . . any suggestions?"

I could hear my heart beating in my ears. He asked for my suggestions—what else could I give him that he had not already heard and considered? I sat my briefcase on the desk, opened it, and pulled out a manila envelope.

"What's this?"

"Something I've been working on since the Asian financial crisis. It's about as finished as I can make it for now. I intended to show it to you someday—maybe when you started to ramp-up your re-election campaign."

President Taylor opened the envelope and pulled out the document. "Plan B?"

"MY, MY, WE had a little scuffle today," Jimmy Wilkerson said to Douglas Halperin, the minority leader of the House of Representatives. "I hope the secretary wasn't seriously hurt."

"She's the only sane person in the president's administration." Haperin scowled. "While I like a good fight, this one won't . . ."

Wilkerson interrupted. "Hey, turn up the TV. We have a replay on CBS."

The tape began as the Treasury Secretary walked from the doors of the Treasury Department building. Fallon Connelly hadn't even reached the steps outside Treasury when several protestors started yelling at her.

"What are they yelling, Doug?" Wilkerson fiddled with the remote.

"It's not something you would say to your mother, Jimmy." He chuckled.

The replay showed the secretary walking toward Executive Avenue with her head down. As she stepped in between the metal barriers in the street, the crowd closed in toward the barriers. The crowd pressed tighter together as it moved against the barriers, angrily yelling what sounded like obscenities and pushing until they forced one panel of the barrier over onto its side. First one, then many more protesters stumbled over it, and surged towards the secretary, pushing her toward the protestors on the opposite side. She banged into opposite side barrier and fell over with it into the crowd. Protestors surrounded her, yelling in her face. Someone kicked her and knocked her brief case out of her hands. When she reached over to pick it up and started to get to her feet, another protestor pushed her back to the ground with his foot.

"Did someone spit on her?" Halperin asked.

Suddenly five White House security guards surrounded her. She was pulled to her feet by one of the guards while the other guards barked at the protestors to back away, their hands on the guns holstered at their waist. The guards and the secretary moved quickly out through the space they had cleared and into the protective boundary of the White House grounds.

"Wow. Turn on Fox, Doug. Let's see how they're spinning this," Wilkerson said.

The screen filled with tight shots of clusters of protestors, instead of the wide angles the other networks had. A wide-eyed, shellacked blonde with a tight sweater reported the story, doing her best to sound serious and credible.

"Love that one," Halperin commented. Wilkerson chuckled.

"Protesters fed up with President Taylor's economic stimulus package and his socialist regulatory legislation lashed out today in a protest of unprecedented size across the street from the White House. Almost 10,000 people showed up to protest the debt and the likelihood of a higher tax burden on future generations to pay for the president's stimulus program and regulatory reform. The Treasury Secretary was inadvertently caught up in a scuffle between proponents and opponents of the president's policies. A White House security detail drew their guns and roughed up several protesters as they rushed in to escort the secretary to the White House. One protester said that the Secretary of the Treasury yelled obscenities at them as she made her way across the street to the White House."

"I didn't know Ms. Connelly had a foul mouth." Wilkerson laughed.

"That's just Fox crap, Jimmy." Halperin muted the volume on the TV with the remote. "You saw what really happened on CBS. I'm surprised the police didn't bust it up. It looks like Taylor is learning how to handle these situations."

"We've got other traps in mind. Eventually he'll lose that calm exterior. Then we'll show him up for what he really is—an incompetent, hot-headed half-breed." Wilkerson leaned back in his office couch. "The tide is turning, Douglas; so much for the liberal agenda. The American people are convinced it's a failure. Now, we have to keep dragging our feet on the rest of the president's agenda—pound home our message of deficit and debt. The economy will stagnate; there will be no job growth and people will get even more disillusioned. That will put us back in the majority this year. Taylor and his entourage of intellectuals won't be able to turn things around quick enough to change the outcome."

"Do you believe there's a chance the president will give back some of the unspent stimulus funds to help reduce the deficit?"

"He's not wired to think that way. He'd just as soon go down with his ship." Wilkerson put his feet on the coffee table.

"What does the Treasury Secretary think?"

"She's seen the worst side of excessive government spending. She worked at the IMF. I am certain she is making the appropriate arguments to the president. She knows the medicine the government will have to swallow sooner or later. I think the president will listen to what she's telling him after the midterm election. She'll have a plan in hand and the political will of the American people behind it."

"You know, if some of the Tea Party candidates win their primaries and the general election, we'll have to figure out how to bring them into the tent," Halperin interjected. "Some of their positions are a little over the top, and they don't seem to be beholden to anyone."

"It's Washington, Doug. They'll want to be re-elected after they've been in office a few months and the contributions from corporate donors start coming in. No matter what they say publicly, they'll end up doing the right thing. I've seen this kind of populism before. They'll come around."

61

October 2010
Toronto, Canada

"WHY DID YOU want to meet at your house, Father? What is wrong with the telephone?"

"I've just gotten back from a trip down south, and we need to discuss some changes to our plan—in private."

"You don't trust the phone?"

"Not with this, and neither should you when it comes to our other business ventures."

Anton considered the need for secrecy. As he thought about it, he and his father never discussed Deep business other than face-to-face and in a private setting. But phone-tapping seemed outside the realm of reality. Maybe his father was becoming paranoid with his elder years. Or maybe he always was, and Anton was just first realizing it.

"Really, Father. We don't have the NSA in Canada."

"Oh, yes we do, Anton. They just go by another name. But to the point. Have you seen the latest polls for the U.S. election?"

"Of course. I review what we print and broadcast. It looks like the Republicans will take back their House of Representatives but will fall short in the Senate."

Anton had been following the polls conducted by their media operation. As the weeks went on and with the election nearing, they also showed Republicans would take control of several key governorships and state houses. That would serve them well in redistricting efforts after the

U.S. census when they could cement and increase their gains in their House of Representatives.

"And that is where we come in. We think we can move up the timetable of our plan if the Republicans take both houses and completely control the U.S. Congress."

"How can we influence the outcome of the election at this late date?"

"No one is talking about vote rigging. It would raise too much suspicion."

"Then what are you suggesting, Father?"

Thomas poured a whiskey from the crystal decanter setting on the dark green marble kitchen counter. He took a deep drink, while looking at his son.

"We need to discuss one of our little side businesses."

How many businesses was his father involved in anyway? Was this another media company or something else? Anton was tired of his father's cloak and dagger conversation. "Why do I need to hear about another one of your business ventures?"

"Our business, Anton," he insisted. "You have been chosen to run our next operation, and this business will be useful to you."

"If you know what needs to be done, why me?"

"Consider it a test—a test of loyalty and commitment."

62

November 2010
Toledo, Ohio

PATRICK CONNELLY SAT at the long table in the kitchen of the Toledo firehouse eating a microwaved lunch of leftover franks and beans. He was reading the sports section of the *Toledo Blade*, checking the scores of the college football games from Saturday. Ohio State had won again over archrival Michigan 37-35. Suddenly the siren blared.

"Connelly, we got an explosion and fire. Let's go," the chief insisted as he stood in the doorway to the fire station kitchen, already outfitted in his boots, hat in hand.

Patrick left his plate on the table and rushed to the lockers, grabbed his gear and hopped aboard the truck that was already moving out of the firehouse.

"What we got?" Patrick yelled above the blare of the siren to his fellow fireman riding with him on the running board of the red truck.

"Looks like a car explosion, one passenger," he yelled back, grabbing his hat just before the force of a hard right turn almost flipped it from his head. "EMT reports one injury at the scene. Car's still burning."

"Know what happened?"

"That's why we're going." They held tightly onto the bar as the truck raced forward. "Us and the chief. We put the fire out; the chief investigates."

The fire truck wound its way through the light Sunday traffic of Toledo, siren blaring, slowing but not stopping for red lights at the intersections.

Within fifteen minutes Patrick could see the flashing lights of police cars and an ambulance. A white, late model sedan sat at the intersection, flames still leaping through the broken windows of the vehicle, driver's side door open.

The fire engine squealed to the rear of the car. Patrick and his mate hopped off quickly and uncoiled the hose connected to the water tank of the truck. The fire was out in minutes.

"Where's the driver?" Patrick asked the chief who was talking to police on duty.

The chief held up his hand for Patrick to hold on and finished his discussion with two Toledo cops. Patrick stared at the open ambulance door. The EMTs were placing a body in a black plastic bag.

"The car's a goner," his mate said.

"So is she." Patrick nudged his mate and nodded toward the ambulance.

"What is it, Connelly?" the chief asked. He had finally finished his discussion with the cops. Patrick kept staring at the black bag in the rear of the ambulance. He already had his answer.

"IT WAS A hit job, Mikey," Patrick insisted over the phone the day after the newly elected senator's car exploded. He popped a beer from the fridge and took a seat at the kitchen table.

"You don't know that yet."

"The fuck I don't." What did Mikey know about bombs and fires? Just because he ran a business he thinks he knows everything. "I was on duty and responded to the call when it came in. I know a bombing when I see it. Even the chief says so." Patrick took the first sip of his beer and quickly felt his tension relax. "Who would want to take out the new senator and a woman for god sake?" As far as Patrick was concerned, the whole damn country had gone nuts.

"I don't know, Patrick," Mike answered. "Just look at all those demonstrations before the election—people carrying guns at those political rallies. We're all angry over the mess the country's in, but now we're going to start shooting each other?"

Patrick remembered the TV clips of the demonstrations before the election. Nut jobs carrying pistols strapped to their waists. Their signs were downright vulgar—pictures of the president with a swastika and a Hitler mustache; their violent shouts were even more so.

"It's amazing no one got shot. But the senator . . . this was premeditated—a bomb for Christ sake." Patrick recalled what the chief said after they got back to the station: "Takes some know-how to build one of those things."

"Yeah, you might be right," Mike finally agreed. "It wasn't some angry protestor who did it, that's for sure. Why aren't they blowing up one of them Wall Street guys, not a brand new senator? She hasn't done anything yet."

"Then who would want to do it?"

"Someone who thought she'd be working against them I guess. But her not being in the Senate isn't going to help me any—you know with my business."

"Hey, that's right." Patrick remembered that his brother was still trying to get government funding for his surge protectors. "You talked with her during the campaign about your surge protectors and that government bill."

"Yeah, she said she would support the energy bill if she got elected. Now I got to start all over with a new senator."

"SHE WON BY ten points. I can't just appoint one of our own to the seat, Thomas."

"Listen, Governor, you won your second term; you have four more years. It's your last term and people will forget by the time it is over," he insisted. They had done the hard job. Now this governor did not have the guts to take the next necessary step? "This is important to us. It gives us a 51 to 49 majority in the Senate, and with control of the House going to us, we cannot only stop the president's agenda, but begin to implement ours."

"Okay, I'll give it some thought. We still have time before the new session of Congress. We have a lot to get done here in Ohio during the next four years, and after my term I have larger ambitions. I don't need a lot of distractions and negative press."

"Governor, I do not think you understand what I am saying," Thomas pressed on, his voice low but firm. "We appreciate your agenda and your ambitions, and we will support you in more ways than you can imagine, but there is nothing to think over. We need this done . . . then we will help you with your objectives."

The governor was silent. He recognized the importance of keeping this particular ally in his court. Still, his citizens were reeling from the tragic death of a popular newcomer, and he knew he was going to come under fire if he appointed someone from his own party instead. "I'll need a lot of support—now and later. A friend in the press would be useful to deal with the fallout, and support our agenda for the state. And after my term," he added pointedly.

"That can be arranged and much more. We do not often have opportunities like this. This one cannot get away from us." Again there was silence between them. "We know you will do the right thing, Governor."

63

"WELL, JUST HOW much thought did you give it, Governor? The senator-elect was just buried last week," David Milestone said. He folded his *Wall Street Journal* and leaned forward with his elbows on his desk, covering several documents he had started reading earlier that day.

"David, I believe it's important to give my state some certainty as soon as possible after this terrible event. There is no reason to drag out the decision." Yeah, Milestone sighed, give them certainty; that's more important than their wishes. This governor was just one more bully—cut from the same cloth as the Wall Street bankers and hedge fund managers who had turned the economy into their own personal casino. He felt like just hanging up on him.

"But her opponent? A Republican? She won by ten points. Doesn't that tell you your constituents preferred a Democrat?"

"It tells me they preferred Maria Cantwell to her opponent—nothing more. She got 55% of the vote; that means that 45% of Ohioans wanted her opponent. After the campaign he's a known entity to the people."

"It also means that a majority of your constituency voted against his positions." Milestone felt his anger rise along with his voice. In this guy's world, the will of the people meant nothing.

"And almost half of them agreed with his policies." There was a long pause. "David, I've made up my mind. I was only giving the president a courtesy call before I announce tomorrow. I have to go."

"But, Governor . . . hello . . . Governor?" Milestone slammed the receiver into its cradle and threw the *Journal* against the wall opposite his desk. This was only going to make things a lot tougher. That guy has some balls. He reached for his Blackberry to text President Taylor.

"I REALLY DO not want to meet with them, especially Wilkerson with that smug little smirk on his face. He's going to enjoy this." The president finished signing letters of condolence to the families of two Army Rangers recently killed in Afghanistan.

Jimmy Wilkerson and Douglas Halperin sat outside in the waiting area, full of themselves and the big GOP win in last week's midterm election. The tragedy in Ohio had been conveniently subsumed under their gloating at adding another Republican senator to their ranks. The whole thing stunk, and Milestone was as sick of it as Taylor.

"You want me in the room, Mr. President?"

"Absolutely, David. And feel free to smack either of them up along the side the head if they give you an opening." The president straightened his tie and flashed one of his increasingly rare smiles.

"How do you want to play this; I mean do you want to draw a line in the sand today?" Milestone put the letters the president had signed into a folder for later.

"Last night I thought we should just politely listen to what they have to say, and not give them the satisfaction of knowing what we might be considering." The president leaned back in his chair.

"And this afternoon?"

"I'm more inclined to remind those idiots that the President of the United States has the power of the veto. They're the ones that keep touting the Constitution." He moved things around on his desk.

Milestone knew he was stalling. Good. Let those bastards wait. "You don't think they could override?" The frequent discussions on Congressional rules and strategizing around them often gave him a headache. Filibuster, cloture, veto—he much preferred running campaigns to managing the office.

"In the House, maybe, but not in the Senate. They don't have the two-thirds needed."

They had such a powerful agenda lined up for the next two years, but if the GOP was as serious about stonewalling as they had been the last two, they both understood the president might as well forget about it.

"So, a stalemate."

"That's what they've done to us for the past two years—kept us from moving forward enough to get this economy turned around. We can be as entrenched as they've been."

Milestone was dubious; that was not why Taylor was elected, and they both knew it. "But that could affect your re-election chances next year, sir. The people want the two sides to work together to get things done."

"Do you really believe the American people want Republican solutions, eliminating Medicare and Medicaid, education grants, spending on infrastructure, cutting taxes for the rich . . . again?" He looked at David directly.

"Frankly, I don't know what the American people want, other than jobs and some stability and security so they can get back to their lives," Milestone admitted. "They don't know if your policies or those of the other side are right. All they want is results and they are sick of crises."

"Damn it, David, the one thing I regret is holding back, trying to compromise to bring some of the other side on board."

It was a rare admittance from the president, and Milestone knew how hard it was for him to say. After the huge wave of positive energy that had pushed them into the White House, what had gone wrong? Had they failed to lay out their policies to the American people? Or did they just misjudge the openings they gave the other side to twist everything to their own advantage?

"They never intended to compromise on anything, Mr. President. Made it look like they would, but in the end they dug in their heels, walked away, and kept us from doing enough to turn things around before the election. They led us down the primrose path, and now they have us over a barrel." The talking points of the Republicans over the past two years paraded through his thoughts. "You got to hand it to them. They stayed on plan and message and held their troops together."

"Well, David, maybe it's time for us to get back on message ourselves."

"I'm sorry, sir, I don't understand." Milestone looked at the president. Were they going to shift strategy, while the new House Speaker and Senate Majority Leader sat outside, waiting for their meeting?

"Instead of reacting to their agenda for the next two years, and we know exactly what it's going to be, don't we . . . I mean, those two assholes are going to come in here bellowing about how the American people have given them a mandate for smaller government and less taxes, and oh, by the way, that just happens to mean drastic cuts in federal spending, with thousands of low-level government workers laid off, and cuts to unemployment benefits and Social Security and Medicare, which the voters somehow never realized was going to actually impact their own ability to receive the benefits they've paid in to all these years—oh yes, we know what they're planning. But what if we take the initiative? What if we flood the halls of Congress with our message instead?"

"Nothing would pass, Mr. President." He hated himself for saying out loud what he had been thinking. Taylor was finally getting enthused about his agenda again, he was starting to look like he did two years ago, when he was deep in campaign mode.

"Of course it wouldn't, but at least we could show the American people a clear alternative to the crap they've been pushing," Taylor insisted. "And we can certainly point out the consequences of their programs."

"But that means nothing will get done for the next two years. The people will punish you for it in 2012. Might as well not even run for re-election."

"And if I give into what they want, and the people see where that leads, they'll punish me for caving in. And besides, maybe the whole running for re-election thing needs to be rethought. What if I insist on following through with my agenda even if they stonewall it? And tell the American people I'm willing to run the risk of not having more time in office to stay true to the principles they elected me to enforce?"

Milestone sucked in his breath, pretending he didn't hear that part about rethinking re-election. "Like I said, Mr. President, between a rock and hard place."

Taylor pushed his chair away from his desk and stood. Milestone breathed a sigh of relief. The old glow was back; he could feel it. Shit, he could even see it.

Taylor's voice was firm and decisive. "I'm inclined to start the election campaign right now, David. Let's show them we can be just as entrenched as they have been. Hell, I can give press conferences and position speeches every month. Hammer home our message over and over again just like they've been doing."

Now this was a job he could deal with, Milestone thought. If they just framed the next two years as an extended re-election campaign . . . "And let the chips fall where they may."

Taylor laughed and looked at his watch. "You are full of clichés today. I guess we've kept them waiting long enough," he said still laughing. "Show them in, will you?"

David Milestone went to the door and motioned the two soon-to-be majority leaders into the Oval Office.

"Gentlemen," the president said, pointing to the two stiff side chairs in front of the desk. "It's your meeting. What's on your minds?"

Both Wilkerson and Halperin looked at each other, obviously surprised by the shift in protocol.

"I have another meeting in fifteen minutes, gentlemen, so let's get going." The tone of the president's voice was matter-of-fact. He shuffled some papers on his desk; Milestone stood by, waiting and watching.

"I'm sure you agree that the American people have spoken and want a reduction in government spending and an immediate downsizing of government in general," Wilkerson began. "Our primary goal has to be getting the debt and deficit under control."

Taylor looked up from his desk and glared at the leaders. "Is that what the American people said, Senator?"

Milestone could hear an edge of sarcasm in the president's voice. Yes, yes, yes, he thought. We can do this.

"I wish I had the ability to read the mind of every voter in the last election. Most of the Congressional races were not that far apart. And you didn't win the seat from Ohio, Jimmy."

The senator cleared his throat. "That is what our candidates campaigned on and they won, Mr. President."

"Like I said, most by slim majorities, and one convenient death, and as I recall they campaigned on a number of issues, including Second Amendment remedies. I guess that's one campaign promise your guys have kept."

Wilkerson started to object, but the president cut him off. "Most importantly, your candidates promised jobs. So what are the specific pieces of legislation to create jobs you want to discuss?" He crossed his arms.

Milestone watched the men squirm. Maybe they thought they were coming in here to do a victory dance, but it definitely wasn't panning out that way.

"Well, we know that all this government spending is crowding out the private sector and preventing job growth. That has to stop. And we need to reduce taxes to encourage investment in private sector jobs." Wilkerson's voice grew more confident as he ticked off the items on his agenda. "Finally, the newly passed financial reforms will choke off capital from the banks and reduce their ability to lend at a time when we need to infuse capital into the economy. We need to repeal that legislation and . . ."

"Excuse me, Senator, but interest rates are the lowest they've been in decades, the banks have the money to lend, countries and institutions are buying U.S. T bills and bonds at the lowest interest rates in fifty years, and the major corporations are sitting on trillions of dollars in cash." The president's reputation for cool recitations of fact was cemented on such displays. "Exactly how is the government crowding out the private sector? And the banks have plenty of capital to lend. The Fed and the Treasury have made sure of that, but there aren't enough people and businesses wanting to borrow."

Wilkerson leaned forward in the stiff chair. "With all due respect, Mr. President, that situation is soon to change. These huge deficits are going to drive up interest on the debt *and* inflation, and those buying our debt will soon retreat. And if we enforce some of the laws passed in the last session, a good part of the derivatives market may move off shore. That means trillions of dollars lost from our economy."

The president smiled. "Clichés. You really don't understand economics do you, Senator?"

"I understand we have unsustainable debt." Wilkerson's chin jutted out. Milestone made a few notes.

"Japan is the second largest economy in the world, Senator," President Taylor pointed out. "What is their debt level?"

"I don't see what that has to do with the . . ."

"Japan's debt level is almost twice their GDP. But their economy keeps growing, maybe not as fast as they want, but growing nonetheless. And their unemployment level is half of ours, and their economy a third the size of ours."

"I take it then that you are not going to be receptive to reducing our deficits and debt."

Wilkerson was growing more and more agitated, while Halperin sat there silently. Milestone wondered if they were planning to play good-cop bad-cop; maybe Halperin would swoop in to save the meeting with some calm words of appeasement. Fat chance, he thought.

"That's not what I said. Of course, we have to be fiscally responsible and do what we can to reduce expenditures in the midst of the biggest economic crisis we've seen since the Great Depression—a crisis that your party and the lack of financial regulations and enforcement got us into. But am I going to agree to draconian spending cuts at a time when the economy is just starting to get on its feet again? No, Senator, I'm not. And I am not going to reverse the financial regulations we passed earlier this year and let the banks take us into the ditch again. If that's what the big banks and derivative business need to survive, then let them go to other countries and drag them down."

"Mr. President, the people have spoken!" Wilkerson insisted. Halperin remained mute.

"And like I said, they want jobs and a stable financial system. They also want an energy policy that takes us into the future, as well as sensible regulations that protect the air they breath, the water they drink, the food they eat, the toys their children play with, their rivers, their oceans, their national parks. That's what I'm going to try to give them, along with a host of other things I promised two years ago."

"Surely, given the state of our economy you cannot be seriously considering . . ."

"Oh, but I am."

"The Congress will never support your agenda, I can assure you," Wilkerson sputtered.

"Well, that's your option, Senator. But that doesn't mean I have to support yours. We'll have the next two years to debate our positions, then we'll see what the American people want in 2012."

"Surely, you . . ." Wilkerson started, but was cut off again.

"Bring me sensible proposals that have some semblance of a compromise and deal seriously with the country's problems, and we will discuss them. Anything more, gentlemen?"

The men looked at each other, Wilkerson huffing audibly, Halperin's eyes narrowed, his lips pressed together tightly.

"Okay, your fifteen minutes is up. Good day."

The president looked back to the paperwork on his desk, waiting for the men to leave. When they closed the Oval Office door behind them, David Milestone cleared his throat.

"Did you really want to throw down the gauntlet?"

"Is that what I did? I didn't mean to. I hope they didn't take me the wrong way." He grinned, took off his jacket and rolled up his sleeves. Even though it was almost 5:00, he looked like he was preparing for some long hours at his desk.

Milestone started to leave through the rear door to return to his office. "David, what are your plans for dinner?"

"Same as always—work late, go home, and eat a pot pie."

"Have dinner with me upstairs. We need to outline the State of the Union."

"Is he nuts?" asked Douglas Halperin once their limousine pulled out of the gates of the White House.

"Or sly as a fox." Wilkerson was seething with anger for the way he was treated in the meeting. He would get his revenge. "He's going to use the next two years to draw a sharp contrast between his positions and ours. But he's right about one thing—borrowing *is* too cheap right now. Until we do something about those low interest rates, we'll never be able to starve big government." Wilkerson slipped back into the seat of his limousine. "And it sounds like he will likely force our hand on the budget issues."

"Into a government shutdown? We might be blamed for that. Look what happened in the Clinton era." Halperin frowned.

"Ultimately, I don't think this president has the balls for that, Doug. But, if he wants a fight, so be it. What I know for sure is, if we don't stand firm, the people who elected us won't be there two years from now, and we cannot get elected without them." This definitely wasn't the Clinton era. This time they would not capitulate.

"But there is some good news," Wilkerson continued. "If there is a government shutdown, the administration will have a harder time enforcing its new regulations on the banks, oil and gas producers, or any of our constituents. They will be thankful for that."

"And you don't think we'd be blamed for the short-term pain? It's the people who vote, Jimmy, not corporations and banks."

Wilkerson agreed that here there was uncertainty, and they had to be cautious. "We have to craft our message very carefully—keep it concise, and all of us have to stick to it. Ordinary people end up believing simple phrases that they hear over and over again." He paused, framing his thoughts. "You have to keep in mind that the majority of American people don't stay at home during the day watching the cable news shows. Most get the sound bites on the network news. Hell, only a small percentage have college degrees and a lot of them never graduated from high school. We press a simple message on our audience: spending beyond our means, taxes destroy job creation, government's too big and stands in the way of the private sector, and the debt will turn America into a Third World country. Then we'll refine it based on circumstances on the ground."

"WELL, STEPHEN, IT certainly sounds like the president is digging in his heels. He understands that our planned budget cuts will water down a number of his reforms, including the new financial regulations. I think repeal is beyond what we can accomplish until we replace him with one of us," Wilkerson asserted.

"Then we need to put pressure on the president to keep those regulations in check," Russell said. "He has a lot of flexibility in what they'll look like. Surely the Treasury Secretary can have some influence."

"Even if we passed a repeal bill, the president would veto it," Wilkerson countered, "And if we cut off or reduce funding for its implementation, the president will veto the budget bill, and that would leave us with a potential government shutdown. We're not sure how that would play with the American people. It might put our chances in 2012 in jeopardy—for Congress and the Presidency."

"Getting rid of those regulations is our top priority, not the political aspirations of the party, Jimmy. If it takes the threat of a shut down to put pressure on the president to back off, then so be it."

"And what if the president doesn't back down and makes us responsible for a shut-down? Holding a majority in Congress and taking back the White House is the only sure way you'll get financial reform repealed. So our political aspirations, as you refer to them, should be on *your* priority list."

Still, Russell had a point. A government shutdown could pressure the president on the regulations. But who did he think he was? It was time to remind Russell of the power of Washington politics, which he was pooh-poohing.

"Even if we succeeded in cutting off the funding for the regulations, the president still has tools at his disposal to make your life difficult, Stephen," Wilkerson continued with his familiar smirk. "The Treasury and the Fed could increase capital requirements and the Fed Funds Rate. They could start poking around in your derivatives business, too, Stephen. We know Taylor's thought about those. Surely, you don't want that."

Russell remained silent for a long moment. "I understand you, Senator, see what you can do. It sounds like Jude Anders still has Taylor's ear in spite of the Treasury Secretary."

"That may be," Wilkerson acknowledged. Anders and Connelly, they were the two wild cards, although getting Connelly into Treasury had been a big help. "It's hard to say. The president is holding his cards pretty close to his vest. We're not sure who he's listening to."

"You find a way to keep those financial regulations from getting out of hand," Russell said. "I'll deal with Anders."

The new senate majority leader hung up the phone. Without intending to do so, he may have killed two birds with a single phone call.

64

December 2010

"WOW, JUDE, WE haven't had lunch in almost a year, outside of the White House cafeteria. What's up?" Fallon slipped into the booth at our favorite lunch spot in Georgetown. Little more than an upscale burger joint, it offered high-backed booths, dimmed lighting and low-level background music. That meant just enough of a sense of privacy for a sensitive conversation without feeling like you were hiding something.

"I just wanted to have lunch with my favorite single woman. What's unusual about that?" She was right; it had been ages since we had met for lunch outside the office. We both knew that doing so was usually code for needing to speak a little more freely, but I hoped she'd let me ease into it gently.

"So Lex isn't your favorite anymore?"

"Well, next to Lex, but what they say is true: once they leave for college . . ." Adjusting to the empty house was one thing; realizing that she was having a daily life as a young adult was something I was having a much harder time getting used to.

"Ah. The chick has left the roost. Mikey is about to face the same thing." Fallon had managed to flag down a passing waiter to ask for coffee before we had even settled in. She tore open a packet of Equal and stirred in some artificial creamer. "How's she doing at Princeton?"

"She's doing fine, but every time I press her on grades . . . well, you know. How are things going with Michael?"

"He's treading water, waiting for Congress to pass the GRID Act. Thanks to Anton he has a good private investor who's keeping the lights on; he can pay his house payment and insurance premiums—he's okay. I just wish Congress would get off their butts."

I smiled, glad to hear that things were working out for Mike . . . for now. "You know it's going to be tougher now that the Republicans control both houses." Environmental issues were bound to get skewered, even one with irrefutable science behind it. "There's talk of some fairly draconian budget cuts."

"While I agree with a number of the cuts the Rs are talking about, Mikey's product is linked to national security. It stands a good chance." She put on her reading glasses and scanned the menu, effectively ending that line of conversation. And she was right, I had no appetite for the same kind of discussion we always had at work.

"Fallon, there is something I wanted to talk over with you," I said, stirring my coffee.

"I should have known—you want my advice. Does this mean you're buying?" She grinned at me.

"Don't I usually? Anyway, I got a call from Princeton yesterday."

"Lex?" She leaned forward slightly; she looked concerned. "I thought you said she was doing okay?"

"No, no. The call was from the chair of the Department of Economics. They want to know if I would be interested in an honorary professorship with a one-year visiting-teaching assignment." The call had more than surprised me; it left me with a string of unanswered questions.

"You're joking. Really?" She put her menu down and took off her glasses. A waiter appeared but I waved him away for a few more minutes.

"What? You think I'm not qualified?"

"Of course you're qualified—the IMF, Fed, a master's degree from Georgetown, a White House position. It's not unheard of, especially with someone of your stature. No, it's just that you already have an important position." She lowered her voice and leaned over the table. "Why would they think you would be interested in their offer?"

Of course, she hit the nail on the head. That was my first question too: why would they even offer it if they didn't think I'd accept?

"You're seriously considering it, aren't you?" She leaned back, a look of amazement on her face.

"At first no, but last night I thought at least I should look at it," I said, not really sure if I was trying to convince her or myself. "I've done about what I can on the Economic Council, and with the Republicans regaining power, what will we accomplish over the next two years?" To be honest, I was already burned out. Sure, I wanted to help craft a new industrial policy and a new trade policy with the Chinese, even strengthen the financial reform legislation, but what were the chances of getting anything through Congress? Two more years already felt like a slog.

"And you're thinking you could be closer to Lex? You better ask her if she wants that."

"Yeah, you're probably right. I wouldn't want to live with her, but at least I could see her more often—you know, a coffee at the student union, an occasional dinner. The pay is good enough. Anton is taking care of her tuition. I can still afford the living expenses." I had been obsessively going over the numbers, hoping that would give me a clear picture one way or the other, but the reality was already sinking in. I wanted to go. I wanted to be closer to Lex, and I wanted out of the White House.

"On the surface it sounds like a good fit." She sipped her drink and set the cup back on the table "You know, Jude, you've been dealing with crisis after crisis for most of your career. Maybe it is time to do something with a little less stress. But as much as I hate working with you . . ." She winked. "You've become like an old piece of furniture—hard to part with."

I SUSPECTED FALLON would encourage me to take the offer. In spite of what she said, she was tired of our disagreements on economic policy, and frankly, thought I had too much of the president's ear. She would have more power if I were out of the picture. But what would Anton say? I trusted his opinion more than anyone's when it came to career and life decisions. I lit up a smoke outside the White House, shivering in the late afternoon chill, and called him on my cell phone.

"I think it is a wonderful offer, but remember what I told you," Anton scolded.

"You mean about how someone can get me out of the way without killing me." That issue had also kept me up all night. More than the money, more than the slog of D.C. gridlock, there was the very real prospect of being played . . . or worse.

"Yes, Jude, that conversation."

"Well, there are a number of people who would like me out of the White House, even Fallon, probably, but she doesn't have the pull to get me the Princeton offer." I took a drag on my smoke and wished I was wearing my gloves.

"Just knowing that someone may be pulling some strings is all you need to know. You have to ask why would they want you out of the way and, I guess, do you care?"

"Rolling back financial reform would be the only reason that makes any sense for getting rid of me. The president will veto any attempt, but of course the Republicans could refuse to fund its implementation. That will be part of the whole budget confrontation this year."

"And will your president cave in on the budget if you are not there?"

"He'll compromise on some items, but not that one. The American people would kill him in the next election." I chuckled. "And so would I. I've told his chief of staff as much."

"Is there anything else you need to get done in your position as director?" Anton's tone shifted with the specificity of his question. I paused, thinking about Sasha and how she would grill me about details.

"There's plenty I would like to get done, but with the make-up in Congress, none of my initiatives would pass. We're pretty much at a standstill until after the next election."

"Sounds like you've made up your mind." His tone was perceptibly lighter. I looked out over the crisp White House lawns; the streetlights came on, even though it wasn't quite 5:00.

"Not yet, but I am seriously considering it."

Of course, I was going to take it. My gut instincts weren't always right, but this time I was sure. Maybe someone did want me out of the way; maybe I wanted to be out of the way myself.

65

February 2011
Columbus, Ohio

"I AM NOT negotiating with them," the governor of Ohio said to his chief of staff. He threw the files onto his desk. He had his marching orders; it was time to stop pretending they were all on the same side.

"Then how are you going to get concessions on pay, benefits, and pensions? If we're going to balance the budget, we have to get those concessions."

It was the same old story, every year, and here was his own right-hand man expecting him to just fall in line with the status quo. Maybe he needed a new chief of staff.

"They've been raping us for the past thirty years. My predecessors have always given into their goddamn demands. They're bankrupting the state, and I am not going to be held hostage like my predecessors. Not again; never again."

"Then what do you plan to do, Governor?"

He seemed visibly diminished by the governor's defiant statement. Good. Maybe he could get the same reaction from the media.

"We're going to take away their right to negotiate. We'll make them cover their pension shortfall, pay their fair share for healthcare, and tie their salaries to a percentage of state revenue collections. And that means they going to have to take a pay cut this year to cover our shortfalls."

The chief of staff raised an eyebrow. "That requires legislation, sir."

"I'm not stupid; I know that," he barked. "Senator Bowers has drawn up the legislation. He'll be submitting it next week. We control both houses. I want you to be the point man. You get the representatives and senators on board. And let me know who might be resisting or straying from the program."

"Ohio is a heavily unionized state, Governor. This is going to create an uproar the size of Texas."

The governor stared at his chief of staff, wondering again if he had the right man.

"There are a lot of people out there who want government to tighten its belt, and when they hear the deal our public employees have, we'll have plenty of support. We get this done early, then we have four years for those who get pissed off to calm down." He sat on the corner of his desk and folded his arms. "Things will be better by then, and they'll applaud us for being fiscally responsible."

"And the media? What do we do about them?"

"We can get our propaganda out just as well as these union bastards. You keep our troops in line. I'll take care of the message."

February 18, 2011
Toledo, Ohio

PATRICK CONNELLY HELPED himself to a second can of beer from the fridge and headed into the living room to watch TV. Elena had her hands full trying to get a batch of macaroni and cheese into the three kids, but he had just completed his usual 3-day shift at the stationhouse and he was beat. She always gave him a pass on taking care of the kids when he got home, but he knew he'd have them full-time the next two days, until he went back to the house.

"Hey, try to keep it down to a dull roar in there, I wanna catch the news," he hollered to them as he settled into his favorite chair and flicked the remote on to CNN.

"The debate on Capitol Hill intensified today as Republicans insisted on spending cuts to reduce the deficit, while Democrats said the federal revenue raised by eliminating corporate tax loopholes and tax breaks for oil companies would more than triple the spending cuts proposed by Republican law makers. With an estimated budget deficit of $1.65 trillion this year and a debt of over $14 trillion, both sides are seeking means to cut federal spending or increase revenues, yet neither party seems willing to compromise. While the debate goes on over next year's budget, another debate is beginning over the debt ceiling for this year. Unless the ceiling is raised, the Federal Government would have to curtail spending on a number of critical programs, including Social Security, Medicare, and defense. A more onerous option of defaulting on the government's debt is considered by insiders and economists as totally out of the question, given the potential global economic consequences."

The reporter, who wore an incongruous purple tie with his grey suit, had an appropriately serious expression, although Patrick knew as soon as the story changed, so would his facial expressions. He sipped his beer, trying to make it last. Used to be, he didn't think twice about helping himself to a second or third beer. These days, he tried to make the 12-pack last at least through the week.

"Meanwhile in Ohio, the governor indicated he would support a bill introduced by Republican lawmakers to repeal collective bargaining for public employees, including teachers, firefighters, and police. The state is projecting a $8 billion shortfall next year, and reducing pension and benefit obligations are key to cutting the deficit, the governor said. He stated his case for the bill, saying union representatives have historically refused to negotiate pensions and benefits in good faith."

"That's a fucking lie!" He bolted upright in his easy chair.

"Patrick, watch your language around the kids," Elena called from the kitchen.

"But it's a lie." He wondered if he had heard right.

"What's a lie?"

"The governor says we refused to negotiate over pensions and benefits to help balance the state's budget. We've offered to negotiate, but he refused. The son-of-a-bitch."

Elena came into the living room, drying her hands on a dishtowel. "It sounded like they're going to cut your pension and benefits. We already lost over 40% of our IRA in the crash."

"They lost the employee pension funds when the state gambled them away in those hedge funds, and now they want us to pay in more and extend our retirement age to cover it," Patrick fumed. "And they want us to pay a larger share of our health insurance premiums, too."

"You're kidding me. We already pay over $700 per month out of our pocket. How much more do they want us to pay?"

"Fifteen percent."

"And where do they think we're going to get the money for that, Patrick? I've already put off buying new jeans for the boys because of the increase in our mortgage payment."

"And guess what?" Patrick added, unwilling to meet his wife's eyes. "Our governor wants us to take a temporary pay cut, too . . . 3%, until the economy turns around."

"And when are the insurance companies going to take a pay cut? Something's got to give here." She stalked back into the kitchen, resignation in her voice. "And I'm sick of it being us."

66

February 21, 2011
Darien, Connecticut

"JOSEPH, HAVE YOU been following the news?" Benjamin sipped his whiskey, sitting comfortably in the wing chair in front of the study's fireplace—a familiar and comfortable meeting place for he and his comrades.

"There is too much news these days," Joseph replied. He watched the fire blaze, thankful for the warmth on his aging bones. "Which piece are you referring to?"

"The ruckus over the public employee unions in Ohio."

Joseph had been following the events in Ohio each morning from the *New York Times*. But he had had a couple of private conversations with the governor as well.

"Yes, my old friend, it is about time. Did you know that labor unions now only control 12% of the U.S. workforce, with public employees being most of what is left?" he said, recalling the statistics the governor had given him last week. "When those unions are destroyed, so will the American organized labor movement."

"They have been with us for almost what? 150 years? It has taken since Reagan to dismantle them."

"Some things take a long time," Joseph nodded, "especially things that require a different mindset."

"Like the financial restrictions of the New Deal?"

Joseph smiled. "That took us more than seventy years, Benjamin. It is understandable given the chaos and hardship of the '30s. People have long memories. Sometimes we have to wait for them to forget."

"Or die." Benjamin chuckled.

"So how long do think it will take to tear up their social contract?"

"Many cherished institutions of American society are nearing their end, Joseph. The social contract, as you refer to it, like the labor unions will be the last to go."

"But maybe sooner than we thought possible. As we speak, our friends in the U.S. Congress are moving our plan forward."

Benjamin's typical wry smile vanished. "That is a long shot at this point. To be sure, James has crafted a good strategy and message, but I doubt it will happen . . . not yet." He swirled the whiskey in his glass. "Still, the message paves the way."

Joseph shifted in his chair, trying to find comfort from the sciatica that plagued him daily in his elder years. "You know, Benjamin, when we helped Reagan into office, I thought sure we would see some real progress in our direction. That's the promise he made. But instead, he was more concerned about hastening the end of the communists, even though their fate was inevitable with or without his actions. And honestly, when the Democrats became more fiscally responsible in the 1990s, I thought our current plan was doomed. But that half-wit came through in the end, of course with the help of our guy on the inside. Two wars, tax cuts, and a drug program that were not paid for all ran up the debt."

"What is it he said?" Benjamin's wry smile returned. "Deficits don't matter."

They both laughed.

"And the greed of our Wall Street compatriots and our money in the derivatives market, egging them on," Benjamin continued. "When the financial crisis hit, there was no choice but to bail out the banks. And the ostriches in Europe have only postponed the inevitable with their typical indecision. When the U.S. economy falters, theirs will crumble like stale cake."

Joseph leaned toward his old friend seated next to him. "I told you years ago that Anders might still be useful. And so he was in his counsel to Taylor. We knew what he would do."

"Yes, and now deeper and deeper in debt."

"If our plans in the Middle East pan out, we can play the oil futures game as well as any. A foreign policy crisis and escalating gas prices will pressure this president to give into the program. Thomas and Anton have had more than a little success in some countries."

"And, if need be, our friends in the rating agencies are poised to put even more pressure on Taylor," Benjamin added.

Joseph sat back in his chair, sipping his whiskey. So many things would likely be accomplished within his lifetime. This he never expected and made him feel slightly triumphant. "Within five years, labor unions will be a thing of the past. Within twelve years, the safety net." His aged voice grew more confident with each word. "The belief in individual rights and democracy fostered by the union movement and the freedom provided by the security of the safety net will be gone. When children's memories fade through their adult years and are no longer passed along by their grandparents, then we will take back our land *and* our heritage."

"But without king or queen this time," Benjamin asserted with a mocking laugh.

"And when the shining light across the pond fails . . ."

"We will restore our legacy, at least on this side of the globe." A serious look crossed his face. "A frightened people will be more easily controlled in the short term. Even in these so-called democracies, we can coerce the votes we want from the ordinary people, at least until they realize their problems are too deep and complex for a democracy to solve."

Yes, Joseph thought, ordinary people. "Those who hope for security and stability in their lives. And the others who never have enough—both easily manipulated."

"And our friends on the other side of the globe . . . they will claim a vested interest, and insist on their own prescriptions."

"And we will remind them how we helped to position them!" Joseph slapped his hand on the arm of the chair. "And we will remind them that they still rely on us to meet their people's needs."

"That will not last forever, Joseph. They will eventually create their own self-sustaining hegemony in the East."

"That will be beyond our time, my good friend." He tapped his wrinkled fingers on the chair's arm. "It will be up to our younger members to create a plan."

67

Washington D.C.

"MY GOD," FALLON said aloud as she listened to the news report after a long day at work.

"The governor of Ohio also announced today plans to reduce state corporation taxes by 8% in order to attract more businesses into the state. 'This will create thousands of jobs for the state,' the governor said. This comes on the heels of his announcement yesterday to cut state employee salaries, increase the amount they pay for insurance premiums and pension benefits, and limit their collective bargaining rights. Union leaders said today that they will fight the governor's actions."

She hadn't seen the news in almost a week, having worked very late each night. The headlines she scanned on-line held no hint of the depth of this new chaos. She reached for the cordless phone and dialed her brother's number.

"Elena, it's Fallon." She pulled a Lean Cuisine out of the freezer and stuck it in the microwave. "I just heard the news about what's going on in Ohio. Is your governor for real?"

"Yes, Fallon, he's for real, and he intends to cut Patrick's pay and increase the amount we have to pay for health and pension. That's about as real as it gets for people like us."

Fallon had heard rumors, mostly from Jude, that several states controlled by the Republicans after the election intended to take harsh austerity measures to balance their budgets. Of course, Jude also reminded her that these actions were the result of the stimulus money running out that was given to the states after the financial crisis.

"What is this country coming to?" Fallon asked, not quite sure how to respond.

"Well, you should know," Elena's voice rising. "You financial wizards and politicians keep talking about spending cuts, while the rest of us ordinary Americans lose most everything we have gained in our lives. How do you think we can afford to pay more for healthcare and replenish the pension fund after you banking types squandered our money? Christ, the governor here wants to cut Patrick's salary by 3%. We got hit with another increase on our adjustable-rate mortgage payment. Where are we going to get the money to pay our bills?"

"It's not me, Elena. We're trying to do what we can here in Washington." She slipped off her heels and kicked them under the kitchen table. First Mikey, now Patrick. She had thought Patrick would be safe with his union contract, but apparently not.

"Yeah, right," Elena continued. "Looks to us like all you're doing is helping your friends on Wall Street. You political types can't even pass that bill Mike needs to keep his business afloat. What about him and his family? He could lose his business and his house. Then what?"

Elena was wrong; Fallon knew economic growth would eventually benefit Main Street once the banks were stable and the corporations saw enough certainty to start hiring again. Even so, she felt the warm flush of shame rise in her cheeks.

"Mikey's okay for now."

"For now, but what about next year? The rich are getting richer and the rest of us are being forced to live like a Third World country. How long do think this can last before the people rise up? It's happened in other countries. Don't you think for a minute we're going to put up with this for much longer."

Fallon was stunned by Elena's anger and her threats. She was talking about revolution.

"Is Patrick, there? May I speak with him?"

Elena dropped the receiver on the counter without saying goodbye, which sent a shock into Fallon's left ear. She could hear Elena shout for her brother.

Her sister-in-law just didn't understand; the situation was too complicated for someone without the background to appreciate the complexity. She took a half-full bottle of white wine out of the refrigerator and poured herself a generous glass.

"Hello," Patrick answered.

"I just heard the news on TV. The pension and pay cuts are pretty severe. Is your union going to fight them?" The microwave finally beeped; she pulled out her steaming whatever-it-was and dumped it on a plate.

"If we still have a union, Fallon. I guess you didn't get that the governor is going to take away our bargaining rights—make us go along with whatever he decides."

"Oh, come on, he can't just disband a union."

"I guess you haven't been paying much attention, 'cause that's exactly what his bill does. And the asshole legislators are going to pass it."

It had taken the firefighters in Ohio fifty years to get their bargaining rights. Fallon didn't understand a whole lot about unions, but she knew private companies couldn't just disband a union because they didn't like bargaining with them. How could a state government?

"Can he really do that, you know, I mean legally?"

"We'll fight him on it, but our union boss says if they pass the law, it's over. Seems like only us ordinary people are taking the hits these days."

"We're all making sacrifices, Patrick."

"Sacrifices, my ass. You think you're somebody special, don't you, Fallon, with your goddamn college degree and your highfalutin' job. If it wasn't for that guy Dad knew, you'd be here in the trenches with us. We could teach you a thing or two about balancing budgets without enough money coming in to cover the basics. I think you forgot where you came from."

She ignored the budget balancing remark. Patrick had no idea that she spent her entire career working on just that. But it was the other thing he said that rang in her ears.

"What guy?"

"The guy that got you into Harvard and paid for it." She caught her breath. What was he talking about? "For a college-educated woman, you're pretty stupid."

"You're nuts. I got a scholarship to Harvard."

"Yeah, right. And why do you think they'd give you a scholarship? It's not like you was the valedictorian."

For the first time Fallon became consciously aware of a fact she had never considered. She had always just assumed she got a scholarship. That's what her father told her. But Patrick had a point. She had As and Bs, but she was not at the top of her high school class. And given where she went to high school, even straight As wouldn't have meant that much to Harvard.

"Who is this guy you're talking about?"

"Jesus, Fallon, I don't know his name. Pop did, and he took it with him to the grave. Ask Mom, she might know."

"You're serious." She watched the cloud of steam curl up from her plate and then dumped it in the sink.

"If you don't believe me, ask Mikey. He'll tell you. I gotta go to bed. I'm on duty tomorrow."

68

March 3, 2011

THE PRESIDENT OF the United States stepped up to the podium in the White House pressroom. This would be the first presentation of several proposals he promised the opposition leaders in their meeting last fall. He was ready to use the bully pulpit to draw a sharp line between his positions on the issues and theirs. Taylor knew none of his proposals would pass, but at least they would provide a platform for next year's election.

"Today I am submitting a bill to Congress that puts our country on a road to energy independence. We all understand the need for energy independence. It is vital to our national security and to our environment. The goal of our bill is to have alternative energy sources, including wind, solar, and geothermal, providing 40% of the nation's electric needs by 2020, and 60% by the year 2035. To do this we are prepared to fund development of alternative energy sources at 50%, and require the utility companies of the country to contribute an equal share without substantially passing off their costs on to the American citizens. This will be a public-private partnership in which both taxpayers and the private sector equally invest in our energy future."

He spoke about research and innovation, geothermal and electric storage, short-term energy credits for natural gas, and EPA standards for fracking, which often led to toxic byproducts in ground water.

Taylor could hear the clicking of digital cameras around the room. He felt the hot lights on his face and the sweat bead up on his forehead. He knew if he listened closely, he'd also hear jaws dropping around Capitol Hill.

"Finally, our bill requests $5 billion dollars over the next five years to modernize our country's electric grid, including the deployment of smart grids around our major metropolitan areas to more efficiently use the electricity we create, and the full implementation of the GRID Act that protects electrical transmission from geomagnetic interruptions."

"I know my opponents will ask the same question they have been asking for over two years: how do we pay for this bill? We are proposing a solution to that as well. By eliminating the $4 billion in tax breaks that currently go to oil companies each year, we can substantially fund our plan. With their record profits over the past twelve years there is no reason to continue these incentives, especially since the oil companies have failed to explore or develop oil resources on over 60% of oil leases already granted by the Department of Energy. And with regard to those leases, the DOE is issuing notices to those companies today, directing them to begin exploration within twelve months and begin drilling within two years. If they do not meet these deadlines, the Department of Energy will revoke their leases."

WILKERSON GOT UP from the couch in his Senate office and turned off the TV. "Well, the president is certainly fulfilling his promise, Douglas. The bill goes to you first. What are you going to do with it?"

"It will never get out of committee, Senator. The president knows that. You won't have to deal with it, if that's what you're worried about."

They both chuckled.

"So what do you think of Ohio rolling back the public employee unions?" Wilkerson asked, prying to learn just how much Douglas Halperin knew or suspected.

"The governor and his legislators are holding firm. I admire that. It amazes me that he's been able to hold his Republican team together in the face of the protests and recall threats. Not a single defector." Halperin got up from the couch and helped himself to a bottle of water from Wilkerson's office fridge.

"They should be an inspiration to all of us here on the Hill."

Halperin nodded in agreement.

"Without union support, you stand a good chance of picking up additional seats from Ohio next year, Doug. It could even put Ohio back in our camp. That could help put our presidential candidate over the top," Wilkerson added. "How are your guys in the House doing on our budget proposal for next year?"

"We're making it public next month. Along with the cuts in discretionary spending, we've decided to lay the big issue on the table this year—Medicare. But the new group of Tea Partiers insists that we bring up the tax plan, too. People might think we're going too far."

Wilkerson had heard those rumblings. That was a risk, cutting Medicare and the top income tax rates at the same time. Maybe they should deal just with the spending cuts, and do the tax cuts, or at least make the current tax cuts permanent, after they retook the White House next year. It might be easier and more palatable to the American people.

"You can't move them off that position?" Wilkerson asked.

"Trust me, I've tried. I have never seen such religious fervor by nearly the entire group of freshman. If I don't include the tax cuts, they'll throw me out of the speakership." He scowled.

"Well, we'll have to gauge the reaction to that one. Still, the American people might be so afraid of the debt and unemployment—of becoming a Third World debtor nation—that we can convince them that drastic spending cuts *and* lower tax rates are the only solutions to get the economy on its feet again and create jobs. It's worked with the Tea Party," he said with a slight chuckle. "It may work with independents."

"Do you really believe that, Jimmy?" Halperin's voice was low, and he looked at his colleague through heavy lids.

Wilkerson was taken aback. "Which part? Of course, we need to get our debt and deficit under control."

"I mean the tax cuts?"

"While I don't necessarily agree with the timing on that, if we don't cut revenues, we won't have the pressure to cut spending and reduce the size of government. The two go hand-in-hand; sooner or later it's the only way."

"We already have a revenue shortfall," Halperin insisted. "Reducing tax rates in the middle of this recession will only make the deficit worse if the economy doesn't start growing."

Wilkerson looked at the house majority leader. Sometimes he wondered if Douglas really believed in the agenda they laid out two years ago. It was obvious Halperin did not understand the deeper agenda; fundamentally he was too committed to American political institutions.

"Taking away the funds to run government is the only sure-fire way to keep it under control. And we both know that a small government won't have the resources to interfere with the private sector."

"So our constituents can operate with fewer regulations."

"That's why we're elected, to serve the people who sent us here." Wilkerson smiled. He hoped that would be the end of it.

"But if we're serious about cutting the deficit and reducing the size of government, we have to look at defense," Halperin went on. "It's too big a share of the budget."

"Hold on now. I know what you're saying, but we have constituents in the defense industry too. They have supported us for years and would be none too happy about big cuts in their programs. I understand we may have to target some cuts here and there, but we just can't take a meat clever to entire defense programs." Now he was getting worried. What if Doug went rogue on him? They'd been through that before; they didn't need another embarrassment like that. "We don't need to lose defense-related jobs. Remember we have some of our governors relying heavily on the defense contracts that go to companies in their states, even in your district, Doug. We could very easily get ourselves sideways with a whole lot of our supporters."

Halperin pressed on. "That only leaves Social Security. If we touch that, the seniors are going to clobber us next election. And we'll never get cloture in the Senate anyway—the Democrats will filibuster any bill to change it."

Of course, Halperin was right. Hopefully, their numbers in the House and Senate would be large enough after the 2012 elections to kill the remainder of the social contract. But they would probably need the presidency as well. Getting enough votes in the Senate to override a veto was too much to ask for.

"Look, Douglas, this is the time to get the social programs under control. We have been afraid of cutting them for years, always conceding in the eleventh hour. Let's put Social Security on the table this year as a program that has to be revamped if we're going to seriously deal with the debt and deficit, but not propose any changes until we win back the White House. We need to raise the awareness of people so they'll be less resistant to the changes once we take a vote on them. Then we'll play it the same way as Medicare—we grandfather in those over fifty so they won't be impacted by any changes. That'll kill most of the resistance from the seniors."

Wilkerson continued. "Right now we have this president in a box. His numbers are low. People think he's too far left of center." Wilkerson recalled the latest poll showing almost 40% of Americans thought he was a socialist. "Taylor believes the American people want him to compromise in order to get something done. If he fails to go along with us, at least on a large portion of our agenda, he will have failed to find a way to get things done, and the people will vote him out next year for lack of leadership and mismanagement. We need to push him as far as we can and see what we can get."

"So we give in on Social Security and Medicare for now, and he gives in on most of the other cuts in our budget. In the meantime we've started the conversation on the social programs."

"Exactly. We might even be able to get him to agree to make the current temporary tax cuts permanent." Maybe Douglas could eventually learn the art of political tactics.

"But what will we do if the president vetoes our budget and shuts down the government?"

"If he does that, he'll get the blame." Wilkerson shrugged. "The people know we have to deal with our debt and deficits, and we'll be giving them a credible plan. It will be Taylor's decision to shut it down. If he does that, it makes our chances even better to take back the White House." Wilkerson began to find this conversation tedious. Why should he be sitting here having to convince the guy who was his partner on running the congress about their agenda at this late date? And yet, Halperin still brought up his doubts.

"The debt's still going to get bigger in the short term, even with our proposed budget cuts; even worse with tax cuts. And it looks like we're going to be forced to raise the debt ceiling again before we take a vote on our budget. It's going to be tough convincing the freshman members of my caucus to raise it without the president agreeing to our proposed budget. Hell, some want to insist on a balanced budget amendment to the Constitution as a part of any debt ceiling deal."

"Yes, I heard that. That one would never pass the Senate, but the threat of a default on the full faith and credit of the United States, now, that will put pressure on the half-breed and those progressive Democrats in Congress. They're cowards fundamentally, and won't want to play chicken with that, not like the budget." Wilkerson placed his hands behind his head. "Ultimately, the debt ceiling may be our best lever to passing our budget initiatives, Doug. That's why we need to get our budget proposal on the table soon, before we hit the debt limit. It's going to be an interesting debate."

Wilkerson leaned back in his office couch. He and his friends had talked about the prospect of not raising the debt ceiling and concluded, should that happen, it would only exacerbate the situation. Government spending would be drastically curtailed, the American economic engine would grind to a halt, and unemployment would rise. Even the threat of a default could cause the country's credit rating to be downgraded and interest rates to rise substantially, limiting government borrowing far more than any austerity budget would do, while digging the government further into debt. The negative effects on the global economy and the debt issues in other countries would exponentially increase, creating fear of a collapse around the world. He smiled. Let it come to that. Their goals would be realized much quicker than planned.

69

ANTON SAT AT his desk, the phone in his hand, for several minutes before dialing. Business was business, and he was in a very good position at the moment. He wasn't even sure of the reasons for his hesitation, but this was not a call he was looking forward to.

"I am sorry, Michael, but it is pretty clear your Congress will not pass the GRID Act this year. The budget proposed by your controlling party in Congress has completely stripped funding for infrastructure improvement projects in their new budget proposal, and the provisions for your electric grid protection were not included in the national defense portion of the budget."

"I know, Anton." Anton could hear the resignation in Michael's voice. "Fallon gave me a heads up a couple of days ago. I assume this means your investors can't carry my business any longer."

"They believe it is a bad investment at this time. I am sorry. But when the investors came in and you filed a patent for your surge protector design, you gave the investors a 50% stake in your patent rights. They are willing to buy out your share." He planned to wait patiently while his offer was considered and was surprised when Connelly responded immediately.

"What are they willing to pay?"

"Not enough to keep your business going, given the current economy I am afraid, but it is probably enough to wind down your business and pay your family's living expenses for a couple of years."

415

Anton knew how these kinds of circumstances often played out; so rare was the individual who could see the loss of a business as an opportunity for fresh new start. He waited.

"Okay, I'll talk it over with Jean," Michael finally said. "Get back to me with a figure as soon as you can."

"I will, and, Michael, I truly am sorry."

Anton hung up the phone and gazed out the window of the small office in his house. The winter snow had completely melted with the last warm spell. He knew what his father would say about Michael losing his business; he'd consider it a necessary short-term casualty that sometimes occurs if they are to achieve their ends.

GOOD MORNING, MR. President," Milestone said as Mitch Taylor entered the Oval Office.

"Morning, David. Are we ready for our briefing?" He had already been to the gym and was pumped up and ready to go. Declaring his intentions had been the best decision he'd made in months; every day felt like a new opportunity instead of the exhausting march it had become.

"First, you have a national security meeting at noon to go over the Middle East situation."

"Any news from the negotiations yesterday?" Taylor had been keeping track of the debt ceiling debate, sometimes calling in late night strategy sessions with his closest allies. It had been a hell of a struggle and the American people were losing patience.

"No good news, sir. There was still no movement last night. The other side won't give an inch."

Six weeks of intense negotiations with members from both sides of the aisle in both houses of Congress, and they had hardly seen any movement toward a deal to raise the debt ceiling. How far would the opposition take this, he wondered? But debt-ceiling issues have always been resolved before, many in the eleventh hour.

"Have you talked with the leaders on our side of the aisle?"

"They're not willing to move any further, and they certainly aren't going along with a balanced budget amendment." Milestone took a seat in front of the president's desk, a folder opened in front of him. "They may go along with a cap on our debt as a percent of GDP, but not unless the other side gives on a hike in the tax rates. With the conditions currently attached to the Republican debt ceiling bill, they're going to recommend a 'no' vote to their caucus."

"Our party will get slammed for that." Taylor leaned back in his chair.

"The proposed cuts are too onerous for them to swallow. They want a clean debt-ceiling bill and debate the budget bill separately. I think we can explain that to the public."

Taylor turned his swivel chair and looked out the windows of the Oval Office. He knew he couldn't push his party any further. They had gone as far as they could without sacrificing their core beliefs—and so had he.

"A clean bill would have bought us a little more time to influence public opinion."

"I think the other side knows that, sir."

"What are our next steps, David?" he said while continuing to look out at the White House lawn. "I refuse to turn Medicare over to the insurance companies. At least the Republicans are not clamoring to turn Social Security over to Wall Street."

"Not yet."

He turned his head and looked at Milestone. "You and Jude Anders. You still believe Medicare is just the foot in the door?" His counsel had almost always been spot on; rare was the occasion when David had been wrong, or Anders for that matter.

"Yes, sir. We've already given in on Medicaid in the negotiations."

"You know, we could solve those problems by instituting a mandatory universal health care program." This was one more of his initiatives that he still regretted not pushing harder. "The Europeans, Japanese, and Taiwanese, even the Swiss, have done it. It works. Why can't the other side see that? For that matter, why can't the American people?"

Milestone closed his folder and pushed his chair back from the desk. "They've bought the propaganda—more big government controlling health care decisions and more debt. Are you going to hold your position on financial reform? Some of ours in the Senate may be prepared to roll back some key provisions; at least go gentle on the regulations. They're getting a lot of pressure from their contributors."

"And put us in jeopardy of this happening all over again?" Taylor swiveled his chair back to face his chief of staff. "Yeah, it might make the economy improve for a while, but in three to five years we'd be right back in the ditch. No, not on my watch."

"Mr. President, we have to face the reality that the debt ceiling may not be raised. Milestone paused. "We need to start making plans. Have you talked with the Treasury Secretary?"

"Connelly says we have to cut Social Security, Medicare, Veterans benefits, EPA and the regulatory agencies first. If that doesn't get us below the ceiling for the remainder of the year, we'd have to look at Defense. We cannot default on the principal and interest on our debt. No options."

"You could order a pull out from Afghanistan," Milestone offered. "That might give us more flexibility in dealing with the Middle East crisis."

"That would make some in our party happy, wouldn't it?" The president picked up a paper clip and started twisting it out of shape.

"There are some good arguments for it."

"I know. Trust me, I've thought of doing it many times, but the Defense Secretary and the generals are against it. You know, the end of American military superiority—a slippery slope. And no one can give me a clear direction on our current Middle East problems. Any military action there will cost money too."

"But the debt ceiling could give you the leverage to get out, even over the objections of the military. You would have no option. And I guess it provides cover for no U.S. military involvement in the Middle East situations."

Taylor in fact had considered giving the order to get out of Afghanistan before the debt-ceiling vote. That would have sent the message that he intended to protect the safety net first. But that would only ramp up a new set of criticisms: weak on national defense and not willing to face up to our *real* debt and deficit problems—the safety net. The opposition was already calling him indecisive over current events in Yemen, which was seeing an unprecedented escalation of unrest. Even if he did give the order to withdraw, it would take months. Not quick enough to help with the debt ceiling, and it wouldn't be enough to cover the fiscal shortfall.

"I'm afraid they have us over a barrel, Mr. President. The only good thing is that when Americans start feeling the pain, they're likely to blame the Republicans more than us."

"And the Democratic members of Congress who support the other side, I hope."

"Should I have the Treasury Secretary prepare a detailed plan, sir? At most we have a week."

Taylor remained silent. Opening his desk drawer after a moment, he slowly pulled out a manila envelope and set it on his desk. He stared at it.

"What's that?"

The president looked at the hand-written label on the center of the envelope. "Plan B." He looked across the desk at Milestone. His mind was made up. "Get Connelly working on a plan."

"Yes, sir." Milestone turned to leave the Oval Office.

"Oh, and David,"

"Sir?"

"Get Jude Anders back here. I want to meet with him tomorrow."

"But, sir, he's at Princeton."

"Tell him I need him . . . to execute Plan B. He'll understand. Oh, and tell him to pack a bag. He's going to be here a while."

70

THE PRESIDENT'S NATIONAL security briefing began at its scheduled time in the Situation Room of the White House. The key players were seated at the long table surrounded by large flat-screen monitors: Vice President Collin Sanderson, National Security Advisor Brice Fullerton, Secretary of State Willis Donner, Secretary of Defense Robert Boyd, and Chairman of the Joint Chiefs Walter McMillan.

"Be seated," President Taylor said as he walked in the room and his administration rose from their chairs. These things were all business; no one wasted any energy on small talk. He started right off with the Middle East unrest. "Colin, have you talked with President Choles?"

"Yes, Mr. President. He believes the protests in Sana and Adan are under control. He's seen these kind of protests before in Yemen; says things will quiet down in a week or so."

"That may be true for the cities," Brice Fullerton interrupted, "but our satellite reconnaissance shows a massing of rebel forces near the Saudi border. The King has ordered troops to the border to prevent a rebel incursion into the Kingdom. The Saudi Air Force has been mobilized and is flying surveillance sorties."

"What kind of weapons do the rebels have, Robert?" the president asked his Defense Secretary.

"Mortars, ground-to-air missiles, tank-buster missiles, jeeps, and some troop-carrying trucks—mostly pickups." Dry and often dour, Robert Boyd was mostly a numbers man; Taylor was grateful he didn't have to suffer through displays of bravado every time he opened his month, unlike some defense secretaries he recalled.

"How far to the Saudi oil fields?"

"Three hundred miles to those furthest south, sir; five hundred to the Ghawar oil field—the big one," Boyd answered.

"Have the Saudis taken defensive positions around the oil fields?" No matter what these governments said about their problems, eventually it all came back down to oil. Who has it; who wants it.

"They do not have enough troops mobilized to protect both the Yemen border and the oil fields. They believe if they can prevent the rebels from entering the Kingdom, they won't have to worry about the oil fields." This was news to Taylor; since when did they not worry about the oil fields?

"Unless Al Qaeda sympathizers within the Kingdom decide to sabotage them," Fullerton chimed in. "Have there been protests within the Kingdom?"

"None so for," answered Secretary of State Donner. "The King has increased the citizens' stipend to discourage protests by a large segment of the population and is talking publicly about moving up the timetable for democratic reforms. That doesn't mean Al Qaeda won't try, but they don't have much of a foothold left in the Kingdom."

"What about the other countries in the region?" The president asked.

"Small protests in Syria, Jordan, Libya, and Egypt. The governments are not cracking down, except for Libya." Donner said. "There may be something brewing in Iran, but reports are sketchy."

"What have we communicated to the presidents and the kings?"

"Same message, Mr. President. You need to expedite democratic reforms or risk being overthrown by populist movements."

"They'll do that only when forced to. What else?"

"Oil is up $10 per barrel since yesterday," Collin Sanderson answered. "Fear of significant upheavals in the Middle East is causing speculation on the Commodities Exchange."

"But there is no shortage of oil at this point."

"Speculators are looking to make a killing, Mr. President. They're betting on a disruption in oil supplies."

Taylor rubbed the back of his neck and loosened his tie. Reeling in speculators, it was an almost impossible job. The marketplace had turned into one giant casino. "Can we put a stop to the speculation?"

"We've looked into that before," the vice president said. "The Commodities Futures Act prohibits the government from interfering in the derivatives contracts market. The Chairman of the Commodities

Trading Commission is monitoring the situation as best she can, but the agency still has no authority over the oil futures speculation as long as it is within the law. We didn't get that piece in the financial overhaul bill."

Visions of long lines of cars snaking out of gas stations and around the block, a common sight when he was a kid, rose up in his mind. "Gentlemen, I think you all know we don't need another crisis just now. Christ, of all the times for the Arab world to rise up against their dictators."

An Air Force officer knocked on the open door to the Situation Room. "Sir." He came to attention and saluted.

Taylor looked toward the doorway. "Captain, this had better be good."

"Yes, sir," the captain said. He handed Taylor a piece of paper.

Taylor read it and looked up at the Chairman of the Joint Chiefs. "What is a Solar Energetic Particle Event, Walter?" He held out the paper for McMillan to read.

"According the US Air Force Weather Agency, it's a solar maximum event caused by a coronal mass ejection four hours ago." McMillan said after reading the alert, a trace of urgency in his voice.

"What the hell does that mean?"

"Given you have been notified directly, Mr. President, it means that there has been a major solar eruption and a solar magnetic field is heading for Earth with a high probability that it will impact the United States." McMillan turned to the captain, "Get Lieutenant Colonel Schmidt on the com."

"Yes, sir," the captain snapped. He moved to the phone and began dialing.

"I thought these kind of things hit the North Pole and created a light show. Why am I being notified?" The men around the table shifted in their seats. Vice President Sanderson checked his Blackberry; Fullerton and Donner followed suit.

"That is what I am trying to ascertain, Mr. President."

"Lieutenant Colonel Schmidt," a husky voice announced over the speakerphone in the Situation Room phone.

"Schmidty, this is Walter, what's the target and ETA of the SEPE?"

"Two to five days, sir; target east central Canada, possibly stretching down to the U.S." The men in the room were silent.

"Where in the U.S.?"

"We cannot pinpoint it exactly, sir."

"Come on, Schmidty, best guess based on current data?"

"Anywhere between Grand Rapids and Buffalo we think." A sudden shuffling of papers on the conference table ensued as the men prepared to head to their offices. Taylor tried to picture a map with a line stretching between Michigan and New York.

"Stretching how far south?" McMillan asked.

"That's even more difficult to predict. Toledo, Cleveland, maybe Columbus, Indianapolis, Pittsburgh."

"When can we be more certain on time and location?"

"We're monitoring it hour by hour, sir."

"I want an update every four hours."

"Yes, sir. Should we initiate operation CONUS?"

"Put everyone on alert," McMillan replied. "Have you notified your counterparts in Canada?"

"Ten minutes ago, Mr. Chairman."

McMillan pushed the button to disconnect the com and looked at the president. "Depending on the force of the solar wind and strength of the magnetic field, this could be a problem."

"What kind of problem?" Taylor asked, an uneasy feeling settling in his gut.

"I am not apprised of all the details, sir. We need to get that from NASA. And we need to alert Homeland Security. They need to inform the governors of the potentially affected states and the power companies."

"Are we talking blackout, Walter?" Taylor rubbed the back of his neck again. What was he just saying about not needing another crisis?

"If it is severe enough, sir."

"For how long?"

"It all depends, but a smaller event in Canada knocked out their electric grid for almost a day. If it's powerful enough and had a direct hit in the U.S., it could effect one or more cities."

"Get the directors of NASA and Homeland Security on the com, now," the president ordered. "And, Walter, what is CONUS?"

"HELLO, JOSEPH, HOW are you?" Fallon was surprised to hear the familiar voice of her mentor on the phone; except for that brief call of encouragement when she had been offered the Treasury job, it had been years since she had heard from him.

"I am doing well, Fallon. I take it you have got something you can sink your teeth into these days."

Fallon laughed. "I think the operative word is 'sink'." She closed the folder of documents she had been reading at her desk and pushed it aside for a moment.

"My, my, well, I am quite sure you can handle it, if anyone can. But that is not the reason for my call. I was curious if you are planning to attend the alumni meeting next month?"

Ah, even Joseph had been pressed into service by the nation's most aggressive alumni association. She searched through her emails for the invitation.

"I really doubt it. We're in the middle of a small crisis. Haven't you heard?"

"Yes, Fallon, I read the papers. Do you think we will get some resolution among the disputing parties?"

"I think so. Most of what is going on is just politics and posturing. There are enough smart people on the Hill to not let it come to . . ."

"You are most likely correct in your assessment," Joseph interrupted. "But what if calmer heads do not prevail?"

"We are working on a plan, as you would expect." She continued scrolling through her emails. Damn, where was that thing? "It will make giving in to the spending cut demands look like a picnic. I hope you don't need your Social Security check or Medicare."

"I would gladly give them to someone who needs them, you know that." His voice was gentle. "I feel sorry for the ordinary people of this country."

"There's no help for it, Joseph. We just don't have the money to keep them afloat." She did feel sorry for the ordinary people. Her own brothers were struggling, although she didn't appreciate the way their wives had begun to treat her, as if the crashing economy was somehow her personal responsibility. And her own portfolio had taken a hit; it's not as though she was immune.

"I am most concerned about the government living up to its obligations," Joseph went on. "That would be a terrible thing for our country, if they did not. Who knows, you might have to work with the IMF again, Fallon." She could hear a smile in his voice.

"Don't worry about that. The president would never default on our bondholders—betray the full faith and credit of the United States. We were all raised to know that we have to pay what we owe. That's part of our culture."

"I am glad to hear that. You people in Washington wouldn't want to give an old man a heart attack."

"Come on. You're not old, and don't worry."

It was so nice to hear his voice; it had been too long. She used to see him frequently, especially when she was a student at Harvard. Joseph had been there for every milestone in her career, and they were long overdue for a visit. She'd see what she could arrange.

"Thank you, Fallon. I'll give your regards to the alumni committee. We will miss you."

71

Present Time
Katapola, Amorgos, Greece

THE SOUNDS OF the fishing boats in the harbor leaving for their first run of the day, and the morning sun streaming on my face through the open window woke me from a very deep sleep—the best sleep I could remember having in years. A tray with a pot of coffee and rolls awaited me outside the door to my room. I sat outside on the balcony having my first breakfast on the island and watching the daily activity in the harbor until it was time to get ready.

I looked in the mirror of the bathroom, readying to shave after my shower. My blondish hair had turned white around my temples; I had deep wrinkles along the sides of my mouth and hairline cracks emanating from my eyes and cascading down my cheeks. When did I start to look so old? Perhaps I hadn't paid enough attention to my physical appearance in the last two years, or else all these lines in my face were new. I stood there looking at the can of shaving cream in my left hand and finally returned it my Dobb kit. I collected my things and headed to the lobby.

"Your driver's name is Jacobi, Mr. Anders. He speaks English fairly well. Ask him for anything you need. He and his family are very well connected throughout the island," the hotel clerk told me as I checked out.

"Thank you. I'll come back for a stay after I get settled in Lagada. I would like to see more of Katapola." I signed the bill and pushed it across the desk.

"I would be happy to serve you," he said as he handed me his card. "Call me when you wish to make a reservation. Good day, Mr. Anders."

I dragged my luggage outside. Jacobi was parked in front of the hotel in a small dark blue sedan. I thought of the last time I was assigned a driver—Argentina. A host of memories rose to the surface but I tamped them down. Now was not the time for that journey again.

"Good morning, Mr. Anders. I help with luggage." Jacobi grabbed my oversized roller bag and wrestled it into the open trunk. "Please," he said, pointing to the front passenger seat.

"I need you to take me to Lagada to drop off my luggage, and then back to Chora to pick up a motorbike rental." I threw my backpack in the back seat of the car.

"We go Chora first, to bike rental shop. On the way. Quicker, use less gas. I have rack. I put on back of car."

Of course, why did I feel like I had to tell him how to do his job? Yet another ingrained habit I was going to have to lose.

"Really? That would be great if you wouldn't mind."

"Is no problem."

I hopped into the front seat and we drove away from the hotel and toward the mountain that overlooked the town.

"You must go Ormos for food. No stores Lagada," Jacobi announced as we wound our way through the narrow streets of Katapola.

"Yes, I had heard that might be a problem, but I think I can manage. I can carry most of what I need in my backpack. I don't need much."

Jacobi was quiet for a while as he wove the car out of town. "Mr. Anders, I have daughter, Aglaia. She shop and cook for you—has car. Not charge much."

I had heard about the generosity of the locals, but what I really wanted was to be alone. On the other hand, having someone who knew the food, what was fresh, spoke the language, I could see how that would make things easier.

"Shopping sounds good, but I would rather cook myself. Maybe an occasional meal."

Jacobi immediately pulled out a cell phone and made a call; his Greek was fast, and I hadn't heard it enough yet to grow accustomed to its awkward syllables. "She bring you some food for tonight," he said, slapping the phone closed. "You talk tomorrow."

"Wow, thank you. I do not speak Greek."

"Her English okay. Aglaia teach you Greek, you teach Aglaia good English."

"I'll try."

My stay in Greece suddenly took on the plot of more than one movie. I guess it was okay for me to hope that she was young and pretty. Might as well take the fantasy for the full ride.

"How far to Chora?" I asked him.

"Small kilometers, but road twisty. Take time. You look, I drive."

The landscape was arid, and the climb to the top of the old volcano that created this island was steep and twisty, just like Jacobi said. I cracked my window and lit up a smoke, almost dropping it on the floorboard when Jacobi took one of the hairpin curves a little too fast. He looked over at me and laughed. We gradually wound up the side of the volcano and the brush turned into scrub pine trees. There were flowers and wild grasses and the air cooled. We were many kilometers above the Aegean Sea, which I could see behind me when the little trees did not obscure the view. Chora was on the other side of the volcano, where the view would be of the south side of the island.

I could tell we were nearing the summit. There was more brush and the landscape got rockier. I lit another cigarette and waited to see what was on the other side.

72

May 19, 2011
Washington D.C.

AROUND 9:00 IN the morning. I got a call from David Milestone, requesting that I meet with the president—urgent, he said. I had just gotten out of the shower. I didn't have class until 1:00, but I had planned to run a few errands. When David told me it was about Plan B, I dropped my towel and finished the conversation with him wet and naked. I had been following the debate in Washington, but never seriously considered the president would implement the plan.

"Of course, I'll be there this afternoon, David. Thank you for calling and please tell the president I look forward to seeing him," I said in my most formal voice, considering my current state. I quickly dressed and rang my administrative assistant to cancel my 1:00 pm class. I felt like a character in a movie, telling her I had an urgent meeting with the president. "At the White House," I added for emphasis, although god knows I didn't need to.

At 10:00 I left my apartment in Princeton and took a cab to the train station in Philadelphia to catch the 11:15 train to D.C. It was nearly 1:00 by the time I arrived at the reception room to the Oval Office where I was told the president was still in his national security briefing. Even on the train, I felt a growing sense of anxiety. By the time I made it to the White House, I was grateful for the pause.

A little after 1:30, the Chairman of the Joint Chiefs, Secretary of Defense, and National Security Advisor came out of the door to the Oval

Office. The look on their faces was stern, and there was a sense of urgency in the air, but each greeted me cordially with small talk about my new career until David came to the open door of the office.

"Jude, good to see you. The president is ready for you."

"Mr. President," I said as he got up from behind his desk and came over to me. I reached out to shake his hand; he hugged me instead.

"Thank you for coming, Jude. David, can you leave the two of us alone?"

"Yes, Mr. President." Milestone shot me a questioning look and headed out the back door of the office.

President Taylor picked up a manila envelope from his credenza and motioned me to the couch in the center of the room. He sat down across from me and tossed the envelope on the coffee table that separated us.

"You know, when I first read this, I really did think you were a crackpot." The president's voice was easy, his demeanor calm. Considering the urgency of David's phone call, and the looks on the faces of the security advisors, I was a little confused.

"And now?"

"Let's just say that now I see the same options as you. Nasty medicine in either case."

"Two lines, both leading to the same point eventually." I wondered what had happened that led him to consider it now, as opposed to last week—or last month.

"Yes, but as you say in this paper . . ." he nodded toward the manila envelope on the table, "better to get the pain over sooner rather than later. Coming all at once, like you recommend, is going to set the global economy on its lips. Countries, corporations and creditors are not going to have a lot of time to react. That gives us some time to put things in place to soften the blow and prevent them from making the situation worse, as you suggest in your paper." He gestured again to the envelope on the table. He had apparently read it very carefully.

"If you're going to implement Plan B, you have to advise the leaders of the major economies," I noted.

"Yes, of course, but not yet—right? Christ, this can't leak out. If it did, the panic would be worse than the actual effects."

"Agreed." I couldn't be sure if he was referring to my part in the last leak we had dealt with or not. Regardless, I knew it would not happen again. I tried to keep my voice as calm as Taylor's, as though this was just an ordinary conversation. "A couple of days in advance should give them and their finance ministers some time—not enough time for them to fully prepare, but enough to start considering what steps they will take. They will likely take some of the same actions as we do."

"I hear Congress intends to direct how I implement the cuts if the debt ceiling is not raised. How do we handle that?"

"Well, Mr. President, you can get counsel from the attorney general, but my research says Congress has appropriation authority, which directs you how to spend—on what and how much—but it cannot tell you what to cut when you run out of money and they refuse to extend your borrowing authority. If they try to pass a new appropriations bill with specific language on cuts . . ."

"I veto it."

"Exactly."

Various individuals would have to be notified of the actions the president was planning to take if he were to implement Plan B; many would try to stop him. "Have you talked with Fallon Connelly about this?"

"No. I have her working on a detailed plan for the cuts everyone expects if the ceiling isn't raised. When I do tell her, I'll say Plan B is just a contingency plan, that I want to explore the implications of all my options."

I was surprised at his strategy; keeping Fallon out of the loop was probably necessary, but it made me more than a little uncomfortable. "She's not going to like it," I insisted, knowing that Fallon was committed to the tried and true prescription for dealing with debt. But we had our debate in front of President Taylor last month. Apparently she had lost.

"I know." His grin had the slightest hint of boyishness about it. "Now, let's get to it. I need the sequence of steps beginning now, through my announcement, and then after—first days, weeks, and months. I want to predict as much of the fallout as I can." He paused. "And since you've become quite the prolific writer these days with your blog, I want your help with my speech."

It turned out I had become a pretty good writer, especially about the issues we were facing. When I took the teaching position at Princeton, Anton hired me to write an occasional piece for a blog his media company had created. I didn't need the money, but it gave me the opportunity to hone my views and maybe influence public opinion from an entirely different platform. I had worked for the government most of my entire career; it was a nice change of pace. We decided to call the blog *Economic Justice*.

73

May 20, 2011

"ANY WORD FROM the White House?" Jimmy Wilkerson asked his secretary as he walked into his office after a meeting with his Republican Senate Caucus.

"No, Senator." She looked up at him, her hand on the phone. "Should I call David Milestone?"

"Not now. Get Doug Halperin on the phone, will you?"

The senator stepped into his private office and looked at his desk, covered with stacks of files. So much for the paperless office. The vote would be taken next week. Whether the president and his compatriots capitulated or not, the era of big government and the social safety net were over. A smug grin ran from one side of his face to the other. He knew they could wait until the last minute to cut a deal, but the longer he and his colleagues held out, the greater the fear of default. Once again he mused at how the plan would work.

The rating agencies would use the fear of default as an excuse to threaten to downgrade the U.S. credit rating. They were looking for any leverage they could use to get the administration to back off on regulations that made them liable for misrepresenting the ratings they issued on mortgage-backed securities during the housing boom. And a downgrade of the credit rating would increase the likelihood that bond markets would insist on higher interest rates on Treasuries. That would place an enormous drag on the economy and guarantee a high cost of government borrowing for many years to come. They would finally starve the beast, he thought. The economy's anemic growth would stall and begin a retreat. More jobs would be lost, and all of this economic bad news would double their chances of taking back the White House next year.

Still, in the back of his mind he was convinced Taylor would eventually capitulate. The president didn't have the stomach for completely slashing his social programs or playing roulette with the debt ceiling. But this time there would be no compromising. Taylor was trapped one way or the other. He had to play it their way, and they would defeat him next year.

His phone intercom buzzed. "Mr. Halperin is on line one, Senator."

The senator took off his suit coat and flung it on the couch, then picked up the phone. "Doug, are you ready for the big day?"

"We've waited a long time, Jimmy. My guys in the House are chomping at the bit to take the vote."

"Make sure they don't look too smug about it," Wilkerson cautioned. "We don't want the American people thinking we're insensitive to the pain that's coming their way. Have you heard anything from the White House this morning?"

"Not since negotiations broke off last night. It's been almost two weeks since they last gave in on anything. I don't think the White House or our friends from the other side of the aisle are going to give any further. We're in the eleventh hour."

"Will you be working over the weekend?" Wilkerson reached into his office fridge for a bottle of water.

"We are willing, but there's been no word from the Oval Office. They may be trying to intimidate us by pushing us right up to the deadline. That tactic won't work this time."

"So be it. It's their fault if negotiations fail, and we'll make sure the public believes just that."

"I did hear that the Treasury Secretary is working on a plan for cuts if the ceiling isn't raised."

"Really?" Surely, they weren't actually going to go through with it, Wilkerson thought. "That may be just a ruse to put pressure back on us. Have you got the bill together directing the Treasury on which obligations to pay first?"

"It's ready to go—defense and our foreign debt first. Anything left over gets funneled into reduced funding for Homeland Security; nothing for the other government departments, Social Security or Medicare. They will have to furlough the employees from the regulatory agencies. Nothing gets done until a budget deal for next year, which is four months off, or they acquiesce to our budget terms."

"Either way we'll have it our way. I think you and I need to get together to refine our message a little before the House takes its vote."

"Are you thinking a formal press conference or the usual ad hoc thing, Jimmy?"

"Given the magnitude of the event, we should plan a formal press conference, say thirty minutes after the vote to raise the ceiling fails and the House adjourns. But let's make it just you and me. Like I said, we don't want any of our crackpots showing their gleaming smiles behind us." Yet another lesson they had learned the hard way since the midterms.

"Do you want me to come to your office?"

"Yes. Let's do it at 4:00."

Jimmy Wilkerson stared at the files on his desk. Yes, they would win this battle—Check and Mate.

PRESIDENT TAYLOR STRODE back into the Situation Room. At his side were Homeland Security Secretary Natallyeh and Chief of Staff David Milestone.

"What's the latest on the solar event, Walter?" Taylor asked.

McMillan turned toward the door, and stood stiffly at attention—a habit from his years in the Marines. "I received an update thirty minutes ago, Mr. President. We've caught a break on the ETA. Looks like Sunday."

"And strength and location?" Taylor took his seat at the conference table.

"Both still difficult to estimate, sir. This is a big solar ejection, but what happens when it hits the Earth's magnetosphere is not really predictable." McMillan punched in some coordinates in his PC. A map of North America appeared on the large TV screen hung on the west wall of the Situation Room. "We are still looking at an area west of Toronto."

"How far north? Detroit is west of Toronto." Detroit, Toledo, Cleveland, Pittsburgh, and Buffalo . . . he had looked at the maps himself last night, honing in on who exactly would be affected.

"And a little south. If we are lucky this thing will hit north of Lake Huron, in Canada." McMillan zoomed in on the map and drew his pointer over the Great Lakes.

"And if we're not lucky? How far south could this thing go?"

"It's not just where it hits, Mr. President," Homeland Security Secretary Natallyeh interrupted. "We have to analyze the electric transmission sources for our population areas in Michigan and Ohio. If Detroit is getting electricity from Canada and the storm hits in Canada, it could take out the line transformers between the plant and the city. If it hits Michigan, it could impact northern Ohio."

"Have we done the analysis?"

"In process, sir. We're reviewing our options for rerouting power around the areas potentially affected."

"What else could the solar storm interrupt?"

"NASA is moving a few satellites in geosynchronous orbit away from the impact area, so we should be okay there, and the space station is nowhere near the projected entry point," Walter McMillan answered. "That being said, it could affect gas pipelines—give unreliable pressure readings."

Taylor raised an eyebrow. Pressure readings were key to keeping things from blowing up.

"Who notifies the pipeline operators?"

"The governors of the affected states," Natellyeh responded. "That's part of what we will communicate to the governors."

"What about our nuclear power plants? Are we in danger from more than damaged transformers?"

"Sir, there are two plants that might be in the projected impact zone and two more just outside of it," the secretary responded. "Each of these plants have diesel power backup in case of an electrical failure throughout the grid. But we should advise the governors to shut down the plants as a precaution—in case of any anomalies."

"So what are you telling me? Could the plants be affected or not?" It was imperative he had an idea of the scope of this crisis. Every decision he made from now on depended on him knowing as accurately as possible what he was facing.

"We've reviewed our nuclear plant disaster response plan, and believe there is at most a negligible possibility of a nuclear incident. Our biggest concern is what do we do if we lose electric service to a major city. We don't have the time or resources to immediately evacuate, say, cities like Detroit or Cleveland. An outage of significance will create food and water shortages, not to mention the looting aspect. Sir, I think we should have

FEMA begin staging supplies in the area. It will take a couple of days to get supplies together and transport them."

Taylor thought of Hurricane Katrina and the shameful lapse in proper response. His chance would be different. "Do we have enough supplies for a million people?"

"We maybe able to get enough food and water together to help a million or so for at most a few days." Natallyeh's voice was flat; she was probably thinking about Katrina too, Taylor thought. "We would need to start moving people out of the area if the outage was prolonged beyond that."

"Walter, do we have an evacuation plan?" He turned his gaze to McMillan. He liked McMillan; he was always clear and concise on every point.

"Yes, sir, we have a plan for every major city in the country; that's the purpose of CONUS. CONUS will assist with distribution of supplies, law and order, and command the evacuation, if one is required," McMillan responded. "This is not like a nuclear attack; we can keep the citizens in place until the event, and then assess the extent and duration of the damage to determine next steps. But the secretary is correct about staging supplies." He paused. "Sir, FEMA has the powers to act by Executive Order, but given the potential magnitude of the disaster, we would be on more solid footing with the public if we invoke the National Emergencies Act. If we're going to go that route, we need to do it soon."

President Taylor hadn't thought of that. He tried to remember the conditions under which he could invoke a state of emergency, and how long he could keep it in effect. It could provide broader cover for other actions they might need to take down the line.

"Well, maybe declaring an emergency would be the right way to go." He looked directly at David Milestone, hoping he would get the point.

"Yes, sir, it could be useful," Milestone replied. Taylor thought he saw David acknowledge what he was thinking. Was it a wink, or just a blink? "But we need to notify Congress that you are declaring a state of emergency under the National Emergencies Act."

Yes, Taylor thought, that might be a problem with this Congress. Still . . . "Not just yet, David." The other advisors were looking at him curiously.

"Wait until the event occurs?"

"No need to create alarm unnecessarily." Taylor was sure David got the gist of where this was headed. "But we do need to inform our legislative leaders and the governors of the affected states that the storm is coming. Walter, notify FEMA and CONUS to start moving supplies to the staging areas in Indiana, Michigan and Ohio, and, David, get the governors of Michigan, Ohio, and New York on the phone. A conference call with all three. Then I need a communications plan for the public."

"And the congressional leaders?" Milestone asked.

"Call them to the White House for a meeting this afternoon."

"Before or after your national security meeting, Mr. President?"

"Shit. I forgot about that. Does anyone else have a crisis to deal with?"

IT WAS 4:00 pm when I got a call from David Milestone. The president had a couple of things to discuss with me, and asked me to join him for dinner. At 6:00 I met the president in the Oval Office before he, a thin black binder he was carrying, and I went upstairs for an informal dinner.

"I need to bring you up to speed on a couple of things, Jude," Taylor said as we left the Oval Office and walked under the colonnade that bordered the Rose Garden to the entrance that led to his private quarters. "Things that may impact Plan B."

"Have the Republicans agreed to raise the debt ceiling?" I hadn't heard that, but I knew that there were a number of behind-the-scenes negotiations underway.

"No, nothing that simple, I'm afraid."

He paused as though waiting for another question from me, but I had no idea what to ask. "We have a couple of national security issues."

"Sir?"

"You know about our problems in Yemen?" he asked as we entered the elevator to the second floor.

"Yes. Bits and pieces." There were protests in the cities of Sana and Adan, but the army had secured the cities. Brutally, some said. More importantly, a band of rebels probably linked to Al Qaeda held control of the northern, mostly desert part of the country. They had made frequent incursions across the border into Saudi Arabia over the past few days. Word was they intended to try to take over some of the Saudi oil fields to disrupt global oil supplies.

"Well, the Saudis have offered us $5 billion to provide ground assets to assist them with fighting an insurgency that is now threatening to take over the Ghawar oil field. Our Saudi friends don't have enough ground forces to fight off the incursion from Yemen *and* protect the field."

That was news. I had thought the Saudis had a large army. I knew they didn't like to get their hands dirty. Was this just a way to get someone else to do the hard work?

"Is $5 billion enough?"

The elevator door started to open, but the president pushed the button to close it again.

"That's not the point. They will give us more, as we need it. But how can I commit troops to yet another war when we might be implementing Plan B at the same time, even with the Saudi money? You've seen the impact the latest uprisings in the Kingdom, Libya, and Iran have had on oil prices. A full-blown war with significant American troop involvement would likely lead to even more speculation. And that's without even considering our own recession and the weariness of the American people. We've been at war for ten years as it is; the coffers and our spirits are drained."

The Saudi offer was more than new information; it could potentially be a game-changer. I could certainly see the potential impact on oil prices. I needed some time to think through the effects on Plan B.

"You said there were a couple of security issues?" We were still in the elevator, perhaps the only place the president felt truly protected from being overheard. "What else?"

President Taylor remained silent for several seconds. I waited as patiently as I could, although the import of the moment was not lost on me. I assumed Plan B was in his binder, along with whatever he needed to do to make it happen.

"Listen, Jude, what I am about to tell you cannot be discussed with anyone other than me."

"Of course, Mr. President." I thought of Sasha. Surely he knew.

"On Sunday there is a high probability that the north-central U.S. will be hit by a geomagnetic storm."

"Is that related to the solar flares reported several days ago?" I wondered where he was going with this, but as he spoke, it dawned on me. Natural disaster.

"Yes, but what has not been reported is that the strength of the waves headed toward Earth is something we have not seen since we began tracking such events." He thumbed the black binder but did not open it.

"Where exactly do we expect the solar storm to hit?"

"The exact location can't be predicted precisely, but we believe in the vicinity of the U.S.-Canadian border above Detroit. We're not certain what areas will be impacted, the number of people who might be without power, or for how long." The president leaned against the elevator wall.

"Are we talking hours or days, sir?"

"Jude, we could be talking months, maybe even a year or longer." His voice was calm. His eyes were on me. I thought of Hurricane Katrina and the breadth of that crisis, which was never fully reported to the American people. This could be worse, much worse.

"But people can't live without electricity," I replied, "at least not for very long."

"I'm glad you appreciate the magnitude of the situation." He righted himself and released his finger from the close-door button in the elevator. "We've been staging emergency assets to help, but if there's a direct hit on our transformers, or even power plants, god forbid, we will have a long-term problem that will require us to evacuate a large segment of the population in the area."

We walked down the hallway through the family sitting room and into the kitchen. The president flipped on the light. The kitchen had a black and white tiled floor, walnut-colored cabinets, and a white counter that wound around a food preparation area in the center of the room. I had never been in the kitchen before; my only time in the private residence was at a New Years party last year. The president opened the door to the family dining room and looked in for a moment. It was empty and dark; he pulled the door closed again.

"It will take billions to fix the problem if the event hits us."

"At a time when we don't have the money and Congress won't raise the debt ceiling," I responded. The financial implications of such a disaster were almost beyond comprehension. "And if we default on our debt, no other country will lend us the money to rebuild."

"That's why we're talking, Jude," he said, setting the black binder on the counter. "I met with Wilkerson and Halperin earlier to advise them of the situation. The only way they will raise the debt ceiling is if we give in on their spending cuts in the proposed budget."

"Even in the midst of a major catastrophe and emergency? You are kidding."

"I wish I were. Like climate change, maybe they just don't believe in the potential consequences. They said they were at the end of the line, and they mean it. No more debt. We have to pay our way from the money we take in."

"And taxes?"

A tired look overtook his face and he sighed. "They still want to cut them further."

Taylor opened a cabinet door and pulled out a bottle of scotch. "Drink?"

"Sure, two cubes."

I shifted into high gear. This was the kind of problem I actually liked solving, and I wasn't going to waste a minute. "Do we manufacture the equipment needed to repair the damage to the grid in the U.S.?"

"I am told most of the companies that build the transformers are in the U.S. Why?" he asked as he handed me the drink.

I took a sip of the scotch. "Well, the Treasury can print enough money to cover the costs of repairs. We'll have some control over the value of the dollar within the boundaries of this country. It's when we have to buy goods or services outside that the debt becomes a significant issue. And as you read in Plan B, we will never get our economy to recover until we get our foreign trade imbalance under control. The more we make things here, the less we import, the less our trade deficit, and the less obligations we would have to our creditors."

"So you're telling me Plan B not only helps with our import-export imbalance, it actually can help us repair any damage caused by the solar storm?" He leaned against the refrigerator and loosened his tie.

"In more ways than one. We can cover the costs, and we can put a lot of people back to work. That's the only good thing about catastrophes—more jobs."

"What about needed parts that aren't made here?"

I thought about his question for a minute. "We create new companies funded by our new investment funds, or foreign companies can choose to open manufacturing facilities here. It might take a little longer, but in the long term . . ."

"I get it." Taylor sipped his scotch. "And the Saudi situation?"

"Well, there's no doubt that turmoil in the Middle East, especially in the countries you mentioned, will drive up the price of oil in the short run. You can already see the impact on the oil futures markets, even though currently there is no shortage. Plan B will drive prices the other way once the global economy adjusts to what has happened. But that won't last forever."

"Meaning?"

"As we discussed, Plan B will push the world economy into recession, maybe a full-blown depression, for a period of time until it adjusts to the new economic principles. That recessionary force will dramatically reduce the demand for oil globally and the price will fall until the global economy sorts itself out."

"And the speculators will lose their shirts," the president said with a wry smile on his face.

"You win some, you lose some. It's difficult for me to feel sorry for them." I grinned, lifting my glass in salute. I turned my thoughts back to the uprisings in the Middle East. "Mr. President, foreign affairs is not my bailiwick, but I have always found it interesting that we tout democracy and free-markets until some country that controls the resources that are necessary to run our economy—or the interests of American corporations—decides to pursue free elections. The turbulence in the Middle East has been going on for decades. Strong-arm dictators have held those societies together; insurgencies will likely persist until all the people believe they are getting a fair shake. Eventually, they'll have to go through their own mid-life crisis, so to speak, find their own equilibrium. Maybe the time is now with everything else going on?"

Taylor set his drink on the counter and gazed at the ceiling. "A geomagnetic storm that might make at least one major city uninhabitable, uprisings in the Arab countries threatening the energy source that drives the world, and a global economic crisis all at the same time." He looked directly at me. "That's going to cause a whole lot of chaos all at once throughout the world."

I swirled my drink in the glass. Yes, there would be chaos, at least for a while, but chaos also provided opportunity.

"You're probably right, sir. But we can use that chaos as a cover to take the necessary steps to insure the success of Plan B."

"The cover of chaos. I like that."

The president picked up the black binder and slid the book across the counter toward me. "Jude, I need you to read this and tell me what other actions we can take to reinforce Plan B."

I picked up the binder from the counter, opened the black cover, and read the title page: *National Emergencies Act*.

74

May 21, 2011
Monroe, Michigan

"YES, SIR, I understand the cost of shutting down Fermi 2 and restarting it after it cycles. But as a precaution, isn't that the prudent thing to do? That's what Homeland Security is recommending." Frank stared at the NRC award on the opposite wall of his small office that he had received last year for five consecutive years without an incident at the nuclear plant he managed. He held the phone an inch away from his ear. Eddelston always talked loudly, especially when he was stressed.

"I've talked this over with the governor, Frank, and he agrees. We don't know when or where this solar thing will hit, and besides, we have backup power in place that gives us plenty of time to bring down the reactor if that storm takes out the grid."

"But, Mr. Eddelston," Frank persisted, "we're not sure how the reactor and its systems will handle any anomalies."

"Shut down No. 2 and we would be cutting off 20% of the State's power source. Neither the Governor nor the shareholders want that. If this storm misses us we would have deliberately created an electricity shortage. I am not going to take the heat from the citizens or the shareholders over that one. If this thing hits us, then we'll decide what actions we need to take."

Politics and money, Frank thought. What about safety? "But . . ."

"Frank, do what I tell you," Eddelston interrupted, "or we'll find another plant manager who will." There was a long silence. He had been threatened by Eddelston before. Maybe after this is over, he'd retire. "And, Frank, don't bother calling your friends at the NRC. The decision to shut down or keep operating is a state and local decision."

Washington D.C.

"MOST OF THE people think you are being alarmist, Mr. President," David Milestone read from a sheet of paper. "The poll taken last night indicates over 70% of Michigan and Ohio residents do not believe the geomagnetic event will significantly disrupt their lives." The early morning sunlight was streaming through the windows of the Oval Office.

"What about the local police departments?" He looked at the Secretary of Homeland Security. "I hope they are taking the warning seriously."

"The governors' offices inform me that all the local police forces and firefighters have put extra men on duty and cancelled leaves," Secretary Natallyeh replied.

"We have CONUS forces positioned outside of Detroit, Saginaw, Flint, and Toledo," McMillan added. "The Canadians have forces positioned near Toronto, Windsor, and Hamilton, but they believe this time they can weather the storm. They've beefed up their grid after the '89 outage."

The president leaned forward in his chair and put his elbows on the desk. "What's the ETA on this thing, Wally?" McMillan never had notes; never carried a file with him to these meeting. He held all the relevant information in his head, at the ready whenever he needed it. And if he didn't know something, he told you so—straight up. Maybe that's why Taylor had such complete confidence in him.

"We should start to see the storm interfere with the Earth's magnetosphere late morning or early afternoon tomorrow. From that point on, we don't know where it's going to go or how long it will take before we know the extent of the impact."

"And the evacuation plan?"

"Operational for Detroit, Flint, and Saginaw, Mr. President," the Homeland Security Secretary responded. "We're waiting on the impact before we make plans operational for Toledo, Cleveland, or any of the other target cities. FEMA supplies are stationed outside the impact area. We can start moving within an hour after the event."

"Nuclear plants?" the president continued, going down his checklist of all the critical components of their preparedness plan.

Natallyeh's face was stern. "The governors of Michigan and Ohio refuse to shut down the plants that may be in the path of the storm. But the NRC claims there should be no consequence to the plants. They have backup diesel power generation to keep cooling the fuel rods and to give them time to shut down the reactor if necessary."

"It is within their jurisdiction, Mr. President," David interrupted.

President Taylor swiveled back and forth in his chair. He went down the checklist in his mind. "So what else do we need to do?"

"Your declaration of a state of emergency is ready," David answered. "We've alerted the news networks that we will cut into scheduled programming for an announcement once we know the impact of the storm."

If it came on Sunday afternoon as it appeared it would, he'd be interrupting the baseball games. While it would piss off the fans, his announcement would certainly have a large audience. "And between now and the impact?"

"Sit and wait, Mr. President . . . and I guess pray," McMillan responded.

"To which god, Wally?" He grinned. "At least the Saudis seem to have gotten control of Ghawar from the dissidents and pushed the insurgents back into Yemen. Maybe we should choose Allah."

May 22, 2011
Toledo, Ohio

AT 1:43 ON Sunday afternoon, the traffic lights in Flint, Detroit, Toledo, and points in between had no colors. The neon names of restaurants and bars flickered and went black. Major league baseball games being watched on TV in eastern Michigan ended abruptly. The Detroit Tigers were playing an afternoon game in Cleveland. The Municipal Stadium lights still blazed as the Tigers and Indians played in the 2nd inning with no score. The lights and control panel of the Fermi nuclear power plant suddenly went dark but recovered within thirty seconds as the emergency generators kicked on. Communications and lights in Firehouse No. 57 in Toledo, Ohio, went out. Patrick Connelly and his crew looked at each other in the dim light from a small window in the firehouse kitchen. This was it.

"Elena, are you alright?" Patrick asked after Elena picked up her cell phone. At least their cellular service was still operative.

"Yea, Patrick, but the lights are out." He could hear the kids squealing in the background; it was all one grand adventure for them.

"You know the plan, right?"

"I'm heading with the kids to Mom and Dad's now. I've got the car gassed up and packed."

"I love you." He watched his crew start to suit up. He knew he only had a minute. "If this lasts through tomorrow, you'll evacuate to Mikey's, right?"

"Mom and Dad will never go." She hollered at the kids to settle down and get in the car. He felt his throat tighten.

"If I have to bring a hook and ladder to drag them out of their house, I will. Call me if there are problems."

"Okay. I love you, Patrick."

"Love you, too, Elena. Be careful on the streets and mind the kids."

Washington D.C.

WALTER MCMILLAN ENTERED the Oval Office and stood stiffly just inside the doorway, a pose all too familiar to Taylor. Milestone stood to left side of the desk, briefing the president on his weekly schedule when McMillan came in.

"Mr. President, we have had the event." It was a simple utterance, one without fanfare or emotion.

"Who's affected, Walter?" Deep in his heart he hoped it was Canada and not the U.S.

"The center was in Lake Huron, north of Port Hope." A glitter of hope arose as Taylor anxiously awaited McMillan to continue. "Grid outages from Saginaw Bay south to Toledo, west to Saginaw, east to London, Ontario." His hope faltered.

"That's Detroit, Flint, Saginaw, and Toledo." Those were major cities that were affected—and all the small communities and farms in between.

"Yes."

"And Cleveland?" Detroit and Toledo were bad enough. Cleveland would make it a catastrophe of unimagined proportions.

"No, sir. The utilities are trying to reroute power to Toledo," McMillan replied in his typical matter-of-fact style. Taylor sighed in relief. "But eastern Michigan is a problem. Transmission lines from Canada to that part of Michigan are down, as are the lines from Ohio north to Michigan and the western to eastern part of the state. We're working on a preliminary assessment on the number and location of damaged transformers."

"Has CONUS been notified?"

"Yes, sir. Plans are operational."

"Mr. President, you need to go on TV," David inserted. "The networks are standing by." That was just like David, always thinking about communicating to the American people.

"How long do I have, David?'

"Fifteen or twenty minutes until you go on air, Mr. President."

He was still in his workout clothes from his late morning exercise. He would have to look a bit more presidential when he addressed the nation. He had ten minutes to change.

"Get Wilkerson and Halperin on the phone. Patch the call into the residence while I change. I need to notify them before I go on air."

"Gentlemen," the president began as he was buttoning his shirt, talking with the Congressional leaders on the speakerphone in his bedroom, "a solar-generated geomagnetic storm has struck the Earth and knocked out the electric grid from central to eastern Michigan and south past the northern border of Ohio. We are awaiting a preliminary assessment of the number of transformers along that part of the grid that could have been damaged or destroyed." He was about to put on a tie but decided against it for a more in-the-trenches look. "We are assisting residents of the major cities in the area and are implementing pre-developed evacuation plans." The next thing he had to tell them would raise their hackles, he was certain. "I am declaring a national emergency by the powers invested in the Executive under the National Emergencies Act. I will forward the

Congress written justification for such invocation as specified under Title III of the Act. I will be making the announcement to the citizens of the United States in five minutes."

"The National Emergencies Act?" Wilkerson gasped. His voice rang through the room on the speaker. "Surely there is no need for that, Mr. President."

"I believe if you read the Act, Jimmy, you will see it was designed for emergencies just like this one."

"Well, we will not agree to it, Mr. President," Wilkerson snapped, "and we will introduce a resolution to that effect under Title V of the Act."

Of course, they would not agree, and the debate would have to be resolved by the Supreme Court—eventually. "Do what you will, gentlemen. See you in court."

75

"FRANK, LOOK AT this." The operator pointed to a rack of gauges in the control panel. "The water temp in the Fermi 2 reactor is rising." Joe's voice, normally a tenor tone, almost rose to an alto pitch. He quickly checked his computer. "It's up eight degrees in the last two hours."

Frank looked at the gauges and the graph displayed on the computer. They lost power a little less than a day ago, and the backup diesel generators had kicked in just as they were supposed to. Eggelston had sent him an email, giving him the particulars of the outage. They needed to keep the plant operational. There was a good chance they could generate power that could be sold to the western part of Michigan routed via Indiana. Since that time Frank and his crew had been performing checks of the equipment and monitors. Up until now, everything appeared to be functioning within tolerances.

"How soon before it reaches critical?" Frank asked.

"At this rate no more than two to three hours."

That didn't leave a lot of time. Should he order a controlled shutdown of the reactor? If he did that and there was nothing wrong, Eggelston would have his ass. Frank ran through a series of diagnostics on the computer. Everything appeared normal, and yet the temperature was rising.

"Are we pumping water into the reactor?"

"According to the readings, the cooling system is functioning normally. Flow rate and pressure are both within specifications, Frank."

Water was getting to the reactor core and with enough force. There were only a few possible causes for a rise in water temperature. "Is there a leak in the core?" He looked at Joe. Was it getting hot in the control room or was he just getting nervous? He loosened his tie.

"Pressure would be down, but it's not." Joe seemed miffed at the anomaly. "Water level in the reactor is at 128,575 gallons—well within limits."

"Then maybe the pressure readings are faulty." Frank hoped against hope that it was the readings that were faulty and not the reactor itself. What else could be causing it? "Who's on duty in the plant?"

"Leffler."

"I'll get him to check the readings at the main control valves," Frank said as he pulled the walkie-talkie from his belt, and started to press the talk button.

"Shouldn't we begin to power down the reactor as a precaution?"

"Eddelston doesn't want this baby shut down unless it's an emergency."

He called George Leffler and quickly made his way to water-cooling area of the plant. He needed to see for himself what the hell was going on.

Washington D.C.

THE MORNING AFTER the geomagnetic storm took out the electric grid in eastern Michigan, President Taylor had been on a satellite link with the mayors of Detroit, Flint, and Saginaw, and he tried to reassure them that he was taking every possible action to assist with the catastrophe. No, he didn't know how long they would be without power. Yes, evacuations would likely be required. They were just beginning to assess the extent of the damage.

Taylor was tired and still in the sweats he put on that morning after a quick shower. He and his team were up most of the night in the Situation Room, receiving reports on the extent of the outages and the movement of troops and supplies into the affected areas. He looked around the Oval Office. Unlike the Situation Room, it didn't have the clutter of coffee cups, soda bottles, and stale pizza from the night before.

The governor of Michigan was just one more of many calls he would have today. CONUS and FEMA were doing all they could to provide relief and protection to the towns and cities in eastern Michigan, and the governor acknowledged that the federal response was well planned and coordinated. Taylor sympathized with what Michigan was going through. He knew what would happen next would tax the will and spirit of the millions of people that lived in that part of the country.

"You intend to evacuate three of my state's major communities, Mr. President."

"Absolute necessity, Governor. Like I said in my address to the nation yesterday, eastern Michigan received the strongest hit. Over 70% of the major transformers are down. There is no potable water, no electricity, no way to pump fuel for vehicles."

Taylor leaned back in his desk chair, phone to his ear. This was one of the few "alone moments" he had had in the past few weeks, and he was spending it talking to mayors and now the Republican Governor of Michigan.

"Excuse me, but why aren't you focused on fixing the electric outages?"

The president let out a small chuckle. "Governor, there are over 140 transformers out in Michigan and surrounding areas based on a preliminary assessment, maybe more when its all said and done. Do you have any idea how long it will take to replace them?"

"I assume a few weeks, a couple of months at most. We need to get the plants up and running again . . . and the people back in their homes." Taylor wadded a piece of paper on his desk and tossed it in the waste can. He was focused on protecting lives and property; the governor was concerned about getting business back to normal.

"We have top priority for new transformers, but there are only about 20% of those needed sitting in inventory," President Taylor said. "The rest have to be manufactured, and that takes a long time."

"You empty out those cities, it'll be one giant ghost town here, not to mention the security issues."

Detroit's long, painful history of looting and violence was not lost on anyone. That's why he sent in the troops—to maintain order. CONUS forces would have to stay well after they evacuated the city, just to make sure. The single chime of the grandfather clock Taylor had selected from storage and placed in the far end of his office announced 1:00 pm.

"I understand, Governor, but it will take at least a year, probably longer, assuming we can come up with the money." Taylor rubbed his tired eyes. "We're working with the utility company to determine which communities we can bring back on line first. Then we'll start moving people back. In the meantime, federal troops will be deployed to the cities to protect property."

"What do you mean, come up with the money? That's what FEMA is for, Mr. President."

"You are correct, at least in part, but in case you haven't been paying attention to the news, the federal government is out of money." Taylor was enjoying the irony in the call. He hoped this governor could marshal enough pressure on his party in Congress to raise the debt ceiling and avoid the impending fiscal crisis. "And your friends in Congress refuse to raise the debt ceiling so we can borrow more to fix the grid. We'll have to wait until next fiscal year to see if we can come up with the money."

"Can't you take money from other sources?" The governor's voice grew louder.

"Like what?"

"Hell, you guys in Washington have tons of cash squirreled away for useless programs." The Michigan governor was just like so many other Americans. They didn't believe the government was really running out of money; they thought it was just being poorly spent.

"There is nothing left in the discretionary part of the budget, Governor."

"Well then, take it away from the entitlements. This is my state, for god sake."

"Your friends are cutting those funds too, Governor."

Monroe, Michigan

GEORGE LEFFLER PLUGGED his remote data device into the port of the main feed water pump just outside the room housing the reactor.

"Jesus Christ," he said, "what did you say the pressure readings were in the control room?" He looked at his boss.

"Within limits," Frank answered. Or at least that's what he was told by the plant operator. He thought back to the data and the operating specs for cooling the reactor core. Yep, the pressure was within allowable tolerances.

"These readings show that we're giving the reactor only 12K gallons of water per minute," Leffler said, panic evident in his voice. "Are we running at full capacity?"

"Eighty percent." In his head Frank quickly compared that figure to the minimum volume of water required to operate the reactor at that capacity—12K wasn't enough. "We should have at least 16K GWPM. No wonder she's burning hot."

Frank got on his 2-way radio with the control room. "Joe, your pressure readings are faulty. We're not pumping enough water into the reactor. The readings here say we're only pumping 12K. Bring down the reactor to match the volume of water we're injecting into the core. She's going to burn up!"

"Crap. On it," Joe responded. "I'll increase water flow too. It'll bring down the temperature quicker."

Frank pulled a handkerchief out of his pocket and mopped his brow. He took a deep breath.

"Good idea. George and I are going to check out a few more things, then I'll be back," Frank said into the walkie-talkie. "In the meantime run a complete diagnostic on all operating controls." Something wasn't right, but what?

Washington D.C.

"SENATOR, WE'VE GOT a problem," the Michigan Governor said flatly to his U.S. Senator. "President Taylor says it will take at least a year to get the electric grid back on line for the cities in the eastern half of the state."

Senator Ryan had been on the phone all morning with his major constituents from eastern Michigan. He had large contributors in Troy that were now living in hotels or with relatives outside the disaster zone; one had moved his family to their second residence in Maui before the event.

Their businesses were shuttered. They were angry and wanted answers. How long was this going to last? What was the federal government doing to get the electricity back on line? What was it going to do to reimburse them for their losses?

"Governor, we've had a major event," Ryan said. "I'm sure the president is being overly cautious in his estimates." He rubbed his eyes and sighed. The governor was the least of his worries.

"Even a couple of months will wipe out our economy. Do you think the factories we have left are going to stay here and wait? Hell no." The volume of the governor's voice rose several levels. "They're heading for Mexico or one of those southern states." The CEOs of GM and Chrysler informed Ryan earlier that they were negotiating plant space in Alabama. Smeldly would like that all right. Fucking crackers.

"Governor, I appreciate your position, but what would you expect businesses to do? It's a free country and free economy." That had been the Republican mantra. Regardless of the pain, they had to live with their principles. "The car companies are going to take a major hit in their production, especially now when they're just getting back on their feet."

"My position!" the governor retorted. "You're supposed to be representing the goddamn state, Senator. And Taylor says they have no money to rebuild the grid."

"You mean the debt ceiling?" Ryan turned to look out his office window. He was glad his family lived in Grand Rapids and was not affected by the evacuations. He didn't have a single relative from the east side of the state. Their families were born and bred in Grand Rapids.

"Yeah, he dropped that card."

"There is no appetite for increasing the debt. Even you said . . ."

"I know what I said, but this is a goddamn emergency. This is no time to worry about balancing the budget."

In his heart, Ryan agreed with the governor, but they had to stick to their principles. What did the governor expect him to do, and how could he get him off his back? "Rumple and I are only two senators. The rest of our colleagues are dead set against more borrowing. We will have to find the money we need from current expenditures." He had his staff combing the 2012 budget to find areas to cut in order to provide funding to fix the grid in Michigan. There were vested interests tied to every line item; cutting any one of them would figuratively and literally take an act of Congress.

"Taylor says there isn't any money left."

For once, Ryan had to agree with the president. After they took control of Congress last year, they'd pretty well cut federal funding to the bones except for defense, Social Security and the healthcare programs. They would have to look there, he was sure.

"I hear you, Governor. My staff is reviewing the proposed budget for next year to try to find the money. I'll discuss it with the majority leader."

"You better do more than discuss it, Senator, or next year you won't need to open a campaign office anywhere in this state."

Ryan hung up the phone and gazed ahead blankly. One day after the storm and the pressure was out of control already. The rest of his week would be pure hell.

"Cynthia, get the majority leader on the line for me, will you?" Senator Ryan asked his secretary.

This whole situation was getting out of hand; he was more inclined than ever to agree with the governor, but he didn't think asking for a handout was going to give him much leverage with his colleagues.

"Senator, the majority leader is on line 1."

"Thanks, Cynthia." Senator Ryan picked up his phone and punched line 1. He was sure Wilkerson would have some ideas on where to find the money even though his staff hadn't so far; at least he might have some words of encouragement.

"Jimmy, I suppose you were expecting a call from me."

"I hadn't thought of it," Wilkerson replied. "But I bet you want to talk about the president's declaration of a state of emergency last night."

"Actually, I want to discuss what we can do to put things back together in my state, and quickly." There were few things Ryan agreed with the president on, but declaring a state of emergency made sense from his point of view.

"Well now, that's going to take some time, Ryan. They have to build the transformers you know. It's not like they're just sitting on the shelves."

"I understand that, and the time it will take, but there are some transformers available that can get things rolling. The problem is Detroit Edison doesn't have the money. With the grid outage and evacuations, they've just lost 50% of their revenue base. And you know the state doesn't have the money. We're still relying on stimulus funds to balance our budget."

"I understand your position, but the whole country is in the middle of an economic emergency," Wilkerson responded. "What do you expect me to do?"

"Find somewhere in the budget to find the money, Jimmy." He was shocked Wilkerson wasn't already on that. Jimmy knew the ins-and-outs of the budget better than any senator.

"The other side will filibuster any attempt to cut into the social programs, Ryan. You know that."

"What about other items in the discretionary part of the budget? Can't we trim a little from a number of programs in order to come up with the money?"

"While I am sympathetic to your position, the line items that are left are already cut to the bone. And many of them are strongly supported by your colleagues."

Ryan bowed his head and closed his eyes. His colleagues, as Wilkerson referred to them, had their own vested interests at heart, over the interests of his state or the country for that matter. Okay, if they were going to abandon him, he would do what he had to.

"Then agree to raise the debt ceiling so we can borrow the money."

"Ah, it always comes down to that, doesn't it?" Wilkerson replied, the tone of his voice reminding him of a scolding schoolteacher. "How can we make our point to the American people if we give in? You know, Senator, there will always be emergencies."

His day was bad enough already. He thought he'd get some support from the senate majority leader. But this, a lecture on austerity? "Enough of the dogma, Jimmy. We're not talking about some pet project earmark for my state. And unless you haven't looked at a map lately, Michigan is a part of the USA." There was a long pause. Maybe the leader had finally got his point.

"Even if I wanted to support you, how many senators do you think will? And let's say you get enough support in the Senate, what about our friends in the House? Good luck with that."

"Then what in the goddamn hell do you propose we do?"

"I don't have an easy answer for you, Senator. We all have to learn to live within our means." Ryan slammed the phone into its base. He put his elbows on the desk and held his head in his hands.

Monroe, Michigan

"FRANK, I'VE DONE a complete diagnostic," Joe said, shaking his head. "Everything seems to check out, but we're getting contradictory data from the control room and what's happening in the system."

"What do you mean?" Frank was still huffing from the hurried walk back from the bowels of the plant. He didn't smoke, but some of the weight needed to go. After twenty-five years of a sedentary job and no membership in a health club, he wasn't in the best of shape, especially for a man of fifty-eight.

"Look at the temperature." Joe pointed to the temperature gauge on the control panel. "I've inserted half of the control rods into the reactor and have increased water flow by 5000 GWPM, but the temp is still going up. It's near critical." Frank looked at the gauge as the needle neared the red area on the meter. He looked over at the water pressure gauge. As Joe said, the GWPM was where it should be.

"How can that . . ."

The pulsating horn of the plant's alarm system blared in the control room and the containment building of Fermi 2.

"What the hell?" Frank said. He and Joe looked at each other, confusion on their faces. The walkie-talkie attached to Frank's belt vibrated with the panicked voice of George Leffler.

"Frank, we got a problem. The core water is overflowing the reactor." It was a puzzle; it didn't make sense. But this was physical evidence Frank understood. They needed to take action—now.

"SCRAM the reactor core!" Frank yelled to Joe above the drone of the pulsating alarm. He punched the two-way radio. "George, get everyone out of the containment building, now!"

Joe slammed his palm down on the emergency button in the middle of the control board to initiate the emergency shutdown procedures. Frank flipped open a red plastic binder to confirm the correct procedures. He and Joe worked furiously for thirty minutes inserting control rods and reducing water flow and pressure. When the rods were completely inserted in the reactor core and the water within the reactor was contained, Frank picked up the phone and dialed the NRC.

76

May 24, 2011
Washington D.C.

MITCHELL NEZ TAYLOR was not wakened from a deep sleep the night before, even though there was almost another catastrophe in Michigan. His team had handled it perfectly without him. Now he was fresh for his cabinet meeting later that day and was being briefed by his chief of staff.

"There was no core breach or damage to the fuel rods. It's going to take them a month just to mop up the radioactive water. The plant will be down for at least six months based on preliminary estimates of the damage. The NRC is on site."

"What caused it?" The president made some last minute notes on the document on his desk.

"NRC thinks the geomagnetic storm damaged the microprocessors in the water control valves and pumps, producing faulty water temperature and flow readings."

"The storm could do that?" He looked up from the document. He recalled something about erratic pressure readings in the briefings before the storm hit, but he thought the plants would have been taken off-line if there was a real risk. Apparently, they were all learning. "But with the grid down, I am not sure the state needs the power anyway."

"Toledo is back up," Milestone continued. "Power was rerouted from northeastern Ohio. It's just the eastern half of Michigan where we have a problem, and Windsor, Ontario, just across the border. Toronto was not effected. They installed surge protectors five years ago." He sat down across from the president.

"I talked with Wilkerson and Halperin this morning about increasing the debt ceiling, or at least agreeing to a short-term income tax to pay for the catastrophe," the president said.

"How did they react?"

"They took the oath—absolutely no tax increases." Taylor leaned back in his chair. If he ever wondered what the GOP agenda really was, he got his answer on that call. Screw their pious talk about responsibility and patriotism. They were all about power, and nothing was going to stop them from getting it.

"And the debt ceiling?"

"There was some opening, but the negotiations ended when they asked me for a commitment to cut entitlements and not veto their repeal of financial reforms. Reluctantly they agreed to discuss our proposal in their caucuses. They are meeting later this week."

"Did you give on any of their proposals?"

How much to give, how much to bend. Taylor's whole term had so far been marked by his ability to accomplish only a few things of substance. He was tired of being hammered for his lack of leadership, and he knew if he gave in to the Republican proposals, they really would have him in a box. No, he did not intend to do their bidding to the end of his term.

"My public position is my position, period, David. No cuts without revenue increases, and no repeal of any of our legislation passed over the past two years."

"At least you won't have Anders threatening to shoot you," David replied dryly.

Taylor looked at David. What did that mean?

"Don't you remember? You took the Financial Reform Act off the table; he said that would be the last straw."

"Oh, yeah, I didn't think of that. I guess I won't need a bullet-proof vest." He smiled.

"Do you think they will raise the ceiling without the concessions?"

"Given the nature of events, they'd be idiots not to. They've got their cover, and they're writing off Michigan next year if they don't go along. The extent of the damage gives them plenty of reasons to raise the ceiling." He flipped through the document on his desk. The reactors, the power plants, millions of private homes without electricity or potable water, gas stations, businesses, schools, office buildings, and what factories were left in the region—everything had come to a dead stop.

"Remember, sir, the people of eastern Michigan won't be there to vote." Milestone pushed himself to his feet. "And the western half of the state votes Republican, mostly. But what do we do with the Plan B announcement?"

"If Congress votes to raise the ceiling, I have no grounds to implement it. But I want to be prepared just in case. When do I meet with Anders and the Cabinet?"

"In three days. Friday afternoon, Mr. President. Due to the crisis, everyone is willing to stay late, even though it's a holiday weekend. I believe they are still expecting Monday to be a day off—depending, of course, on how things go."

May 27, 2011

I HURRIED DOWN the hallway to the Oval Office just before 2:00. I had finally gotten to sleep around 4:00 am and slept through my 6:30 alarm. The cabinet meeting was supposed to start any minute now, but I was still making changes to the president's speech half an hour ago. Milestone let me in the office.

"Here are my latest revisions to your speech, Mr. President," I said handing him a sheaf of papers.

"Is everyone assembled, David?" President Taylor glanced at the speech and tucked it into his meeting folder.

"Yes, Mr. President, in the Cabinet Room."

"Okay, let's go."

I watched the president move through the office, a sense of gravitas surrounding him. All night I had wrangled with that speech, knowing that the he would soon take one of the most serious actions ever in the history of our nation. While I struggled with balancing stern authority with heartfelt compassion for our country in the speech, I recalled how Taylor had been almost stoic in the face of the many converging crises he now faced. Perhaps his Native American heritage had given him a leg up on maintaining focus while filtering out all the irrelevant noise around him.

We walked into the Cabinet room, Milestone trailing behind us, and took our seats around the table. Fallon Connelly and the Attorney General, along with the secretaries of State, Defense, Homeland Security, Energy, Commerce and Education—were already assembled.

Fallon shot daggers at me as I took off my suit coat and sat in the chair. "How could you recommend this, Jude?" We had not seen eye to eye for some time. I was not surprised by her anger. "Do you have any idea what this will do?"

President Taylor interrupted. "Let's keep this civil. No one wants to default on our sovereign debt, but the alternatives the other side is still insisting on will be even more onerous." He turned to Fallon. "Hopefully we won't have to implement this plan. I'm waiting to hear from the leaders of Congress on raising the ceiling in light of the catastrophe. But just in case, let's get on with it."

"At least your brother's business will take off now," I said, hoping a little levity would soften her up.

"His investors bought out his patent last week." Fallon's voice was bitter. "He had no choice given that Congress wasn't going to pass the GRID Act. The investors will make the money, not Michael."

That was news to me. Anton. I just shook my head, amazed by who usually benefited from a dire situation.

"Okay," Taylor interrupted, "the banks first. Fallon."

Fallon snapped her head away from me and faced the president. "Mr. President, the Comptroller of Currency is ready to step in before the banks open the morning after Memorial Day. They obviously cannot cover every institution, but they will take care of the big boys and the largest institutions in the each city over 100,000 populations. The value of big bank assets other than deposits would be essentially worthless as the markets collapse. We'd put them into receivership, and the bank shareholders would take the haircut. Your assurances with FDIC coverage should prevent a run on those banks and the others that OCC can't cover initially." She slapped her folder shut and tossed it on the table.

"And the Federal Reserve, Jude?"

I had worked very quietly with my old mentor, the Fed Chairman, over the past several days, exploring the possibilities for a national U.S.

Bank in the event of another financial disaster like the one in 2008, and the steps the Fed could take to alleviate the financial impact of the Michigan disaster should Congress not raise the debt ceiling. "Purely, hypothetical," I told him, "just in case." I really wanted to tell him the truth and the full extent of Plan B—his input would be invaluable—but I couldn't risk it, knowing that the CEOs of the largest banks sat on the Regional Federal Reserve Boards. It was bound to be leaked. We spent hours reviewing those times in our history when we had a national bank. Establishing one now, especially with the powers of the Federal Reserve, would not be difficult.

"The Fed could nationalize the largest banks under the auspices of the Federal Reserve," I said, deliberately avoiding Fallon's eyes. "The big banks would operate under OCC supervision until the new national bank is established. We could let the community banks and credit unions remain independent for now. The Fed would pump in the appropriate funds to help all of them meet their capital and reserve requirements."

The others took notes; someone let out a loud sigh. I continued.

"Once the OCC took control of the bigger banks, we could begin to implement the program to write down residential and commercial mortgage loans held in the banks' portfolios to the actual value of the property, unless of course we got a legal opinion that we can't do that as a part of your emergency powers." I nodded to the Attorney General. "If not, then we'd wait until the banks are nationalized. We could certainly do it with the mortgage loans held by Fannie and Freddie since they are already in receivership to the government.

Additionally, we would forgive outstanding balances on bank-issued credit cards as of the date of your announcement. Freeing our people from as much of their debt as we can should spur consumption. And we would place payments on commercial loans in abeyance until the economy has stabilized sufficiently to resume payments. Finally, we would suspend all payments of outstanding student loans until we determine whether we could forgive all or part of them." I looked down the table at the Secretary of the Department of Education. He smiled.

"What about state and local governments?" the president asked.

I continued to marvel at the sense of peace around him. Perhaps this was really the opportunity he had originally ran for: the chance to hit the reset button, take everything down to the bone and build it back up the way it should be.

"The Fed could announce monetary facilities to keep them afloat so they could continue to operate and pay for essential services until this sorted itself out, and authorize increases in the money supply as needed." I consulted my notes. "The short-term price controls would help until things settle down. Treasury would only sell T Bills and Bonds domestically, and it and the Fed could establish their value at a level to keep the pension funds that are heavily invested in them whole."

"And restrictions on moving money off shore?" The room was silent.

"In place," Fallon responded. "Not a dollar would move from individuals or corporations from U.S. to off-shore banks unless it is hand carried. But as I have told you, Mr. President, international credit markets will freeze up. No international source would lend to us or to anyone else for that matter. Capitol markets will sit on their cash until they see where things are headed. A lot of that cash will be in dollars. Even though the value of the dollar would likely fall, they will cautiously watch what we do to stabilize it."

I looked around at the shocked faces of the Cabinet. This was the first time most of them had heard the extent of our actions and the effects on global financial markets. They had been given just as much information as they needed to cover their areas of the plan and nothing more. Only the president, David, Fallon, and I had the complete picture and understood the implications. I tried to consider the consequences as best I could, but there was a lot of uncertainty in how markets, creditors, and countries would react.

Fallon continued. "To prevent speculation, we would temporarily suspend trading of currency and oil futures on the exchanges. All private trading of derivatives would be halted, and when we resumed trading, it would be done only on a public exchange, and we would limit commodities futures trading to only those parties that have a legitimate need to do so." She seemed deflated, as though her energy had leaked out of her, even though this was an action she had supported in the past.

I knew this action would not get rid of the Commodity Futures Act—the disastrous bill that allowed the banks into the derivatives market and created a shadow banking system outside the control of the Federal Reserve. It was the final straw that broke the back of our financial system. But the president didn't have the power to repeal laws under his emergency powers. Still, using his emergency powers to insist that all derivative trading be done on a public exchange would put it in a cage as long as the president retained those powers.

Fallon continued describing part of the plan to stimulate the economy by announcing several publicly-held investment funds to attract private capital that would support needed infrastructure projects, education and R&D.

"We're also kicking around a small business investment fund to attract money for startups and ongoing operations of small business," she said. She seemed slightly optimistic about these creative options, which I had suggested to her primarily to secure her cooperation with Plan B. "We think right-minded, patriotic Americans will want to put their money there—like the Liberty Bonds during WWI. Wise international investors will probably invest, too. They would be safe investments with better guaranteed returns than they can get in the market, which is going to be in the toilet."

"How long before we can get these funds up and running, Fallon?" Taylor had been quiet as he listened to Fallon's presentation. Occasionally he'd jot down a note but for the most part, he seemed content to take it in.

"Within a month, two at the outside. I have a team working on prospectuses and operational mechanics as we speak."

President Taylor quickly riffled through several pages of what I realized was my speech and made some marks with his pen. "Jude, any chance we can shorten the timeline for enforcing the import tax on foreign-made products?"

This would be one of the more controversial uses of the president's emergency powers. Even I wondered if it would hold up in court. Only the secretaries of Treasury and Commerce and the Attorney General knew about this proposal, and the other Cabinet members looked at each other in amazement when I discussed the plan.

"As you know, sir, it would be our policy that products sold in the U.S. must be made in the U.S., or face a stiff import tax to offset the cost of making the product here. This policy would likely shock global corporations and companies, especially those that have moved their manufacturing offshore. We have to give them appropriate lead-time to re-establish manufacturing facilities in the U.S. Frankly, I thought one year was fairly aggressive. But we could insist they demonstrate that they will comply with the order by building or renting plant facilities, say within six months. If we didn't see progress by that time, we could impose the tax."

"If we didn't let them know we are serious about it, they'd find a way to delay until the elections are over, or at least until the Supreme Court ruled on my powers under the Emergency Act," Taylor responded, ignoring the discontent he could feel in the room around him. "No, we're giving them six months. This is still the largest economy in the world; they're not going to walk away from that."

Both the president and I firmly believed that bringing those jobs back, coupled with the infrastructure work to repair the electric grid and highways in the near term, would bring down unemployment substantially over the next year. We expected that the infrastructure investment fund and the increased revenues from people going back to work would help fund the needed projects. But there were a couple more major sources of revenue that most in the room hadn't thought of.

"If we liquidate and nationalize the major U.S. banks, the government assumes ownership of the bank deposits, loans, and other assets," I noted. "Interest on loans and the profits generated by other bank-held assets would accrue to the U.S. government. That's the profits that used to go to the bank CEOs and shareholders. Additionally . . ."

The Secretary of Energy jumped in. "We'd revoke all leases and nationalize the exploration, drilling, transport, and refining of oil and natural gas under the president's emergency powers. The revenue from any oil or gas extracted from U.S. sources would also go to the Treasury. We know our oil resources are limited, but we are rich with natural gas."

I remembered what Allende had done with their natural resources in the early '70s. I could hardly believe we were now considering implementing our own nationalization program.

"That is still a lot of revenue," I insisted. "And if we got our tax program through, we'd have even more. Until we got things in place, we'd print money to keep the economy afloat."

"There is a lot of doubt as to whether I have the authority to do anything with taxes under my emergency powers," the president inserted. "We have an army of attorneys going through all the emergency statutes and how they've been used in the past. At a minimum, we believe we might have the power to temporarily suspend some of the loopholes and special tax breaks. But, if I have the authority, we would raise tax rates, if only to put money into our investment funds to cover the repairs to the electric grid. I'd insist that the upper 2% of the income earners pay 40% of their total income, including dividends and interest in taxes. We're also considering a transaction tax on all securities sales to discourage any massive sell-offs and options speculation to help stabilize the markets. If none of that flew, we'd have to wait until tax rates automatically go up at the end of next year." The president looked at the members of his cabinet seated around the table. "We all have to remember that if we implement Plan B, we won't have principal or interest on our external debt to worry about anymore. That's a lot of money." He smiled.

"Good luck with buying oil to support the economy," Fallon interjected, her voice dripping with sarcasm.

"We have an energy rationing program that could be implemented within two days of the announcement," the Energy Secretary responded. "Mr. President, at your direction, we have developed a Marshall Plan to expedite the development and deployment of alternative energy sources. A lot could be done the first year of the plan. And, Madame Secretary, you should know that the price of oil would fall like a rock once the global economy goes into recession. And with the current unrest in the oil-producing countries, we believe they would be willing to sell us their oil, even in dollars. They know it takes money to run their governments, too."

One by one each cabinet secretary briefed the others in the room on how they would implement their components of Plan B. They and their lieutenants had worked many long, difficult hours over the past several days to pull together their aspects of the plan. I could see the weariness on their faces, and in many cases, fear as well. None of us knew how this might turn out.

"And security?" President Taylor looked across the table at the Homeland Security Secretary.

She cleared her throat. "The FBI and U.S. Marshall Service have their plans in place. The National Guard has already been activated in every state in case we have to declare martial law. They believe the activation is a part of your declaration of a state of emergency. Their activity and that of the local authorities will be coordinated under CONUS command. We would give the lead to the local authorities first and see how it plays out, sir."

"Hopefully, my speech would help to keep people calm and temper violence." He paused, and I'm sure I wasn't the only person in the room thinking about what he just said. "No one has been able to reason with the Tea Party people. God only knows what they might do. And the armed forces, Robert?"

There was a long silence. Secretary of Defense Boyd shifted in his chair. "At your direction, I have already given the order to withdraw our troops from Afghanistan within two months, and accelerate removal of remaining advisory forces from Iraq. The Afghan President called me a . . . well, you can imagine. Our NATO allies are onboard. I'll announce the troop withdrawal next week. If we move forward with Plan B, the only foreign U.S. bases that would remain open are in South Korea and Kuwait, and we have agreements from those countries to cover our costs. All non-essential military equipment programs and contracts would be suspended indefinitely. I'd hate to be a congressman from any of those districts. And yes, even though I am one of them, I will do everything I can to put this reduction in our national defense posture at the feet of the Republicans."

The president smiled warmly at the secretary. "Thank you, Robert. At least you put your country ahead of your politics."

"How have our allies reacted, Mr. President?" Fallon asked. I glanced at her; it appeared she was attempting at least a conciliatory posture.

"Well, the Tory Prime Minister from Britain reminded me of the hit his economy would take given their banks' debt exposure to Ireland, Portugal and Greece, as well as the U.S.—that is, should we go forward with Plan B. If we do, I don't think we would be allies with them again until Labour takes over next year. The average Brit would cheer us, as would a number of other so-called socialist countries. Of course, France and Germany had a similar reaction. Their banks would have to be put in receivership given their debt exposure. They'd have to take many of the same actions as we are planning."

"They won't be free to implement a number of those actions without consent from the European Union. What has the E.U.'s Finance Minister said?" I asked.

"They're discussing it, Jude, but I suspect the E.U. would fall apart, just as you predict. At least the countries would be free to do their own currency adjustments and move forward unconstrained by E.U. currency rules. The E.U., as well as the global economy would be over, at least for now."

We could reasonably predict how most Western economies would react and the actions they would take, but there were still a couple of wild cards out there. "And China?" I asked.

The room was completely silent. We looked around at each other, wondering who would answer. Fallon finally responded.

"The Chinese are quietly selling as many T Bonds as they can without creating a panic, even though we have not informed them of any of our potential actions. Obviously, none of the major economic powers will buy them because they know what might happen. Third World economies are buying at a steep discount, thinking they're getting a good deal."

We all exchanged looks and nodded. There were some things we could manage, and other things we knew we could not. We were going to have to be content with the extent of our responsibility and let the chips fall where they may. David cleared his throat and suggested we adjourn.

President Taylor, David, Fallon, and I headed to the Oval Office to cover a few remaining issues.

"Mr. President, do you believe the Supreme Court will rule in our favor on the State of Emergency declaration?" I asked while we were settling into the comfortable chairs in the president's office.

"We have grounds with the Michigan disaster, but the specific economic actions we are planning under its cover . . . well, the Attorney General has doubts, at least on insisting we bring back jobs to the U.S. and taxes. He believes the import tax is valid; we've used something similar to it several times throughout our history. Still, if the Court rules against the emergency declaration, even that piece would fail."

"We'd need to push our agenda fast and hard before the court rules, and delay the Court's decision as long as we can—until their next session in October." Milestone interjected, taking a seat on the couch. "But we are on solid ground with the other steps—those grounded in existing law."

"Have you set a time for the announcement, Mr. President," I asked, "if we go through with Plan B?"

"Like I said at the outset of this meeting, first things first." He removed his suit jacket and loosened his tie. "Let's see what Congress is going to do. I expect something from them soon."

"Mr. President, even if Congress does not vote to increase the debt ceiling, surely we can deal with this without implementing Jude's Plan B."

It was clear from Fallon's comment that I would be the one deemed behind this course of action, even though the president made the decision. That was fair—it was my plan.

"And what would be the result, Fallon," the president answered, "follow the same path as Chile, Argentina, South Korea, Thailand? Have your IMF and our creditors claiming every ounce of flesh they can into the foreseeable future, like Europe did with Germany after World War I? Austerity leading to a deeper recession, followed by even more austerity." He frowned at her.

"But South America and Southeast Asia made it through their crises," she persisted.

"Did they? Look at them today; what would their economies be like if they hadn't followed the IMF's program and defaulted on their debt instead? And their economies are miniscule compared to ours. Do you really believe those remedies for fixing our debt problems will work here? No, they won't—not if you care about the people who live here—the ones who will get slammed by those approaches."

He paused, and I could see him pulling together the internal energy he relied on when he had given his campaign speeches, his nomination acceptance speech, his inauguration speech. The man had a power that set him apart from the rest of us; he had a calling. He knew his place in history and he was ready to seize the moment. The hairs on the back of my neck stood up when he fixed his gaze on Fallon and spoke again.

"Our people have been pawns, and I'm not going to make them pay for the excesses of a few who controlled the board. There are a number of reasons we got ourselves into this position. Much of it was our own doing—all of us should have known better. But there are others who have taken advantage of our weaknesses and our inability to control *our* frailties, or *their* actions. And now things have gotten so fundamentally out of balance that traditional prescriptions won't fix our debt problem or the global economy." He paused and looked the Treasury Secretary square on. "And I refuse to turn our economy into some form of oligarchic feudalism or our country into a Corporatist State."

"Do you really believe Plan B is going to fix those problems?"

"No, Fallon, you missed the point," he continued. "Plan B wipes the slate clean and gives us a chance to start over with a new set of economic principles."

"And what makes you think you and Jude Anders know enough to create a new economic framework for the world?"

I looked at her. I knew Fallon Connelly, and she was not going to give up without a fight.

The president started to respond, but I interrupted. "Listen, we have our own ideas, but other thinkers around the world who have wrestled with the same issues will add their voices. If we're going to have a global economy, we have to do this together. If not, then we'll move on our own. Plan B is only the trigger—a short-term plan and a broad outline for a different kind of economy. The key is that we are not going to be strapped into outdated frameworks that don't work anymore for the American people or those of this planet."

Fallon looked at me for what felt like an eternity. Finally, as I saw the last spark of our friendship dim in her eyes, she busied herself packing up her folders. She was the first to leave the room. President Taylor caught my eye; I could see him gently shaking his head.

"EVEN IF I GET 100% of Democrat votes, I can barely get us over the line, Jimmy," Douglas Halperin asserted as he settled into the couch in Jimmy Wilkerson's Senate office. "But I'm not sure I'll get that. The Minority Whip says he has some holdouts too . . . in Georgia, Mississippi, and Texas. Without those votes, we can't pass it. And he was clear as day—we'd have to give a lot more to muster the votes we need from the other side."

"I've cobbled together enough votes to get it through the Senate, but there is a problem." Wilkerson moved behind his desk and took a seat.

"What's that?"

"You know the new senator from Missouri?"

"The Tea Party guy?"

Wilkerson could tell from the look on Halperin's face that he knew something crazy was coming. Doug had his hands full with the Tea Party Caucus in the House. He'd been dealing with their antics since the beginning of the year.

"Yeah, that one. He's been quiet until now; seemed like he went along with us except for the abortion crap. Actually, I thought he was a reasonable man. But now he says he will filibuster any bill which we introduce to increase the debt ceiling."

"Even if we give him some assurances with the '12 budget?" Halperin was incredulous.

"Says he and his wife prayed on it all last night. He believes the solar storm was God's wrath for our moral and economic failures as a nation, and God has instructed him to do all in his power to stop the ruin."

Halperin sat across from Jimmy Wilkerson with his mouth open. "Does he understand what this will do?"

"I don't know what he knows or doesn't. He's no economist for sure. All I know is that he claims he is doing God's work."

Halperin rolled his eyes. "What do we do now?"

Wilkerson would say he had done all he could. He had plenty of cover when the House failed to raise the debt limit. He had done his job—impeccably.

"We take our votes. You're first. Hopefully, I won't have to vote."

May 28, 2011

PRESIDENT TAYLOR AND I were in the Oval Office going over last-minute adjustments to his speech that would announce Plan B to the nation. Both of us secretly hoped the other side would be reasonable and find some way to increase the debt limit, especially in light of the disaster Michigan now faced. Milestone knocked once on the door and entered.

"I just got off the phone with Wilkerson," he said shaking his head. "The House doesn't have the votes to extend the ceiling, and there's a Republican senator who will filibuster any attempt to raise it; catastrophe or not."

Taylor leaned back in the couch, put his hands behind his head, and gazed up at the oval ceiling. I wondered what he was thinking. I just sat there watching him take measured breaths. This was the moment of reckoning—the single moment where you decide. I held my breath, waiting. Taylor dropped his arms, his hands slapping his thighs. He looked at me across the coffee table that separated us.

"Are you ready, Jude?"

I got up and paced the rug of the Oval Office. "No one in their right mind could be ready for this." My own fear and doubts overcame me, but I had seen the results of the other path. No, not again; not this time. "What time will you make the announcement to the nation?"

"We have it on good information that the House and Senate leaders are planning a press conference after the vote in the House late tomorrow. Frankly, I doubt it will get out of the House," the president said. "We'll be ready to go, but we are not going to announce anything until they start their news conference. Then we'll preempt them with my speech from the Oval Office." He grinned.

"Whose idea was that?" I asked.

"David's, of course." Milestone stood at the door, a smile spreading across his face.

77

May 29, 2011

JIMMY WILKERSON AND Douglas Halperin, leaders of Congress, took the podium in the Capitol pressroom following the debt ceiling vote in the U.S. House of Representatives. The vote to raise the debt ceiling failed in the House by a large majority, with several Democrats voting not to raise it as well.

Jimmy Wilkerson stepped to the podium with Halperin at his side. "This is a grave period in American history," the Senate Majority Leader began. "This irresponsible president has refused to . . ." Wilkerson faltered slightly as several members of the press began checking their buzzing Blackberries. "To do what is right for this country. He is now leading our economy into dangerous territory, rather than giving into the will of the American people and dealing seriously with our debt and deficits. His actions have . . ."

Wilkerson's remark strayed off in mid-sentence as the camera lights were turned off. The Blackberries of the press corps were now buzzing furiously. He looked over at Halperin, who showed him the message on his phone, while most of the reporters rushed out of the room.

Every television set in the country that had tuned into the majority leaders of Congress in the Capitol pressroom had now switched to the President of the United States of America, sitting at his desk in the Oval Office of the White House.

"My fellow citizens of the United States of America, tonight I am announcing a series of steps to deal with the grave crisis facing this great country."

78

May 31, 2011
New York, New York

IT WAS THE day after the Memorial Day holiday, a sweltering Tuesday when the U.S. markets would finally open following the president's announcement to the American people on Sunday evening. Stephen Russell's Blackberry began ringing text messages at 4:05 am. He was already up and showered, awaiting the inevitable reaction to the president's speech.

He and his team of investment managers had met all day on Monday, trying to develop a strategy to minimize the damage. When the U.S. markets opened they would move as many bond investments into cash as they could, and then into gold. U.S. allies had been quietly selling Treasuries since the end of last week. Now everyone would be selling T Bonds. But there was no market for them. The Chinese had dumped over 40% of their bond holdings in the last three weeks and most of the rest before the markets closed on Friday.

By 5:00 am Russell was dressed in his double-breasted blue pin-stripe suit with red, blue, and green rep tie and headed for his office on Wall Street in his Lincoln limousine. He began making mental notes of everything he was going to have to deal with when he got to the office.

"I need to dump my repo assets and quickly," he muttered to himself, scrolling through the emails on his phone.

In spite of their meetings yesterday, he was beginning to have second thoughts about the strategy he and his team had agreed to. They still held a bundle of Treasuries. Should they hold them and wait for them to come back, or sell them for pennies today? They'd backed a few large investments with T Bonds; the investors were going to ask for more cash to back them up. What else could they sell to make up the difference? "Fucking Taylor," he said aloud in the back seat of his limo. This was going to kill his bottom line.

He switched to CNBC on the silent screen of the TV embedded in the seatback in front of him; the anchor looked as though he had been up all night. The U.S. markets hadn't opened yet, but he got a glimpse of what had happened overseas yesterday and again today; it wasn't pretty.

By 6:00 am Russell was in his office surrounded by fresh flowers. The phone had all eight lines flashing at once. Wasn't anyone going to answer them? He knew he wasn't the only one here. Someone was brewing fresh coffee; he could smell it. He punched line 1.

"Stephen, we have futures sell-offs in ten of our major money market funds. They each hold a lot of short-term Treasury debt. This is going to break the buck. There's going to be a run on all the money-market funds. What do you want to do? All the institutional investors are pulling out." The voice on the other end of the line was panicky; it sounded like too many cigarettes and not enough sleep.

"What the fuck do you expect me to do?" he said as he hung up the phone. This they expected, and there was nothing they *could* do to prevent the sell-offs in spite of President Taylor's assurances to protect domestic bondholders invested in U.S. Treasuries.

Russell punched line 2.

"Stephen, our oil derivatives are in the tank. We've lost over 50% of the futures value. They're suspending futures trading at noon. What do you want to do—hold or sell?"

Russell was about to say 'sell', but paused. He hadn't thought about the oil derivatives. Turmoil in the Middle East would cause the price to go up; global recession caused the price to go down, a devalued dollar made the price go up. Which way will it go? He considered the options.

"What's the current price?"

"Down 30."

"Buy all you can at that price or lower," he barked as he hung up the phone.

Russell punched line 3.

"Good morning, Stephen, I hope you're having a good day." Jonathan Peter's usually smooth voice had a jagged edge to it he hadn't heard before.

"Go to hell, Jonathan. So what are you running this morning?"

"Well, Stephen, I have officers of the Office of the Comptroller here in my office, awaiting to escort me out of my building. I am no longer running anything. I really hope you're happy."

"I had nothing to do with this, Jonathan," Russell exploded. "Call the fucking president if you want to whine in your morning coffee."

"You forget, Stephen, since TARP, you're a bank too. I'll see you in the soup line, my friend."

The door to Stephen Russell's office burst open.

"Sir, put down the telephone," barked an officer of the Comptroller of the Currency. Russell dropped the phone receiver and it clattered on the desk. His stomach rumbled and he wondered if he might lose his morning coffee. "We are here to escort you out of the building. You are no longer in charge."

Russell picked up his briefcase and was forcibly led out of his office, down the elevator, out of the lobby and onto the street by the OCC officials. Protestors and the media had gathered outside the office of his investment bank. Russell stood there in shock, looking at the anger in the faces of the protestors and listening to the yelled obscenities from those who were surrounding him.

A man dressed in khakis and a plaid shirt with unkempt hair walked slowly but steadily toward him. Russell caught him from the corner of his eye as he reached for his cell phone to call his driver. He fixated on the person moving at him, while punching the speed dial on his Blackberry. As he neared, Russell could see the brown stubble covering his face. He stepped back, but the man kept coming. Russell stood his ground, punching his speed dial button over and over until the man was suddenly in his face.

"Adios, motherfucker!"

Russell felt a searing hot pain in his abdomen as he watched the backside of the man disappear into the crowd.

"What's going on?" he asked himself as the yells of the crowd blurred into a hum.

He reached down to his stomach to the point of the pain, and pulled his bloody hand up to his face as he dropped his Blackberry and collapsed on the sidewalk.

Washington D.C.

"WHAT DO THE polls say, David?" President Taylor stood at the window of the Oval Office, gazing on the peaceful lawns. In the background, a small television tuned to cable news, its volume muted against the hysteria of the anchors, showed crowds of people swarming the financial district in New York.

"It's early, but so far 43% in favor of your actions, 29% opposed." Milestone checked his Blackberry again, just in case it had changed in the last few minutes.

"What about the other 28%?"

"Stupidly undecided, sir." Milestone grinned. "I think it fair to say that approvals will be near 50% by the end of the week."

"That means our friends in Congress will have a tougher time turning back the declared state of emergency." He turned from the window to look at his Chief of Staff.

"Don't kid yourself, Mr. President. They will vote it down. And you will ignore their vote. And then we are both off to the Supreme Court." He picked at a cheese Danish he had snagged from the White House cafeteria on his way up to his office.

"The Attorney General already has plans to delay that as much as possible."

"Still, you will need those emergency powers for at least a year. He can't delay it that long. The rumor is that several of the global corporations have their lawyers working on legal challenges to your policy on producing goods in America, and the oil companies have publically declared that they will fight nationalization. Both will try to use their friends in the courts to delay Plan B's implementation."

"You mean, until after the election next year." Milestone was right; they didn't want a quick decision from the Supreme Court, which was likely to rule against his use of emergency powers. "Then we'll implement the import tax. We've given our global friends six months to decide on which way they're going to go. If they want to waste it on legal debates, so be it. But we need to put as much of the program in place, quickly so the people can see its benefits, like the Wall Street bank CEOs being removed from their offices by the Office of the Comptroller—a federal government agency."

"Looks like the people are already seeing some of the benefits," Milestone said, pointing his Danish at the TV set. Taylor reached for the remote and turned up the volume. Stephen Russell, CEO of PRI, a Wall Street investment firm and bank, was escorted out of his office and surrounded by reporters, TV cameras and angry citizens. He suddenly dropped to the ground.

DAVID MILESTONE USHERED Fallon Connelly into the Oval Office. Everyone on the team had done their best to remain cordial with each other during a tense time, but Fallon had alienated almost the entire cabinet. She began to wonder if she would be able to keep her job or if Taylor would consider her expendable too, just like the bank CEOs.

"The Dow is down over 5000 points, the S&P over 400," she said, ignoring the president's wave towards a chair in front of his desk. "The NASDAQ is at 1200. Trading was suspended at 11:00 am. Who knows where the bottom will be."

"Thanks for the good news, Fallon. Did you expect something different?"

"No, Mr. President."

"What's happening globally?"

"Greece, Ireland, Portugal, and Spain have all declared they will default on their debt. They will likely sever their ties to the E.U. Thailand, Indonesia, Argentina, Italy, and a host of Third World debtor countries are likely to default as well—probably all of them when this is all said and done. The IMF and the World Bank will be bankrupt."

"Again, did you expect something different?"

"No. It seems Jude's plan is proceeding according to plan. But the chaos this is causing . . ."

"We have just broken the bottle, Fallon. It will be a while before we can put the pieces together."

That phrase sounded familiar to Fallon, then she remembered: it's what she had said to Jude about the Indonesia account when Suharto was overthrown.

"What is the response from the European Union?" The president asked.

"Their finance ministers are meeting today and tomorrow. The E.U. doesn't decide things quickly. It will be at least two months before they decide they cannot continue their currency in its current form, or their legal organization for that matter."

"And China?"

"China is silent, sir."

Taylor paused, wondering what was happening there, in the second largest economy in the world. It would likely take weeks or months before the dust settled and a clear picture emerged.

"What's happening with the banks?"

"The OCC has taken over the target banks," she stated, keeping her tone level. "You may have heard Stephen Russell was murdered outside his investment bank this morning after he was escorted out."

"Do you expect surprise from me, or maybe sympathy?" His voice was hard. "Glass will be everywhere; some people will get cut. Do you think the other side would have any greater sympathy for us had we chosen their path?" Taylor picked up a document on his desk and begin reading.

"No, sir. No, I do not." She turned from the desk to see Milestone holding the office door open for her.

"Happy, Mr. Economic Consultant to the President, or whatever your title is these days?" Fallon snapped, standing in the doorway of my office.

I wasn't surprised to see her, nor surprised by her tone. I looked up and searched her face. This was a Fallon Connelly I had never seen before. What was it—anger, frustration, loathing?

"I won't be happy until we turn things around."

"Really? Wasn't that what the Republicans were trying to do—face the debt issue head on and get the economy back on course, before the president cut them off and took matters into his own hands?" Her look was pure daggers.

"But at whose cost, Fallon?"

"You don't think the same people will end up suffering?"

"Of course there will be suffering, but this time everyone will have to bare some of the pain; like the bank CEOs who got us into this mess. If I knew in 2008 what I know now, and had the guts, I would have told the president to vote against TARP, and nationalize the financial institutions of this country then. I bet you don't know that I almost did that. Now we have a little correction to make—this time in favor of the taxpayers. The people's money in the banks is safe, and part of their pension funds are protected, for now. And corporate CEOs will have to answer to their shareholders."

"How long will the people's investments be safe?" she countered. "What will they be worth in a month with the market in free fall?"

"The market will recover, and we will get the economy back on its feet," I said firmly. "This time markets and the economy will work as they should—for the benefit of all the people. If I didn't believe that, I wouldn't still be sitting at this desk."

"Fucking idealistic tripe." She shot her words out like bullets. Her eyes flashed, and the color rose in her cheeks. "When you're gone and Taylor is gone, things will pick up where they left off. The forces that drive our economy are part of human nature. You can suppress them, but you won't kill them. What you think you can change, you have only postponed and made even worse."

"It's too late to revert to the old prescriptions for economic growth," I said, rising to my feet. "Within a month the people of this country, and maybe those of other countries, will understand what has been done and where it can lead. They'll get it, Fallon, and once they do, no one will be able to just switch off the vision."

"Jude, you *are* a fool." Fallon turned to walk out of my office, but stopped as she reached the door. "How could you believe that one man's ideas could change the economic history of the United States, much less the world?"

I looked at her and shook my head. Was she so entrenched in her view of the world that she couldn't see what was happening around her?

"It's not me who will change the economic history of our country. It's demographics. The future of the world doesn't belong to you and me anymore. It belongs to Lex's generation and the next generation of immigrants, and in *their* vision, Fallon, America's economy is not controlled by plutocrats and oligarchs."

79

Toronto, Canada
June 1, 2011

"YES, JOSEPH, I know what it means," Thomas said as he leaned feebly against the marble counter in his kitchen, the years defeating his body and his spirit. "We are still assessing the damage. And there is the woman; calmer heads could prevail."

"Not with Anders in the president's house! I was so hopeful—and in my lifetime." Joseph sighed deeply. "I thought we had moved him out of the way." He shifted his weight to his other leg to relieve the stabbing sciatic pain shooting down his right side to his ankle. "How could a single person disrupt our plan? You know the odds, and I do not believe in coincidence."

"Surely, you do not believe Anton . . . his work in Ohio and the Middle East confirms his loyalty." Joseph saw the old fire rise in his friend's eyes for a moment but it did not last. Having come so far . . . perhaps this really had undone them all.

"It is not me who questions his loyalty, Thomas, but some of the others . . . you can understand their suspicions." Joseph shook his head. "Anton and Anders. What was the chance of them ever meeting, much less becoming friends? And then Jack, positioning him at the IMF."

"He was just trying to help Anton's friend," Thomas said as he reached into the cabinet for a glass and filled it with tap water. "He could only see the slightest resemblance, having raised Anton from an infant. And then, when he discovered they had the same birth date . . ."

"That may be. But you should have left well enough alone, Thomas, after you found Anton by bribing your way into his sealed adoption records. I am sure Jack and Laurel were quite pleased when you just showed up, his natural father, out of the blue."

"They were happy that I was . . ."

"Before or after you took a 40% stake in his business?"

"That had nothing to do with it." Thomas shrugged his shoulders like it was no big deal.

Joseph laughed. "With Jack's business failing, and his stake in Anaconda Copper enough to bankrupt him after Allende's nationalization program, I am sure he was more than happy to have you involved in Anton's life." Joseph sagged onto the stool at the counter. "Of course, you knew that Jack's suspicions were likely correct. You knew there was another, but you should have just let it be. Really, personally searching through Massachusetts vital records just to be sure—how pathetic." He had gone over the long trail of connections last night. They had made mistakes along the way, but this one . . . when they could have prevented it . . .

"And once you confirmed Anders' identity, you suggested that we consider him too. After all, by that time he was in a position that could benefit our efforts. When he quit the IMF, we should have just let him go. But we didn't. He had other opportunities; he would have been out of our way, but it was your insistence, Thomas, that we give him another chance. He would change, you said, as he got older and lost his youthful idealism. So we secured a position for him at the Fed—at your request." His voice had risen considerably and Thomas had stepped back a bit under the assault.

"But even you agreed . . ."

Joseph struggled to regain his composure. "Yes, yes, I know—we all agreed that he might be useful even if he did not become one of us."

"At least at the Federal Reserve we could maintain a watchful eye."

"But when he went to work for Taylor, we lost that control. I blame myself for giving in to your sympathies. Deep down my instincts told me that he would be a problem, especially given his relationship with Anton."

"You think Anton knows who Anders really is?" Thomas began pacing the large space of the kitchen. "I don't believe it—he would have told me."

"But if he does know, that would certainly confirm our suspicions about how Anders seemed to anticipate our moves."

Thomas began to speak, but Joseph interrupted. "We discussed this years ago, when we admitted Anton to the Deep. We all agreed."

Thomas looked down at his kitchen floor. "Yes, I know," he said with a heavy sigh that rang in Joseph's ears for what seemed like an eternity. Thomas returned his gaze. "Do you want me to arrange it . . . with our usual resources?"

"Under the circumstances, I think it better if I do that. I will let you know this evening when and where." He checked his watch. "I have to go. My flight leaves in an hour."

JOSEPH LEANED BACK into his limo's soft leather seat, made sure the glass was up and took out his cell phone. He thumbed in the number and gazed out the window; the airport was not far and he did not have much time for this call.

"Have you given anymore thought to the discussion we had yesterday?" He asked as soon as his call was picked up.

"I believe we have to go along with the president's plan. If we refuse or drag our feet, that could easily put us on the outside with limited influence or authority, and opening up a fight with the executive might end up betraying our position, or at the very least, weakening it going forward."

"I had pretty much concluded the same," he said. "But I had another thought. This state of emergency thing, it could work to our advantage. What if someone else with the right values was sitting in the White House, with Connelly at his side?"

There was a long pause. Joseph looked at his cell phone to make sure he had not lost the connection. "Are you still there?"

"Yes. I was considering your question."

"And?"

"Someone from our side in the White House would give us other options, but I doubt Taylor's emergency proclamation will be upheld by the court. Our influence there is limited."

"Yes, you are probably correct." Joseph poured a whiskey from the small bar in the limousine. "There is another matter."

"Yes?"

"Anton and your protégé. We need to correct our mistake . . . before things get totally out of hand."

"Do the others agree?"

"I wanted to inform you first."

"And Thomas?"

Joseph sneered. "He understands what must be done."

"Well, that is a pity. I am quite fond of him actually—like the son I never had."

"I know." Joseph paused. "Do you think Anders found out?"

"About the plan? I have no evidence of that, but he left my employ over two years ago. Who knows what he may have learned while in the White House?"

"Or from Anton."

"If Anders knew, Anton would be a likely source."

"Thomas does not believe that."

"Do you, Joseph?"

"What difference does it make whether I believe that or not? We need to minimize the damage. I do not foster revenge, but business is business."

"Too bad he never worked out."

"Wrong set of values." Joseph laughed. "From his mother's side, of course."

Joseph hung up and put his cell phone in his suit coat. Perhaps they had pushed things too quickly, an error often made by older men anxious to achieve their ends within the length of their timelines. He leaned back in the seat and smiled. Maybe all was not lost. He could see another way.

June 2, 2011
Toronto, Canada

ANTON GLARED AT his father. He had called early while Anton was getting dressed for work. The fact that his father insisted they talk face-to-face led him to believe that this was going to be Deep business.

"What is so urgent that could not wait?" He stood impatiently just inside the foyer of Thomas' house. "You will be at the board meeting on Monday, and I am going to be late for the editors review this morning."

"I need you to go to Washington tomorrow. There is an opportunity to purchase one of the local TV outlets. Getting our feet into that market, especially in these times, would help our bottom line."

Anton started to object. Thomas held up his hand.

"I know, I know, members of the board of directors are supposed to stay out of the day-to-day operation of the company, but the deal will not be available for long; from what I hear, the price is right—a benefit of the crisis."

"Why don't you go?"

"Really, Anton, you know how hard it is for me to get around here, much less get on an airplane and fly to the States. Anyway, you could visit your acquaintance while you are there."

"Jude? He is much more than an acquaintance."

"Yes, yes, of course he is." Thomas paused; it was as though some thought had carried him to another time and place, or maybe, Anton thought, at his age he had lost the thread of his thinking. "But it would be helpful to have some inside information on President Taylor's plans—something he has not yet announced. As you know, our plan, well, it is not proceeding as we hoped."

Anton narrowed his eyes. This had nothing to do with the deal in D.C.; this was Deep business after all. "What type of information could be useful at this late date?"

"Well, what other actions the president might be considering under his state of emergency declaration, for example, and how long he may try to keep it in effect."

"I am not certain Jude is privy to that information, and if he were, I doubt he would tell me."

Thomas gazed at the streaks of morning sunlight spreading across his foyer floor. "You are probably correct . . . still, what harm in trying? Knowing what is coming might influence our decisions."

"You have never asked that of me before, Father, to use Jude to gather information for our benefit." Sure, he had passed on information over the years that, if Jude acted upon it, might benefit their plans, but using him to . . .

"I have never had to, Anton. But our situation is somewhat desperate, and frankly the members of our group are none too pleased with how things have developed. You can appreciate the impact on our portfolio."

"Some portfolio—debt."

"It is our currency, Anton. Remember your loyalties." Thomas' voice was stern.

"Oh, I remember them, Father, and do not forget they have been tested."

"Yes, yes I know." Thomas held Anton's glare. "I am sorry. We are all on edge right now. Still, there are those who question how Anders could have anticipated our moves."

"They think I told him?" Anton bristled.

"Not many of us believe in coincidence, Anton, you know that."

"Whatever Jude knows, he figured it out on his own. I can assure you he knows nothing of the Deep or our plan."

His father's response was measured. "Okay, I believe you. Enough said."

Anton wondered whether he could ever believe anything his father—or anyone else in the Deep—ever said. They stood in silence; their eyes locked on each other, for another long moment before Thomas turned to the console table and picked up a white envelope.

"I have come into possession of a couple of tickets to the *Follies* performance at the Kennedy Center." His voice was smooth, as though their conversation never happened. "You can do our media business, then you and Anders could attend the show that night. What do you think?" He held the envelope out to him, but Anton made no move to take it.

Use his friend, just like Sasha did, as a conduit of information? And for what? To salvage a failed plan; a plan that even he was unsure he fully understood or agreed with. Had anyone ever just walked away from the Deep? He was sure if they had, they would not have lived to tell the tale; his own options were limited, indeed. But he had not spent decades under his father's tutelage for nothing.

"I am sure Jude could use a few hours away from the madness he has helped to create," Anton said as he took the envelope from his father and carefully tucked it into his jacket pocket. "I will ask him."

"Madness . . . Our thoughts exactly. Please enjoy the performance. Oh, I almost forgot." He turned back to the table and reached for a slim box. "Francis gave me this hideous pink tie for my birthday. You know how I hate pink. Perhaps you would like to wear it to the performance. It would be appropriate for the venue."

A tie? When had his father ever given him a present, even a re-gifted one? Anton took the box and looked at the deep wrinkles of his father's slightly bowed forehead.

"Just one question, Father."

"Yes, Anton, what is it?" He looked up at Anton.

"If it benefited the Deep, would you kill your own son?"

His father's eyes shifted slightly but quickly directed their focus on Anton's face. "What a silly question, my son. You mean more to me than anyone."

Washington D.C.

"I DON'T HAVE time to talk right now, Anton."

I hadn't talked to Anton in weeks. Usually I was glad to hear from him and looked forward to sparring over a few drinks, but like everyone else in the White House, I was up to my eyeballs just trying to hold everything together.

"Of course, I understand. But I am in town tomorrow and have a couple of tickets to the *Follies* at your Kennedy Center. Surely you could take a few hours off . . . to clear your head."

A lot of late nights had left my eyes red and gritty; I looked away from my computer screen for a few minutes and rubbed them. "Things are a little intense here."

"I am sure President Taylor would agree that the appearance of calm would be a good thing from White House officials at this difficult time. And besides, I need to know when you will resume your blog postings. We do have a contractual agreement."

I had never intended to hold him to that agreement; to me, the writing was something between friends, and while the checks were appreciated, my lifestyle didn't really require quite so much padding. Besides, I had been far too wrapped up in the day-to-day management of an economy in chaos to wax poetically about political or economic theory.

"You have a great way to spin things to get what you want, my friend," I told him after a minute. "By the way, Princeton has respectfully requested that I withdraw from my post. I think I'll still have a job in the White House as long as I can bear it, at least until after the next election if things go badly."

"I guess that would be expected, Jude. Does that mean you will indulge me with a few hours of your time?"

"A quick dinner first at the Old Ebbitt, your treat?"

"With a '92 Bordeaux, of course."

Frankly, he was right. It had been too long. An evening off would be good for me, although I didn't think President Taylor would have much to say about me making an appearance in the audience of the *Follies*.

80

June 3, 2011
Washington D.C.

ANTON AND I met at 6:30 at the Old Ebbitt Grill, still as elegant as it was the first time we met here so many years ago. Due to the hour, or perhaps the economic crisis I had helped to engineer, we were the only customers in the restaurant. The performance at the Kennedy Center started at 8:30, giving us plenty of time for a nice dinner.

"To us, my brother," Anton toasted.

"And to single malt," I offered, lifting my glass.

"One more thing we have in common, Jude."

"A scotch? From a single barrel?"

"Definitely. Two glasses from the same barrel." A warm smile crossed his aging face. "And a good cure for the ailments of life."

I had been feeling every late night, every panicked news report, every early morning strategy session. My gut was messed up, I smoked too much and sleep came only if it was accompanied by a couple of scotches and some Advil PM.

"Well, thank God for scotch because ailments are part of life, especially at our age."

"And how is that going, your life?"

Typical Anton—getting right down to what was on his mind. "How do you think?"

"I think as you expected, Jude." His voice was calm but his gaze direct.

"You are too wise, Anton, but actually, things are somewhat better than expected. Oil futures dropped through the floor just before the president suspended trading on the Commodities Exchange by non-interested parties." It was a hollow victory. We had watched the markets on a small screen in Milestone's office while Taylor readied for the moment of suspension. No one made a sound when it was done. We just shuffled off to our respective desks, most of us probably wondering if we really had any idea what we were doing.

"Well, I am glad I do not invest in futures." He sipped his drink, his eyes still on mine. A typical Anton response—he always says what he doesn't do. And most of the time I didn't believe him. "But tell me, how does this state of emergency thing work in your country?"

"Not for long, I'm afraid. Congress has rejected the president's declaration." I ran my finger along the edge of the now-familiar menu. "Damn, if the Ohio senator hadn't been killed, we could have made it stick."

"Maybe you should knock off one of the Republican senators." His eyes seemed mischievous. I couldn't remember seeing that look since our student days in Toronto.

"I don't think that would work," I said, uneasy with the topic. "There are only four states with Democrat governors and Republican senators. And only two of those states allow the governor to appoint a new senator."

"Sounds like you have thought that through."

"Just wild musings . . . in my free time," I managed a chuckle. "Anyway, even if one of the senators disappeared, the Republicans would still hold a one-vote majority until a new senator was appointed. I doubt we have that much time. At any rate, the president is ignoring Congress's rejection. Now it will end up in the Supreme Court for resolution."

That had been our plan from the beginning; full steam ahead and damn the torpedoes. I knew it was the right choice, considering how polarized and ineffectual Congress had become, but it was still tough waiting it out. All we could hope for was that enough had been set into motion that legislative wrangling would not be able to stop it.

"And how will your Supreme Court decide?"

"The opposition holds a 5 to 4 majority. How do you think?"

"I think you will lose, but I have always wondered about something." Anton idly swirled his drink, his eyes on the ice cubes in his glass. "What happens if you have only eight justices on the Court? You know, if something were to happen to one of them?"

This was not a topic I was enthused about pursuing any more than knocking off a senator, and I was hoping Anton would get off this track. The Ohio senator's death was still unresolved. An undercurrent of fear ran through the hallways in the Capitol, that was certain.

"The president appoints a new justice, but he or she would have to be confirmed by the Senate." I sipped my drink and pretended to read the menu.

". . . which is controlled by your Republicans by two votes?"

"Yes."

"So what happens if the Republicans refuse to confirm your president's appointee?"

"Until they agreed on a candidate, the Supreme Court would be left with only eight justices to make a decision on any particular case."

"Evenly split, four from their side, four from yours? A stalemate?"

I looked at him with mild curiosity. "I hadn't thought of that. I suppose you're correct, assuming the missing justice is from the other side."

"Interesting," he said. "Do you like my tie?"

Grateful for the diversion, I had to chuckle. I wasn't planning to mention it, but had certainly noticed it the moment I entered the restaurant.

"What, you do not like the color pink?" He looked down at the tie, a faux-scowl on his face.

"As a matter of fact I do, but I don't think it becomes you."

"Really? And I do not think you look good in red and black rep ties either."

I lifted up the end of my tie and let it fall on white linen tablecloth. "What's wrong with this?"

"I am afraid it is more my style than yours. Don't you think it is a bit too conservative for you, especially now?"

I laughed. "Our relationship has finally come to this—ties."

Anton undid the knot of his tie and slipped it from beneath his shirt collar. "Here. Let's trade."

"Finally you have a good idea." I undid my tie and we exchanged them at the table under the watchful eyes of the wait staff.

Anton's cell phone rang as he was trying to retie my tie, now his. He looked at the caller ID.

"Excuse me, Jude, I must take this call, and I might need to use the mirror in the bathroom to adjust my new tie. Go ahead and order dinner for me, will you? The usual, steak *au poivre*, medium rare." He got up and left for the men's room with his cell phone to his ear, the tie dangling in his other hand.

A SLIGHT FIGURE in a black costume for tonight's performance made her way up the ladder to the catwalk holding the lights above the stage. The catwalk sat above the top edge of the curtain and provided a clear view to the rows of seats in the theatre. She counted the rows from the front until she reached ten. Then she counted the seats in the center section, starting from the left aisle until she reached numbers nineteen and twenty. Once the audience settled in she would count again to be certain. Of course, he could be in either seat, but she had one more piece of information. She crouched down low on the catwalk and blended into the black background of the stage ceiling. Now she must wait and remain unnoticed, then disappear at the end of the performance during the curtain calls.

ANTON ENTERED THE men's room, already well into the phone conversation. "Yes, as we discussed yesterday. I will leave the method up to you, but we need to do this soon." He kept his voice low and peeked into the stalls to be sure he was alone. Thank god the Old Ebbitt had finally done away with that archaic attendant tradition; the last thing he needed was a grizzled old black man in a white jacket handing him a paper towel. He listened to his caller for a moment.

"Preferably within a week, but I understand the timing must be right," he said, studying the striped tie in his hand.

"Just take care of it. I have already arranged things on your end as I did the last time. This will be our last discussion of the matter." He ended the call, draped the tie around his neck and looked at his reflection in the mirror.

ANTON RETURNED TO the table with a smile on his face and my tie neatly done in a double Windsor.

"Sorry, Jude. I promise that will be my last business call for the evening."

I poured him a glass of '92 Saint Julien. Considering how empty the place was, I expected dinner to arrive quickly, which was good because not only was I hungry, I was already feeling a little buzzed.

"Sorry, I couldn't wait," I said as I lifted my half empty glass in a toast. "To us."

"To us, Jude."

I was surprised to see his hand shake just a little as he lifted his glass.

Anton and I finished dinner and the entire bottle of wine and caught a cab from the Old Ebbitt Grill to the Kennedy Center. If I had been with anyone else, I probably would have begged off the rest of the evening and gone home, let the wine lull me into dreamless sleep. Instead, while we waited for the lights to dim, we exchanged stories, from our days and nights at the Student Union at Toronto University, to my excursion to Buenos Aires. We even talked a bit about Sasha and what that little detour had cost me. When the performance began, I let the color and pageantry lull me into a quiet peace. It had been a very long time since I had allowed myself to relax and be swept away by music, dancing and costumes.

I was grateful to be sitting here with Anton. I had known him since we were both twenty-two. How many people do you know that long in your life, other than family? My mother was dead, as were Jack and Laurel and Anton's real mother. Still, his father, now well into his eighties, hung on tenaciously.

As the performance went on, more musings danced through my mind. Our two lives had become so intertwined over the years. At least the Vietnam War had one good outcome—our paths had crossed as a result. Anton came from privilege and became the CEO of a major media conglomerate; I was a lower-middle class kid raised by a single parent who grew up to have the ear of the most powerful man in the world. And here we were in the beginning of our later years, best friends, or as Anton put it, more like brothers.

My life had been good, and certainly meaningful. In spite of how I disparaged the leadership of my country most of my adult life, I had been blessed by this land of opportunity. But that opportunity was now at risk, not so much for me anymore, but for Lex and subsequent generations. I had done what I could; was it enough to provide for their future?

I had no regrets really, but now was the time to focus on my daughter and the rest of my life without the next crisis to confront. After so many years, could I really do something other than trying to solve the world's economic problems, and what would it be? I had often thought about writing a book. A novel, perhaps, where my only-too-real life did not have to intrude.

The show was almost over; we had been laughing non-stop from the beginning of the performance. Anton looked over at me and smiled. He looked at peace, and I felt the same way—something I hadn't felt in years.

A few minutes later, we all stood in applause as the curtain closed. I turned to Anton. He was still seated, his chin tucked into his chest. Perhaps the wine and the steak had finally overcome him and he had fallen asleep.

"Anton," I said, as I jostled his shoulder trying to wake him. The house lights came up. I saw a red stain blooming on his white shirt, just next to my red and black rep tie.

81

Fall, 2011
Toronto, Canada

LEX LAID A single white rose at the base of the tombstone and backed away to stand next to me. Tears were trickling down her cheeks. She had never lost someone close.

"Dad, I never knew you and Uncle Anton had the same birthday." She wiped away a tear as she stared at the inscription.

"Yes. I remember when we found that out." I handed Lex my handkerchief. My tears had yet to come, but I knew they would. "Anton's adoptive mother invited me to his twenty-third birthday party while I was living in Toronto. He got the gifts, but we both got a toast. I think that's one reason Anton often referred to me as his brother."

"Wow, that's amazing." She clutched the hanky, now covered in smears of black mascara. "I mean you being best friends, and born on the same date."

"Life is full of coincidences, Lex."

"I'll miss him, Dad." She started to weep again.

Tears welled in my eyes. I let them come. "Me, too. Ready to go?"

"Yes. This is just too sad."

I put my arm around her as we turned to leave, and was surprised to see a white-haired old man in a black trench coat about thirty feet away. He appeared to be staring at us. As we started to move away from Anton's grave, he walked toward us, his steps feeble but determined. As he approached, he called out. "You are Jude Anders." It wasn't a question.

I froze. "Yes, I am, and who . . ."

"I am Thomas MacDonald, Anton's father."

Unnerving as his sudden appearance was, I was sorry that this had to be my first chance to meet him. I had heard many stories about this man—that he was successful, tenacious, even ruthless. I remembered Anton chafing sometimes under what seemed like a short leash while he tried to run their business.

"Nice to meet you." I shook his hand warmly. "This is my daughter, Elexus."

He stared at her intently and took her hand. "Very nice to meet you, Elexus. Anton was very fond of you." Lex nodded, tears still coursing down her cheeks.

"This is our first opportunity to pay our respects," I said. He was deeply wrinkled but his gray eyes were sharp. Even with his age I could see traces of Anton in his face. "We never received word of a memorial service."

"There wasn't one, Mr. Anders—Anton's wishes."

"Of course, I should have expected that. Sounds like him."

"Yes." He looked hard into my face.

"We will miss him dearly." I gazed back; his eyes were deep-set and cold.

"So will I. Anton would appreciate your sympathies." There was nothing sympathetic in the way he looked at me. I felt very protective of Lex suddenly.

"We need to be going, Mr. MacDonald." I hoped he couldn't hear in my voice the anxiety I was beginning to feel. "We have a plane to catch. It was nice meeting you."

"Yes, after all these years." He looked again at Lex, and I tightened my arm around her shoulder as we hurried past him.

When we got to the car I looked back for a moment. Thomas MacDonald stood with his back to the grave; he continued to watch us as we drove away.

82

Present Time
Lagada, Amorgos, Greece

WE SAT ON the small patio of my rented house, listening to the Aegean Sea crash into the rocks below. It was nearing sunset. We had just finished coffee and were now enjoying a small glass of ouzo. I smelled the fragrance of the liqueur. I had never tried it back home, but now I was developing quite a taste for it.

Several nights a week, Jacobi's daughter came to my house, her arms laden with fresh bread, fruits, and vegetables from the village market. Oftentimes, she had a fresh fish caught that afternoon. Her English was much better than her father had let on; as I unburdened myself of my story, I rarely had to explain or simplify my words.

"Do they find who kill Anton?" Aglaia asked.

"Not yet." At least this was the latest news from Lex in her last letter. There was no internet or cell-phone service in Lagada. If you wanted that kind of connectivity to the broader world, you had to travel to Katapola.

"Who do you think do it?"

"I think the shooter got the wrong man," I said quietly as I gazed out over the water. "We may never know who or why."

How many times had I retraced the events and conversations of that evening? I was still haunted by the thought that someone wanted *me* dead, not Anton. Who might have been behind it, and how did they get it wrong? The image of Vasco so adeptly retrieving the white envelope from my jacket pocket that afternoon in Buenos Aires popped into my mind.

What was in it, and why did Anton want me to meet Vasco? Somehow I always felt that Anton had had a hand in that little adventure. Did he lure me to the *Follies* too?

"He was your friend." She shook her head; her voice held the same sadness that I had felt earlier over dinner as I recounted the events surrounding Anton's death. It was almost as if she really knew him and was grieving for him along with me. I had noticed how patiently she listened as I dumped out so many details of my life. She took it all in with so much sincerity; there didn't appear to be a self-centered bone in her body.

"Yes, he was my best friend." After all he had done for me, I could never believe Anton would set me up, certainly not for a hit job. He was the only real friend I ever had.

There was a long silence between us. I sat staring at the glass of ouzo, thinking of Anton.

"So much killing in your country, Judas," she said finally. "Representatives from your capitol; governors of states; heads of your banks."

"Yes, Aglaia, bankers and politicians. I think many of them deserved it—those that had a hand in causing and perpetuating the crisis for their own selfish goals, regardless of the suffering they were causing to the people of my country."

I remembered what the Federal Reserve Chairman said to me at the outset of the crisis: people either become slaves or they revolt. Some of the people had exercised their Second Amendment rights.

"Even your head legal justice." She shook her head, and I understood her dismay. Under normal circumstances, no one could condone murder; perhaps we had lost the distinction between the means and the ends they were supposed to achieve. "What wrong did he do?" Her look was penetrating, and I didn't know how to answer.

One more mysterious car bomb. But that killing didn't come from populist anger. Actually, it helped us to continue the state of emergency, but who was behind it? Ever since the Chief Justice had been blown to bits in his car on the way to the Supreme Court, I had thought often about my conversation with Anton the night he was murdered. How did he put it? *A stalemate.* The death of the justice was too convenient. Was it just one more coincidence for me to add to the long list of coincidences between us?

"He was in the wrong place at the wrong time," I said finally with a shrug I wished could relieve me of my sense of guilt. What else could or would I say? If Anton had a hand in it, it would be his secret; a secret he took with him.

Both of us were silent. Perhaps we were each trying to understand the events of my country from our own perspectives. Aglaia's countrymen had suffered from the burden of their own debt and then from the global economic crisis I had helped to create, but their response hadn't been violent. After our declaration of Plan B, Greece followed suit by defaulting on their debt over the objections of the E.U. It took them less than a month to withdraw from the Union and re-establish the *drachma* as their currency. The government quickly established an import tax on all foreign goods that could be produced in the country, and began funding new businesses to start up that production quickly. With their devalued currency, tourists were returning and exports were rising. Slowly but surely, people were getting back to work.

"Your president, he wins your next election, no?" Her voice was lighter, and I could tell she was trying to lift my spirits as well as hers. I managed a small smile. I was touched.

"He is ahead in the polls, but it's a long time before the election. There's a lot that could happen between now and then, even though things in my country are improving."

"But, Judas, I do not understand. If your work makes things better, why then do you leave? Does not your president need you?"

The conversation President Taylor and I had had before I turned in my resignation ran through my mind. I had become the focal point of the opposition's demand for a return to fiscal responsibility and the free-market system that were, as they claimed, the foundation of American exceptionalism. Taylor was being portrayed as a pawn of the "socialist policies" pushed on him by his advisors, and as a tyrant for declaring the state of emergency. Maybe I had become an obstacle in his bid for re-election.

And while I wanted to see Plan B through to the end, I had been ready to step aside some time ago. The president never asked me to resign, but I understood, as did David Milestone, how my position in his inner circle would likely only hurt his chances. And then there were the threats.

We couldn't do much to keep me out of sensational news stories following Anton's murder; I was sitting right next to him in the audience at the Kennedy Center, after all. But when White House security took the unheard-of step to provide me with Secret Service protection—not to mention my almost constant fear for Lex's safety—my decision was pretty much made up.

"I was being used by the opposition as the poster boy for what they claim is wrong with my country. Anyway, the president and his team are doing just fine without me." I had told Fallon that others would lend their voices to creating a different kind of economy, and many throughout the country and the globe were doing just that.

She looked up at me; she seemed confused. "But if things get better, why then are so many of your people still fighting what you are doing?"

Only last week I had received a brief note from David Milestone. He related some of the latest legal attempts by the global corporations to undo our American jobs policy, and the lawsuits filed by the oil and gas companies that had held leases on U.S. lands. Both would take years to wind their way through the courts. I had tried to explain the intricacies of the legal wrangling to Aglaia that afternoon when we picked up my mail. The president had no choice but to issue orders to impose import taxes on those non-complying corporations, but the revenues from oil and gas production were adding substantially to the Treasury.

"My country has become too polarized. The two sides refuse to compromise." I gazed out to sea and the sunset shimmering on the water.

"But if your people do not work together to solve problems, then nothing will get done," she insisted. "There will be no progress."

"Or one side will eventually gain control and force its policies on everyone. In some ways, just like we are trying to do." Deep down, I had to admit that was the essence of our strategy. Hold control for long enough until our policies were so firmly entrenched that the majority of the people would not want to return to the mantra that had taken control of America so many years ago.

Something bothered her; her eyes had grown dark again and I wished I could just put my arms around her, comfort her in some way. I could see she was struggling to find the right words.

"But that is *turannia*."

"Huh?" The word had a familiar sound, but I couldn't quite . . .

"You know, Judas, absolute power over the will of your people."

It took me a moment to find my words; it was hard not to agree with her. "To some it might look like that, but my people still get to vote in the next election; they can reject the president's program. We are still a democracy. Besides, what are the alternatives? As you say, nothing would get done."

"But your people will work together again. They must understand that they have to do that."

"I hope so, Aglaia, but I have my doubts."

"If they do not, then what will happen . . . to your country?"

She looked at me over the rim of her glass as she sipped. I guess that was the question.

"It will probably whither and decline," I spoke softly. "Some say it's already begun. If we don't find a way to move forward together, my country will go the way of ancient Greece, the Roman Empire, and other great civilizations in human history."

She sat quietly, holding her glass of ouzo with both hands, like a child. A last few beams of sunlight streaming through the broken clouds in the western sky illuminated her dark complexion. From that first afternoon when she had brought me dinner, her natural beauty was not lost on me. Now, after weeks of conversation with her, I could also see the beauty of her mind . . . and her heart.

"Why must this happen, Judas, the rising and the falling?" Her look was curious, like that of an anxious pupil awaiting the answer to a long-pondered question.

"I guess we've lost our sense of purpose," I began. "Maybe we've gotten too obsessed with the material things of our world." I looked out at the darkening sky. A warm breeze blew up from the sea. "Or maybe we, as a society, can no longer balance the tensions that have always existed in America."

Or we could no longer understand each other; it was as though each side spoke in a different tongue, like the voices of Babel in biblical times. Who knew? I was tired of trying to understand my country. Certainly, history would provide reasons; that's what history did. But maybe there would be no definitive causes of the final chapter of American greatness. Maybe we had just reached the end of our line.

"And so you come here to escape the wars between your peoples and your declining."

Again her words were direct and insightful—something that, before my journey, I wouldn't have expected from a native of Amorgos, so remote from the sophistication of big cities. But I shouldn't have been surprised;

this was Greece after all, the home of Plato and Aristotle, and many other great thinkers of early Western civilization.

"Another civil war? You may be right." Anton had alluded to same thing that Christmas in Toronto. "If there is any hope at all, it will be with the next generation."

"Your daughter?"

"Yes, like Lex. Her friends, her colleagues, her peers."

She sat quietly. Finally she spoke again. "She finishes university, no . . . in England?"

"Anton took care of that, thankfully, and me too. Otherwise Lex couldn't go to Oxford to finish her studies and I would not be here." At least Lex would be safer outside of the U.S.

"You mean he give you money?"

"Something like that." My words caught in my throat for a minute. Aglaia poured us each another glass of ouzo, a drink that couldn't have been more different from the vintage Bordeaux that Anton so favored. "It's called a trust." Trust was exactly what Anton and I had.

It was yet another surprise I learned of after Anton's death, that he had provided for Lex and me for the rest of our lives in a way I could never have anticipated or achieved myself.

"Will you go back to your country after your visit here?"

Her voice was soft, and as I looked at her, she lowered her eyes. She had remained steadfastly in my employ; there had been no suggestion in the least that I was interested in anything other than her fine cooking and occasional company. Yet here we sat together on the patio, each with two inches of liquor in a chunky juice glass, and I wondered.

"I don't know, Aglaia. It's only been two months."

I looked away. What was she really asking me? And what did I really want? There was nothing left for me in the States and Lex was in England. I could go there. But here in Amorgos there was the sun and the sea, and a way of life far away from the rancor of the world. And for now, at least, there was also Aglaia. I knew I had to decide soon.

"You say you work no more. What will you do? I mean with life."

Again her question surprised me. I had been asking myself the same thing all the way to Amorgos and every day as I hiked down to the Aegean Sea and back. I got up from my chair and pulled the Zippo from my pocket, considering her question, cigarette dangling between my lips. I kept saying I was going to quit, but here I was, still smoking and now developing an appreciation for the pungent flavor of Turkish tobacco readily available in the local *ayopá* in Ormos. I looked at my old friend in my left hand. The last ray of sunlight flickered on its metal. It was scratched and dented, but still worked . . . even after all these years. It had served me well. I lit the cigarette and took a sip of the ouzo Aglaia had poured. Standing at the rock wall that bordered my small patio, I watched the last vestiges of sunlight retreat from the southeastern shore of Amorgos. I could feel her hand's light touch on my shoulder. Tears started to well in my eyes, but I held them back.

"It's not the end of my line," I said, when I could speak. "I have one dream left."

Washington D.C.

FALLON CONNELLY PUSHED some files around on her desk and stared at her computer screen. The hallways were quiet. She still had her job and her paycheck but there was nothing else she recognized about her life. Jude had disappeared and her colleagues avoided her. She dutifully prepared reports and met with President Taylor regularly, but she felt like she inhabited a shell that had belonged to someone else. Even her brothers rarely talked with her anymore. She punched the blinking light on her office phone without taking her eyes from the screen.

"Fallon, this is Joseph." The thin voice was barely audible over the speakerphone.

"I haven't heard from you in a while." Her own voice sounded tired in her ears. "How are you, old friend?"

"Old for sure, and frail, I am afraid." His voice got stronger. "But young enough to buy you dinner. Are you free tomorrow evening?"

"I didn't know you were going to be in town. We are a little busy around here." She reached for her Blackberry on the desk, and quickly scrolled through her calendar. "Yes, I think I have time for a quick dinner. Is there something special you want to talk about?"

"Nothing special. I just want to make sure you are okay and to catch up on the goings on in D.C. You know I do not get out much anymore.

But I know what has happened is not to your liking. Perhaps we could discuss some options."

"Not to my liking? That is an understatement." She tossed her Blackberry onto the desk and sighed. If anyone had options, it would be Joseph. He had been with her through every career move she'd made. If he could come up with an option that didn't include perpetuating Jude Anders' mess, she'd be all for it. "The president is running things, Joseph, not me."

"But Mitch Taylor may not be president for much longer, my dear."

"He's ahead in the latest polls, if you haven't noticed."

"Yes, Fallon, I read the newspapers. But it is many months until the election; a lot can happen between now and then, and I have never relied on polls to predict the future."